Not A Day Passes

Alison Clarke

Pen Press

© Alison Clarke 2011

All rights reserved

No part of this publication may be reproduced, stored in a retrieval system, or transmitted in any form or by any means, without the prior permission in writing of the publisher, nor be otherwise circulated in any form of binding or cover other than that in which it is published and without a similar condition including this condition being imposed on the subsequent purchaser.

First published in Great Britain by Pen Press

All paper used in the printing of this book has been made from wood grown in managed, sustainable forests.

ISBN13: 978-1-78003-289-4

Printed and bound in the UK
Pen Press is an imprint of
Indepenpress Publishing Limited
25 Eastern Place
Brighton
BN2 1GJ

A catalogue record of this book is available from the British Library

For Emily

One should examine oneself for a very long time before thinking of condemning others.

~Molière

Author's note

I have known about aspects of *Kate's* story for almost twenty-five years, in particular how she came to be inextricably linked to *Evelien van der Post,* despite the fact that the two women never knew each other. The details remained sketchy until I met Kate in person a few years ago, by which stage she was in her late seventies. What she revealed had a profound effect on me and I felt that hers was a story that ought to be told.

For almost fifty years, *Kate's* life had been blighted simply because she had the misfortune to be born into the era she was. As a woman of high principles, when she found herself facing the most difficult of decisions she knew that no matter which choice she made she would be harshly judged by a hypocritical society quick to condemn and slow to forgive.

Living in today's liberal society we take for granted our freedom of choice, which perhaps makes it difficult to appreciate the pressures placed upon someone like *Kate*, and to understand the motivations behind the devastating decision she felt compelled to make.

I do not wish to detract from the reader's enjoyment of the book by revealing how the story ends, but I hope that, like me, you will feel uplifted and inspired by *Kate's* courage and determination.

Not A Day Passes is, however, a blend of both fact and fiction. The events surrounding Kate and Evelien, as well as Jim, Richard, Helen, Clare, Matthew and Michael Prosser are largely true, although aspects of characterisation are not. Most, but not all, of the remaining characters are based on actual people, but their personal experiences have been fictionalised. Any resemblance to the experiences of actual persons, living or dead, is purely coincidental. In several cases locations, and in all cases proper names, have been changed.

Acknowledgements

I would like to thank all those who have helped in the writing of this book, in particular the people who encouraged me most, Michael, Dorothy, Claire and Virginia. I would also like to thank *Kate* and *Evelien's* families for allowing me to tell their story. I hope they feel that I have done it justice.

Prologue

Plymouth, October 2002

To the casual observer, it was an event so wholly unremarkable it barely merited a cursory glance; but not to Kate Prosser, who understood the grim consequences of ill judgements and rash decisions only too well. Too often it seemed, despite her best intentions, she had merely succeeded in directing her life along a pitiful path rutted with pain, regret and profound guilt. And now she was on the brink of making the final crucial decision; a decision she prayed would, at last, chart a course to absolution and deliver the inner peace she so desperately craved. But it was a risk, for she knew that there was every possibility she was merely paving the way to further recrimination and bitter disappointment, and there was no means of knowing how it would transpire. She shuddered as she felt the cold breath of fate exhale on her once more.

She lingered beside the post box, needlessly checking the address she had so carefully copied onto the crisp white envelope, but it bought her some precious time; time to change her mind, walk away, and leave well alone. She had noticed neither the darkening sky nor the tears of soft autumn rain that had begun to fall, until they started to smudge the ink and threatened to deface her clear, neat handwriting. It prompted her to act. She reached forward, placed the letter deep inside the narrow slot and held it aloft. She heaved a deep reproachful sigh as she withdrew her trembling hand and with it the precious missive. She simply couldn't let it go. She stood, gripped by indecision, blankly staring at the box with her hand still hovering in the slot.

She turned her head, begrudgingly, in response to a muted, attention-seeking cough and was confronted by a tall willowy woman flanked by two young children, a girl and a boy. Each child was standing in eager anticipation, impatiently holding their mother in one hand and a picture postcard in the other. Kate briefly glanced at the woman before lowering her gaze towards the smiling, expectant children. Her heart skipped a beat as she felt her hand open automatically, and the letter dropped from her grasp. It was gone.

'I'm sorry, I didn't realise you were waiting,' she muttered tersely, her mind still focused on the letter now nestling at the bottom of the box. The young woman smiled in silent response. Kate nodded in polite acknowledgement, touched the box for luck, then slowly turned to cross the road.

Head down, deep in thought she picked her way along the soggy, leaf-strewn pavement. As she reached the corner she glanced back. The trio had gone. In the distance, the bright red pillar box stood alone in silent witness, Kate's darkest secret enclosed within its bowels. A postman was kneeling on the damp ground, mindlessly shuffling the contents into a thick grey sack. Kate suddenly felt an overwhelming urge to run back, to explain that she had made a terrible mistake and needed to retrieve the letter, but it was hopeless; she was too old and it was too far. All she could do was stand and stare. She watched, powerless, as the postman stood up, closed the little door and carelessly tossed the sack into the back of his van. Then he was gone.

Kate was gripped by sensations of relief and trepidation in equal measure as she remained gazing into the distance, oblivious to the rain now tumbling down on her from above. Her thoughts, firmly focused on the past, were jolted into the present by the muffled sound of her mobile phone. She fumbled in her pocket and pulled out the wretched thing.

'Hello,' she answered cautiously, hoping she had pressed the right button.

'Oh, hi Mum, it's only me. That's novel, you've got it switched on for once.'

Kate grimaced but ignored the impertinence.

'Are you on your way back yet? We were hoping to get off soon.'

'Hello, Matthew, yes, on my way now. Sorry, I didn't realise you were in such a hurry.'

'Well we weren't, but Becky has decided she wants to stop and get some things for the flight, which means we're a bit tight on time now, but we don't want to leave without saying goodbye. How long do you think you'll be? Oh, nearly forgot, did you actually post it?'

'Yes, of course I posted it,' she replied indignantly.

He continued on breezily, her reply barely registering with him. 'Listen, do you want us to drive over to meet you? You must be getting soaked. Did you even take an umbrella with you?'

'No, I forgot to bring one, but I'm fine thank you. I'm just round the corner, almost home; honestly there's no need to come to meet me,' insisted Kate.

'Okay then, if you're sure. Tell you what, Becky and I will start loading the car which will speed us up a bit.'

'That's fine; I'll see you at the house. I should be there in about five minutes,' Kate replied.

'Alright, see you in a moment. Bye.'

Such an inane conversation, reflected Kate, as she struggled to turn off the phone, realising that she was still trembling. How unemotional and matter of fact he'd sounded; so like his grandmother in moments of significance. He must have known how high the stakes were, what it all meant to her; why couldn't he be more like his twin?

His detached, dispassionate, enquiry seemed to rasp awkwardly against the emotional charges still pulsing through her body. She knew only too well that moments earlier she had been on the verge of turning back without posting it at all; she had thought to tear up the carefully constructed letter. Maybe it was the sight of those children that had helped to steel her resolve, but she was riddled with doubt. What if her revelations destroyed years of cherished memories, and he hadn't known the truth about her? What right did she have to wreak havoc in someone else's life simply to salve her own conscience?

'What have I done?' she whispered to herself in harsh admonishment.

A torrent of turbulent thoughts tossed round her head as she began to walk more briskly towards the house. She turned into the gravel driveway, raised her still shaking hand and waved in silent greeting to Matthew and Becky who were standing in the pouring rain rapidly shoving their bags into the large boot. Becky ran towards her, kissed her warmly on the cheek, Matthew hastily embraced her, both jumped into the car and then they were off.

Nothing in their world had changed.

Chapter 1

Plymouth, summer 1943

Kate opened her eyes and blinked sleepily in the half-light as she struggled to focus on the familiar ceiling. A butterfly was fluttering against the window pane. She was momentarily distracted by the tap-tapping of its wings as it tried in vain to escape. From somewhere downstairs the small realities of everyday life refocused her thoughts as the usual morning sounds beckoned her back.

She forced a toe from under the shiny eiderdown and felt the summer. Her south facing room was dimly lit; the sun would flood through the window and light up the room properly once the shutters were back. She knew she should get up, open the window, and let the poor creature fly free, but the cosy bed held her in its grasp. She lay lazily listening to the muffled sounds from below. She began to drift off again wrapped in the comfortable cocoon of clean cotton sheets and warm woollen blankets. She awoke with a start as the familiar sound of her mother's clipped voice cut across her reverie.

'Michael, would you like some tea?'

Michael Aldworth stretched out his legs contentedly, folded his hands behind his head and sighed as he leant back in his favourite chair. Accustomed to years of seeking solitude in environments of endless people, he had taken a rare opportunity for time alone, lost in one of his beloved classics.

His thoughts were distracted by Kate's tread on the stairs; the middle ones always creaked. He glanced at the clock, ticking contentedly on the marble mantelpiece, and mentally noted the time; 11.15. He shook his head. Years of naval discipline ensured that he rose as soon as he awoke; 6.30 every morning; winter, summer, workday or holiday. He considered commenting on his daughter's tardiness but refrained from doing so.

Kate pushed against the kitchen door and flopped down beside the large, wooden table, freshly scrubbed as ever. The kettle spewed its steam as the range, like the sun on a sweltering day, heated an already hot kitchen. Her mother was moving around efficiently.

'So, you've finally emerged,' Sarah Aldworth remarked pointedly. 'Would you make some tea please, and take a cup to your father? He's in his study.'

Kate said nothing as she walked apathetically to the range and pulled the lid off the teapot. There was little need to check if the old tea leaves had been rinsed away but she did so automatically. She tapped the side of the kettle, lifted it off the stove and poured in the first wetting. She noticed how the first drop of water blackened the grey metal interior as the dry dust turned dark. Swilling it around, she threw the black-stained water into the Belfast sink. She carefully measured sufficient tea for three, conscious that her mother was scrutinising her every move. As she poured on the boiling water, and watched the leaves rise to the top then sink again, it occurred to her that the whole process had succeeded in passing another interminable five minutes.

'Tea's ready,' she called to her father half-heartedly. 'Do you want it in here or in the study?'

'In here please,' he replied, setting down his book. He noticed that the leather on his desk was starting to wear; it was a satisfying indication of the long hours worked. He smiled as his daughter entered the room, set down the tea and kissed him fondly on his forehead. He squeezed her arm in a gesture of affection.

Kate returned to the kitchen, slumped back into her chair and wearily watched her mother busying around the kitchen, supremely in control. She sat in silence, sipping her tea as she observed her mother occupy herself with needless domestic chores.

Sarah raised her head from wiping down the now tea-stained sink. 'I don't suppose you've any plans for what's left of the morning, have you?' she asked with barely disguised disapproval.

The question was rhetorical. Kate knew that her mother would have devised a schedule already; a schedule she would avoid if at all possible.

'I'm asking you,' her mother continued without waiting for a reply, 'as I'd hoped you would come with me to visit the Cowans. I bumped into Mrs Cowan yesterday – she sent her regards to you by the way – she's still very upset about Joe.'

Kate sighed. The last thing she felt like doing, on a sunny Saturday morning, was visiting the elderly couple. In June, a quick but devastating raid had killed the Cowan's only son, Joe. Joe's mother had cradled her son, at the end of his life, as lovingly as she had held him at the beginning. His body had been crushed by the weight of masonry. Joe had arrived into the world three weeks late and had departed it sixty years early. The resultant brain damage from a difficult birth had meant that, at eighteen, he was still totally dependent on his parents. In Kate, Joe had found a friend and mentor. Kate had helped him to gain the rudiments of reading and writing, but it was all for nothing; Joe had become another futile victim in a never-ending war.

'Do I have to?' Kate challenged, knowing the answer already. 'I never know what to say to Mrs Cowan. I know how difficult it must be for her, for all of them, but I feel so awkward visiting there now.'

'Well I think it's important they know we care; they've suffered enough as it is. I really think you should come with me,' Sarah stated emphatically. 'You know how fond Joe was of you, how fond they all are. A visit might take their mind off things; I think they'd be very hurt if you didn't come with me. Mrs Cowan mentioned how much they appreciated the help you gave Joe, how much he had looked forward to his lessons with you.'

'Well, that was to prove a pointless waste of time, wasn't it?' snapped Kate, annoyed at her mother's less than discreet attempts at manipulation.

'Kate, what a thing to say! How can you think that giving Joe the benefits of an education was ever a waste of time?' scolded Sarah.

'I'm sorry,' responded Kate contritely. 'Look, I would come with you but thinking about it I can't, Bob's coming round,' she protested feebly.

'Well, I don't suppose he'll be here until later on this afternoon,' Sarah retorted sharply. 'We'll be back long before then, there's plenty of time. What are you two planning to do anyway?'

'I'm not sure really, we've nothing definite arranged; thought we might go for a ride on the bicycles if the weather stays this good. If we do can we take a picnic?'

'I don't know if you can or not but you may,' corrected Sarah with a schoolmarm brusqueness that displayed her barely suppressed irritation.

Kate carried on regardless. 'Don't know; we might just go to the pictures if we can't be bothered to go to all that trouble,' she mused vaguely.

'Well, I'm sure Bob will have something much more concrete planned. Come on, hurry up, eat some breakfast, get dressed and then we can get going,' demanded Sarah curtly.

Secretly Sarah had been pleased when the friendship between Kate and Bob, formed in their earliest childhood, had apparently started to blossom into something more. Michael had been less enthusiastic, leaving his wife in no doubt that he thought Kate would be better employed in ensuring that she gained a place in college, without the inevitable distractions that Bob Thompson would bring. She had only turned seventeen after all.

'But he's such a steady boy and we know his parents so well. Look how stoically he took his rejection by the RAF,' Sarah had remonstrated. 'He's just what Kate needs to keep her feet on the ground and keep her away from worse possibilities. You know how headstrong she can be.'

Michael had remained unconvinced, though privately acknowledged that, with the arrival of so many Yanks the previous year, many fathers would have welcomed a Bob Thompson with open arms.

As expected, Kate spent what was left of the morning visiting the Cowans.

Chapter 2

Plymouth, summer 1943

'Oh, hello Bob, how did you get in?' Sarah turned her head as she opened the oven door, on hearing Bob's brief, hesitant knock. Flustered, he responded apologetically to what he read as disapproval for coming in uninvited.

'Hello, Mrs Aldworth. Sorry, I hope you don't mind. Mr Aldworth was just going out when I arrived, he said it was fine to come on in.'

'Don't mind at all, just curious,' Sarah replied lifting the contents from the oven.

'Something smells good,' commented Bob, overtly sniffing the air.

'Thank you. I've baked a cake; wretched dried eggs, I'm afraid, but it doesn't look too bad. Will you stay for some?' Sarah offered brightly.

'Thank you, I'd love some, but I believe Kate is keen to go to see some American picture on at the Gaumont. Features Humphrey Bogart and some German-sounding woman, Ingot something or other, can't quite remember her name. It starts at three o'clock so we'd better get going or we'll miss the bus. Would you and Mr Aldworth like to come?' he continued chattily, glancing at his watch.

'No thank you. I'm afraid Kate's father is not a great one for the pictures. He's only interested in the real war, on the newsreels I mean, and once they have run out so has his patience. Perhaps if you can recommend this one he could be persuaded; somehow I think he might value your opinion more than mine. Ingrid Bergman, by the way, is the German-sounding woman and actually she's Swedish,' Sarah corrected.

Bob was embarrassed by his blunder but encouraged by her flattery.

'I'm afraid my expectations for it aren't that great so I might have to embellish my account of it if you're to succeed in your plans, Mrs Aldworth.'

Sarah was still smiling at him when Kate appeared at the door pulling on her cardigan.

'What's amusing you two?'

'Your persistent lateness,' retorted Bob.

'No point in rushing to wait. What are we doing this afternoon anyway?'

'Thought you wanted to see that picture on at the Gaumont, though if you don't hurry up we'll miss the bus. It goes in ten minutes.'

'Fifteen actually,' replied Kate, screwing up her nose and sticking out her tongue in mock triumph.

'Kate, really, I despair, when are you finally going to develop some decorum; you're seventeen not seven for goodness sake. Honestly I don't know how Bob puts up with you,' sighed Sarah.

'He doesn't mind, do you, Bob?'

Bob glanced at Sarah to gauge his answer and reckoned that his support was unquestionably expected.

'Well I suppose your mother has a point. I don't mind for myself, so much, but other people tend to notice things like that,' he replied obsequiously.

'For crying out loud, Bob, you're far too worried about what other people think. I'm quite happy to let them take me as they find. Mind you, you didn't seem so bothered about your reputation when you were caught nicking from…,' she continued mischievously, grinning as she nudged him in the ribs.

'Do come on, Kate, we need to go.' Bob shifted uneasily as he cut her off mid-sentence and ushered her to the door, turning as he went.

'Goodbye Mrs Aldworth. I'm sorry we couldn't stay for cake, I'm sure it's delicious.'

'Another time, Bob; make sure you bring Kate home,

straight after the picture. Her father and I don't like her being out after dark.'

'Of course.' He held the door for Kate and followed her out. He was intensely irritated as they hurried towards the bus stop. He disliked being rushed almost as much as he disliked being put in a bad light, and Kate had a knack of achieving both. Sometimes he felt she deliberately provoked him in front of her mother merely for her own amusement and he was stung by her disloyalty.

'Why on earth were you going to tell your mother about that... that incident? No one is supposed to know about it. I told you in confidence,' he snapped.

'Oh, for goodness sake, Bob, it was years ago. You were ten years old. She wouldn't care about that now.' Kate looked at him in surprise.

'Well I care,' he responded sulkily. 'I hate it when you try to belittle me in front of your mother.'

'I wasn't belittling you. For God's sake, grow up! It was said in jest. I didn't realise it was such a big deal. After all, when you told me you seemed so damned proud of the fact.'

Kate's black eyes flashed in irritation. Sometimes she felt that the years had dissolved away and that she was back with the petulant boy of their childhood.

'There's no need to swear, Kate. Your mother's right, sometimes you do lack... what was that word she used... 'decorum', I think it was. Why can't you be like other girls?' he accused.

'Well I tell you what, Bob Thompson, find one of them and take her to the blasted pictures. No doubt she'll swoon in your arms and enjoy the lecture. I've had enough of you and your moods for one day, thank you very much. I'll go in and see it by myself.'

'You wouldn't dare,' he goaded.

It was the incentive Kate needed. She turned on her heel and walked decidedly towards the bus stop. Bob glared at her and considered calling after her.

No, he thought, if that's how she feels let her go. She'll come to her senses soon enough and even she wouldn't go on her own. I'll call her bluff.

He watched as the bus turned the corner and slowed in response to Kate's raised arm.

Kate paused, knowing the trouble she would be in for going on alone, with the constant threat of air raids. Bob Thompson was sure to make it a point of honour to inform her parents. She hesitated as the bus drew up beside the stop, her determination momentarily suspended.

'Are you getting on, my luvver?' the conductor called out to her.

She stepped forward boldly. The conductor rang the bell as Kate blindly found the closest vacant seat, sat down and chin set, stared straight ahead. The bus passed Bob, still standing on the pavement, watching in disbelief as the oily fumes enveloped him. Kate was shaking from a heady mix of anger, fear and excitement; the cause was undefined but the response was clear. She felt the first prick of tears and bit her lip to hold them back but with little effect. She opened her bag and pulled out a crumpled, fraying handkerchief, sniffling surreptitiously as she wiped her eyes.

'Are you okay, honey?'

Kate blinked and felt her face redden in response to the enquiry. She half-turned her head in a fruitless effort to hide her face as she continued to hold the handkerchief to her nose.

'I'm fine thank you. I've just received some bad news that's all. I'll be better in a moment,' she fibbed.

'Hey, I didn't mean to pry, but you look so upset.'

This time the nasal tones in the voice struck her as she turned to look at him properly. He met her gaze, his eyes crinkled at the edges in concern. He felt her tension and attempted to lighten the atmosphere.

'I was surprised that you chose this seat when the bus is almost empty – guess I thought it was my lucky day.'

Kate felt her pulse quicken and for once paused to consider her response. Her mother's warning voice rang in her ears; as if she weren't in enough trouble. She quickly glanced around to assess the likelihood of discovery, but there were no obviously familiar faces in the immediate vicinity.

'I'm sorry, I didn't check before I sat down.' Kate felt her face burn and her stomach freeze. 'I'm quite happy to move seat if you would prefer it.'

'You sit just where you are, honey; this could have been a lonely journey for both of us. Was that your guy I saw standing looking kinda forlorn on the sidewalk back there?' he asked mischievously pointing backwards with his thumb.

Kate fought to constrain her blush and narrowed her eyes as she struggled to interpret the strange words. He misunderstood her reaction.

'There I go again, prying where it ain't wanted.'

'No, no, I don't think you're prying, it's your accent… it's so…so American. You sound just like Humphrey Bogart,' she laughed nervously, before thinking how idiotic the observation must appear.

His eyes lit up, encouraged by her response.

'So you like Humphrey Bogart? I believe his latest movie is on in town. Maybe you've seen it? I hear it's one for the ladies, but I reckon in the right company I could be persuaded to sit through it.' He looked at her and she swore he winked.

Kate was unsure how to cope with a situation that, although undoubtedly of her own making, was becoming increasingly difficult. The encounter was exciting and daring, but she felt uncomfortable sitting on a bus happily chatting to a complete stranger and a Yank to boot; she was fearful of discovery. She checked again to see if she knew anyone on board.

'Mmm, no, I haven't. In fact I was intending to see the matinee this afternoon, but my friend couldn't make it, so I think I'll wait until another time,' she stuttered in reply.

'Would that friend be standing a mile back wishing like heck he was sitting where I am? I'd be happy to take his place.'

He raised his eyebrow and broke into a wide smile which framed perfect white teeth.

Kate was torn between feelings of indignation and fascination. Only last week her cousin Rose had entertained her with stories about 'those randy Yanks'. The oft repeated warnings about their free thinking and free ways were apparently true, and she had been shocked to realise that Rose was not passing on second-hand gossip. Kate had sought to appear relaxed at the revelation; she would not have allowed Rose to consider *her* so conventional as to openly disapprove, but inwardly she was taken aback. Apparently, Rose had easily dispensed with the values that Kate herself took for granted. She was determined that, as in all other areas of her life, she would guard her independence, and that if and when she chose to allow anyone to take the same liberties with her, it would be firmly on her own terms.

Her mind raced as she sought to buy time. She was strangely perturbed by this encounter with a man who was talking to her as an equal. She had always given the impression of years beyond her age. The lipstick she had carefully applied in the hall just before leaving, and well out of her mother's range, added to the illusion of a confident, independent woman. He was not to know that, in reality, she was only seventeen and was travelling into the city with every intention of watching a picture on her own but in full expectation of a severe ticking off when she arrived back. She was enjoying the attention, the intimation of attraction, the independence and the defiance. What harm could come of it? There would be dozens of people milling around and it was still early in the day. Besides, now that she thought about it, it would look so strange to sit watching it on her own. She hadn't dared to look at him properly, but she knew that he was waiting for a response.

'Thank you, but I don't think so, I don't know you and I don't think my parents would approve.'

15

As soon as she said it she immediately regretted it; now he would be reassessing her and realise his mistake that it was a schoolgirl not a woman who was sitting beside him.

'I beg your pardon, ma'am,' he replied. 'I didn't mean to suggest anything improper. I'm not sure my parents would approve of my inviting a young woman I'd just met on a bus to a movie either.'

Kate shot him a look expecting to see ridicule in his eyes, his intention irony, but instead he met her with a full blown wink this time. She was completely thrown but was desperately trying to maintain her composure. This complete stranger, with his strange accent and unfamiliar words, was flirting with her. Despite her outward appearance she still had the experience and judgement of a girl. She was lost and unsure how to proceed. The easiest option was to deter him with her youth, but that went against every screaming urge. After what seemed an interminable pause, she regained sufficient confidence to reply.

'I'm sorry. I suppose, if you can bear to sit through it, well… I don't see why we shouldn't go together. After all, you could have been sitting in the next seat anyway. Thinking about it, it would appear worse to go on my own, wouldn't it?'

The apparent confidence of her reply disguised the tremor in her voice. Kate hoped that, if indeed he did notice, he would think she was still recovering from her upset. She wanted to add that he should understand it was not something she would normally contemplate, allowing a complete stranger to accompany her like this, but she concluded that this would appear unworldly.

'Well, I think I should be flattered,' he offered with mock indignation. 'It isn't every day a gal lets you know that your company is preferable only to being on her own. I can assure you that, from where I'm sitting, watching a movie with you is not something I feel I'd have to bear. I'm Art Willis by the way.'

He beamed at her and held out his hand. She immediately noticed the insignia on his shoulders.

Kate felt the omnipresent blush intensify as her mind began to race. 'Crikey, he's a Lieutenant, what on earth am I doing? I've offended him…Art? I wonder what that stands for?'

'I'm Kate Aldworth,' she replied simply, shaking his hand.

She stood up, with girlish impatience, as the bus jolted to a halt. Art instinctively reached out his hand and placed it under her elbow to steady her. The gesture was gentlemanly and simply done, but he kept it there as he stood himself and guided her out of the seat. She could feel the warmth of his hand as he gently but confidently took control of her. It seemed natural and comforting to have this strong, handsome man take the lead and she happily complied with his guidance. He stepped off the bus before her, then turning, reached out and took her hand to help her down. Normally she would have skipped off the step and jumped back onto the pavement. Something in his gesture slowed her pace as she gracefully pointed her toe and reached towards the ground. She could feel herself straighten as she turned to thank him.

'So where's this movie showing?' he enquired brightly.

'It's only a short walk from here, up this street and round the corner at the Gaumont.'

They started walking naturally in tandem, and she noticed how seamlessly he moved her to the inside of the pavement. His manners were impeccable. Her concerns vanished as she now actively sought to see whom she might meet in the company of this handsome, young American. He was about six foot two, slim and walked bolt upright. Kate, for once, was glad that she had stretched up suddenly in the last twelve months and, at five foot eight, was now the tallest girl in her year. In her heels she felt sophisticated and graceful and was able to match him stride for stride.

'Hey, what you say if we skip the movie and go for one of those famous Devon teas? My shout. I think I'd like the chance to get to know you properly, Miss Aldworth, and we can't talk during a movie.'

He spoke with authority but without any hint of overbearance. She felt that he genuinely wanted her consent to any change of plan. In Kate's limited experience, men were of two types: those like her father whose views she accepted without question and those like Bob whose views she regarded with indifference. Art was different; he balanced the strength of her father's opinions with the compliance of Bob. She was enthralled and felt like she was floating along, making little contact with the pavement.

'Alright then. Shall we walk towards the Barbican?' Kate offered tentatively. 'Perhaps you'd like to see the spot where your forefathers departed these shores; follow in their footsteps.'

'Is that a hint?' Art asked straight-faced. 'Hey, all you had to do was refuse the tea.'

She looked at him flustered. 'Oh no, I'm sorry, I didn't mean it like that at all, I just thought that you'd like to…' She stopped mid-sentence as she met his grinning face.

'You're joking,' she laughed, realising how needlessly tense she was feeling, and what easy company he was proving to be.

'Well, I reckon I could risk a visit to the shore without the fear of being press-ganged,' Art jested as he stepped aside and allowed her to lead the way.

They walked towards the city's historic quarter making their way through the morass of crumbling buildings and rubble-strewn pavements, their shattered remains testament to the force of Hitler's ambition. It was unthinkable that Drake's city should surrender its skies to an Armada of Luftwaffe. The citizens, proud or foolish, had stood resolute and rebuilt as around them their city was flattened. Hastily constructed modern buildings stood shoulder to shoulder with those ancient Elizabethan artefacts that had successfully managed to shrug off the relentless pounding.

Kate stumbled slightly as they turned the corner into the Barbican and her heel caught in the bumpy cobbles. Art instinctively took her arm once more. With Bob she would have vehemently rejected such offers of support, asserted her independence, but with Art she took full advantage of the opportunity for the renewal of such unexpected intimacy. She silently thanked mother luck.

'How about here?' suggested Art as they approached some tables casually placed on the pavement outside a rather smart looking tea room. They sat down and ordered two of their widely advertised 'speciality cream teas'.

'We're out of jam and cream,' explained the sullen waitress in response to Art's request. 'We've only got margarine, but the scones are fresh. It's the war,' she added witheringly, without any hint of apology.

'Okay ma'am. Two of your famous margarine teas will do just fine,' Art responded cheerily as he snapped closed the menu.

Kate smothered a giggle as the waitress glared at him before flouncing away.

'Well, I hope I've made a better impression on one young English woman,' Art continued, as he turned towards Kate and smiled. 'So, come on, tell me all there is to know about Miss Kate Aldworth. I want to discover everything about you.'

'Not much to tell,' started Kate hesitantly, not sure how much she should reveal about herself to a complete stranger. 'I was born here in Plymouth, lived here all my life. I have a younger brother, James, both my parents are teachers, my father is a Headmaster. He was a Lieutenant Commander in the Navy before that, fought in the last war. When he left he decided to train as a teacher, met my mother at college, they got married, they had my brother and me… I'm hoping to become a teacher too… that's about it. Pretty boring really.'

'I can assure you, there's nothing boring about you,' Art retorted, looking straight towards her. Kate looked away feeling herself redden in response to the compliment. 'So you're a college girl, I might have known, brains and beauty. So when do you finish your studies?' he continued innocently, as the waitress returned with the tea and noisily distributed the cups and saucers.

'Shall I pour?' he offered, picking up the teapot without waiting for a response. 'Never sure how you British do this – is it milk or tea first?'

Kate smiled. 'You decide... strictly speaking, I think it should be tea first,' she added as an afterthought, noticing he was hesitating balancing teapot and jug in hand.

'Tea first it'll be then, ma'am. When in England...' he stated emphatically as he filled her cup and handed it over.

Kate was glad of the opportunity to divert the conversation. She didn't want to correct his mistaken assumption that she was already at college. She was feeling incredibly awkward about disclosing the fact that she was only seventeen and still at school. She looked at him afresh; what age would he be? Twenty-two, twenty-three? Such a gap, but then there were over fifteen years between her parents. But they had been older when they met; the gap seemed to narrow as the years increased.

'So, you're following in your parents' footsteps,' Art continued. 'I'm sure they're real pleased that you're carrying on the family tradition.'

'I'm not doing it to carry on a tradition. It's my choice,' Kate challenged, rather more abruptly than she intended.

Kate was dismayed that he should assume she was seeking to emulate her parents, especially her mother, who was the epitome of boring respectability, so dully conventional. Kate was particularly close to her father; she admired him greatly, but she knew that he also assumed she had decided to follow the career he too had chosen. From early childhood she had felt the pressure of their expectation but was determined to lead her own life. Yes, she was prepared to conform, but when it suited her own purposes. She would train as a teacher, but only because she viewed it as a ticket out of Plymouth; a ticket that could take her overseas, allow her to experience the world and secure her freedom.

Art held up his hands in mock surrender, grinning at her reaction. 'Hey, whoa! You picked me up all wrong; reckon it would be pretty darn difficult to persuade you to do something you didn't want to do. I worked that out pretty quick, I think.'

Kate grimaced. 'Sorry, I didn't mean to sound so abrupt. You touched a raw nerve that's all. You're not the first person to suggest that I'm blindly following in my parents' footsteps. You haven't met them,' she added with emphasis. 'So come on, what about you then? Now that you know everything that's remotely worth knowing about me, and I've made a complete fool of myself, I think it's only fair that you spill the beans, don't you?'

'Oh no… not so fast, you don't get off that easily. I don't think I quite know everything about you yet, do I?' Art teased. 'Like who's the forlorn figure you so cruelly abandoned on the sidewalk back there?'

Kate felt her blush return.

'Oh, you mean Bob,' she sighed as she took a bite of stale scone. The dry dough stuck to the roof of her mouth. She took a sip of tea in an attempt to remove it discreetly. It gave her time to think.

'We've been friends for years,' she continued dismissively, 'as long as I can remember. He's like a brother to me. We were supposed to be going to the pictures together, but he decided he didn't want to see it after all so I went on alone… I didn't want to miss it.'

'Which is why you're sitting here with me now, I suppose.' Art challenged teasingly, daring her to continue, before breaking into the widest of grins once more.

'Alright you've got me. We had a row. But we have been friends for years and that's all, honestly.' Kate smiled sheepishly, avoiding Art's gaze.

'I'll take your word for it.' he responded knowingly, raising an eyebrow. 'He hasn't joined up yet then?' he asked casually.

'No, he can't,' explained Kate, glad that Art had moved the conversation away from the true nature of her relationship with Bob. 'Of course he tried. He applied for the RAF, but they discovered he had a problem with his heart. It was pretty devastating for him. He's applying to join Barclays bank now,' Kate explained simply, not wishing to have to justify Bob further.

Art nodded in sympathy. She looked across at him and smiled. The contrast with Bob could not have been more marked. She had known Art for less than an hour, yet she felt completely at ease. With Bob she had always felt the need to tread carefully. He had been a constant, if unexciting, presence for over twelve years; their relationship seemed to her halfway between sibling and expectation. She was fond of Bob, they had grown up together, and he was someone with whom she could escape the confines of home but, as far as Kate was concerned, that was it.

'So is that me off the hook?' Kate asked expectantly. 'Am I now to discover your darkest secrets?'

She sat enthralled as Art recounted stories of his home in Boston, his views on England, on the war, on life in general. For Kate, each precious second ebbed away like grains in a sandglass; she willed them to flow forever. It was with dismay that, finally, she had to concede how late it was.

'I really don't want to but I must be getting back now, Art,' she stated apologetically. 'My parents will be getting worried... I mean what with the possibility of night raids and everything,' she added hastily.

He looked at his watch and grimaced in disappointment. 'Sure thing, I'll come back with you if that's okay?'

It was more than okay; it gave her a few more precious minutes with him. She didn't want to admit to herself that returning home also meant returning to reality and the likely consequences of her decision to go on alone. How could she be both people in one; a young woman capable of engaging the attention of this intelligent, worldly man and yet a girl who would almost certainly face the chastisements of atavistic parents? Would he dismiss this occasion, so significant to her, as a pleasant afternoon's distraction; one that occupied a few hours during an interminable war in a foreign land and she would never see him again?

To Kate, the journey home had never before appeared so short. She thought back to the many times she had silently sworn at the dilatory women apparently unable to board a bus without fussing over boundless bags, brollies, sticks and steps. During this journey she willed each stop to have an army of invalids, each contributing to the delay that would extend the journey for a few precious minutes. She was so unsure what would happen next; it seemed impossible that she should disembark, wave a desolate goodbye and that would be it. That he should alight with her was equally impossible; what would she say? What would he expect her to do? Where would they go? She could hardly arrive back and nonchalantly introduce a man she had encountered on a bus to her incredulous parents. He would see her for the girl she was. If he should ask to see her again how could she consent? A thousand thoughts exploded in her mind as she felt her pulse race and the unwelcome flush once more begin to invade her face. She so desperately wished to maintain her composure and embrace the decorum that so often appeared to elude her. His voice cut across the barrage as they approached her stop.

'I'm sure your parents will be glad to know that you've got back just fine. Will Bob still be waiting for you?' Kate shrugged in a non-committal response, not wanting to get entangled in another conversation about Bob. Thankfully he didn't press her.

'I need to head back to base, but would you consider it forward of me if I were to request the pleasure of your company again? We're having a bit of a do for the 116th in the Officers' Club next Saturday, inviting some local dignitaries and I would be delighted if you could come. It's nothing too grand. I could arrange to pick you up at around seven o'clock, if that suited. Your parents can come too if you think they would enjoy it. The base commander is keen to get the 'old timers', as he calls them, on board. He reckons all this talk of us Yanks being overpaid, over…well you probably know the rest, is not so good. He wants to prove that us 'all American boys' can behave just as appropriately as your British ones. What do you say?' His prolonged, unbroken speech betrayed an uncharacteristic nervousness. He was anxious to see her again.

Kate's natural reaction was to accept with girlish eagerness, but she contained her natural impulse.

'That's very kind of you Art, I'd love to go,' she replied managing to steady her voice. 'I'll discuss it with my parents, see if they would like to come along too. How can I let you know?'

'Here take my number. You can leave a message for me at the base. I sure hope you can make it. I've really enjoyed your company this afternoon, Miss Kate Aldworth,' he stated grandly. 'Are you okay from here?'

The bus drew alongside her stop. He stood up and led her to the door. He stepped aside to let her pass and, as she did, took her hand and brushed it against his lips. She glanced around furtively to see who might have observed, jumped off and skipped onto the pavement. She turned to watch the bus draw away, observing that he touched his cap in mock salute and continued to grin until completely out of sight. Kate yelped with glee, clenched her fists and started to run.

As she reached the door, breathless, she paused and tried to gather her thoughts and her composure. What awaited her, this woman who was about to become a girl again? She considered her options, appeal to their better nature, brazen it out, apologise for being so independent. She decided that it was impossible to pre-empt her approach until she could see the lay of the land. She opened the door and called a cheery hello; best not to appear guilty she reckoned. After all what was so terrible about having tea in an open place with a very respectable young officer. She heard her mother calling from inside the kitchen.

'Good, you're back, is Bob with you?'

So he hadn't snitched.

'No, just me,' she called. The strength of her voice belied the weakness of her resolve. She walked into the kitchen. All appeared as she had left it. The kettle, sitting idly on the range, still spewed its steam; the open oven door still warmed an already hot kitchen. She sat beside her mother. How could she appear so normal when everything had changed?

'Well, did the picture live up to expectations?' Sarah was reading the newspaper and barely looked up.

Kate concluded it was now or never. Her mouth dried as her palms moistened.

'Actually we didn't go to see it,' she spoke lightly as she looked at her mother to gauge her reaction. Nothing.

'Didn't you? Where did you go then? I thought you were late back considering the picture was at three o'clock. Did Bob decide he couldn't face it after all?' asked Sarah distractedly as she turned a page.

'Bob and I didn't go anywhere, we had a row. I went into Plymouth on my own. Well I started out on my own but it didn't quite work out like that. Please don't be upset with me, I'll explain, it was all perfectly proper and we were never alone. We just sat drinking tea and then I, I mean we, got the bus back. He was a complete gentleman.'

The words spilled out like rounds from a misfired machine gun. Each one was missing its target.

'Slow down, Kate, you're babbling like a baby and making no sense at all. Who sat drinking tea? Where did you go? Where's Bob now?' Sarah enquired setting down her paper.

'You won't understand. You've forgotten what it's like to be seventeen but feeling everyone treats you like an eternal child.' For the second time that day, Kate found herself fighting back tears of frustration.

'What are you talking about? What's happened?' Kate was surprised to see the expression on her mother's face. Her brow was wrinkled, not in its usual stern map of displeasure but in genuine concern. Overwhelming emotions took over as Kate began to cry. She felt her mother's arms embrace her as she buried her head in the nape of her neck. Sarah gently stroked the back of her head, twiddling her hair between her neatly manicured fingers.

'It's not so long ago, you know, since I was seventeen but, of course, I didn't have your confidence and free spirit. Are you upset about rowing with Bob? It's only a tiff. You've had many before and will have many again. He'll be round tomorrow and it will be as if it never happened,' Sarah reassured gently.

Kate submerged herself in her mother's caress. It felt strange but comforting. She lifted her head and tried to compose herself.

'Please don't be angry with me. I haven't done anything wrong, but I know you won't approve.'

'Approve of what, Kate?' her mother hadn't released her arms but Kate felt them tense. Kate took the crumpled handkerchief from her sleeve and blew her nose. Between breathless sobs, she recounted the story of her meeting with Art.

'He's very respectable,' she continued, 'I think his family is pretty much like ours. His father fought in the first war, his mother went to college, they live in Boston. He was a perfect gentleman the whole time and made sure I got home safely. He's invited me to a dance at the Officers' Club as he calls it, next Saturday. He suggested that Father and you should go along as well. You see he's not trying to hide anything and neither am I. Please don't be angry, I didn't plan it – it just happened. Well nothing happened as such, we only talked and drank tea and then we came home.'

The silence, before her mother spoke, seemed interminable.

'You're growing up so fast that, yes, sometimes, I suppose, I forget you're no longer a child but a young woman. I'm not sure I really approve of your being accosted by a complete stranger on a bus, but from what you say he appears to have behaved himself. I suppose he's a lonely young man, a long way from home. Someone's son. He must realise that you're still very young and going to an event in an Officers' Mess would be quite something. I'm really not sure.'

'I know, it scares me a little, well in truth a lot, but I would so like to go. Father and you would really like him, I'm sure you would. Please say I can go.'

'I'm not saying 'yes', but I'll talk it over with your father. He might decide that he would quite enjoy the inside of an Officers' Mess once again, although he'll think it's not quite the Senior Service and an American one at that. I can get round him when I need to.' She smiled conspiratorially at her daughter. 'We'll talk about it tomorrow when I've had time to think.'

She squeezed Kate's shoulder with a motherly touch, as Kate hugged her awkwardly.

'What about Bob?' she continued tentatively. 'You must consider his feelings in this. You've been close for such a long time,'

'I know, I think Bob and I have finally outgrown each other. I'll be kind to him, I promise,' Kate answered compliantly. 'Thank you for understanding,' she added as she got to her feet slowly. The excitement of the encounter, the effort of telling her mother and the relief of the entirely unexpected reaction had drained her.

'I think I'll go to bed now if you don't mind. I feel so tired all of a sudden and I'm developing a rotten headache. Good night, Mother, sleep well.'

'God bless, dear,' Sarah replied as she kissed her cheek and cupped Kate's face in her hands. Something intangible had shifted between them.

Kate climbed the stairs, the middle ones creaked. Had merely a day passed since they had announced her arrival this morning?

Chapter 3

Malta, 15th September 1943

Jim Palmer took a deep draw on his pipe and watched as the smoke, drifting on the breeze, melted into the warm air. At his feet, a battered English rose gently swayed, elbowing a native weed in a vain attempt to establish its claim over the bed of foreign soil. The cicadas had begun their chorus of evensong as the sun started to set across Grand Harbour. The sea leapt and glinted like a freshly caught salmon in the dying light. From his vantage point, high on the ramparts of HMS St Angelo, Jim surveyed the scene of perfect calm that was laid out before him; a scene crafted as nature had designed. Below him the sea lapped against the battered fort walls, its healing brine licking the wounds of the ancient edifice, first constructed then destroyed by man.

Jim had been on the plucky little island of Malta for little over a week and was still trying to find his feet. Two weeks previously he had been on a much needed spot of leave in his native Plymouth, having travelled down from battle-scarred London. He'd commiserated with the families of colleagues washed to the bottom of the sea, got drunk, smoked, cried, laughed, loved… relived normality for ten precious days.

He had arrived on the island just in time to witness the remnants of the defeated Italian fleet being escorted into Grand Harbour. There was an air of excitement and optimism in the air and Jim had breathed it in. He had sensed the island's warm welcome from the first moment he had disembarked. Having so far successfully dodged the storms of war, he had found refuge in the relative safety of the little island, like St Paul before him.

His thoughts were disturbed by voices and he turned to see Bill Bates approaching, his arms linked with a small, slim, blue-eyed woman in her early to mid-twenties.

'There you are,' Bill called cheerily. 'We've been looking for you. I'd like you to meet my fiancée, Evelien. We've just got engaged. Still find it hard to believe she's actually said yes.' He looked admiringly at Evelien, grinning broadly.

'How do you do, Evelien? Very pleased to meet you. I'm Jim Palmer, Bill's replacement,' Jim explained brightly holding out his hand.

'In job only, mate, I hope,' bantered Bill.

'I know,' Evelien replied smiling as she shook Jim's hand. 'Bill told me you had arrived, last week I am thinking. I am pleased to meet with you as well.'

Jim tried to hide his surprise. Her English was good but not perfect, the accent was definitely foreign and if he weren't mistaken, German.

Couldn't be, he thought to himself, they'd never allow it. What was she doing here?

Bill began to laugh.

'You too and I always had you down as a man of the world. No need to say anything mate, your face says it all. Mind you, if I had a shilling for every time I've had the 'Jerry' look. Admit it, you thought Evelien was German, didn't you? No, she's Dutch, you pillock.'

Jim felt his face flush, he hadn't reckoned on being so obvious. He wasn't sure, however, that the flush was entirely due to his gaffe. Evelien's eyes were a vibrant pale blue, her aquiline nose was slightly too long but somehow it added definition to a face that was moulded with the smoothest skin he had ever seen. Her blond hair was shimmering in the fading light. An Aryan look if ever he could define one. Her smile indicated that she had fully comprehended his assessment of her and she was now looking straight at him through her piercing blue eyes. There was an air of sensual, continental confidence about her that he had never encountered before, and it unnerved him.

'Evelien's a nanny to an English family who live here in Malta, name of Brown. Isn't she fantastic?' continued Bill gushingly. Jim was lost for words. To concede, he felt, would betray the overwhelming instant attraction he was desperately trying to conceal, but to deny would offend.

'You're a lucky man,' he offered feebly. It sounded so hackneyed he immediately sought to make amends. 'Are there many more like you round here, Evelien?'

Jeez, he had made it worse, it sounded like he was spotlighting every unattached woman who happened to be waiting expectantly for the next boatload of fresh faces to arrive.

'I don't think I am understanding you completely. Do you mean are there many nannies in Malta? There are some, but I think I am the only one from Holland,' Evelien replied pleasantly.

'I don't think that's what he meant at all,' interrupted Bill noticing Jim's embarrassment, 'but I'll spare his blushes. Hands off, mate, she's taken.' Evelien continued to smile at Jim, ignoring Bill's dig, but she hadn't failed to notice how Jim had first looked at her.

'We thought it would be a good idee for you to have someone to help you to get to know peoples once Bill has gone away tomorrow. I have been living here since before the war and know many peoples. It is nice, yes, to not always be with men in uniforms, I think? You must forgive me, my English is still not as good as I am wishing it to be,' she apologised coyly, noticing a slight look of bewilderment on Jim's face.

'It's a lot better than my Dutch,' interjected Jim. 'Yes, that would be great. Sure you don't mind, Bill?'

'No, I agree it's a good idee,' he grinned, gently mocking Evelien's pronunciation. 'Reckoned it was a two-way street and you were a safe bet. Evelien can help you find your feet, get you settled in and you can keep her out of mischief,' he added teasingly, winking at her. 'Want to join us?'

The thought was tempting but, as Bill was due to depart the next day, Jim thought it pertinent to allow them time alone so declined the invitation. He lit a match and tapped the tobacco gently with his forefinger as he watched them walk away together. Evelien's slim hips swayed alluringly as Bill's arm drew her closer to his side. As they approached the corner she turned and waved to him. Jim waved back, pipe in hand.

Hell, he thought to himself, tricky one that.

Jim had enjoyed his fair share of women, the magnetism of a uniform provided its own particular pull, but he had also been blessed with a brain and dark Mediterranean looks. As his leave in Plymouth had readily proved, the tenuous certainty of any personal future in wartime Britain had lowered many defences and there were plenty of young women only too willing to enjoy the company of the handsome young sailor and share their favours. In a world where every sensation was already heightened, he enjoyed the physical closeness of these women, but that is where it ended. He never allowed it to become anything more than a casual act of mutual release from the pain and suffering around him.

He was feeling confused and mightily unnerved by his unexpected reaction to Evelien. The last time he had felt adrenaline torpedo through his veins like that, he had been off the coast of Norway dodging death, as his ship, HMS Penelope, had desperately sought to out-gun the gathering Luftwaffe. Jim prided himself on his self-control, and his ability to present an unemotional, measured response in the most difficult situations. It was this, he believed, that had led to his quick promotion. What was it about Evelien that had caused this uncontrollable reaction in him? Her lack of Englishness, her beautiful face, those eyes, the chase, or simply the fact that he had the distinct impression she too had felt something pass between them? He was flattered. He was disorientated. For the first time ever, he felt like he was floundering in unknown waters.

'Jeez, Jim, pull yourself together, you arrogant bastard,' he said aloud. 'He's put his trust in you, she's another man's fiancée; she felt nothing.' He was neither convinced nor convincing. He turned sharply on his heel and walked briskly back towards his quarters, drawing deeply on his pipe, lost in his thoughts.

Chapter 4

Malta, July 1944

It took all Jim's willpower to maintain a brotherly distance. Evelien's eyes had filled like glistening ice age tarns; tears were beginning to spill over and flow down her beautiful face. He had an unbearable urge to take her in his arms and comfort her. What on earth had happened?

She had been standing waiting for him in her usual spot, just outside the base, but this time his usual cheery wave, on spotting her, had not been reciprocated. His heart had sunk towards his boots; something was amiss and he assumed that, for some unknown reason, she was upset with him. He had walked towards her with a degree of trepidation.

He had spent the day eagerly anticipating yet another blissful evening with her. For months he had tried to convince himself that their relationship was entirely innocent; he was merely remaining true to his word and looking after 'Bill's interest'. But he knew perfectly well that, nine months into his posting, he no longer needed Evelien's help, if indeed he ever had. If truth be told he had fallen hook line and sinker for her. He felt incredibly bad about it; Bill was a jolly decent chap and in no way deserved the disloyalty of a friend in whom he had implicitly placed his trust.

As a pair of naïve, carefree, young cadets happily thrust together to face the challenges of Dartmouth, they could not have envisioned the cynical battle-hardened veterans who would be reunited four years later. Bill had been the first to greet Jim when he arrived at St Angelo and the latter had been mightily relieved to find a familiar face. They had immediately fallen into the easy friendship that had seen them through their previous time together and were soon raucously regaling each other with stories of their youthful conquests and shared experiences. Flippancy had an uncanny knack of diminishing the horror of the intervening years. It had come as something of a surprise to Jim when Bill had introduced Evelien as his fiancée – he hadn't reckoned Bill was the marrying type. But then what man could have resisted her? Jim knew he was playing a dangerous game. Bill had been a hugely popular colleague and it had not gone unnoticed that Jim was spending an inordinate amount of time with his girl. The barrage of crude taunts directed towards him on an almost daily basis, confirmed to Jim that his fellow officers were far from convinced that his motives, where Evelien was concerned, were entirely honourable. Had someone from the unit felt obliged to inform Bill?

Evelien had been anxiously waiting outside the base for over half an hour. Like Jim, she had managed to maintain a façade of perfect propriety, but with each loving letter she sent to Bill, the pangs of guilt increased and the masquerade was crumbling. She felt a full-blown fraud faithfully declaring her commitment to a man whom she now doubted she could ever marry; but she could not bring herself to end it. She knew how much she meant to him and had no wish to hurt a kind and decent man. She had thought herself in love, the war had strangely affected her emotions, but she now knew she had been mistaken. Meeting Jim had proved that; she was completely and utterly smitten by him and was now only too painfully aware what true love meant. But Jim was hard to read. So far his behaviour had been exemplary and he had given her no indication, at all, that he felt the same way. She had not, however, forgotten the unmistakable look on his face when they first met, and surely he must feel something for her, she reasoned, otherwise why would he choose to spend so much time together? Maybe he was simply doing it because he had promised Bill. It would be typical of him; prepared to keep his word even when all reasonable obligations had passed. Her doubts made her all the more reluctant to declare her hand in case he didn't feel the same way she did. Moreover, she feared he would consider her frivolous and disloyal. After all, she had only got engaged to Bill the day before they met. She had concluded that it was best not to take the risk and to continue their friendship on the basis on which it had been established up to now.

'Evelien what on earth's wrong?' asked Jim tentatively as he took her hand in his, careless of the reproachful stares of those around them. They started to walk together towards the waterfront in an effort to distance themselves from the crowds of sailors milling around the base.

She turned to him as she spoke. 'Oh God, it is too awful, Jim. I can hardly tell you. I have found out something terrible, just this hour. My sister… my sister has been taken into prison by the Japanese… I cannot believe it.' She burst into deep uncontrollable sobbing, doubling over in her agony. Jim stopped walking and, tentatively putting his arm around her shoulder, pulled her towards him. She instinctively pressed against him and rested her head on his chest. He enveloped her in both arms, bent over, and buried his head in her golden hair. The unique smell of her aroused sensations he hadn't known existed. He fought against an array of emotions. His innate decency caused him to struggle with the joy of holding her. Was he taking advantage of her in her grief at this God-awful situation? Would an external observer have watched and concluded that he was an opportunist shit? Yet it felt so natural to stand holding her, comforting her. What else could he do? Wouldn't any decent human being do the same in the circumstances? That he knew he was in love with her was a side issue. It was an act of human kindness, irrespective of his feelings for her and she wasn't to know about those.

'I cannot begin to think what she is going through; to have been taken by the Japanese and what Hans says in his letter. It is just so awful,' Evelien continued her voice breaking. 'You don't know her, of course; she seems so strong to the outside world but is really so soft and gentle inside. I am fearing that in her body and in her mind it will destroy her. I cannot even bear to think of it.'

Jim continued to cradle her in his arms and rubbed her back gently, swaying her like a baby falling asleep. He felt her sobs start to diminish and lifting his head, gazed down at her as she raised her head to look up at him. She felt so small and vulnerable in his arms, her head barely reaching his shoulders, like a child.

He smiled at her and her lips parted in a forced response. She held his gaze as he slowly lowered his face towards her. He had only meant to give her an avuncular kiss on the cheek, a gesture of comfort, but she turned her mouth towards him and their lips met. He pulled her closer towards him and kissed her passionately. Months of pent up emotions and doing the 'decent thing' exploded. They were lost in the joy of it.

They pulled away and looked shamefacedly at each other. They knew they had crossed a barrier that should not have been crossed, but it was one that could never exist between them again.

'That was not meant to happen. I'm so sorry, Evelien.' He whispered the words in earnest apology as he held her tightly.

'No, no, it was me as much as you. I wanted it to happen. Oh Jim, I have wanted it to happen since I met you that first night with Bill. I was not sure you felt the same and, of course, there is Bill. I feel so bad about him. And Eliezabeth. It is not right, not right just now, not when I know poor Eliezabeth is suffering as she is. I cannot think about my own feelings when I am also thinking about her pain. Just hold me close to you. That is what I am needing.'

Jim wrapped his arms around her again as they collapsed on the ground, huddled together out of sight of prying eyes.

'Do you want to tell me all about it – would that help? How did you find out?' he asked, gently cradling her.

'I have just been given a letter from my brother, Hans. I think I told you before one time that he still lives in Rotterdam; he is living quite close to my parents. They have all had a terrible time. He put another letter in with his, one he got recently from a man whose name is called Kapitein Christiaen Vendermark. It seems that when poor Eliezabeth was taken prisoner she met him for a short time. It is somewhere in Java, but he has got away.'

'Remind me, what did you say she was doing in Java?' asked Jim cautiously, not wanting to cause Evelien more pain.

'She was working as a baboe, what you in English call a nanny, like me, but she was working with a Dutch family. I cannot remember what I have told you about her before. She is two years older than me. She came to visit me here, at the start of the war, and she was going to try to work here with me in Malta, but her English is not so good so she went to Java. I think her employer, Mr de Groot, did some work for the Government in Holland, but I am not very sure about that. Last time she wrote to me, she told me that she was looking after the two little boys of the family. Her employers were kind to her and she seemed very happy; then we hear nothing from her at all. My family do not know what has happened. We did know, of course, that the Japanese soldiers go into Java in 1942, but we were hoping for the best thing. We thought that, with his contacts, her employer must have got them all out or that they were hiding somewhere. Of course, we also know that many Dutch peoples, women and children had been taken into prison. We just keep hoping that she had got away and would turn up, laughing and happy as she always is. My parents have been so worried, we all have and now this. This is the worst. She would be better off dead.'

'Oh Evelien, don't say that. This Kapitein Ven... what was his name?'

'Vendermark.'

'Yes, Vendermark; well he escaped, didn't he? There's hope then, perhaps she has too,' said Jim trying to reassure her and deflect her thoughts. 'Mind you, thinking about it, I'm pretty amazed. That can't have been easy. I'm presuming he's

Dutch with a name like that. A European travelling through Java…not easy at all,' mused Jim. He was about to continue when he realised that he was probably making matters much worse for Evelien so he promptly changed tack.

'So how did he know about Hans?'

'Well he writes in his letter that she met him very briefly in the…oh, what is its name, where they keep the peoples?'

'A prisoner of war camp?'

'Yes, there. He promised her that, if he ever got away, he would contact Hans to let him know what had happened to her. The things he says in his letter, it would kill my mother to know it all I am thinking. It is too awful.'

'Do you want to tell me what he wrote?' asked Jim gently.

Evelien started to sob again. She dabbed at her eyes, letter still in hand, then held out the crumpled, sodden pages to show to Jim.

'I am sorry, I cannot tell you what he has written. I cannot bring myself to read it again; you will have to read it for yourself,' she mumbled apologetically.

'I can't, Evelien,' he replied gently, glancing at the letter, 'it's written in Dutch. You'll have to do it for me. Come here.'

He took the letter, straightened it out, pulled her in between his knees and as she leant back against him, gave it to her to read. He felt her rhythmical breathing and the sensual swell of her body pressed against his thighs. She sniffed as she started to read, translating it as best she could.

Dear Mr van der Post

No doubting you will be surprised to get a letter from a complete stranger. My name is Christiaen Vendermark. Not long ago I came back to Holland having got away from Bandung prisoner of war camp in Northern Java. I will not take of your time now to go into the facts, but it is enough to say that it was a… mirakel…'

'I am sorry, I do not know this word in English… it is like magic,' she explained apologetically, pointing to the word on the page.

'A miracle?' offered Jim helpfully.

'Oh, it is the same,' she said, expressing her surprise as she continued reading.

'but it is enough to say that it was a miracle in itself, and I thank God for it.

I'm afraid, however, that I find myself the bringer of bad news and that this letter, while it may give you and your family some help, it may also cause you many sorrows. Although it is some months since I was with her, I believe that your sister, Eliezabeth, is alive but I am afraid that, like me, she was taken by the Japanese and her situations are not good.

My knowledge is not much, but as I understand it, Eliezabeth, and the family she worked for, were taken prisoner shortly after the Japanese arrived, in 1942. At first they were taken to another camp; I do not know where that was but I do know that, at some time, Eliezabeth was removed from the rest of the family and was taken to Bandung. I only met her once, for a very short time when we were moving camp, but she managed to push a note into my hand with your name and address and these few informations. Of course she must have known about the attempts to get out and, although it seemed impossible to all of us, she asked that if I managed to get out I would get in contact with you and let you know what has happened to her. I now keep that promise. I could not keep her first note for fear of discovery so I hope I have managed to remember the facts correctly.

I wish I could bring you happiness, and I do not wish to add to your pain, but I must tell you that conditions in these camps are pretty terrible with illnesses such as… dysenterie…'

She paused again and pointed to the page.

'It's the same in English, dysentery,' explained Jim gently.

'How strange,' she remarked, managing a faint smile.

...illnesses such as dysentery everywhere. Many die not only from these illnesses but from the terrible beating every day. We lived, survived I should say, on the most small amounts of food that would not provide enough to eat for a small animal yet alone men and women made to do hard physical work. The Red Cross and the... het Verdrag van Genève...

She looked around frowning. Jim nodded to confirm that he understood. He squeezed her gently in a gesture of encouragement. She carried on bravely; she was struggling to maintain her composure especially as she already knew what was coming next.

... het Verdrag van Genève does not exist as far as the Japanese are thinking.

But there is worse news to come I am afraid. Just before I got out in early March, I learnt that Eliezabeth had been taken from another part of the camp in late February. One day, it seems, the guards stood the young women outside the hutten...the houses. They went on to choose the most beautiful of these, those with the looks most from the west, such as light skin or blue eyes. You will understand why Eliezabeth was chosen. The prisoner who told me could speak some Japanese and worked where they kept the women. He heard the soldiers laughing and shouting as the women were taken away in a truck. They shouted that they hoped they could visit them soon in their 'special house'. He was sure that this meant the women were to be used as ... as prostituees...'

41

She stopped reading and turned her head, staring at him, her eyes glistening, her face etched with pain as she sought to see if he understood what the word meant. There was no need for translation. It was as deplorable in Dutch as it was in English.

'Oh Evelien. Why did your brother want you to know all this?' Jim lamented, pulling her closer into him and kissing the top of her head.

'I think he believes it is what Eliezabeth would have wanted; certainly this Kapitein Vendermark thinks we should know. Hans warned me about this letter, told me that it had some terrible things and that he nearly did not send it to me. In some ways I wish he had not.' She sighed loudly, her voice sounding strained as she began to read again.

'I cannot begin to think how this news will affect you and your family. I pray that if there is a God left above he will guard and look after her.

Eliezabeth felt you should know about the violence of these men, that the rest of the world should know, so that the fight against such cruelty would continue with power. I felt that you should know the rest. She said, however, that you should only tell your parents that she is alive, and save them from the worst informations. She wrote that she loves you all and thinks about you all the time.

I wish I could bring you happier news but, let us pray she is still safe and you will all meet up again someday soon, when this terrible war has ended.

Yours sincerely,

Kapitein Christiaen Vendermark'

Jim took the letter from Evelien, folded it, and wrapping his long arms around his knees enclosed her within. She bent her head and rested it on his muscular forearm. She rubbed her face against the smooth hairs wiping away her tears. She then kissed it gently. Neither of them spoke. The air was charged with tension; the tension the news in the letter had brought mingled with the tension of their physical closeness. She felt that she had known him forever, this kind strong man who was wrapping her in the womb of his arms. She felt so tired. Eventually she spoke.

'I feel that I could fall asleep for a hundred years and when I wake the world will be clean and new, without pain and cruel things, only filled with love and kindness.'

Jim pushed himself up onto his knees and, turning her towards him, lifted her to her feet. She drooped against him. He kissed her briefly on the lips.

'Let's walk towards the beach and watch the sea, it's good for the soul, healing. It's such a beautiful, balmy night.'

Evelien sniffled quietly, nodded and linked his arm as they strolled towards the bay.

The beach was deserted so they sat in the moonlight cupped together as they watched the incoming tide invade the parched sand, each wave capturing a little more. The day had been unbearably hot and the off-shore breeze was welcome and cooling. The sea hummed its familiar shanty. Jim eventually broke the silence.

'Don't you think there is something reassuring in knowing that the sea has washed these shores for millennia? It was here before us and will be here long after we are but dust. The world will go on without us. We are but a blink in time; when we've finished our journey, packed our kitbag of three score year and ten, it will continue on endlessly leaving and returning to this shore.'

She turned towards him and smiled. 'I am not sure I understand all you say, but I am thinking you are quite a philopospher, yes?'

'Philosopher I think you mean,' he retorted gently.

They burst out laughing. It was good to see her smile again. He grabbed her into him and pulled her down onto the sand. They kissed again and he knew that he wanted her more than he had ever wanted any woman before. Not in the lustful careless manner of his previous encounters, but because he wanted to love her, to please her, to be at one with her.

Jim placed his hand over her breast. He felt her body stiffen beneath his touch. He self-consciously withdrew it.

'I'm sorry, Evelien, I shouldn't have done that... please don't imagine I brought you here to take advantage... oh God, I'm so sorry.'

'Sshh. She held her finger to his lips. You English are all so, how do you say it... proper, older fashioned. Bill was the same at first.'

Jim flinched at the mention of Bill's name.

She reached up and pulled him towards her as she whispered.

'Do you love me?'

'Love you? I can't begin to tell you how much I love you. I absolutely adore you.'

'Me too,' she replied encouragingly.

They shared their love in the moonlight of a foreign beach, as the sea lapped gently at their feet. The cooling breeze fanned across their naked bodies as the war raged unnoticed in another world.

Chapter 5

New York, 4th February 1946

Kate stood on the deck as the SS Argentina ploughed its way through the icy waters of New York Bay. Ahead of her, a roar went up as the Statue of Liberty, bathed in light, came into view, and dozens of girlish screams echoed across the chill morning air. Her heart leapt with excitement. It was the first real indication that she had arrived in America, that she would soon be reunited with Art, and that they could start out on their new life together. Like everyone else, she had been violently sick on the journey across as the ship corkscrewed through the roughest of seas. She stood on deck, under a canopy of countless twinkling stars, breathing in the fresh icy air. She never thought she would be so glad to see land, any land. They had arrived in New York harbour nine long, wearying, days after leaving Southampton; a united sisterhood of bold adventurers, setting out like a band of pilgrim mothers bound for the uncharted waters of a foreign land. They were travelling to a people whom they knew were torn between sentiments of welcome and those of resentment.

As the ship drew alongside the harbour, Kate jostled with the mass of bodies waving wildly while it docked. The noise was deafening as the loudspeakers blared out 'God Bless America'. The biting early morning air froze her cheeks but she hardly felt it, warmed at the thought of seeing her husband of six months once again. She hoped Art had already arrived in New York to take her on the final leg of the journey to Boston and her new home. She couldn't wait to see him, to hold him again and love him completely as they had for a few precious days. They had had so little time together after their wedding, only three blissful days in a hotel in St Austell. Kate blushed as she thought about how little sightseeing they had managed to do; they might as well have stayed in

Plymouth. Art had returned to his unit, and then had left for America almost immediately afterwards. The last time she had seen him, she had been standing disconsolately on the station platform in Plymouth, fighting back her tears as he disappeared behind a curtain of steam. She hadn't been sure when she would see him again.

Art was waiting at the Red Cross Chapter House with so many of the other fresh-faced husbands. He hadn't wanted Kate's first experience of his homeland to be that of a hot and crowded journey on a war-bride train; cattle corralled into carriages that would carry them, like early homesteaders, to the four corners of America. He smiled as he thought about the shy bride he had left behind, the innocent girl who had become a sensual woman in his arms. He could never love anyone as much as he loved her. He couldn't wait to introduce her to his folks. He knew his father would be enchanted by his English rose; his mother would finally have the daughter she had always wanted. His fiery, gentle, independent, beautiful wife was somewhere in the waters off New York. Almost there, a few more hours and he could be with her for the rest of his life. The war was over; he could leave the devastation behind as surely as he had the bodies of his best buddies. He could look forward to a future with Kate and, hopefully one day, children and a life of normality.

A roar went up as news of their arrival at the Chapter House filtered through to the ranks of waiting men. The stringent immigration procedures seemed to be taking forever and tempers were fraying as the patience of war-hardened veterans was tested to the limit. They had lived through some of the most horrific experiences known to man, survived and emerged whole, to be thwarted on the home straight by the seemingly insurmountable obstacles erected by a few overly officious immigration officers. Some had arrived the previous day to find that the ship had been delayed for twenty-four hours. They were tired, hungry and anxious to get home with their wives. Eventually the first few women were allowed through. Art had the advantage of height to be able to see above the seething mass of bodies and check for Kate's arrival. At last he spotted her, her long stride carrying her along. She saw him, standing tall and distinctive above the crowd. He was wearing a light beige suit. She had never seen him in civilian clothes before; he looked distinguished and even more handsome than she remembered. She waved wildly to attract his attention. His face lit up in its familiar smile, framing the perfect white teeth. He moved towards her, cutting through the crowd, like a scythe through a cornfield, and swept her into his arms. He had forgotten the taste of her as they kissed the passionate kiss of lovers reunited at last. Around them the scene was played out a hundred times as husbands and wives, oblivious to the crowds around them, rekindled their unabashed love for each other.

Art began to load Kate's sparse luggage into his father's Cadillac.

'I was worried it wouldn't all fit in,' he commented wryly, shoving her cases snugly into one corner.

'Wouldn't fit in! I've lived in a cabin smaller than that boot for a whole week,' exclaimed Kate, gazing into the cavernous space. Art turned towards her and grinned, observing the look of astonishment on her face.

'I can't believe how little you've packed. No woman I know is going to survive long on the contents of a few small cases,' he teased.

'Well, my darling husband, you can blame your stingy US Navy restrictions for that. I think your famous stores have some making up to do, that's if your wallet can stand it, of course,' she giggled, pressing against him affectionately as she attempted to open the driver's door. He laughed, put his arm around her and guided her to the correct side of the car.

They set off along the highway. The car seemed to roll along on air. The journey was enthralling. Kate peered through the window with a child's insatiable curiosity, wide-eyed and wondering at the passing scenery. The skyscrapers stretching high above them seemed to kiss the sky. She imagined she had fallen through a rabbit hole and arrived in Wonderland, everything was so remarkably oversized. She felt small and insignificant and began to wonder if she really were the same, slightly apprehensive, girl who had departed the shores of England only a few days earlier.

She closed her eyes as the traffic lurched towards them, travelling at extreme speeds on the wrong side of the road. She felt the excitement and wonder of youth as her life stretched before her, filled with anticipation.

'How far is it to your parents' house in Boston?' asked Kate yawning discreetly.

'Not that far, honey, less than a couple of hundred miles I guess,' replied Art sympathetically.

Not that far, thought Kate. Her heart sank; she doubted if they would get there by nightfall. She reckoned it was about the distance from Plymouth to Birmingham, half a day's drive, after the most tiring and nauseating journey. She had been up since before three in the morning to experience their arrival into New York. She just wanted to get to her final destination and fall asleep.

The car swept along the wide open roads, swallowing up the miles. They arrived in Boston, at Art's parents' house, astonishingly quickly. They were there by mid-afternoon. She stepped nervously from the car, keen to create the best of impressions with her new family. Their large wooden house loomed in front of her. Everything around her seemed bigger and better, untouched as it was by the pernicious hand of war. Art took her arm and walked proudly beside her. He had been noticeably subdued in the car, and she wondered if he was also nervous about the meeting.

'They'll love you just as I do, don't worry,' he whispered noticing how the garrulous girl, who had chattered incessantly along the way, had suddenly lost her voice. Art's parents Ed and Nancy rushed out to greet them. Art's younger and much shyer brother Brandon followed a short distance behind.

'Hi honey, you've got here at last, you must be exhausted, you poor thing. Wow, ain't she pretty, Art?' gushed Nancy, enveloping Kate in a bear hug. Ed followed suit with a similar rib-crushing embrace.

'How do you do?' said Kate politely coming up for breath. 'It's very nice to meet you, Mr and Mrs Willis.'

'Hey, it's Ed and Nancy, we don't go for all that formal introductions stuff. Don't you sound so British, just like... darn, what's her name... that actress you know, Ed, prim and proper by all accounts... my memory ain't what is used to be... the one in... oh, what's its name? We saw it not so long ago... *Brief Encounter* that's it,' continued Nancy enthusiastically.

'Do you mean Celia Johnson, honey?' asked Ed helpfully.

'Yes, that's the one. We've got our very own Celia Johnson.'

Kate was pretty sure that with her distinctive West Country burr, she sounded absolutely nothing like Celia Johnson but, then again, all Americans sounded the same to her so she didn't protest.

'Now you come and get yourself settled in. There's plenty of hot water if you fancy jumping in the tub. You can't have had many home comforts on that goddam-awful ship. Am I right, did Art tell me that you were on that old rust bucket for nine long days, or am I imagining that? I'm so glad you've got here safely, honey. Hopefully we'll get the old Art back as well; honestly, he's been that quiet and mopey since he got back from Europe. I can only assume he's been pining for you, honey. Maybe you can get him to tell me all about his adventures. I can't get a darn word out of him on the subject.' She didn't seem to stop to draw breath.

Kate looked at Art. He was staring at his mother. His eyes had turned dark and menacing, like lifeless, stagnant pools; the surface had become dull and unreflective. Kate watched him and felt a shiver run down her spine. She knew that below the surface he had laid to rest a thousand traumas, buried them in the hidden depths. She feared that, if ever disturbed, they would emerge as a putrid, stinking poison.

She had first noticed the change in him when he returned to England from France. Essentially he was still the man with whom she had fallen deeply in love, kind and thoughtful, but he was much quieter and more serious. He had avoided talking about his experiences and she knew better than to push him. It was obvious that his mother did not.

Kate felt swamped by the welcome from Nancy; it seemed so casual and over familiar. She felt uncomfortable calling them by their first names; she feared that it would appear disrespectful. Even she had become 'Mrs Willis' back home, in deference to her new-found marital status. She decided to avoid calling them anything at all in the meantime. It also occurred to her that this was home now – England was in the past. She started to feel the first twinge of homesickness. She knew how much her parents and James would have enjoyed seeing New York and now Boston. She wondered when she would see them all again and if they were missing her.

Kate followed them all into the large, airy but unexpectedly warm house. Nancy showed her up to her bedroom. Art carried her relatively small cases and set them down heavily on the floor.

'I hope you two young lovebirds will be comfortable in here,' Nancy said without any hint of irony. Art looked at her, wishing his mother could be a little less obvious in her observations and a little less exuberant.

Kate blushed when she saw the huge double bed and Art's clothes casually thrown on a wicker chair beside it. Up until that moment, it hadn't occurred to her that, of course, she would be sharing a bedroom with him right under his parents' roof. She hoped that the wooden walls she had observed outside, disguised good thick brick ones inside.

'Have you told Kate yet?' enquired Nancy impatiently.

'Told her what, Mom?' asked Art.

'About the house, of course,' she urged.

'No, I was keeping that as a surprise for later, but I guess I'll have to tell her now,' he replied, slightly irritated that his mother had stolen his thunder. He wanted to tell Kate when they were alone, tell her while she was lying in his arms. It was to be a wonderful surprise.

Kate stood quietly, waiting.

'Mom and Dad have given us a wonderful wedding present, Kate. They're buying us a house. We were waiting until you arrived so you could choose.'

Like the Cheshire Cat, Kate's face had disappeared behind the widest grin. She couldn't believe it. She hadn't reached twenty-one, yet here she was living in America; she was to have her own house, she had Art, her independence. It couldn't be true, she would wake up in a moment and realise she was back in Plymouth, in the claustrophobic clutches of her mother.

'Dad's brother is in real estate, he has some houses I think you would like,' Art explained. 'They're quite close to here… but far enough away to allow us some privacy,' he whispered in her ear as his mother left the room to fetch some clean towels. Kate smiled knowing exactly what he meant. Nancy was very kind, and had made her feel most welcome, but Kate was finding her rather over-zealous. A bit of space between them was just the thing. She began to appreciate her own mother's cool geniality.

Kate was dying to 'jump in the tub', as Nancy had put it so eloquently, to collapse into the large comfortable looking bed and catch up on nine days and nights of broken sleep, but she thought it would appear rude. Art would also have liked to jump into bed with her, but with more carnal purposes in mind. He had to concede that there was little chance of that, what with his mother's enthusiasm and Kate's modesty. It would have to wait.

Somehow Kate managed to make it through the rest of the day, her eyes held open by sheer willpower and youth.

Ed and Nancy took her for a drive round Boston, pointing out the historic buildings. Everything seemed so untouched by the war; every building standing as it had proudly stood for a hundred years. The enormous cars with their unfamiliar names, Cadillacs, Dodges and Chevrolets rolled along over perfectly smooth roads, unblemished by craters and temporary repairs. Kate was too tired to take much of it in, she was desperate for sleep. At last darkness fell. It was Art who suggested that perhaps she needed an 'early night'. She had missed him so much, dreamt of being with him again for so long, but in her heart she hoped that he wasn't talking in euphemisms. She was so tired and felt incredibly awkward about sleeping in the same room as him with his parents listening next door.

Art and Kate wished his parents good night and climbed the wide stairs together. Kate leant against him hardly able to carry her exhausted body upwards. She washed in the spacious bathroom and returned to the bedroom shyly delaying getting undressed while he was in the room. Art was waiting his turn to go into the bathroom. She quickly slipped on her nightdress and was tucked up in bed by the time he returned.

'That was quick,' he commented, looking at her lying in the bed with the bedclothes pulled up under her chin and her dress neatly folded on the chair. 'I was kinda hoping to help you out of that.'

She smiled at him, her eyes half-closed in sleep. He undressed much more slowly and jumped in bedside her stark naked. He put his arms around her and held her close. She felt his excitement. He kissed her tenderly; desperate to transform her into the hungry young woman he had left behind in England. The combination of sleep deprivation and Nancy overdose were too much for her. She felt herself drifting into the sleep of the dead, cradled in his comforting arms. Her first night in America with him passed in sleep-filled oblivion.

Three months later, Art and Kate moved into their smart new home, with a flurry of activity. All day Nancy and Ed helped them to fetch and carry box after box from one house to another. A succession of delivery lorries arrived, bearing the fruits of their shopping labours. As Art's parents finally left the house, Art and Kate hugged and thanked them profusely for all their help and generosity. They closed the door behind them and breathed a huge sigh of relief. At last they were at home alone and this time it was their very own.

They looked around at the boxes piled high in every room, each patiently waiting its turn to be unpacked. They only had a sofa, a bed and some kitchen utensils at their immediate disposal, but it was all they needed for now. Kate couldn't put into words how happy and excited she was. Everything looked so new, so modern and interesting. The freshly waxed floors smelt warm and welcoming. Smooth and easy to clean Formica tops adorned the built in kitchen. A large space stood empty, pre-empting the arrival of an enormous refrigerator. They had an electric cooker, a washing machine, even a percolator to make coffee; she loved having freshly ground coffee in the morning. They had a TV for the sitting room, a shower in the bathroom and a telephone upstairs and down. Kate had every modern convenience possible at her disposal. It was like an Aladdin's cave to her. Her excitement in her new home was surpassed only by the thought that in seven months' time, there would be an even more wonderful new addition. She was expecting her first child.

Chapter 6

Exeter 1946

'Well, here we are, darling, home sweet home, as they say.'

Jim Palmer pushed against the door with his back as he swivelled around to carry Evelien in.

'Oh Jim, put me down before you drop me,' she laughed. 'Why do husbands carry their wives into the house like this anyway?'

'Old Roman tradition, I believe, something to do with their carrying off the Sabine women and it being bad luck to trip on the threshold. Vaguely seem to remember something like that from a distant Latin class.'

He set her down gently.

'I am sure you make these things up just to impress me,' she retorted. 'I would not know if you were telling the truth to me or not, but you are so clever I think it is true.'

She looked at him admiringly, kissing the end of his nose, before glancing around the noticeably small room.

'Not up to much perhaps,' he replied following her gaze, 'but it'll do until we get something better. I can't believe you're actually here with me at last, here in England.'

He held her close and kissed her forehead.

'Mr and Mrs Palmer, sounds good, doesn't it?' he continued. 'We'll be happy here, won't we, Evelien? Happy together, just the two of us and this little house, no bombs, no danger, no sun come to think of it. I hope you won't miss Malta too much. Not quite the same weather in Exeter I'm afraid.'

'No. It is exciting for me Jim, a new life, in a new country and best of all sharing it with you. I do not miss Malta, not yet, and hopefully not ever. I am so happy, really I am. I want to get out to seeing all the places I have only read about in books. Perhaps we are going to London some time, no?

'Yes, we are going to London some time,' he teased, mimicking her accent.

'Oh Jim, do not make the fun. Now I am here my English will be getting much better. You will be seeing.'

'I love it just as it is, it's part of you,' he replied stroking her hair. 'I love you just as you are, my beautiful wife.'

Jim had returned to London at the end of January '45. Before he left Malta, Evelien and he had agreed that they would marry as soon as the war ended; they thought it would be tempting fate to do so before. Everything still felt so precarious that planning a happy and stable future somehow seemed wrong. They could hardly wait, but surely it couldn't be long before the war finally ended, months rather than years they had reasoned. Germany was on the run, the Allies were winning and the end was finally in sight. Evelien had stayed on in Malta with her employers, the Browns, until September, returning briefly to Rotterdam to visit her parents and brother, Hans, before travelling to her new life in England. Hans had still not received any news of Eliezabeth. Even if she were still alive, they couldn't be sure that she had been freed. Terrible stories were beginning to emerge as people made their way back to Holland, but it was all still very confused. Hans had kept the worst from their parents; they seemed so vulnerable and weakened by war that he couldn't tell them the truth.

Evelien had been shocked to witness the aftermath of the war and the ravages of Nazism. Malta had undoubtedly suffered but Holland, it appeared, had simply shrivelled up and died. She listened in horror to her parents' accounts of how they had fled Rotterdam in terror seeking to evade the relentless German bombers, ceaselessly dropping their careless death from above. Her parents had lost everything, but they had been amongst the lucky ones. Thousands of innocent men, women and children had lain dead in the aftermath and the centre of the city that she had known so well, where she had spent her youth, was no more. Even now, five years later, as she walked around in despair, she was horrified by what she witnessed. The city still had an aroma of death, the dust hadn't fully settled. It looked ill and grey.

Emaciated bodies, with cheekbones like knuckles, eked out a living in what had once been a proud and prosperous port. Like everyone else, her parents' staple diet consisted of bread, potatoes and sugar beets; just enough to stave off starvation, but little more. Their sunken faces were testimony to the futility of war. It was over and what had been achieved? Nothing, it would seem, but heartache and destruction. There were no victors; all had lost, leaving only buildings and lives in desperate need of reconstruction. She had no heart to stay; this shell of a nation was not the country she remembered with fondness. She longed to be away from it, to be with Jim, to forget, yet she was filled with profound guilt. Was she abandoning her beloved parents when they needed her most, especially when no one knew if Eliezabeth would ever return? They had lost so much already, perhaps one child and with her departure, yet another. But, if she stayed, did that mean abandoning Jim, for how could he find work in a land where he could not speak the language? She couldn't bear the thought of losing him.

'You must go to England, Evelien. There is nothing for you here now. I will look after your mother and, God willing, your sister when she returns.' Her father's unsolicited words of advice had taken her by surprise. She had not thought to discuss her reservations with him, not at least until she had taken more time to think. For all his fragility, her father's mind had remained sharp and perceptive. She might have known that he would suspect she was considering staying, but he had encouraged a fierce independence in all his children from the earliest age.

'Remember what I once told you; we are a nation of explorers, Evelien, it's in your blood and you cannot escape it. You must go out and grab life, grab every opportunity while you can.' Her father's words had rung in her ears. He had first expressed them on her sixteenth birthday and she had acted on them two years later. Now ten years further on, he was setting her the challenge once again, for he knew that having already drunk from the cup of independence she could not relinquish it now. He had made the decision for her and, in doing so, had salved her conscience.

Filled with a heady mixture of sadness and excitement she had caught a boat to England a week later. She had fallen into Jim's open arms and wept tears of joy for the life to come and sorrow for those she had left behind.

Jim and Evelien were offered a little terraced house on the outskirts of Exeter. They were lucky; houses were a scarce commodity. The house had belonged to an aunt of Jim's father and miraculously had escaped the war intact, standing bravely alone, while many around it had collapsed. Jim's great-aunt, like the house, had managed to survive the war but not pneumonia; she had died in the summer. It was in this cramped, rather damp little house that Jim and Evelien were to start their married life. To them it was a haven of peace.

Demobbed and unemployed, Jim joined the queue of countless others seeking to readjust and rebuild their lives. He had considered returning to Exeter University to finish the Geography degree he had been forced to abandon six years earlier, but he realised that he now had a wife to support and he needed to earn some money. On demob he started to apply for every job he could think of; one that would allow him to use his brain but would not require a degree. It was tough going as thousands of other young men were seeking similar employment. Women, who had so ably stood in and proved themselves in real jobs for the best part of six years, were naturally reluctant to step aside and creep back to the dependency of being a housewife.

'Hello, Evelien, are you here?' Jim called as he opened the door and entered the dark little hallway four weeks later. Evelien ran to the top of the stairs; she could tell from his voice that something had excited him. He looked up and grinned.

'What is it, Jim?' she asked in anticipation. 'Is it a job?'

'It sure is,' he replied still grinning. She skipped down the steep wooden staircase and leapt into his arms.

'What is it? What job? Is it here in Exeter? Will we have to move?' she rattled in her heavy accent, barely drawing breath.

'Yes, here in Exeter, a bloody good job and here in Exeter. It's the one I wanted but I never thought I had a chance. I nearly didn't apply, thought it was pointless... there must have been hundreds of people applied for that job. I still can't believe it.'

'But what is it, Jim? What will you be doing? What is this job?'

'Only creating a national grid of Devon,' he responded with false nonchalance, as he held her hand and led her into the small sitting room.

'A what?' she asked. 'What does that mean? How I wish my English was better, it is so difficult to understand the words sometimes,' she bemoaned as they sat down and cuddled together.

'Sorry, darling, I don't suppose that means much to you. Come to think of it, I doubt if it would mean much to most people, whether they speak English or not. I'm to be part of a new team. We've been formed to create a metric national grid of Devon. That simply means I'll be helping to make new maps of Exeter... well, other parts too in time. I was so sure they would want someone with a degree, but they seem to think I can learn quickly. It might hold me back a bit for a while, but if I can prove myself, well I think I can work my way up. It's a start isn't it?'

Evelien had only understood about half of what he said, but it didn't matter – she was revelling in his success. He was happy and so she would be too.

They were excited about the start of this hopeful new life. They had come through the war relatively unscathed, a few scars perhaps but luckily they were physical not mental, quick to heal. Along the way they had met the love of their lives, someone without whom neither could imagine existing, they had a roof over their head, Jim now had a job with considerable prospects, and his future looked bright. At last they could settle down.

For Evelien her happiness would be complete once they started their family which hopefully, now Jim had a job, would be as soon as possible; she missed the contact with children and needed something to occupy her own eternally active mind.

Jim had never really considered the prospect of fatherhood, but it was obviously so hugely important to Evelien he concluded that he would be delighted if and when it happened.

Evelien soon settled into her married life in Exeter. She created an easy routine for them both and transformed the dull little house into a happy home. He loved the touches she brought to their lives, the unusual objects she had brought from her homeland, embroidered bell pulls, Delft pottery; the unusual meals she made with what little rations they had. She spent most of her time with the many newly married young women living locally. She was shown kindness, respect and a level of acceptance that belied the cold English temperament she had been warned to expect. One by one, month by month, then year by year, the little group was joined by yet another addition; the next generation was growing. In the two years since the war had ended, England's young men and women had made up for lost time and begun repopulating the devastated cities with gusto.

Even though to Evelien they appeared unworldly and somewhat prudish, she enjoyed the company of these naïve, young women, several of whom had lost their own mothers in the Blitz and with them their time honoured mentors. Most had never left the confines of Exeter let alone Devon. Evelien, with her confident bearing and continental manners, seemed to them modern and unconventional. She was an object of curiosity mixed with admiration. Most had so little idea about life, marriage or raising children that they turned to Evelien for much needed advice. She was older than most of them, now in her late twenties and her experience as a nanny led to her appointment as the unofficial baby expert. She enjoyed acting out the role and joined in the collective delight at each new arrival, while waiting patiently for her own turn.

In two years Jim had been promoted twice; his lack of a degree didn't seem to matter anymore and had apparently not stood in his way at all. He was a popular colleague, considered to be organised and reliable but with a twinkle in his eye and a brain to match. For Jim, life was about as good as it got. He was thoroughly enjoying his job. He looked forward to going in to the office every morning and he looked forward to returning to Evelien every night. He was so content he hardly noticed that Evelien was gradually becoming quiet and withdrawn. He assumed that, like him, she was enjoying the best years of their lives. They had money in their pockets, a great many friends and each other's love. They had been able to save some money and were planning to move into a bigger and better house by the end of the year.

At first, her uninhibited love making had both delighted and shocked him. Jim had had his fair share of woman and was no beginner in bed, but Evelien was obviously the much more sexually experienced. She saw no contradiction between her role as respectable wife to the world and daring lover to her husband.

'Do you think there is something wrong with me, Jim?' Evelien asked out of the blue one evening as she lay casually on top of him. Jim looked into her glistening eyes.

'Wrong with you? You're perfect, Evelien. You couldn't be more perfect,' he replied affectionately, leaning up and kissing the end of her nose.

'No, I mean, don't you think it is strange that we have not had a baby yet, that I have not become with a child? We have been married for two years now and, well, it is not as if there have not been plenty of the opportunities. I think there might be something wrong with me.'

'Happy to have plenty more opportunities to prove there isn't, like now again if you like,' Jim teased. She didn't reply.

'But seriously, Evelien,' he continued soberly, 'two years isn't that long is it? I don't know much about these things, you would know better than me. I suppose it takes time that's all. I'm sure there's nothing wrong, it just hasn't happened yet. We need to be patient that's all. Anyway,' he teased wrapping both arms around her and squeezing her tightly, 'I quite like having you all to myself, just the two of us. When the time is right it will happen, nature will take its course, I'm sure it will.'

'Perhaps you are right. I should not worry. You know though that I am not getting any younger. I suppose I am worried that time is walking on.'

'I think you mean marching on you funny, adorable little woman. I do love you and your wonderful Evelienisms. Don't worry about it, you're still a young woman, silly,' he laughed as she rolled off him. He snuggled into her and kissed her, gently. She didn't respond as she usually did.

'Evelien,' he said quietly, holding her in his arms, 'if it's worrying you, why don't you go and see Dr Greene. I'm sure he will reassure you that everything is going to be fine. Why don't you make an appointment to see him; it will put your mind at rest if nothing else.'

'I think I will do that. I am sure I am being silly that is all. Good night, darling, sleep well.'

'God bless, see you in the morning.'

The next day, Evelien managed to get an early appointment to see Dr Greene. He examined her carefully but concluded that there didn't seem to be anything obviously wrong.

'It's so ironic, Mrs Palmer,' he explained, 'I seem to spend half my time dealing with young women who want to get pregnant and can't and the other half dealing with young women who don't want to get pregnant and can't stop. Don't worry, it's early days yet. I can't find anything physically wrong with you, in fact you seem very fit and healthy to me. The more you worry about it, you know, the less likely it will happen. Try to forget about it, enjoy your married life and I'm sure when the time is right nature will take its course and you'll be back here for happy news before you know it.'

It was just as Jim had said, but Evelien wasn't convinced. There was a constant nagging doubt in the back of her mind, a sixth sense convinced her that it would never happen for her, that she would never hold her own child, but she was determined that she wasn't going to allow it to affect her or her relationship with Jim. Life would go on as normal and Jim would never know her doubts.

They moved into their new home two weeks before Christmas. It was very modern and the rooms were much larger than in the little terrace that had served as home for over two years. Almost best of all there was a phone line which meant that, at last, Evelien could talk to her family. The move had given her a completely new lease of life. She felt like a child back in Rotterdam; everything seemed new and ripe for exploration. Better still, in November she had received a letter from Eliezabeth who, most unexpectedly, had decided that she wanted to spend Christmas with them.

Eighteen months earlier, Eliezabeth had suddenly turned up in Rotterdam, completely unannounced. The family had all but given up hope of ever seeing her again. They had received no word from, or about, her since the letter from Christiaen Vendermark in 1944. Many internees had already been repatriated, but no one seemed to know anything about an Eliezabeth van der Post. Her return, therefore, was greeted by her family with equal measures of shock and delight.

Hans had written immediately to tell his sister the good news, but the details he was able to provide were very sketchy. All he could fathom was that she had been extremely ill, that somehow she had found her way to Batavia in Java where she had been picked up by the British and was then taken to Singapore. She was considered too unwell to travel further and was detained in hospital. No one was quite sure who she was. She had no identification and was delirious, riddled with lice and ulcers. It was months before she spoke and was eventually identified as Dutch.

She hadn't wanted to talk about her experience to the family, and no one wanted to intrude on her private thoughts. Anyway, they were all so delighted to have her back it didn't matter; she would tell them if and when she chose to.

Evelien had written back to Hans immediately, explaining that she would jump on a boat and meet them all in Rotterdam; an exciting reunion and Jim could come as well, but Hans had cautioned against it. Eliezabeth was still quite unwell and receiving medical attention in a local hospital. In truth, Eliezabeth had specifically asked them not to allow her sister to see her until she was completely better. Evelien was deflated; she wanted to see Eliezabeth, she wanted them all to meet Jim. She had been excited at the prospect and was annoyed with Hans for being so reticent. She decided she would go anyway; of course Eliezabeth would want to see her. Jim, however, had read between the lines and talked her out of it.

Now, nearly eight years since she had last seen her sister, Evelien was looking forward to making up for all the lost time but, most of all, she would finally have someone in whom she could confide and discuss her omnipresent anxieties about being barren. If she could talk to anyone it would be Eliezabeth. It would be like old times, back at home in Rotterdam, when they used to sit happily chatting into the early hours, sharing everything; their aspirations, their fears, their joint desire to travel and see something of the world. She realised how much she missed her sister's company and how close they had once been.

Evelien worked tirelessly to make sure that everything was unpacked and the house looked its best for her sister's arrival. She wanted Eliezabeth to see how happy she was; she was sure that she would love Jim as much as she did. She had it all planned. Jim had managed to get a whole week off work and had promised to take them all to London. She couldn't wait; what a Christmas it was going to be!

The days flew by far too quickly as she realised how much stuff they had managed to accumulate in such a relatively short time and how much time it took to sort it all. Jim helped as best he could when he came home from work, but Evelien seemed to fill every waking moment unpacking boxes, hanging curtains, arranging and endlessly rearranging furniture, wrapping presents, decorating the tree, hanging up cards. She worked tirelessly. She wanted it all to be perfect.

Eliezabeth was due to arrive on December 23rd. The day arrived long before Evelien felt fully prepared. They decided that Jim would pick Eliezabeth up on his way back from work, which would save him driving the whole way home and give Evelien a bit of extra time to make the final frantic preparations, but when it came to it she couldn't wait to see her sister and the day dragged by. She sat watching the clock waiting for them to arrive, wishing she had arranged to go with Jim to collect her after all. At last Evelien heard footsteps on the path and rushed to open the door in anticipation. She hesitated as the stranger before her met her gaze. Jim was standing behind a pale, thin, middle-aged woman carrying a large black handbag.

'Evelien,' Eliezabeth whispered as she held out her hand. It was a cold, formal and unexpected gesture.

Evelien immediately bent forward and hugged the stiff stranger who had embodied her beloved sister. She pulled away and looked into Eliezabeth's eyes. They were vacant. The face that met her gaze was that of a much older but vaguely familiar relative; it was not Eliezabeth's. This woman did not have Eliezabeth's fresh flawless skin, but a thin covering of fragile, yellowed parchment, framed with brittle, lifeless, colourless hair.

'Eliezabeth, Eliezabeth kom binnen, kom binnen. It is so good to see you. I cannot believe you are here at last. I have so much to tell you and so much to find out,' welcomed Evelien, trying to maintain her composure.

Evelien spoke in perfect Dutch peppered with English. They linked arms and walked together into the hallway. Jim followed behind in silence, he had seen the look of shock on Evelien's face; he hoped Eliezabeth had not.

Half an hour earlier, he had turned up at the railway station, just as the London train was pulling in. He was expecting to meet a tall, slim, dark-haired, continental beauty. Evelien's instructions had been precise. They were to meet under the railway clock at six o'clock. Eliezabeth would be carrying a Dutch newspaper just in case, but Evelien was confident that he couldn't mistake her. He was hoping that she would have the look of Evelien; that air of confidence without arrogance, natural beauty without effort. He had hesitated as he was approached by a slightly cowering woman struggling to carry her case. She had a crumpled newspaper tucked under her arm and was cautiously gazing around obviously looking for someone. Indeed, it was Eliezabeth.

Back in the house, Jim watched as the two sisters sat holding hands, hardly believing that at last they were together again. He decided to leave them alone to talk. There was so much to tell, but he could see that it would wait. The time wasn't right. They needed to get to know each other again first.

Evelien had imagined that they would immediately slot back into the easy conversation they used to share. Thoughts about having a baby seemed to preoccupy her every waking moment, she was so looking forward to sharing her concerns with Eliezabeth but, as she looked across at this shadow of her sister, instinct told her to wait. There was so much pain written in her expression, so much obviously trapped inside, Evelien wondered would Eliezabeth ever emerge whole again.

'I do not know what to say to her,' Evelien whispered in hushed tones as she crept into bed beside Jim that night. The clock in the hall had just chimed midnight, but Evelien was still wide awake, her mind churning over the events of the evening.

'What did you say, darling?' asked Jim, roused from semi-slumber.

'I said, I do not know what to say to her, how to help her. I cannot begin to tell you how much changed she is. It is breaking my heart. I was so looking forward to seeing her and now I can barely look at her.'

Jim turned over and put a comforting arm around his wife.

'She has said so little. I want to help, but how can I, if she will not tell me anything? Why will she not tell me what happened to her? We used to tell each other everything.'

'Perhaps she can't,' Jim responded gently. 'Perhaps she's tried to forget. Give her time; she'll talk if and when she wants to.'

'She looks so different, so old. She is a young woman in an old woman's body. Hans should have warned me properly. He said she had changed but I had no idee. He should have explained. I was so shocked when I saw her. Oh God, I hope she did not notice. Do you think she noticed?' she asked anxiously.

Jim was pretty sure she had.

'I wouldn't think so, it was pretty dark at the door,' he replied reassuringly. 'Try to sleep, darling, it's been an emotional day and you'll need all your strength for tomorrow. Perhaps when she's had a good night's sleep she'll feel more like talking. She was probably tired after her journey, that's all.' But he was not at all convinced and with a sinking heart suspected that it was going to be a long two weeks.

For much of the time Eliezabeth remained withdrawn and quiet, often choosing to stay in her room alone. She seemed too tired and morose to do anything much except sit and stare. The journey from Rotterdam had indeed exhausted her and there was no sign of recovery. She hardly ate, spoke or slept. Jim and Evelien could hear her wandering about in the middle of the night. Through the bedroom wall they could hear her crying out in loud cries of anguish. When she was awake, so was everyone else.

Evelien was concerned but understanding. Jim, however, was finding the situation incredibly difficult. He had looked forward so much to having some time off with Evelien, to spoiling her over Christmas and had assumed that Eliezabeth would slot in happily with their easy routine. They had been invited to numerous parties; everyone wanted to meet Evelien's pretty sister. They had meticulously planned their trip to London and had got tickets for Evelien and Eliezabeth to see their first English pantomime. There was so much they wanted to do and too little time to do even half of it. They had carefully thought through and devised a packed schedule to give Eliezabeth the most wonderful holiday. As it was, Eliezabeth was reluctant to leave the house, and Evelien was reluctant to leave Eliezabeth, so consequently they spent his precious holiday imprisoned in each other's company. To make matters worse, Eliezabeth seemed to have forgotten what limited English she had previously acquired, so Evelien felt obliged to speak to her in Dutch; he couldn't even join in their conversations. His generous nature was being tested to the limit and while he tried to be sympathetic, Jim's resentment of Eliezabeth was growing day by day. Returning to work came as a blessed relief.

Evelien showed remarkable patience. It pained her incredibly to see her sister's descent into this half-life. Encouraged and supported by Evelien, gradually, bit by bit, snippet by snippet, Eliezabeth allowed the truth about her war to seep out. It was horrific, unbelievable and even then Evelien knew that she was only hearing what Eliezabeth chose to share; she was obviously holding so much of it back. Her mind had sealed over so that the truth might never emerge; her memories had been repressed to protect.

Eventually Eliezabeth opened up fully, one dismal afternoon while they sat alone in the sitting room.

'I can hardly think about it, hardly think about it at all,' she began voluntarily in a chilling monotone voice. Evelien looked up in surprise. She had been sitting quietly watching the flames dancing in the grate wondering if she dared broach the subject of the baby with her sister. She had thought Eliezabeth was dozing.

'It's as if it all happened to someone else and somehow their memories have been transplanted into my mind,' Eliezabeth continued. 'I look in the mirror and it's not me that is looking back. I see a stranger... I want to see a stranger, then I can believe that it didn't happen to me. It doesn't make any sense; nothing seems to make sense any more. It hasn't from the day we were set free.'

She sat staring into space as her mind relived the horror of the abuse she had suffered. Evelien waited patiently for her to continue.

At last, thought Evelien. At last she'll tell me and then I can help. Make it better for her. Let her get it out of her system and then she'll be fine. We can get back to normal.

'We couldn't understand it, one day the guards opened the gates... they told us to walk... to walk home,' Eliezabeth continued slowly. 'Home,' she sneered, 'we didn't know where home was... there was chaos everywhere... people screaming at us, attacking us, they kept attacking us…'

'What, the Japanese soldiers? Why would they set you free and then attack you?' queried Evelien, in a vain attempt to keep the stilted account flowing.

'No, not them, not the Japanese... not this time... I mean the local people, the Javanese. We couldn't understand why... what had we done to them? The soldiers told us to run, to run away. We could hardly stand and they wanted us to run. Run where? Where were we supposed to go? They kept screaming at us. Why do you think they were screaming at us?' she asked bitterly.

'I don't know, darling,' replied Evelien helplessly. 'Perhaps they didn't realise who you were; didn't realise that you had been prisoners. Perhaps they thought you were with the Japanese. I don't know. I can't explain it.'

'No, they knew exactly who we were... they didn't want us... they wanted to get rid of us... it was because they knew we were Dutch. They were filled with hatred; first the Japanese and now them. There was blood everywhere, people lying rotting in the streets... I felt so ill... so tired... the heat... the stench of death...'

She paused, lost once more in the agony of her thoughts. Evelien listened with disbelief. She didn't know if she should encourage her to speak or allow her to think. In truth, she didn't think she wanted to hear much more. She wasn't sure that it was helping and Eliezabeth's demeanour was frightening her. She lifted Eliezabeth's hand and squeezed it gently in a gesture of encouragement. It felt hard and cold. A corpse's hand. Instinctively she thought to drop it but Eliezabeth began to speak again.

'I couldn't keep up with them... all the others... they started to run... they left me behind... my legs hurt so much... I was on my own... I was scared and on my own... the English soldiers helped me. They must have found me. They took me to Singapore... I must have been on a boat but I don't remember... I don't remember anything... then I was in a hospital. They helped me to get better... well enough to get back to Holland.'

Eliezabeth looked towards her sister's beautiful face but could not meet her gaze.

'I'm so ashamed, Evelien,' she continued cautiously, averting her eyes, 'I can't tell even you, I can't tell anyone what happened to us; they were like... like wild animals... we were lumps of meat. They beat us every day... and much, much worse things than that...we had so little food... I really can't tell you... I can't begin to remember...We lived in a kind of never-ending hell... they've all tried to help me... they were so kind, the doctors I mean... first in Singapore and then at home in Holland... but there is so little they can do. My body has healed... well partly healed.' Her eyes had remained cold and staring throughout, her face expressionless. She paused. 'Unlike you, I can never have a child,' she added unemotionally.

Evelien swallowed involuntarily. Eliezabeth had unwittingly touched her rawest nerve.

'There was nothing wrong with me, with my body I mean, until they forced a child into me then ripped it out of me,' Eliezabeth continued with unexpected and renewed vigour. 'I'm sorry I can't tell you... I want to tell you, but I want to forget even more. The problem is there's not a time when I can truly forget and yet I daren't remember. I'm imprisoned in my memories as surely as I was imprisoned in that camp. As I said, the body has healed but the memories never will.'

The fire burned in the grate warming the room with a benevolent glow, but Evelien felt chilled to the bone. She wanted Eliezabeth to stop, to tell her she had dreamed it all. It hadn't happened. She was fine. Everything was fine. But as Eliezabeth spoke, the horrible truth had started to dawn on Evelien; the sister she had known, and loved, was probably lost to her forever. She would never return. Confronted by Eliezabeth's stoicism she felt she had to conceal her own emotions. She wanted to reach out and embrace her sister, to hold her close, to comfort her but she could not bring herself to do it; instinctively she knew it would not be reciprocated.

Neither mentioned it again and Evelien could not share her own, relatively inconsequential concerns in the face of such pain, but Eliezabeth's revelations stayed fresh with her for weeks after her departure and affected her badly. She had formed some idea about what might have happened to her; she had thought the worst but, even now, much of the story had to remain in her imagination. She suspected it always would. The shocking transformation in Eliezabeth's physical appearance, and the profound change in her character, could only hint at the hidden mental anguish inside. She had become a two-dimensional version of her former self, painting for the world only what she chose for them to see; a carefully constructed and considered image. There were no longer the spontaneous actions that created depth of character, the blend of anger, joy, fear, envy, love or laughter, borne out of the moment that make us what it is to be human. It was as if the palette of emotions was no longer hers to use at will and she was required to select them with care.

Chapter 7

Plymouth, October 1952

'Shall I take the luggage straight up? Presumably you're back in your old room, Kate?'

Michael Aldworth struggled to lift the two enormous American cases. Big and brash like much of America, he thought to himself.

'Yes, please do, Michael,' Sarah interjected, 'and can you put Clare's in James' old room. Come into the kitchen with me, you two. I want to get to know my lovely granddaughter. Cup of tea everyone?'

'I'd prefer coffee if you have any,' replied Kate. Clare sat diffidently beside her mother, overawed by the entire situation.

'Sorry, I'm afraid your father and I don't really drink coffee but I think I have some Camp Essence somewhere, if that would do. I didn't think. I have plenty of milk in the pantry, I can heat some up. I suppose you don't drink tea in America so much.'

'Not really, but tea will be fine thank you, Mom,' replied Kate, trying to sound cheerful.

Camp Essence, jeez, she thought miserably, turn the clock back twenty years, you're back in good old Blighty. The adjustment was going to be even more difficult than she'd imagined. She hadn't realised how long the after-effects of the war had remained in operation. There was still some rationing for God's sake.

'And would you like a biscuit, Clare?' coaxed Sarah.

Clare looked at her mother, her brow wrinkled in uncertainty.

'She calls them cookies, Mom. I'm sure she would, wouldn't you, honey?' Clare nodded in quiet agreement.

'Yes I suppose she does, I'm sorry it didn't occur to me.

I notice that you've picked up a bit of the vernacular as well Kate. I'm 'Mom' now.'

Sarah was feeling unusually perturbed. Her customary cool efficiency had deserted her for perhaps the first time in her life and she was desperately trying to sound unfazed and casual, in what she was finding to be the most difficult of circumstances.

'Do you both want to unpack and freshen up before we have supper? Don't suppose days in a case will be doing your clothes much good. I've emptied the wardrobes for you and there's plenty of room in the chest of drawers. I'm sure you haven't brought everything with you anyway. I'll start supper straight away. Steak and kidney, I thought, one of your favourites, Kate, if that's alright with you. I thought Clare might not have had it before. Do you make it in America? Well perhaps you cook the same things as here. You can tell me all about it in good time. Perhaps you can show me how to make some new things, American dishes.'

Sarah continued her inane, circumspect chatter. Kate half listened, uninterested, but at least it delayed the inevitable conversation that, to date, everyone had successfully avoided. Michael arrived back in the kitchen. He was slightly out of breath. He sat down quietly at the scrubbed wooden table and started to drum his fingers lightly. The gesture created a welcome distraction from the unspoken awkwardness of the situation.

'Someone mention tea? I would love a cup. What on earth have you brought back in those cases, Kate, a body?'

He emitted a shallow, breathless laugh.

He's aged, they both have, thought Kate. Six years have taken their toll and what on earth is this going to do to them?

'I think I'll take my tea upstairs if that's alright with you, Mom, Clare can help me unpack. She's very good like that,' Kate commented, trying to sound much brighter than she felt. The shy five-year-old smiled at her mother but remained silent.

'Is there any hot water? I'd like to give her a bath and get her to bed early after supper. She's pretty exhausted, aren't you, honey? It's been a very long, trying journey for both of us.'

Kate knew they would want to talk to her, but not within earshot of Clare. No point in putting off the inevitable.

'Yes, there should be enough for a shallow bath. Do you want to go ahead and do it now? It will take a while before supper is ready and then Clare can go straight to bed. I think that would be for the best.'

As ever Sarah had it all organised.

This is going to be so difficult, thought Kate, difficult for everyone. What a mess. I must try to be patient. They have shown me such kindness but how I dread the 'well we did warn you' lecture. I suppose I'll just have to take it on the chin and get on with it. Perhaps when they know it all they will not be so judgmental.

She took Clare by the hand and led her up the familiar stairs. The middle ones creaked. Kate forced a smile. Everything and nothing had changed.

'Will we be living here from now on, Mom?' Clare spoke for the first time since she had arrived in the house.

'For the time being, darling. Your granny and grandpa have been very kind and we will be staying for a little while anyway.'

'But I miss my friends. It's so cold and gloomy in this old house. Why can't we go back to Boston, to our own house? I like our house. When are we going home?'

Her chin dimpled as tears filled her eyes, but she bravely bit her lip to stave them off.

'I know, honey, it's hard for all of us. There are some things that you just don't understand. One day I'll tell you all about it. Just now, I need you to be brave for me and show your granny and grandpa what a good girl you really are.'

She nodded compliantly and continued to walk glumly up the stairs in front of her mother. Kate arrived back in the kitchen. She looked around. On the surface nothing much had changed in the intervening years; the same kettle was still sitting on the same range. Only the dog was missing. Sarah and Michael were sitting at the table sipping yet another cup of tea. Kate sat down beside them.

'She's fallen asleep, I'm afraid, bless her. I don't think she'll wake up again for supper. She's exhausted after the journey, so I'll let her sleep. I don't suppose you've any brandy do you? Do you mind if I smoke?'

Sarah shot a look at her husband but said nothing.

'I do believe there's some left over from last Christmas. In fact, I may join you. I didn't know you drank brandy, Kate?' Michael got up with an arthritic stagger and came back with a couple of glasses and an ashtray.

'Presumed you were abstaining, Sarah?'

Kate elegantly drew on her cigarette before she took a large swig from the glass and set it down purposefully.

'Okay, let's get this over and done with shall we? I know you're trying to be kind, but I can't bear the pretence. It's fine, you can say 'we told you so' – I know you think that.'

'We don't think that at all, Kate. We are concerned about you and our grandchild. You must tell us what you want to tell us, what you feel you can tell us. Your letter said so little, but we read between the lines of course. You must be so tired now and it will wait.'

It was Michael who, unexpectedly, spoke first. Sarah sat unusually quiet. Kate swallowed; it wasn't the reaction she had expected at all. Memories flooded back to the evening when she had returned from first meeting Art as she recalled how her mother had also responded then in the most unexpected manner. She realised that she didn't know them at all and that after nearly seven years, since she'd last seen them, she was making the same unfounded assumptions.

'I'm sorry, I shouldn't have said that. I feel so ashamed, that's all. I know how difficult this must be for both of you, wondering what the neighbours will say, how they'll whisper behind my back, while welcoming me openly to my face. All that sanctimonious sympathy in the pews, disguising a healthy dose of 'well what do you expect if you run off and marry a Yank at nineteen?''

'I think you're being a bit unfair. People will want to help, of course they will and, anyway, it's none of their business,' Sarah declared defiantly. 'This is a family matter. I don't deny that it's difficult for us, but it must be much worse for you. Mostly we're concerned for you and that beautiful daughter of yours. You look so alone, so sad. We want to help.'

Once again, Kate was completely taken aback by her mother's response. She cleared the rest of her glass and held it out for a refill. Sarah glanced at it but, in the circumstances, thought it best to remain silent. Michael poured the remains of the bottle into both glasses.

'That's it, I'm afraid. Don't think we have anything else in the house.'

Kate took another healthy swig and sighed.

'Thank you for being like this, I didn't expect it if I'm honest. It is only fair that I tell you everything that's happened. It is incredibly difficult for me, but I want you to know everything. It's the least I can do and it's best that we get it over and done with. You need to know why I've come back, although I don't really know where to start. It's all been so difficult I tried, really I tried, but it just became too much. If it had just been me perhaps I could have coped, but then I had to protect Clare.'

She observed their raised eyebrows, but they remained silent and intent.

'I've kept so much from you, for quite a few years now, because stupidly I thought I could make it better on my own, that it would come right and I didn't want to admit to myself or to you that I couldn't cope. I was too proud. I should have told you earlier.'

'Well, whatever it is, you're telling us now,' replied Michael sympathetically. Kate smiled at him gratefully.

'I think I loved him from the first moment I met him on that stupid bus, heading into Plymouth, and I honestly think he felt the same. I know I was young, but I really did think about it sensibly. We loved each other so much, and there was every chance he would get killed. We just wanted to be together, completely together. I know you were against my marrying, giving up the chance of going to college but, like me, you both got to know what a good, kind man he was.

'I was so happy when he came back from France knowing that, unlike so many of his friends, he had made it safely through the war. Except I now know that he hadn't. We were making a new life in Boston, then I found out I was pregnant with Clare, Art had joined his father's firm, it was all perfect. The war was over and we had this exciting new life together.

'I don't know when I first began to notice the change in him. I suppose, thinking about it, even before we got married he had become quieter and more withdrawn, not the carefree, cheerful guy who'd swept me off my feet that day on the bus. As time went on, there was nothing I could put my finger on exactly, but he was different, more distracted somehow, distant I suppose. He'd sometimes flare up at the slightest thing, get annoyed over the most trivial instance, like if he thought I'd moved something of his and he couldn't immediately find it.

'I put it down to the upheaval, moving back to Boston after the war, trying to fit into his new job, coming to terms with marriage and then a young baby. I was so happy and I wanted him to be happy too. I loved America from the start. His family were so welcoming to me it was almost like home from home. His parents had also noticed the change in him, but we all said we should give him time.

'I don't remember exactly when it first happened; I was so shocked at the time, I suppose. I tried hard to erase it from my mind afterwards, but I couldn't. Art had come home as usual. He was tired. I'd had an awful day, Clare was teething and had a fever and neither of us had slept much the night before. Art had had one of his awful dreams, which were becoming more and more frequent, and we'd both tossed and turned most of the night. I'd noticed the dreams almost as soon I got to America. He'd wake me up in the middle of the night, shouting out orders, warnings. It was as if he was back in Normandy, commanding his troops. Often he would wake suddenly, shaking, his back soaking wet. Of course I heard some of the words so I guessed what was happening, but he wouldn't tell me what they were about. I also noticed that he'd started to mutter and mumble to himself during the day. I so wanted to help, but he insisted I wouldn't understand. He clearly didn't want to talk about it.

'Most of the time he was the kind, clever, funny man I'd fallen in love with. He adored Clare and he was enjoying working with his father. They wouldn't admit it, but he's his parents' favourite. The business was thriving, we had plenty of money; he'd come home with presents for no reason other than to tell me he loved me; we had a big car, a beautiful three-storey house, a lovely daughter. I couldn't believe how lucky I was. America was everything I'd imagined it to be and more. When I wrote to you about it, I was telling the truth. I wasn't telling you the whole truth, however. I didn't want to worry you and I'd convinced myself that it would get better. Time would heal.'

Kate paused and smiled ruefully before she continued. She had noticed the stolen glances between her parents. She breathed in deeply and started to speak again.

'Anyway as I said, it was just an ordinary day, about five years ago I suppose. I'd put a steak and kidney pie in the oven, one of Art's favourites. How ironic is that? Art loved my English cooking. I'd gone upstairs because Clare had started to cry; her teeth were giving her so much bother. Apart from Art tossing and turning, I'd been up most of the night with her and I was exhausted. I lay down on the bed, thinking it would only be for a couple of minutes, but I must have fallen asleep.

I didn't hear Art come in. I woke to the sound of a dreadful crash. It really startled me. I rushed downstairs to find the kitchen full of smoke and Art staring at the broken pie dish, holding his hand. I rushed to help thinking he'd hurt himself. He looked straight at me his eyes flaring; I'll never forget the look on his face, it was hatred, fear, anger, all mixed up in one. He said the most terrible things to me.' Kate glanced at her mother before continuing.

'He told me I was a stupid, lazy bitch, who'd nearly burned the house down. I couldn't believe what I was hearing. I was so shocked it was so unlike him, but I bent over to check his hand and as I did, he flung it up and sent me reeling. He kicked the broken dish across the floor spraying the walls with the remains of the pie.'

Sarah raised her hand to her mouth in horror; Michael ran his hand through his hair in disbelief. Neither spoke. Kate saw their reactions and swallowed hard; she could feel her throat begin to thicken as she fought hard against the tears that were threatening to weaken her resolve. The images were still so vivid, firmly imprinted in her mind, forever punched into her deepest memory; the remnants from the explosion of meat, kidneys and charred pastry splattered across the floor, the tears of thick congealing gravy trickling down the walls. She cleared her throat steeling herself to continue.

'He was completely out of control. I crashed against the table, hit my head hard and remember lying on the floor, feeling like a... like a crumpled rag doll. I didn't know what to do. I was scared to move in case he hit me again. He just looked at me in disgust and walked out of the house, slamming the door behind him.

'I picked myself up as best I could; I remember I was shaking like a leaf. I just couldn't believe what had happened. That Art would do such a thing.

'Clare had started to cry again so I ran upstairs and clung to her. I felt like I was drowning or suffocating or something. I can't describe what it was like. I really felt like I was fighting for breath – it was truly awful. To be honest, Clare was the only reality I felt. I think I half believed I was still asleep, lost in the middle of some dreadful nightmare, but I was wide awake, lying there scared stiff. I just held onto her. I don't know how long it was, it seemed like hours, but then I heard the bedroom door open quietly. It was Art. I jumped up, not sure what to expect but he rushed over to me, threw his arms around me and started to sob. He was howling like a baby, his face red and swollen. I'd never seen a man in a state like that before.

'I'm so sorry, I'm so sorry, I'm so sorry, please forgive me, can you ever forgive me?' he begged, the mantra continued over and over.

'It seemed like the years of strain were finally rinsing out of him. I held him close. He sounded so lost and frightened. He told me he didn't know what had come over him. Something had snapped inside when he saw the smoke and smelt the burning. He kept telling me how much he loved me, loved Clare, how he couldn't bear to think about what he'd done, kept asking if I could ever forgive him. It spilled out uncontrollably. We sat on the bed and clung to each other. Thankfully Clare slept through it all.

'Then it all started to make sense. He began to tell me about the nightmares he'd been suffering since June '44; unbearable dreams in which he relived the horrors of the landings on Omaha. As he was telling me, I honestly believe he thought he was back there; he was speaking like he was in some kind of trance. I remember his face was deathly white, his eyes wide open, just staring at me. It really frightened me to see him like that.

'He went on to tell me how he'd watched in horror, helpless, as the bodies of his closest friends, Chuck, Buzz, Marty, I'd met them all, had been torn to shreds by the relentless gun fire. His nightmares were full of the most horrific images you could ever imagine; in one of them he described how severed arms followed his every move. They would tap him on the shoulder; the fingers would point at him in accusation, voices whispered in his ear, 'Why are you alive, while we exist in hell?''

Kate paused. She found it impossible to put into words the full horror of the scenes he had described in the most graphic detail to her, but they were etched in her mind forever. For months afterwards they had haunted her, as they had surely haunted him. Her nostrils had filled with the fetid stench of flesh turned to fragment. Bits of dispossessed body had littered the sand. The sea had bled across the beach, sucking and spewing the flotsam and jetsam of human remnants. The images were raw and grotesque. They had threatened to overwhelm him. She had watched his face contort in agony as he relived every gory detail of life, or more accurately death, on that hell-hole of a beach. She forced a grimacing smile in the direction of her speechless parents before continuing.

'I held him close and cradled him. It was all I could think to do. He was still sobbing like a baby in my arms. I've got him back at last, I thought. It was a catharsis. It was the war and it was finally over for him.'

'Oh Kate, what an absolutely awful experience for you; we had no idea, no idea at all,' sniffed Sarah, biting her lip. Kate smiled at her resignedly.

'It was awful; I didn't know how to react, what to say for the best. He told me that, as far as he was concerned, the lucky ones hadn't made it off that beach as they could no longer remember; they no longer had to deal with it or with themselves. He finally admitted to me how utterly lost and alone he'd been feeling but he couldn't bring himself to talk about it to me or to anyone else. He'd been trying to deal with it all by himself; thought it was a sign of weakness, thought real men, men of courage shouldn't feel like he did. He actually believed that. I tried to tell him that he was one of the bravest people I knew, that he could never be weak, but then he hit me with something else.'

Kate paused not sure if she should divulge much more. She felt an overwhelming need to talk, to share her agony with someone else, but she also felt that she was being undeniably disloyal to Art.

'I'm not sure if I should tell you this or not.' She looked up trying to gauge their reaction to what she had already said, before continuing.

'One day… one day, after a particularly bad night, he told me he'd driven his car to The Mystic River Bridge, climbed on the trusses, looked over the edge and was about to jump off. But as he put it, 'I wasn't even brave enough to do that.' I was so shocked.'

'I'm sure you were. Thank God he didn't go through with it, what a dreadful thing to contemplate,' exclaimed Sarah, looking towards her husband in horror. Kate could sense her mother's deep disapproval. She felt the need to jump to Art's defence, to explain that she had only felt shocked because she had no idea how bad things had got for him, and that it was in no way intended as a judgement on him. But she decided against it; they probably wouldn't understand and she couldn't face a confrontation. She decided she needed to change the direction of the conversation.

'Anyway, in the months and years that followed he seemed so much better; he was sleeping and eating well. He'd taken my advice and been seeing his doctor. He was finally getting the professional help he needed and he was learning to contain his darkest thoughts; could almost hide them away in an imaginary room. He reassured me that the nightmares had virtually stopped but if one began, as occasionally happened, he'd learned to wake himself up and avoid the worst of it. It was the happiest time of my life. I loved him so much and I know he loved me too. He was almost back to his old carefree, fun-loving self. Clare absolutely adored him and he her. We never spoke about that day and he showed me nothing but patience and kindness.

'And it might have stayed like that except, about a year ago, he got a letter from a guy called John Gracey; he'd been in Art's unit. He was visiting Boston on business and wanted to meet up. I wasn't so sure it was wise but Art seemed so well and he hadn't seen anyone since he'd been demobbed. He was really keen to meet up with John, especially as he was the only other one from his inner circle of friends who'd made it off Omaha. I was worried that it might bring the memories back to him, rekindle the nightmares, but I didn't want to make a big deal of it, or suggest that I was still dwelling on what had happened previously. They arranged to go out for a drink. I didn't go with them; I thought it best to let them talk freely. Art came back very drunk – it was about three o'clock in the morning. He didn't drink that much normally and he wasn't used to it. I was in bed and Clare was asleep. He came up the stairs, swearing as he banged against the walls, making an awful din. Clare woke up and went out to see what was happening.

'I was angry with him, oh, not only for waking her up but also because I didn't want her to see her father in that state. I'd also expected him back much earlier and had been lying in bed worried sick that something had happened to him. I suppose I was tired and irritable. I'd been feeling nauseous all day and was pretty sure that I was pregnant again, but I hadn't told Art yet or been to see the doctor. I so, so, needed a good night's sleep.

'I'm not sure exactly what I was thinking. I was glad he was home and that he'd obviously had a good time, but I was annoyed and tired. I think I told him he was a disgrace. I can't really remember exactly, but I do remember he was staring at me then he pushed me. I'm sure it was an accident, he hadn't meant to harm me, but I fell back hitting each stair on the way down. I lay on the ground, winded and confused. He just stood there staring at me; then he turned and walked into our bedroom. Clare, who unfortunately had seen it all, immediately ran down to me. She started to scream and kept shouting for her Pop to come and help. Art didn't appear. She helped me up; my back was aching and I'd twisted my ankle badly. I managed to struggle into the kitchen and sat down. Clare got me a glass of water but I was violently sick. She just stood screaming, scared stiff.

'Art didn't appear. I cleaned up as best as I could; Clare was hysterical. I was in agony but, for her sake, I was desperately trying to remain strong. Eventually I calmed her down and she was able to help me up the stairs. I climbed into bed with her and held her close. She was sobbing her heart out. I could hear Art snoring loudly in our bedroom next door, apparently without a care in the world. It seemed like forever as I lay there, wide awake listening to their competing sounds reverberating around in the stillness of the house. I can still hear it clearly. Eventually Clare fell into an exhausted sleep so I limped into the guest room. My ankle was badly swollen and, when I looked in the mirror, there was a deep purple bruise spread across most of my back. I lay down and managed to sleep off and on, but then I woke up and discovered blood on the sheets. I was losing the baby.'

Kate paused in response to the sound of her father blowing his nose. She noticed her mother's eyes were ringed with red.

'Oh Kate, why didn't you write and tell us? You poor, poor dear and that poor child, he must be mad,' choked Sarah, desperately trying to keep her emotions in check.

Kate continued on dispassionately. She felt that she had wept all the tears she would ever weep and was now recounting someone else's story.

'The pains became unbearable and I knew I needed to get to a doctor. Art couldn't drive in that state, even if I could have aroused him, and I didn't want to leave Clare alone with him. I had no option but to call his parents. They were so wonderful but, of course, now they knew everything. We were all so worried about him. Art was distraught when he realised what he'd done to me, our lost baby, Clare. He couldn't recall anything about the night at all, not even having been out for a drink with John. Of course, I reasoned it could all have been an accident. I didn't know if he'd deliberately pushed me or not. Clare was so upset she didn't sleep properly for weeks. She couldn't understand why her father hadn't come to help, why he'd hurt me and she wouldn't go near him.

'Then the nightmares started again. He kept muttering in his sleep; I caught snatches of his self-loathing. Increasingly he became morose and introverted, even more so than the time before. Some days he wouldn't even get out of bed; he'd refuse to go into the office. He stopped washing, shaving or eating. Eventually he stopped sleeping. I tried so hard to be a good wife, to support and help him; in sickness and in health, I really believed it, but it was becoming intolerable; he was so cross and irritable with Clare all the time, smacking her hard for the most minor misdemeanour. I tried to intervene, to protect her, but then he would become angry with me, told me I was raising a spoilt brat.' Kate hesitated before adding reluctantly, 'Sometimes, he would hit me too.'

'Oh no, Kate, not that, not you as well. Did he hurt you badly?' Sarah was finding it difficult to know what to say. Michael remained wide-eyed and silent.

'Not badly, he didn't mean to do it, he was always so sorry afterwards,' replied Kate feeling the need to defend the man she still loved.

'His parents helped me so much, I thought we can all get through this; I'll get back my kind and loving husband and Clare her doting father. I don't know how long I could have gone on. If it had only affected me I think I would still be there to support him, but I haven't told you the worst.'

'Goodness, Kate, what on earth can be worse? This is awful. I don't know what to say. Can you believe it, Michael? He's ill. He must be ill. This is not the Art we got to know, the man we entrusted you to. It's the war, it's corrupted his mind. What on earth else can there be?' Sarah shook her head from side to side in stunned disbelief. Kate didn't comment but looked at her mother with a resigned look before continuing her story.

'The final crunch came a few weeks ago. It was then I realised I had to leave. His parents were so kind, they said I could stay with them, but I wanted to come home, at least for the time being. I wanted to be with you. I've never needed you both so much in my life.'

Kate fought back her tears as her mother reached across the table and clasped her hand. Her mother's love had always seemed so practical, not at all sentimental, so the gesture was all the more remarkable. Kate lit another cigarette before she spoke.

'It got to the stage where Art hardly left the house. The doctor no longer seemed able to help. Give him time and love, he advised. How much time, I kept thinking, how much love? He would sit in a chair and stare at the walls. I had to force him to eat. His parents came to visit every day, which gave me a chance to get out for a while, do the shopping, get my hair done, normal things that made life bearable.

One day I realised I needed some onions for a recipe I was making. I could get Art to eat a little of his favourite dishes and this was one of them. Clare was having a nap upstairs and, as usual, he'd fallen asleep in his chair. I didn't usually leave him alone in the house with Clare, but I thought it would be fine to nip out for ten minutes. There was an accident on the way and I got delayed. I still wasn't away that long, no more than twenty minutes I guess. When I got back Art wasn't in his chair. I called his name, but there was no reply. I ran upstairs and noticed that Clare's door was open. I went in. He had his back to me and was leaning over her bed; I thought he was lifting her up. It was then I noticed he had his hands around her neck, and he was strangling her.'

Kate paused as she heard her mother's sharp intake of breath. Her parents were sitting listening, completely dumbfounded, rendered speechless. Kate carried on talking.

'She was struggling violently. I could see her little feet kicking out from under the blanket. I screamed and he turned. I rushed towards him like... like a tank and shoved him out of the way. His eyes were staring; he wasn't focusing on me at all. He looked completely confused and dazed. I ran over to Clare. She was coughing, her eyes were bulging, there were bright red finger marks around her neck but at least she was alive. I grabbed her, ran downstairs and did what I thought I had to; I called an ambulance and the police. It was then I decided I had to come home. I just couldn't take it anymore. My biggest concern is for Clare. She's normally so full of life, talkative, smiling and happy, but she's been so quiet ever since that day. She hasn't spoken about it at all and I don't know if I should encourage her to talk it through or just let her try to forget it. She hardly mentions her father; I just don't know what to do for the best anymore, I feel so alone and frightened.'

Kate buried her head in her hands and leant her elbows on the table. She felt her father's gentle arms lift her up.

'You're home now, love. We'll take care of you both. You can stay here as long as you wish, you know you can. It will all work out well, you'll see.'

The concern in his warm reassuring voice made her want to wail. Kate wished to appear strong for them, to act like the independent woman she'd always believed herself to be, but inside she was screaming like a child.

She looked across at her mother who was weeping silently. Kate had never seen her appear so lost; she looked pinched and old, the fight gone out of her. It was obvious she didn't know how to respond.

'I love you both, you know. I can't thank you enough for how you're dealing with this. I wish it could be so different, but I suppose it is how it is. I don't know what's going to happen, whether I will ever be able to go back. I don't even know what will become of Art. They put him in a hospital, a mental asylum full of men just like him. Men who did their bit, who thought they were the lucky ones, the ones that got away. Except, as Art said, they didn't, did they? They sacrificed their lives too; the war is still raging for them and will never end.

'I feel so bad about it, he's a good man, but I have to protect Clare, get her away from it all at least for the time being. That bloody war, so many victims whose names will never appear on any roll of honour.'

Her parents sat staring at her, dazed and silent.

Kate stood up suddenly in an attempt to break the unbearable tension; she put on a brave face as she stated cheerfully, 'Enough, from now on the only way is forward. I'm going to be strong for Clare, we all are. It's her future as well as mine and there is a future, I know there is.' Her parents nodded in soulful agreement. The gesture broke Kate's resolve.

'I'm sorry, I really can't talk about this anymore tonight, if you don't mind. I don't think I can eat anything either, I'm afraid. I'm sorry, Mom, after all the trouble you've gone to. Do you mind if I just go to bed?'

'No, it will keep, of course, if that's what you want to do. Would you like some hot milk?' offered Sarah thoughtfully.

'No thanks, Mom, I just need to sleep, I really am so tired, the journey I suppose. It's been such an exhausting day. I love you both; thank you for being so understanding.'

Kate leant over and kissed both her parents tenderly on the cheek. They hugged her in turn. 'Goodnight. I'll see you both tomorrow. We can talk more then when I'm rested. I'm so sorry to bring all this on you. Sleep well, God bless.'

'God bless you too, dear,' responded her father cheerlessly, as Sarah got up slowly to re-boil the kettle.

Chapter 8

Plymouth, October 1952, evening

Kate crept into Clare's bedroom and, still fully clothed, lay down gently beside her sleeping child. She felt exhausted but knew that for her, sleep was a distant hope. She decided she would lie quietly and rest for a little while. She needed to feel her child's soft, warm presence. She reached over and placed her arm across the slight body, feeling strangely comforted by her rhythmical breathing. She envied her contentment, her unwavering capacity to close her eyes and drift into instant restful sleep. She carefully pulled the heavy eiderdown over them both. It felt cold and unwieldy to her touch.

The pain of reliving the story had sparked her mind into the most unwelcome frenzy of activity. The images that for so long she had managed to snuff out were being cruelly rekindled in all their vivid horror. She was longing to sleep, to blank out the fearful thoughts swamping her mind, filling her head with doubts and feelings of overwhelming loss, but the darkness surrounding her could not provide the distractions she craved.

In her youth, Kate had revelled in the excitement of the unknown; the future had dangled in front of her as a world filled with secret promise. She had been happy to drift along, carried on a tide of endless possibilities, rudderless and carefree; a submissive and compliant protagonist. What scant decisions she had consciously taken had been light and carefree, impulsively spawned and carelessly delivered. They had served her for the day and the morrow would look after itself. Even the decision to return to England had been made on impulse; she had given little thought as to what would happen afterwards. She had simply felt compelled to get them both away from Boston, from Art, and to return to the sanctuary of England. She had realised how desperately she needed her parents; their love, their wisdom, the security they could offer. She hadn't dared to think further ahead.

She had arrived in England with what belongings she could fit into two large suitcases. She had assumed the visit would be temporary. Now, lying in the chilly darkness, having returned to the familiar surroundings of her childhood home, the impact of what had happened was beginning to dawn. The future reared before her ugly and menacing. Her glass, forever half-filled with boundless optimism had drained away, and was now half empty. No matter which way she looked the road ahead was filled with obstacles and pitfalls.

Kate felt utterly lost and alone, unsure which path to take, which way to turn. What should she do for the best? She was acutely conscious that the choices she now made would no longer affect only her, for her future was inextricably linked with two others, Clare and Art. The decisions she made would inevitably chart the course of their lives as well.

She felt crushed by the burden of responsibility. Should she stay in England or return to Boston? And what about Art? Had she deserted him in his greatest hour of need? But if she returned to give him the love and support he needed, the support he deserved, and the love she still felt, what about Clare? Above all she had to think about Clare... Should she damn their daughter to a life with, or a life without her father? Could she ever truly trust Art with Clare again, for there was little doubt, had she not returned when she did, he would have strangled her. It didn't bear thinking about... but what would happen to him now? Perhaps he would be charged with attempted murder, the murder of his own child? Surely they wouldn't punish a man who had put his life on the line for others and been destroyed by the experience...? No, they would realise that he was out of his mind, made mad by the war... But would he ever get better, become well enough to come back and live with them? She couldn't be sure, but then what did life hold for them both here? England was a foreign land to Clare, but she was still young, she would adjust quickly, but how would she support her? Where would they live, for it was clear that they couldn't live here forever; it would drive them all mad. The room felt gloomy, the bed slightly damp. The air hung thick and heavy, laden with the moisture of an English autumn. This house, the home she had loved as no other, these walls that had embraced her throughout her youth, now felt like strangers hemming her in with their cold unfriendly presence. She realised that it was no longer her home, it was her parents'. It was filled with the remnants of their lives, not hers. She longed for the warm modernity of her beautiful home in Boston. She longed for the life she had had. She longed for the husband she had once known. But they no longer existed and probably never would again. How could she ever settle back in England? She had tasted the fruits of another life and it was hard to accept that they would never be hers to savour again. It all seemed so impossible. She longed for the oblivion of sleep.

She lay listening to the faint mumble of the voices beneath her. Her parents were trying to talk softly. She knew that she would be the sole object of their conversation. She strained to listen, to hear what words of comfort or condemnation they spoke. She couldn't make them out. What were they thinking? They had been so kind, but she felt that she had let them down terribly; she seemed to be letting everyone down. What a mess. How had all that pent up hope and expectation come to this?

Kate knew she should get up, get undressed, go to her own bedroom and leave her sleeping child alone. But Clare felt so warm and comfortable while the room felt so cold and uninviting. She felt so tired and listless she couldn't be bothered to get up. She felt her eyelids slowly close under the weight of sleep. Clare rolled over and gently nudged against her, waking her with a jolt. It took Kate a moment to remember where she was. She braved herself to slide out quietly from beneath the clothes, but she was immediately hit by the chilly air. She crept slowly into the bathroom, shivering. She glanced at herself in the mirror. The face that met her looked pale and drawn. As she studied her reflection, it occurred to her that six years previously she had left this house as a fresh-faced excited girl; she had returned a troubled, ageing woman. She turned the hot water tap and splashed her face with the emerging icy water. She brushed her teeth mindlessly and wiped her mouth on a moist towel.

Standing in her own dimly lit bedroom she quickly changed into the inadequately thin nightdress she had selected with a much warmer, centrally heated environment in mind. She jumped under the covers, pulled them up over her head and huddled herself into a ball, willing herself to sleep. She stretched out a foot and felt a, now tepid, hot water bottle; the practical remnant of her mother's endeavours to air the bed. It immediately transported her back to childhood. Heavy, silent tears of hopelessness rolled down her cheeks and landed on the freshly laundered sheets. She felt the weight of despair envelop her as she drifted into fitful sleep.

Chapter 9

Exeter, November 1952

Jim stood beneath the station clock and checked his watch. So it wasn't fast, it was ten o'clock. Evelien's train had been due in fifteen minutes before; it must have got delayed. She would be exhausted when she finally arrived.

He thought back to the last time he had stood beneath this clock waiting for the London train. He remembered how curious he had felt, but also how uncharacteristically apprehensive, as he anticipated meeting Evelien's sister for the first time. He had hoped, rather than expected, that she would be exactly as Evelien had described her; a fun-loving, beautiful young women, as dark as Evelien was blond, slightly taller than her younger sister but just as slim and with the same vibrant blue eyes. Thinking back, Evelien's brother, Hans, had sought to warn his sister regarding the changes in Eliezabeth's appearance and character, but his words of caution had gone largely unheeded.

'Of course she will have aged,' Evelien had reasoned with Jim. 'I have not seen her for many years and no doubting she will think I have aged too. What does Hans expect? He says she is quiet; well, he was never able to talk to Eliezabeth, so why he thinks that is strange I do not know. Two weeks with me and I am sure the old Eliezabeth will begin to show. She can put all those horrible things out of her mind at last. Anyway, it is years ago now. She will have fun with us and soon forget.' How wrong she had been.

On that occasion, Jim had stood on the platform and studied each of the weary passengers as they alighted from the train. No one he had spotted remotely fitted Evelien's description. He had begun to think she must have missed the train but decided he should wait a little longer, remain standing beneath the clock as arranged, just in case. He recalled the shiver of shock he had felt when a woman of indeterminate age, bent over like an old hag, had cautiously approached him as she struggled to carry her case. With dismay he had realised immediately that it must be Eliezabeth; it couldn't be anyone else, but he had known instantly what an enormous impact her obvious demise was going to have on Evelien. They were not going to enjoy the Christmas either of them had anticipated.

He still felt pangs of crushing guilt when he recalled his rising resentment towards Eliezabeth as the long days and nights of that awful fortnight had dragged by, and the happy release he had felt when she finally departed. At one stage Evelien had suggested that her sister should extend her stay; he was ashamed to remember his immediate but unspoken curse. He knew Eliezabeth had deserved his sympathy not his censure. He was a patient man but, my God, it had been difficult to maintain an even keel.

Naturally curious, and in an attempt to understand what Eliezabeth might have gone through, he had visited the local library the day after her departure to see what he could find out. The librarian had looked somewhat bemused when Jim made his initial enquiry. She had no idea what he was talking about. She had written to London to see what they had but to Jim's surprise there was no information available. He was left to wonder.

And then there had been the most unexpected aftermath. Throughout Eliezabeth's stay Evelien had been unusually distant towards him, but Jim had gallantly put it down to tiredness and her understandable shock at seeing the dramatic change in her sister. It had taken Evelien weeks, indeed months, to recover from the visit. She had lost all interest in him, callously brushing off his usual overtures of affection; she had resentfully rejected all intimate contact. It was as if the act of love had become an act of violation. She was filled with an irrational rage which he felt was in danger of transforming his sensual young wife into a frigid stranger.

There was no doubt the experience had put an incredible strain on both of them but gradually, through his patience and understanding, he had got his wife and her love back. But how would she be this time? Would this visit to Rotterdam, to see Eliezabeth once more, set her back again?

At last he heard the roar of the engine as the station master announced the London train's arrival. He gazed anxiously along the platform watching for Evelien to disembark. Her expression would tell him what he needed to know. He waved with delight as he saw her step from the carriage. She returned his gesture, smiling weakly as she ran towards him.

'Oh Jim, you do not know how glad I am to be back and to see you,' she whispered with tangible relief as she wrapped her arms around him loosely.

'How's it been?' he asked tentatively, gently pushing her away to study her face.

'Awful, just awful, worse than I ever expected,' she replied, closing her eyes and shaking her head slowly from side to side. 'Take me home and I will tell you all about it. I just want to get home. I am so tired.'

Jim's heart sank as he lifted Evelien's case and curled his other hand around her elbow in a gesture of support. He noticed she hadn't kissed him. It was the response he had been dreading.

'Do you want to talk about it now or wait until you've had a good night's sleep?' asked Jim kindly as he opened the car door and Evelien climbed in.

'Do you mind if I tell you when we get home, when I can relax and talk to you properly. I do not want to talk about it when you are driving.'

Jim shut his eyes momentarily. So he should anticipate the worst.

'That's fine, whenever you want,' he replied reassuringly. 'Tell me as much or as little as you can,' he added, reaching over and hesitantly squeezing her leg with affection. He was relieved when she rested her hand on his.

It had been two months earlier when Evelien had suggested that she should go to Rotterdam to visit her family. It was her parents' 40th wedding anniversary on the 26th November. It had been over two years since she had last seen any of them and she had reckoned it would be a good opportunity for everyone to be together for a happy occasion. Jim had agreed, but reluctantly. He had work commitments so couldn't go. He wasn't at all convinced that it was a good idea for Evelien to go on her own; there was no knowing what she would find. He had suggested that they should delay a visit until the spring, when the weather would be better and they could both travel together. But she had made up her mind.

Jim had been to Rotterdam once before; Evelien and he had gone for a week during the summer of 1950. Given Evelien's previous reaction, Jim had been reluctant to encourage her to see Eliezabeth before then.

Evelien's family had been warm and welcoming towards them both, but Jim had come to realise how much Evelien's parents were struggling to deal with Eliezabeth's situation. They appeared reluctant to discuss her at all and focused all their attention on Evelien.

Eliezabeth had moved out of her parents' house six months earlier and was by then living with Hans. Jim, of course, couldn't be sure what the relationship had been like prior to the war but he sensed that, in some unspoken way, Eliezabeth's parents blamed their daughter for having put herself in harm's way unnecessarily. They clearly thought that she should have got out of Java earlier. Quite how was not clear. Jim was sure that they loved their eldest daughter but he had concluded that, for them at least, out of sight could largely mean out of mind. Eliezabeth had proved a difficult house guest and they had been somewhat relieved when Hans had decided that she should move in with him. They were getting too old to deal with her unpredictable and fluctuating moods. They couldn't understand why she could not simply put it all behind her and focus on the future.

They had all suffered dreadfully during the war but life had to go on.

During that summer trip of 1950, Evelien had discovered the true extent of Eliezabeth's on-going problems. The day after they arrived, she and Jim had spent an unexpectedly pleasant day with Hans and Eliezabeth as they all enjoyed a relaxing river trip along the Meuse. The apparent improvement in Eliezabeth was remarkable, although Jim felt that her initial greeting had been overly and inappropriately effusive. She had flung her arms around him and kissed him squarely on the lips. Throughout the day she had remained in a most peculiar state of heightened euphoria. At first Jim thought she had been drinking, but he couldn't smell anything on her breath. He couldn't quite fathom what was going on.

They had all returned to the van der Posts' house in the early evening, but it wasn't until nearly midnight that Jim and Evelien had managed to escape to the privacy of their bedroom. Jim was mightily relieved. He was already tired from the previous day's travelling, but mostly he was drained from the extreme mental effort required to communicate even the most basic of things to his in-laws, none of whom spoke good English.

'Well, that went a lot better than expected,' he had commented, sighing as he lay back on the bed and closed his eyes with fatigue. 'Don't you think Eliezabeth was in unexpected good humour? She must be feeling much better,' he had continued sleepily.

'Well, you know why of course,' Evelien had replied unusually sharply as she stood undressing.

'No. Why?' Jim had asked, sitting up immediately, puzzled by her response and looking at her quizzically.

'It is the medicines she is taking. She takes too much. Hans told me today.'

'The what?' he had responded, rather taken aback.

'The medicines. The what do you call them - drugs.'

'What drugs?' he had queried incredulously not quite following her meaning.

'For her pains. She takes the drugs. What we call *morfine*.'

'You mean morphine? When on earth did she start taking morphine?'

'In the hospital in Singapore. They gave it to her there. She has been taking it since. She is always with pain. The doctors think it happened when they took the baby from her body. She got an infection and it has left her with terrible pain. She did not tell me about it when she came to visit us; I had no idee. Hans says she takes too much, all the time. He thinks she has become, oh, what do you say in English when you feel that you must take the medicine?' she had asked frowning.

'Addicted?' Jim had offered disbelievingly.

'Yes, addicted. He thinks she has become addicted. She tries to hide it from him, and from my parents, but he knows.'

'But surely the doctors must know how much they are giving her. How can she take too much? They would know. They wouldn't allow it.'

'Hans is not sure, but he thinks she gets it somewhere, not from the doctors. She disappears and he does not know where she goes. Sometimes it makes her very sad but other times, like today, it makes her very happy. Did you see how she talks like she has had too much wine?'

'Well, yes, I suppose, I just thought she was tired.'

'No, it is not that, although it does make her tired too. Hans is not sure what to do. If she is with pain then she needs it but the problem is she needs more and more to help. He is worried that it has got out of the control.'

'Goodness. What next? Poor Eliezabeth, it's just one thing after another…'

'It is not her fault, it is what those men did to her. They caused all this, not her,' Evelien had interrupted curtly, mistaking his meaning.

'Sorry, darling, I didn't mean to suggest that it was Eliezabeth's fault,' Jim had apologised, worried at the sudden change in Evelien's tone and realising how on edge she appeared. 'Look, if there is anything I can do to help, I'm more than happy to do so. You know that. It's just that I have no idea about morphine or how to stop her taking it, if indeed that's the best thing for her. Can't Hans talk to the doctors?'

'It is very difficult; if she will not admit that she takes too much, how can he prove it? I'll talk to him tomorrow,' she had replied decisively, obviously keen to close the conversation.

Following his fruitless visit to the library in Exeter, Jim had remained determined to discover what Eliezabeth had been through. It had occurred to him that as she now lived with Hans she may have confided in him. Jim had seized his opportunity a couple of days later when, after a particularly trying day with Eliezabeth, Evelien had gone to bed early.

Jim's assumption had been right. Gradually over the course of many months Hans had encouraged Eliezabeth to talk. Although his brother-in-law's command of English was limited, with patience, a modicum of intelligence and much gesticulating, Jim had managed to piece together a pretty clear picture of what had happened. Jim had lived through some harrowing personal experiences, and considered himself hardened and inured to the worst atrocities of war, but even he had been stunned and sickened to the pit of his stomach by what Hans had revealed.

It seems that Eliezabeth was only one of several young women, some Dutch but most not, who were taken from their camp one day in early 1944. At the time they had no idea why they had been selected or where they were going. For hour after painful hour they had crouched in the back of an ancient, rickety truck. As they rattled along the pitted, pot-holed tracks, the harsh bare boards had battered against the bones protruding from their backs and buttocks. Their nutrient-starved bodies had been stripped of the cushioning curves that had once defined their femininity. Scorched from above by the searing sun, with neither water nor shade, they had arrived at their destination bruised, burnt and bewildered.

It didn't look anything like the camp they were expecting, more like the beautiful home Eliezabeth had lived in with her employers, but it was filthy inside, and by the time they arrived, already full of frightened young women. As she staggered through the door Eliezabeth had been overwhelmed by the suffocating heat and the stench of fear. She had almost fainted. A ladle filled with lukewarm, sour tasting water had been tipped into her mouth.

Longing for rest, the women had been dragged outside and forced to stand in the arid heat as a sneering soldier had taken their photographs, one by one. They had assumed it was in case they tried to escape. By the following morning, however, their gaunt images were on open display at the front of the house. The women were scared and bemused, unsure what to make of it all.

It would not be long before they discovered their fate. At noon a truck had arrived crammed with soldiers, mostly officers. They had assembled outside, noisily selecting their victims from the grotesque rank of portraits. Eliezabeth had not understood why until she heard the screams of terrified women rising above the cries of jeering men. She had sat shivering in terror knowing that it could not be long until it was her turn. With what weakened strength she had, she had kicked and ferociously fought against her first assailant, but he had beaten her brutally with the butt of his rifle and raped her anyway.

One young victim had screamed for her mother as a drooling brute stole away her innocence. Barely twelve years old, she had valiantly sunk her teeth into the fleshy cheek hovering above her and been bayoneted to death in view of them all.

Those who refused to cooperate were deprived of food, water and sleep. Starving and dangerously dehydrated Eliezabeth had held out bravely for three long days but stupefied, and in fear for her life, she had finally succumbed to her fate. Day and night for four hellish months she had been routinely and viciously raped. Even the doctor who examined her weekly had taken his turn.

On discovering that she was pregnant two of the guards had pummelled her abdomen in a vain attempt to dislodge the developing foetus. She had been carted away to another camp where a doctor had performed a crude abortion. Awake throughout, the pain had been excruciating. And then she had fallen perilously ill with a fever. She had longed for death. Thankfully they had not returned her to the house.

The more he heard, the more incensed Jim had become but it had also intensified his guilt. He knew he should have shown greater tolerance towards Eliezabeth in Exeter. No wonder she had told Evelien so little and continued to suffer so much. No one could have experienced such brutality without developing irrevocable physical and mental scars. Thoroughly ashamed, he couldn't bring himself to tell Evelien even the little he had managed to discover.

They had left Holland, to return home to Exeter, before anything much had been resolved with regard to Eliezabeth and her morphine addiction. If truth be known, as he kissed Eliezabeth goodbye, it had occurred to Jim that she was much better off in drugged oblivion. Deep down, however, he had known that it was unsustainable.

And now from Evelien's demeanour, and what little she had said at the station this evening, it would appear that, contrary to what they both had been led to believe, the problem still remained largely unresolved two years later.

The late night traffic was surprisingly light as Jim drove home. He parked the car and carried Evelien's case into the house. She followed him in wearily.

'Have you eaten? Would you like a hot drink, or a cold one for that matter?' he asked, trying to remain bright as she followed him into sitting room and lay down jadedly on the sofa.

'No thank you, but you have one if you want. Then come and sit beside me; I need you to sit beside me.'

He decided to forgo a drink. He gently lifted her legs as he sat down and rested them along his lap. He stroked them casually as she began to talk. She didn't object.

'It has got much worse than I thought. When Hans said she was much better he was not telling me the truth,' she explained in a tired, deadpan voice. 'The drug, the morfine, she is taking so much now she hardly knows what she is doing most of the time. One day, about a year ago, I think, Hans found where she was hiding it. He took it away. She screamed at him but he would not give it to her. He says it was terrible. She was too hot, then too cold, crying and crying. And then, when he still would not give it to her, she started shaking, kicking out her legs like this.' Evelien twitched violently in Jim's arms, like an epileptic in a seizure, as she re-enacted what Hans had told her.

'And then she began to vomit, she had terrible pains, bent over with them and – what do you say when you have a bad stomach, going to the toilet all the time?'

'Diarrhoea?'

'Yes, that. She was so weak, so he made her eat something, but one hour later, gone,' she explained, graphically flicking out both hands in a gesture of disgust. 'It frightened him so much he gave it back to her. He reckoned she was better off with it. She made him promise not to tell the doctors or me. She thought I would not agree.

'I should have gone to see her long before now but I think they were not encouraging me on purpose, so they told me she was much better. I only had to take a single look at her and I knew there was something terrible wrong with her. But at least she is not in pain. I tried to talk to her, to tell her to get help but she begged me not to say or do anything. She is so afraid the doctors will put her in a hospital, stop her from having it. So what can I do?

'She has been through so much, at least when she takes it, it helps her to forget. I still think we should tell the doctors but Hans does not. I even think he must get it for her now because I do not think she is able, but he would not admit that. My parents know nothing about it. She does not want to see them. She looks so terrible. So thin, her face is like this.'

She placed her hands against her cheeks and drew them in distastefully like she was sucking gall through an invisible straw. She shuddered as she began to speak again.

'It broke my heart to see her. I do not know what to do. Do not you think we should tell the doctors? Hans and I do not agree on this. He got very cross with me. Told me I could not understand what it was like. He says everything is so good for me I cannot know what it is like for her.' She screwed up her nose as she spoke. 'He says I live here in England in my happy house, with my happy husband and one day with my happy children. How could I know how terrible it was for her when she did not have it?'

Evelien's voice was edged with ill-disguised sarcasm as she mimicked her brother's accusations. 'I was very upset by what he said. It hurt me very much, especially about the children. What does he know about how much I suffer? I did not want to talk to him about it after that. He will have to decide by himself from now,' she finished determinedly.

'Oh Evelien, I'm sure he didn't mean to hurt you. It must be incredibly difficult for him, trying to cope with it on his own. I don't know what's for the best. I know nothing about taking morphine. Hans obviously thinks it's better to leave her as she is. I haven't got a clue. Look, why don't you go and talk to Dr Greene? Surely he must know what to do. Why don't you have a word with him and see what he says? Or if he doesn't know, he must know someone who does. There must be people in England like Eliezabeth. It would put your mind at rest if nothing else.'

'Perhaps, but I think there is little I can do. I will have to think about it. Maybe tomorrow, when I have had a sleep. I am so tired now, I cannot think.' She paused then smiled at him as she squeezed his hand. 'I missed you so much. I do not like when I sleep alone. Come on, come up to bed with me. It is late.'

She pulled her legs from beneath him, sat up, cupped his face in her hands and kissed him fondly.

He climbed the stairs with a considerable sense of selfish relief.

Chapter 10

Plymouth, April 1953

'Well, I guess that's it then, Art wants a divorce. He's doing it for my sake, Mother, I'm sure he is. He's doing the honourable thing, releasing me, taking the blame.'

Kate handed over the lawyer's letter.

'I never thought it would come to this, Kate, even if I did suspect you might never go back to America. Divorce, it's such a big thing. Is this really what you want? You need to think carefully about it, dear, for it affects Clare as well.'

'I know. The truth is I still love him, Mother, miss him terribly and worst of all can't help feeling that I've let him down. Sometimes I think I should have returned to Boston, tried harder, not given up so easily. But then I think how could I have gone back? I couldn't have allowed Clare to grow up like that. Do you think I was wrong in deciding to stay here? I really don't know what to do for the best.'

'Only you can know that, Kate. It won't be easy for you whatever you decide. All I can say is remember that what you have done, you have done for Clare. There's no doubt about it, she does seem very happy here and we don't know how it would have been for her if you had gone back. It would appear that England is as much her home now as Boston ever was. She's happy at school and has made lots of new friends. But even if you've decided that you won't be going back, dear, you don't have to get divorced. You never know what the future might bring.'

'I don't know; I really don't. Divorce does seem so final, so shameful, but perhaps it's for the best. But you're right about Clare, she's happy here and America is a distant memory for her. She never talks about it, you know. She rarely mentions Art anymore, come to that. Perhaps that's not a good thing; maybe I should talk about her father more. But to go back…

My heart tells me to take a chance… my head tells me that I can't take the risk. What if he never really gets better? How could I ever leave him alone with Clare? I can't allow her to grow up needing to fear her father. This way she will have a secure world around her with people who love her and I can start to build a new life. But I'm fully aware of the stigma that will be attached to me and therefore her; always to be known as the child with no father; the child with the divorced mother. All those 'decent' parents who will see us, or see me, rather, as a bad influence. It's so unfair on her; she doesn't deserve any of this.'

'Neither do you, Kate,' her mother added emphatically.

'Perhaps not, but I'm the one who has to take responsibility for the decisions I've made. I know I could just continue as I am, keep my options open, so to speak, but perhaps a divorce would allow me to make a clean break, stop me wondering what I should do. Make the decision final. For all I know, Art may not want to have me back, wants the divorce for his own sake... Perhaps he's not doing it for me at all, as I first thought; perhaps he's doing it for himself. Maybe he hates me for leaving him, thinks I abandoned him; simply gave up and ran away when things got tough, perhaps they all do.'

'I wouldn't think that is the case at all, Kate. His parents have never suggested that he feels like that nor that they do. I'm sure they don't. They understand that what you did you did for Clare.'

'Maybe you're right, but I can't help feeling that I've let everyone down, myself most of all. You know, I want to do something to make Clare proud of me, make you all proud of me; get my life back on track. I know I haven't said anything, but I've been thinking that I might try to go get into college, train as a teacher as you'd always hoped. Perhaps this is the incentive I need.'

'Is that possible, Kate? I think that would be wonderful, but would they take you at your age?' asked Sarah brightly.

'I've made some initial enquiries and there is no reason why I can't apply. I'd need your help with Clare though.'

'Of course we would help with Clare. We'd love to help. Oh Kate, I'm so pleased that you want to do this, create a future for both of you. I'm sure James would help too, when he can, of course. He adores his niece. I must go and tell your father, he'll be delighted. Not about the divorce I mean; the world is changing so rapidly, I feel so old.'

Kate sat and reread the lawyer's letter with mixed emotions. If she were honest with herself, she couldn't envisage ever returning to America. She missed Art dreadfully, loved him as much as ever, but it all seemed impossible; she had to protect Clare and allow her to grow up in relative normality. She hadn't dared contemplate divorce. She still felt the bind of her marriage vows, for better for worse. Had she deserted him when he needed her most? She'd had several letters from his parents since that awful day, loving, chatty and comforting. Her mother was right, there were no words of condemnation; they knew she had done what she thought was best. According to Nancy, Art had spent six months undergoing some horrendous treatment which involved inducing seizures using electricity. Kate wasn't sure that her mother-in-law could have got that quite right, but apparently he was only one of the many veterans undergoing the same treatment in the Boston State Hospital. He had periods when he was doing well, could think and act relatively normally and he would be discharged, but then something would suddenly trigger an irrational bout of violence and he needed to be restrained and readmitted. The good news was that there weren't going to be any charges brought against him. The authorities recognised that he was a very sick man; sickened by war. They feared he would never become the son he had been, he was a shell. They were happy that Kate was settled with her parents but missed them both dreadfully.

I can't take Clare back, she thought. What if it didn't work out and I had to return to England yet again. It would be doubly disruptive for her and God knows what effect that would have in the long term. It's too risky. It would be best if I consent to the divorce and then we can both get on with the rest of our lives.

Kate took out the application forms that had arrived a few days earlier from Romney College in Exeter. She knew that the deadline for her application was only a few days away, but she hadn't been sure what to do as she still wasn't convinced that she should stay in England. Now it seemed that Art had made the decision for her. They were staying. She scanned down the first page:

Name………………………………………

Marital Status……………………………

Oh damn, she thought to herself, labelled already. Why the hell did it matter what her marital status was?

She pondered for a moment. What was she to fill in? Was she still to consider herself married? Would she still a Mrs if she became divorced or did she automatically revert back to being a Miss? She sat twiddling her pen then eventually wrote married. After all she still was.

'What a pointless question,' she said out loud.

It was eight weeks before she got a reply. One morning she was coming down the stairs when she heard the post fall on the hall tiles and on picking it up she saw the official-looking letter addressed to her. Her hands shook as she opened it while walking nervously into the kitchen clutching the rest of the post. Sarah was busy washing the window with a soggy newspaper and white vinegar, buffing it to a brilliant shine. She turned her head when she heard Kate come in.

'I've heard from Romney,' Kate declared with relief, 'they want me to go for an interview next Friday; can you look after Clare for me?'

Sarah wiped her forehead with the back of her hand and smiled. 'But that's great news. I'm so pleased for you. Of course we'll look after Clare. What on earth are you going to wear? Not too much red lipstick mind you, I don't think it would go down too well.'

As ever my mother, thought Kate.

'No, of course not. I think I'll wear my navy suit, the American one father likes me in so much. Do you think it would be suitable? Do you think I'll need to wear a hat? I don't think I have one that matches it.'

'I shouldn't think so. Young people don't seem to bother so much these days. That will look perfect, yes, strike exactly the right note. It's quite unusual, perhaps, but I think that's not a bad thing. We're both so proud of you, the way you have coped, the way you have been there for Clare, it can't be easy. I do hope it goes well for you dear,' responded Sarah, much encouraged.

On the Friday of the interview, at her mother's insistence, Kate caught a ridiculously early train. She hated being early as it always seemed such a waste of time, idling around waiting for the main event to happen. It was a strange quirk about her mother, one who never knowingly wasted a minute, but insisted on being far too early for everything. How on earth was she going to fill her time wandering around nervously trying to keep the interview out of her mind? Of course the train was on time, no delays, no stoppages and she arrived at her destination with two hours to spare.

I'll get a paper and find a little tea shop somewhere close by, she thought, I may well get asked about the latest events I suppose. Now I wonder which way is it to the College? I'll have to ask someone.

She looked around to see whom she might approach and saw a tall, thin man about her own age approaching, his face buried in a paper. He was wearing a hat and a neatly pressed, if rather ill-fitting grey suit, but he looked respectable.

'I'm sorry to disturb you,' she called out as he came level with her, 'I was wondering if you could tell me the way to Romney College.'

He glanced up from his paper, irritated to have been interrupted on his way. He turned towards her to reply.

'Bob, Bob Thompson!' she exclaimed, 'It's me, Kate, Kate Aldworth.'

It took him a moment to register. 'Kate, how lovely to see you, what on earth are you doing here? I thought you were in America. Are you back to visit your parents? Are they both well?'

He was stilted but friendly enough. He obviously hadn't heard anything. Surprising, thought Kate given the Plymouth grapevine, but then both his parents had died the previous year. When she had enquired about Bob, her parents had told her that he had moved away and they hadn't seen him since his mother's funeral.

'Yes, both very well, thank you,' she replied politely, 'I was sorry to hear about your parents, Bob. Are you working here now?'

'Thanks. Yes, I'm in the local branch of Barclays, it's at the end of the street, the red brick building you can just about see at the corner. I'm Chief Clerk now; done quite well for myself, I suppose,' he added rather immodestly. 'But what are you doing here, are you on your own?'

He was looking around obviously expecting to see her husband.

'It's a long story, Bob, have you got time for a chat? I could do with some company.'

'I've got half an hour before I need to be back, that's all, I'm afraid. I don't want to be late, sets a bad example to the junior staff you see, and the manager takes a very dim view of that. It's so good to see you again.'

He hasn't changed she thought, still dedicated, deferential and dull.

He took her to a small chintzy tea shop, full of whispering

old ladies. He dithered over the menu before ordering two tea cakes and a pot of tea. Even so, Kate was glad of his company, she still felt a strange affection for this boy who had unwittingly become a man.

'So you're Chief Clerk now, that's quite an achievement, Bob. Well done.'

'Yes, I'm pleased, thank you, Kate. Not to detract too much from my efforts, I hope, but the bank was so short of experienced clerks after the war that I got my chance. I've worked hard, but it has paid off. But enough about me, what are you doing here? Where is your husband; Art isn't it? Has he travelled with you? I've often wondered, by the way, what does Art stand for?'

'Arthur, of course. No he's not here with me, I've come back alone. Well not entirely alone, I have a daughter who's six, but she's with my parents this afternoon. It didn't work out,' she said simply.

She didn't want to tell him everything, she felt she owed her loyalty to Art, and she feared that this fundamentally weak man would pass ill judgement on a man she still loved, and whom she reckoned was worth at least two of him.

'I'm sorry to hear that. I did wonder at the time when I heard you were getting married so quickly, but I'm genuinely sorry.'

Kate winced. He had to say it, didn't he? she thought. She detected an inkling of gloating, but perhaps she was being unfair. Tactless rather than malicious was Bob. They chatted happily about nothing in particular until, glancing at his watch, he suddenly jumped to his feet knocking the sugar bowl over as he did.

'Crikey is that the time? Sorry, I've got to go, I mustn't be late back. It was great seeing you again, really it was. Look me up if you do get into the College, a familiar face, eh?'

He dashed out leaving a trail of sugar footprints on the grubby linoleum. Kate sighed as the waitress handed her the bill. She paid realising that she still hadn't managed to buy a paper. She turned in the direction of the College and started to walk aimlessly. She found it easily enough. It was located in a quiet residential area in the city, about a mile from the centre, and was set back from the road in its own grounds. What she assumed was the main administrative building was built in red brick, its frontage almost semi-circular. Around the College building was a beautifully manicured lawn, in the middle of which stood a perfectly symmetrical ancient looking horse chestnut. The building appeared to be relatively modern in comparison to the grounds which seemed to have been laid out in a much earlier era. It had a welcoming atmosphere and she felt more than ever that she wanted to belong there.

On entering the College she was shown into a small, slightly fusty-smelling room by a plump middle-aged woman, her hair neatly pinned behind her head in a perfect bun. The walls were papered in a now yellowing stripe. The carpet on the floor bore the hallmarks of countless polished shoes.

'You're rather early for your interview I'm afraid, Miss, I mean, Mrs Willis, but you are welcome to sit in here until it's time. You'll be meeting Dr Murphy. I'll collect you and take you to his room when he's ready.'

Kate sat down and opened the paper she had eventually managed to buy. She sat for some time scanning the pages for something topical, something worthy of discussion. There didn't seem to be anything in particular of note. She put the paper down and sat wracking her brains trying to recall the names of the cabinet ministers, what was happening on the world stage.

What on earth will they want to ask me? she wondered. Having lived in America, for the best part of seven years, she felt she had lost touch with events in the land of her birth.

The door opened and she half expected to see the officious secretary coming back to collect her, but instead she was confronted by a tall, formally dressed woman, in her early fifties, Kate guessed. Following behind her was a small, slim, mousey girl of about eighteen.

'It smells fusty in here.' The older woman spoke rather too loudly to suggest any pretence at discretion. She nodded at Kate in acknowledgement and sat down heavily, patting the seat beside her with her gloved hand, indicating that her companion should do likewise.

The younger woman sat down compliantly. She was very pretty but pale and looked around the room anxiously as she started to cross and uncross her legs in an effort to get comfortable on a sofa that was too deep for her relatively short legs.

'For goodness sake, sit properly, Mary,' the older woman commanded. The younger woman glanced at Kate and blushed. Kate felt for her.

'I'm Kate Willis,' she said, as she got up to shake their hands. It was a gesture intended to defuse the situation more so than to acquaint herself with this unpleasant, overbearing woman.

'How do you do, Miss Willis?' came the icy reply.

'Actually it's Mrs Willis,' Kate replied defiantly.

'I'm Mrs Coates and this is my daughter, Mary. I presume you are also here for an interview. Are you American? I thought I detected a slight accent.'

'No, I'm English, I was born and brought up in Plymouth, but I lived in America for several years. I returned to live in England last year,' Kate replied pleasantly.

'Ah, that might explain your unusual suit, if I may say so. It is somewhat more casual than I would have expected for an interview and you're not wearing a hat. No one seems to know how to dress anymore.'

She sat purse-lipped casting a critical eye over Kate. By now Mary was visibly cringing, sinking ever deeper into the seat, humiliated by her mother's rudeness, but she didn't dare to speak. The door opened to reveal the officious secretary, just in time to prevent Kate saying what was really on her mind.

What an insufferable, arrogant busybody, she thought, how dare she harangue me like that? That poor girl, she'll go

113

feral if she ever manages to get in here. Freed at last from the shackles of that, that… harridan.

She was fuming and needed all her self-constraint to regain her composure on entering Dr Murphy's room. He stood up as she entered, peering at her over a pair of half-moon glasses which were perched precariously on the end of his nose. His hair was white, with an unusually low side-parting. What was left, he had grown sufficiently long to allow it to bend over and shield the entire top of his head. A shaft had escaped and bobbed freely, like a pump handle, as he walked towards her to shake her hand. Kate bit her lip and stifled a laugh. He held the tips of her fingers in a damp, limp shake.

'Please take a seat, Mrs Willis. I'm Dr Murphy. I need to ask you some questions about your application to join us here at Romney. May I begin by asking you why you wish to enter the noble profession of teaching?' He was formal and cold, but Kate had anticipated the question.

'It is something I've considered doing for many years, Dr Murphy,' she replied confidently. 'My parents are both teachers so I've always had an interest. In fact I helped to teach a young handicapped boy to read when I was, I suppose, only twelve or thirteen. When I had my own daughter, I realised how important it was to feed her insatiable appetite for knowledge and –'

'I see, I wanted to ask you about that,' he interrupted rudely. 'I see from your application form that you're married, I hadn't realised that you also had a child. How do you expect to concentrate on your studies with the responsibility of bringing up a child and looking after a husband, Mrs Willis?'

Kate smarted. 'I've thought carefully about that, Dr Murphy. My parents, who also live in Plymouth, are now both retired and have offered to help me in looking after my daughter.'

'Am I to understand then that your husband will be moving here with you and you will leave your child alone with your parents, or are you intending to abandon your husband as well for the duration of your studies?'

It had started worse than Kate could ever have imagined.

Now or never, she despaired. I have to be honest with him; it will only make matters worse if they find out later on that I have not been completely candid.

'Dr Murphy, my husband and I are separated, he lives in America. We are in the process of getting divorced. My daughter and I both live with my parents now.' There, she had said it. She had held her head high. She had tried to sound upbeat and unapologetic, but she was dying inside.

He put his pen down slowly and looked at her hard, raising one of his long, whiskery eye brows.

'I must tell you that I find this news most disturbing, Mrs Willis. In my opinion, teachers have a duty to maintain the highest moral standards, both professionally and personally. We have the most delicate young minds in our hands, minds that could so easily be contaminated by those who are in a position to influence them. We must be very careful about whom we allow to enter our profession. A divorced woman would not be our first choice.'

Kate couldn't believe what she was hearing; she felt that she had been transported into some parallel Dickensian world and that she was actually being interviewed by beadle Bumble. She fought the urge to stand up and make a hasty exit, but somehow managed to retain her composure for the second time that afternoon and considered her response carefully. She spoke slowly in measured tones.

'I agree, Dr Murphy; I have always tried to live my own life by the highest moral standards and indeed was brought up by my parents to do so. I believe that I continue to instil those values in my daughter and would wish to do so with any child I had the privilege of teaching. I also believe, however, that life is not mapped out by a single set of rules and that morality is not an absolute. One man's morality is another man's problem.'

She paused momentarily on noticing his look of incredulity. She cleared her throat before continuing.

'Sometimes we are forced to make a moral choice that must by its nature negate another. To those who would judge our actions, it may not outwardly appear that we have taken a moral stance at all. I believe, however, that the selfless motives behind such stances can be intrinsically more moral than the conventions by which we are generally judged. It's a case of *let him who is without sin cast the first stone*, I suppose.'

Kate sat bolt upright with her hands neatly folded in her lap and continued to look straight towards him, outwardly entirely composed. He lifted his pen without speaking and started to write. Eventually he set it down, dipped his head and once more observed her over his glasses. His face by now was expressionless.

'I can't say that I approve at all of divorce, Mrs Willis. Indeed I firmly believe we have a duty to abide by the vows we have made before God, for better, for worse, but I must admit that I admire your spirit. I also admire your obvious ability to put forward a coherent argument, although I cannot agree with its sentiments. You're obviously a bright, articulate, young woman. I feel that in this case I must consult with my colleagues and cannot make a decision by myself. This is a highly unusual situation, but despite my reservations, I believe you may have much to offer the teaching profession and we may make an exception. If we do accept you into Romney, let me be clear – it will be on the understanding that at all times we will expect you to demonstrate those exemplary standards of behaviour that you have extolled so eloquently just now. I don't believe that there is any merit in putting the remaining questions to you as I think we both understand each other quite well. Good day to you, Mrs Willis, you will hear of our decision in due course.'

Kate was dumbfounded. There was still a chance, if indeed she still wanted a chance after this. She got up and thanked him politely, her dignity intact. He nodded, but remained in his seat writing. She made her way to the door, turned the handle and walked into the hallway struggling to pull on her gloves. Her heart was pounding and her palms were sticking to the soft leather. She walked back slowly towards the reception room and as she passed she glanced in to see Mary Coates still sitting in the shadow of her mother. God help her if she gets him, she thought. What a day!

A letter arrived three weeks later. She had been accepted.

Chapter 11

Plymouth, September 1954

Kate looked across at Clare who was sprawling on the bed bouncing her feet up and down on the mattress and following her mother's every move. Kate's heart sank as she made a final sweep of the room, checking that she hadn't left anything essential behind. She hated the thought of leaving her child again but she had no option, the new college term started the following day.

'You'll do as Granny asks you to, won't you, darling, you'll be a good girl for Mummy?' said Kate, as she lay down on the bed beside her child and held her close. She watched as Clare's large brown eyes started to well up. She was trying so hard to be brave and grown up.

'Do you have to go back Mummy? I miss you so much when you're away. Why can't we all just live here with Granny and Grandpa?'

'I know, darling, and I'm going to miss you too, but I'll be back before you know it; only five days and then I'll be here again. You think about something nice that you would like to do on Saturday and we'll have a special day together. Anyway, you know how much Granny, Grandpa and Uncle James spoil you when I'm away, even though they deny it,' Kate teased. She tried to sound light and convincing as she tickled Clare, but she was finding it hard to control her own emotions. Clare emitted a sad laugh.

'I've got to go now or I'll miss my train, I'm afraid. Are you coming to the station to wave me off?' Clare nodded tacitly.

As her train pulled into the station, Kate considered the now familiar Sunday ritual; church, Sunday roast, afternoon walk, pack, drive to the station, journey back to college. She could hardly believe that she was now entering her second year at Romney. The first had flown by. Still, leaving home hadn't got any easier. She hated those last few minutes, standing on the platform with them, waiting to say goodbye. Clare was standing beside her, holding her hand, shuffling her feet. Kate turned towards her father and hugged him; she could feel his ribs protruding through his jacket.

He's getting smaller and thinner, older and paler. He doesn't look well, she thought as she pulled away from him. She turned to Clare and attempted to lift her up.

'You're getting too big now; I swear every time I try to lift you, you've grown an inch,' she puffed as she half hitched her onto her toes and kissed her forehead.

She climbed into the carriage, pulled down the window, called goodbye and watched them as the train pulled slowly out of the station. Clare ran along the platform to the very end waving her arms wildly in the air. Her father, now slightly stooped, limped along behind her, trying without success to keep up. His grey hair was tossing in the draught created by the departing train. He raised his hand in a slow goodbye.

She sat back in her seat and contemplated her return to Romney. She reflected that her first year had gone particularly well and that she was enjoying the course immensely; in fact, if she were honest with herself, she was really looking forward to getting back, despite missing Clare so much. Far from being a hindrance, having a child had given her an insight that evaded many of the younger, less experienced students. She found the course challenging but interesting and her brain was buzzing with ideas.

She had excelled in her first teaching practice, discovering that she had a flair for producing interesting, stimulating lessons. The headmaster had virtually offered her a job as soon as she qualified. Her college tutors had commented that her essays were trenchant, original and showed maturity and insight. She felt confident, knowing that she could more than hold her own amongst her younger contemporaries.

She had seen Dr Murphy around the College, but he didn't seem to remember her or, if he did, he chose to ignore her which suited them both. She was popular with the other students, many of whom were fascinated by her life in America and she believed that she had inspired many sheltered young minds to seek adventure away from familiar shores. She felt like she had become an older, wiser sister guiding and inspiring her young contemporaries while maintaining her youthful exuberance. After all, she was still only twenty-seven; it just seemed to them that she had already lived an entire life.

She had met up again with Mary Coates on her first day and, since then, they had become firm friends. She had arrived at the College early, her mother's inevitable influence and had been sitting at the window of her college room observing the other students streaming in; excitement, nervousness, tearfulness, happiness, every emotional condition had been laid out before her. Many were tasting freedom and independence for the first time and she could almost smell their anticipation. She had thought back to when, with those same mixed emotions, she had arrived expectantly in Boston all those years before.

Her attention had been drawn to the sound of a car horn blaring. A large black Austin had pulled up close to the College entrance and was causing an obstruction. It was the infernal mother she had noticed first, the same hat perched on her head like an abandoned crow's nest. She was remonstrating with the driver of the other car, refusing to budge until their cases had been off-loaded. Kate had watched the scene unfolding before her with amusement.

Later, exploring the accommodation, she had walked past Mary's room and had overheard the barking orders emanating from behind a closed door; she had recognised the booming voice of Mrs Coates. She had decided to give the owner a wide berth until she was sure she was well and truly off the premises.

She had met up with Mary at supper; she had discovered her sitting alone looking lost and frightened while around her, new acquaintances and lifelong friendships were being forged. Young women were warily eyeing up young men, who were in turn lustily eyeing up young women. It was a hive of activity, buzz, youth and promise.

Kate had introduced herself pleasantly. 'Hello, it's Mary isn't it? We met briefly when we both came for our interviews. I see you also got a place. It's exciting, isn't it? Do you mind if I sit beside you?'

Mary had looked up and it was a moment before she seemed to recognise Kate. She had blushed; Kate hadn't been sure whether this was due to her natural shyness or was as a result of her recollections regarding their previous encounter.

'Oh yes, I do remember you now. I'm sorry, but I can't recall your name, I'm afraid. Yes, please sit down. I don't know anyone here at all. Do you?' Mary had spoken quietly as if she didn't want anyone to overhear.

'Kate, Kate Willis,' she had replied as she held out her hand. 'No like you, yours is the only familiar face in the room; we shall be strangers together.'

Mary had smiled and that had been the start of their close friendship. In this their second year, Kate and Mary were moving into digs together. At first Mary's mother had been less than happy about the friendship, believing that Kate was a bad role model for her impressionable daughter. Kate had been somewhat gripped by the irony of this. That Mary had continued her friendship with Kate, despite her mother's remonstrations, had been the first sign of her growing defiance and independence. Finally out of the perpetual reach of her mother's iron grip, Mary's initial shyness had given way to a steely determination to live her own life. It was Kate who had stepped in to control some of Mary's growing liveliness and wilder antics. With her new found confidence and the leashes untied, Mary was proving a popular girl around college with many male admirers. As an American friend had once told Kate, 'College is a bit like being a kid in a candy store, except you're the candy.'

'Be careful, Mary,' Kate had warned, 'give an inch and they'll take a mile. I'm far from being a prude, but let it be on your terms not theirs.'

Mary had shrugged off the advice, life was for living. Kate firmly believed, however, that much of Mary's bravado was for show and that underneath it all she was still a virgin.

Mary had thrown herself fully into college life, clubs and parties. In reality, however, she was still a naïve girl. Kate liked her a lot and felt protective of her. She smiled as she recalled Mary staggering back to college from a night at the pictures, arm in arm with her latest beau, her mouth wide open to the elements in the mistaken belief that it would expunge the smell of cigarettes. She needed to hide her habits from her mother who had made it abundantly clear that she did not approve of the three vices; cigarettes, alcohol or unmarried sex. Perhaps Mary reminded her of her younger self, a young woman also wanting to throw off the shackles of parental constraints and she enjoyed the small part she could play in undermining the dominating force of Mary's mother. Kate deliberately smoked in front of her.

She was looking forward to the relative freedom of moving into digs. It was the one aspect of the College she disliked, the 'boarding school' regime of the accommodation, the restrictions on visitors, signing in and out at night, being guarded and checked in like a child. Kate's accommodation was 'policed' by a draconian, live-in spinster Miss Edna Hurd. A formidable teacher during the day, Edna Hurd believed that her bounden duty was to protect the innocence of her young charges at night. She dwelt in a flat at the entrance, her hearing finely tuned to the sound of forbidden footsteps. A heavy, masculine tread would result in a flanking attack on the unsuspecting victim, a severe ticking off and an entry in her pretentiously named notebook 'Recalcitrant Rebels'.

Kate and Mary were moving into the top two bedrooms of a small, three-storey, red-bricked terrace which was owned by a middle-aged war widow called Rita Steele. For several years her niece had lived in the house with her, although more recently Mrs Steele was there on her own. Her niece had got married in July and moved out permanently. Bob Thompson had found the house for them.

As he had suggested on the day of her interview, Kate had looked him up shortly after she arrived at Romney and she had seen him often during her first year. It was a welcome connection with home and her parents. They had got used to sitting, happily chatting about things in common as she brought him news of the latest hatches, matches and despatches in Plymouth. Since his parents had died, Bob had lost contact with his home area and he enjoyed gossiping about people with whom they had both grown up. After his initial curiosity, Kate was surprised that he had been sensitive enough to avoid enquiring about Art. They were now divorced, but she got a letter from his parents every three months or so. He was still very unstable and tired easily. He suffered from irrational outbursts, often becoming aggressive before going through periods of deep depression. They hoped that one day they might see Clare and Kate again but they never pressed her.

Kate realised that Bob would have liked to resume their childhood romance, but she had been careful to keep it on a strictly platonic footing. After Art, Bob was a poor substitute, but he was reasonable company; he knew the city and it was a safe way to develop a relatively quiet social life away from the wilder antics of her fellow students.

Bob had got to know Rita Steele after the war. Her husband Stan's family had banked at Barclays for years, but he had been killed at Arnhem. She had struggled to come to terms with his death and had turned to Bob for financial help; it was he who had suggested that she should consider taking in lodgers to boost her income. She had always been reluctant, but Bob had persuaded her that Kate and Mary would cause no problems and could, in fact, provide some welcome company when she was on her own. She had finally relented, mainly as a result of meeting Kate, whom she reckoned was more mature than most of the students she encountered and was unlikely to disturb her peace. Kate felt some responsibility, therefore, for the introduction and so was determined to keep Mary in line.

She had agreed to meet Mary at the house. When she arrived, she was pleased to discover that Mary was already settled in and was happily sitting, sipping tea with Mrs Steele; her mother, thankfully, was nowhere to be seen. It irritated Kate that she allowed herself to be intimidated by Mary's mother. She was the only person who had ever made her feel like that.

'Fancy a wee cuppa, Mrs Willis?' Mrs Steele enquired as she showed Kate into the sitting room where tea and home-made cakes were laid out on a tray, covered with a crisp white cloth. Kate noticed the faint Irish accent.

The room was small but meticulously tidy; it smelt of wax polish. Two Staffordshire dogs sat grinning at each other across a sunken, tiled hearth. On the mantelpiece, a row of diminishing brass candlesticks, laid out like a family of matryoshka dolls, flanked a large wooden-framed photograph, from which stared a small, stocky man in Army uniform. Mr Steele, Kate presumed. Mrs Steele had lit a log fire, which hissed and sparked illuminating the room in the dying light. A large religious tapestry decorated the wall above the fireplace. Every possible space was utilised, with just enough room for an old fashioned, close weave sofa and two armchairs to sit snugly together. They were backed with embroidered, beige-coloured antimacassars. Everything gave the impression of being used for the first time. In fact, the whole room looked like an artefact from another era which had been unwittingly captured in a colourless still life painting.

Mrs Steele seemed friendly enough; she had obviously made an effort to make them feel welcome, but she was formal and uncomfortable. Kate sought to lighten the atmosphere.

'A lovely room, Mrs Steele, and it's so kind of you to light a fire especially for us. Not that I think you don't normally light a fire,' she continued apologetically, trying to recover from her faux pas. Mrs Steele raised an eyebrow but didn't speak.

'Well would you like a wee cup while it's still hot?' she enquired dryly.

'Yes please, Mrs Steele,' Kate replied, winking surreptitiously at Mary who was grinning at her behind their host's back.

'Miss Coates has already unpacked her belongings. She has taken the front room; it's the larger of the two, I'm afraid. When you've finished your tea, I'll help you to take your cases up.'

Mary looked at Kate apologetically, with a wide-mouthed grimace. 'I'll explain later,' she mouthed as Mrs Steele got up to pour the tea. 'My mother.'

She had said it all.

'Well, I suppose we ought to set some house rules,' said Mrs Steele as she handed Kate her cup. Her hand had a nervous shake which caused the tea to spill over into the saucer. Kate politely ignored it. 'I'm sure we'll all get along fine,' she continued, 'but I believe it would be best if we agreed what suits everyone from the start, don't you think?'

Kate felt for this small, nervy, birdlike woman who was clearly finding it difficult to adjust to her new found role of landlady.

'I think that's a very good idea, don't you, Mary?' Kate confirmed with conviction, looking straight at her friend.

Kate could see Mary weighing up the situation and seeking to gain the advantage; she wasn't going to allow her new found freedom to be eroded unnecessarily.

'Of course, but I suppose we're all adults here and understand that we all have to rub along together. It's a new experience for all of us.'

Kate thought it would be churlish to point out to Mary that, strictly speaking, at nineteen she wasn't yet technically an adult.

'I think what we want is to respect each other's individual needs,' continued Mary confidently, 'I'm sure you won't want your life turned upside-down by our arrival, Mrs Steele, and Kate and I just want to be able to complete our studies in peace and to feel at home. Of course, we would expect to help you with the chores and anything else you want us to do.'

Kate looked at her askance.

What's she up to? she thought. Which hole in the skirting did that shy, fidgety mouse disappear into and when?

Mrs Steele seemed somewhat relieved that everyone had reached agreement so easily; she was unsure how these things worked.

'Well, I suppose that's what I want as well, Miss Coates, I don't presume there's any need to set formal house rules. Let's see how it goes shall we?'

And so it was that no rules were ever set and Mary, for the remainder of her time at Mrs Steele's, came and went as she pleased, absolutely in line with being 'at home'.

'What were you up to down there?' challenged Kate as they stood chatting in her room later that evening.

'I was not about to replace 'Hitler Hurd' with 'Stalin Steele', or my mother for that matter.' She grinned at Kate and looked round the room.

'Could do with an update don't you think and what's with all the religious stuff?'

Kate shrugged.

'Still, it's clean and I don't think we'll have too much trouble with Mrs Steele, do you?' suggested Mary, as she looked behind the curtain, ran her hand along the windowsill and examined the results.

'Think she's far more likely to have trouble with you,' teased Kate, observing Mary with amusement.

'Strange little woman isn't she? Where's that accent from do you think?' Mary continued chattily, without waiting for Kate's reply. 'Sorry about the rooms, that was Mother's idea,' she added defensively as she noticed Kate open the small chest of drawers and ram in some clothes. 'She seemed to think that as you would be going home every weekend you wouldn't have so much stuff with you. Mind you, I've no intention of going home unless I have to. This is home now. I'm happy to swap rooms if you'd like though.'

'No you'll need the space to get on with your studies… in peace.' Kate added pointedly. Mary made a face and laughed.

'I think this is going to be fun, don't you? Shall we go out and explore the area?'

'Not tonight, Mary, I'm tired and I still haven't unpacked everything; there's plenty of time to explore, even for you. I'm going to finish off here and get an early night if you don't mind. I'll see you in the morning.'

'Okay. Get the hint,' replied Mary, as she squeezed past Kate and opened the door. 'Give me a knock will you, don't want to be late on my first day back. Sleep well.'

Kate smiled at her as she left. She unpacked the rest of her clothes and set her suitcase on top of the little mahogany wardrobe angled into a corner. The room was much smaller than she was used to, but she was sure she could make it homely. She lifted two small photo frames from her case and set them on the chest of drawers which doubled as a dressing table. She stood admiring the first one which was of Clare. She picked it up and kissed the glass before replacing it carefully.

'Goodnight, sweetheart,' she whispered.

She lifted the second one and studied it closely before clenching it against her breast. It was of her wedding day. Art was looking at her lovingly, his handsome face smiling into hers. They had so enjoyed the day, everyone had, a day of light relief in the grim, grey reality of that dreadful, useless war. She recalled her wedding night, his gentle hands caressing her as he made love to her for the first time. She would never forget the feeling of togetherness as they became one. Would she ever experience that feeling again? She opened the top drawer of the chest and placed the photograph under her clothes.

'This one is for my eyes only darling, my memories.'

She wondered if she would ever see him again. Clare hardly seemed to remember her father. She had never mentioned the night she had watched Art push Kate down the stairs or the day she had woken to find his hands tightening around her neck. It was a blessing, Kate supposed. But had she erased the memories or simply suppressed them? It was hard to explain to Clare why they weren't still living with the kind, loving daddy she felt she wanted to describe, but she believed she couldn't tell her the truth, not yet. Perhaps when she was older she would tell her the whole story. Kate knew she still loved Art and always would. She wondered did he ever think about her. In that distant land did he also lie in bed projecting images of her against the still darkness? She tried to recall her earliest memories of him; remember a time when he was strong and well; the fresh smell of his skin, the feel of his hair brushing against her cheek, his kiss. She had slept in his arms experiencing the comforting warmth of his presence throughout the night. But that had been so very long ago. Long before she had abandoned him in Boston; oh, to have the old Art back.

She lay down on the hard, rather lumpy mattress, pulled the blankets under her chin and reaching out turned off the bedside lamp. She felt the cold trickle of tears on her cheek as she tried to get warm in the lonely little bed. Turning her head, she began to weep quietly into her pillow. Her swollen eyes grew heavy as she eventually drifted into a fitful sleep.

Chapter 12

Plymouth, October 1955

Kate pulled her coat tight around her neck as the already biting October wind cut across the yew-lined graveyard. She tugged at her gloves and took Clare's cold little hand in hers. She squeezed it gently as she looked across at her mother's steely expression, her head bowed in prayer.

'Forasmuch as it has pleased Almighty God to take unto himself the soul of our dear brother here departed, we therefore commit his body to the ground...'

The vicar's chilling words echoed across the graveyard as she watched her father's coffin slowly descend into its final resting place. She imagined her father inside, listening to the proceedings, his arms neatly folded across his chest, his eyes closed in slumber, a wry smile on his lips, his pale face looking to the sky. His final bolthole; he had found his sanctuary at last.

Three days previously she had awoken to Mrs Steele's gentle shaking, 'Mrs Willis, wake up, there's a telephone call for you; it's your brother, James.'

Kate had woken with a start and glanced at her clock; it was only seven o'clock. She immediately thought the worst.

'What is it? What's wrong? Is it Clare?' Rita hadn't replied.

Kate had ripped back the bedclothes and ran staggering down the narrow stairs still half asleep.

'Hello James, it's me, what's wrong? Is Clare alright?'

'Clare's fine, Kate, but you must brace yourself for some bad news.'

'What is it, James? Tell me...is it Mother?'

'No, she's fine...it's Father, Kate...he passed away last night.'

Kate inhaled sharply. 'Oh God, no, not Father. What happened?'

'He died peacefully in his sleep. Mother woke up in the middle of the night and found him lying in bed beside her.'

'How awful... is she okay?'

'Yes, she's coping. It was a terrible shock for her, but she's fine. Luckily I was at home. Doctor Davidson has been... he's given her something to settle her.'

'I can't believe it, James...what do they think it was? Had he been feeling unwell?'

'No, I saw him last night... he had supper, went to bed at his usual time, nothing unusual at all. Dr Davidson thought it was probably his heart, but we may never know. I think you should come back as soon as possible though. Do you want me to drive over there to get you?

'No, no, don't come all this way; Mother will need you there with her. I'll let the College know what's happened and catch a train home as soon as I can. Where's Clare now?'

'She's here, but Mother thinks it's best if she goes to school as normal. That's if she'll go. Is that alright with you?

'Yes...yes, I think that's probably best, let her go to school...yes, you're right; best to keep her busy. How has she taken the news?

'We haven't told her yet. She's still asleep...we thought you might want to tell her.'

'No, not over the phone...I can't tell her like this ...I couldn't...she really loved her Grandpa; she'll be very upset. Will you tell her for me? Do you mind? Tell her I'm coming home and I'll see her later, and give her a big hug from me.'

'Alright, I'll get her up soon and Mother and I can both tell her...do you want to speak to Mother now?'

'No, I don't think I could face that ...I'll wait until I see her. I just need time to think...oh God, I can't believe it. I only saw him on Sunday, he seemed fine then. I just can't believe I'll never see him again.' She choked back her tears. 'Tell Mother I'm coming home. I'll be there as soon as I can...see you all later.'

'Alright, she'll understand... we'll be waiting for you.

Take your time… sort out whatever you need to. We're fine here for the time being…have a safe journey. Are you sure you're going to be okay?'

'Yes, I'll be fine. Thanks for telling me, James, it can't have been easy. I'll see you all later then…goodbye.'

'Goodbye.'

Kate had replaced the receiver and with her back against the wall had slowly slid down it until she was sitting on the cold, tiled floor. She was numb from shock. A reel of terrible inflictions had succeeded in projecting through her brain in the time it took to run down a flight of stairs and the news was as bad as she had imagined.

'Is everything alright, Mrs Willis?'

She had looked up to see Mrs Steele's concerned expression. She was holding a cup of steaming tea.

'It's my father, Mrs Steele…he passed away in his sleep. My mother found him in bed, earlier this morning.' Kate could hardly shape the words. Her voice shook with emotion.

'I'm sorry for your trouble.' Rita had spoken with genuine meaning, as she shook Kate's hand. Kate had thought it a strange, rather formal gesture.

Is there anything I can do?' she'd continued.

'No, thank you, I'm going to get the train home as soon as I can. I'll have to let the College know…perhaps Mary could take a message for me. Actually, come to think of it, yes, there is something you could do for me please. Would you call Bob Thompson? I'm sure he would want to know.'

Kate had arrived home to find her mother busying herself greeting friends and relations. They had cried in each other's arms. Her father was lying in his coffin in James' old bedroom. As she tentatively entered the room, Kate had noticed how it already held the faint aroma of death mingled with fresh flowers. The strangely sweet, sickening scent had seeped into her nostrils. She feared that this scene would forever taint her father's memory. Kate had never seen a corpse before and was wary of the experience. She had walked cautiously towards the casket, catching her first glimpse of the still, pale profile. Snow white lace, fringed his frame. Kate had gazed down at his peaceful face; it was smiling in death. She had bent over and kissed his forehead but the unexpected intense coldness had caused her to recoil. She had rested her hand on the solidity of his chest; it had remained resistant to her touch.

'Never to hear his voice again, or feel the warmth of his embrace. That's the worst bit,' she had whispered, looking over at James. 'He'll never know me as a qualified teacher, will he? He would so love to have seen that, been able to advise me, guide me. I've got to do my best for him now and make him proud; perhaps he will watch and guide me from above.'

She had pulled a handkerchief from her sleeve. Even after all these years it was a less than freshly laundered one.

The next few days had passed in a blur of visitors, funeral arrangements and occasional laughter. Bob Thompson had arrived by car, not long after Kate. He had taken a couple of days' holiday just to be with the family. Kate's mother had remarked how marvellous he'd been, ferrying relations to and from the station, collecting groceries, making sandwiches, handing out tea; being there when they were all physically and mentally exhausted.

'I think he still holds a candle to you, Kate,' she had challenged, as they sat alone together the evening before the funeral.

'I know, Mother, but I could never feel for him what I felt, what I still feel for Art. We're friends and that's all. We're childhood sweethearts who grew up, then grew apart. I don't think about Bob like that.'

'Being friends first can lead to happy relationships, you know, and it would be good for Clare to have a father. I don't suppose you'll ever see Art again.'

'Not now, please, Mother, let's just get tomorrow over and done with and then perhaps I can think about the rest of my life.' Sarah complied and nothing more was said.

The day of the funeral passed like clockwork, largely due to Sarah's guiding hand. Kate decided she should go back that night especially as James had agreed to stay on with their mother for a couple of days. She had her final teaching practice coming up in just over four weeks and she was missing some important lessons; she didn't want to fall behind. She was determined to do as well as possible; a good grade would stand her in great stead in the competitive and sometimes incestuous battle for jobs.

Bob offered her a lift back in his car and she accepted. She felt that his company would help to distract her from the unbearable emptiness she was feeling at the loss of her beloved father, but the journey seemed to take for ever. The wind had really whipped up during the afternoon and rain was beating down like a flurry of arrows. There was flooding on the road and, cautious as ever, Bob didn't want to skid. The snail's pace of his cold little car continued for mile after interminable mile. It was well after midnight when they finally arrived back outside Rita's.

'I can't go in now, Bob,' Kate sighed looking up at the dark-filled windows. 'I'll wake everyone up and they'll only feel the need to ask about the funeral. I don't think I could face that tonight.'

'You can come back and stay in my spare room, if you like. The bed is already made up. I don't mind at all,' Bob suggested.

'That's kind of you, Bob. Do you know, I think I will. I don't suppose you have any brandy? I could really do with a drink; it's been a long trying day and I'm pretty cold.'

'I know, sorry about that. Your luck is in though. A warming drink would be just the thing.'

He smiled across, squeezed her arm and turned the car towards his own house.

You know, he's not so bad, she thought, Mother is right, he has been a tower of strength these last few days. Perhaps there's more to him than I give him credit for.

The house was as cold as the car but Bob put a match to the fire, which was already laid in the grate, and soon there was a warming glow cheering the room. They sat beside each other on his cramped little sofa, each clutching their drink, laughing as they recounted stories of their childhood and reminisced about a shared past.

They roared with laughter, the sombre tension of the past few days ebbing away with each glass of brandy and the ease of each other's company. The freshly opened bottle soon seeped away to just over half full. Kate felt emotional and tired. She rested her head on Bob's shoulder and felt his arm pull her towards him. He felt as warm and alive as her father had felt cold and inert. She realised that, apart from her father and James, she hadn't felt a man's strong arms around her for a very long time. It made her feel alive. Her head was woozy from worn emotions, lubricated by the brandy and she staggered a bit as Bob helped her up the stairs. He showed her into the spare room, but she pulled him down beside her.

'Stay with me, Bob. I feel so alone,' she mumbled, her eyes half closed in exhaustion.

A confusion of her father, Art, Bob, charged round her head as he leant over, cradled her in his arms and kissed her. She didn't resist. The emotional swirl of the day seemed to have spiralled into this one moment. She watched as he slowly undressed; his thin, white body emerging from under his clothes. She stripped off and jumped in under the sheets beside him, shivering. She rested her cold feet between his wiry legs as he pulled her towards him.

'Kate, darling, you must know that I have always loved you.'

She didn't react. She didn't seem to sense very much at all, apart from the warmth she was slowly regaining from his body. He kissed her again and she responded automatically.

The culmination of their childhood love was swift and perfunctory. Kate felt completely unmoved. Bob kissed her forehead and, rolling over, pulled the precious blankets off her. She crept towards him to ward off the cold, wrapping her legs around him, tugging the clothes to reclaim her share. He read it as affection.

'Good night, Kate, love you.'

She didn't reply.

Kate woke early the next morning. It took her a moment to realise where she was. She groaned. Her head thumped and her tongue felt dry and furry. She looked across the bed towards Bob. A dried white dribble trailed from his mouth. She pushed herself up and, scraping her abandoned clothes off the floor, got dressed quickly in the cold bedroom. As she bent over her head continued to thump. She went into the bathroom, splashed her face and rummaged around until she found some Beecham's Powder in the small neat bathroom cabinet. She stared at the pale reflection in the mirror.

'What have you done you stupid, stupid woman?' she admonished.

She could hear Bob still snoring as she made her way quietly downstairs to the kitchen. She gulped down a large glass of water before mixing and downing the little sachet of white powder. She shuddered as the bitter compound tingled on her tongue.

She sat at the table with her head in her hands.

God, she thought, if Father is watching me from above what must he think? What a stupid, stupid, thoughtless thing to do.

She heard Bob's tread on the stairs and turned to see his sheepish face peering around the door.

'Morning,' he croaked. His hair was standing on end and he had obviously found a pair of pyjamas along the way. He looked vaguely comic; the drawstring was hanging like a monk's belt and the buttons were in the wrong holes.

'Morning,' she responded lethargically.

'Don't think that was meant to happen, was it? Not that I regret it. How's your head?' he replied somewhat cheerily.

'Awful, I feel like there's a gang of navvies wielding sledge hammers in there,' Kate forced in reply. She lifted her head and met his gaze. He was grinning at her.

'Please don't take this the wrong way, Bob,' she continued, 'but I wish last night hadn't happened. It was tiredness, the day, the emotion, the brandy, I don't quite know what. I'm very fond of you, Bob, you know that, but I want us to be friends and that's all, just as we were. Can't we pretend that it never happened and go on as before?'

She could see the hurt spread across his face, as his grin disappeared. She knew what he felt about her, she had always known but in the cold light of day it was better to make it clear that she believed it had been a mistake. She had unintentionally led him on enough as it was. She felt terrible, both emotionally and physically.

'I see,' he responded simply. He sat down at the table beside her and put his head in his hands. He didn't speak.

Kate wished he would rage, storm out anything but this silence. She looked at him and called his name quietly.

'Bob, I'm so sorry, I really didn't want to hurt you, it… it just happened I suppose. I think perhaps I should leave.'

She stood up slowly and started to walk towards the door. As she passed him she rested her hand on his shoulder and squeezed it gently. He remained impassive, staring down at the table. She climbed the stairs and collected her bag from beside the bed. As she started to descend, she saw him standing at the bottom looking up at her; he smiled a resigned smile.

'It's alright, I've always known you didn't feel the same way about me as I do about you; you never have. I don't want to lose your friendship. I suppose my hopes were raised that's all. Do you need a lift?'

'Thank you, that's very kind of you. You really are a good man.'

As she reached the bottom, she wrapped her arms around him and hugged him gently. He responded awkwardly, leaning his head on her shoulder.

'Enough of that,' he replied, 'come on, I'll get dressed quickly and then we can get going.'

Neither spoke as he drove her back to Romney. He pulled up outside the entrance gates.

'Are you alright from here? I'm sorry, I would take you right in, but I'm concerned I might be late.'

'That's fine, thank you. I can manage from here.'

She opened the door and stepped onto the pavement.

'Bye,' she called as he started to drive up the road. He waved but didn't reply.

Chapter 13

Teaching Practice, Exeter, November 1955

'Are you feeling alright, Mrs Willis? Sit down, come on quickly, sit down ...' the headmaster's words failed to hit their mark in time.

Kate was desperately struggling against the black veil, rapidly descending in front of her eyes. She shook her head in a last ditch attempt to stave off the familiar sensation, then nothing. She fainted.

She came round to find the anxious face of the headmaster, Joe Madden, pressed close to her own as he crouched beside her. She was lying prone on the floor.

'Mrs Willis, Mrs Willis, can you hear me? Are you alright? Oh my goodness, someone get her some water. Don't worry children, she's going to be fine. Miss Taylor, get the children back to the classrooms as quickly as possible. Could someone please hurry with the water...' Joe Madden was trying to disguise the sense of panic that was filling his mind.

'I'll fetch some, Mr Madden, I'm sure she's only fainted; she looked awfully pale before she fell,' came the calm reassuring response of Joyce Armstrong.

Kate was only half consciously aware of the commotion surrounding her. Joe Madden's anxious voice; the whimpering of six dozen unsettled school children, Angela Taylor's commanding voice as she took control, ushering the gathered mass out of assembly. Kate had unwittingly managed to turn this, her final teaching practice into an unscripted drama. She felt the cold press of the glass against her lips as Joe Madden raised her shoulders off the floor.

'Have some water, Mrs Willis. Here you are, I'll hold the glass for you, try to take a sip.'

She struggled into a half-sit, half-slump and attempted to drink. The cold water spilled over her lips as the over-tilted glass dribbled its contents down the front of her blouse. She spluttered as the first gulp of water entered her windpipe. She felt a wave of nausea creep over her and knew that she was going to be sick. She retched and spewed the remains of her breakfast into the headmaster's lap. She felt his hand instinctively jerk away from her shoulders, but he managed to hold her upright. She groaned from the discomfort of the stomach wrenching spasms and with increasing awareness of her total humiliation.

She had been half way through reading the story of John the Baptist to the assembled school, when the first wave had come over her. Initially, she had managed to stave it off, but her mind was swimming with the realisation that it would probably return. She had been there several times before, in childhood, and knew that she should sit down and lower her head. But how could she in front of all these children? No, she would just have to fight it; but it was a lost cause

Now, lying on the floor of the small school room that doubled as canteen and assembly hall, Kate groaned as she attempted to stand in a vain effort to regain what little dignity was left to her. Mr Madden, oblivious to the stench and staining on his suit, helped her to a seat.

'I feel so awful, Mr Madden, how can I apologise enough. I don't know what came over me, it was all so sudden,' Kate whispered through dry, vomit-tainted lips.

'It's alright my dear, don't even think about it. Are you feeling a bit better?'

Joe Madden's voice was calm and understanding. Angela Taylor arrived in a flurry of efficiency, tin bucket, mop and sawdust in hand. Kate cringed at the sight.

'Let me help,' Kate breathed the words as she tried again to raise herself up.

'You stay right where you are, soon have this cleared up, don't you worry,' commanded Angela Taylor. 'Mr Madden perhaps you will want to go home to get cleaned up? Mrs Armstrong and I can manage perfectly well here. We'll soon have your class usefully employed. Mrs Willis, I think we should get you home to your bed as well. You live near Romney College don't you? Let's think; what's the best way to get you back there? There's the bus, but I don't think that's such a good idea and, anyway, I'm not sure there's one back to the city at this time of day. Do you know, Mrs Armstrong? I think you should call the doctor as soon as you get back, Mrs Willis; you're as white as a ghost.'

From Kate's perspective, despite being a young woman, Angela Taylor was her mother personified; calm and practical in the most difficult situations. Kate longed to get back to Rita Steele's warm and comfortable little terraced house and go to sleep. Joe Madden interjected, regaining his position as the appointed leader.

'No need to worry about bus timetables, Miss Taylor, if you're sure that Mrs Armstrong and you can manage here, I'll take Mrs Willis back once I've been home and cleaned up a bit. In fact, come to think of it, you'd be best to come back with me now and then I'll take you on from there, save a journey back. I'll get my wife to make you some hot sweet tea and an arrowroot biscuit, that's the thing.'

Kate was grateful for his kindness but nearly retched again at the thought of anything passing her lips.

'That would be so kind of you, but I hate inconveniencing you like this. I'm already so embarrassed about the situation.'

Kate could feel some of her strength returning as the awful realisation of the full extent of the event began to sink in.

'Glad to help, I just hope you're feeling better soon, and back with us, Mrs Willis. We were enjoying having you as part of our merry little band.'

He was so unbelievably kind and forgiving that Kate wasn't sure whether his sentiments were making her feel better or worse. He helped her out to his car, glancing towards the school as the sea of inquisitive faces, pressed against the classroom windows, rapidly receded to the sound of Joyce Armstrong's practised bellow.

Kate arrived back at Rita Steele's having successfully avoided the persistent, but kindly, offers of hot tea. Mr Madden knocked on the door and explained all to an incredulous Mrs Steele.

'Come on my wee girl, it's into bed for you. Don't you worry, Mr Madden, I'll fetch Dr Greene and he'll soon have her back on her feet. She doesn't eat enough and she worries that much, you know. Comes back here every night, grabs something to eat and then she's straight back in that room of hers, working until dear knows what time. I'm not surprised it's caught up with her eventually.'

She closed the door behind the headmaster and helped Kate up the stairs, turning her back as Kate struggled out of her clothes and collapsed into the bed.

'I'll do you a nice, wee, hot water jar and you get some rest. Would you like some tea?'

Kate didn't know whether to laugh or cry – more offers of tea, the great British antidote for all ills. Mrs Steele left her to sleep. She was dozing when she awoke to hear voices below and the sound of Dr Greene's tread on the stairs. She had tried to insist that it was probably only flu, the weather had been so changeable, lots of the children had come down with it and all she needed was rest and fluids, but Mrs Steele was having none of it.

'I know when someone isn't right,' she protested, 'and you're not right. You're that pale and wan.'

They had grown close over the last year and Kate felt an ever growing affection for this odd, lonely, little Irish woman with her strange colloquialisms, half of which still remained a mystery to Mary and Kate.

'She's in here, doctor,' Rita Steele spoke quietly, knocking gently as she simultaneously pushed open the bedroom door. 'I'll leave you to it. I'll be downstairs, Dr Greene, if you need anything. She's not well, I'm telling you. She's not well,' she continued as she pulled the door gently behind her.

'Thank you, Mrs Steele. Let's have a look at the patient then. I believe you fainted, Mrs Willis. Do you want to tell me what happened?'

'I'm not sure really. I'm on my final teaching practice at the moment, Dr Greene; it's my last year at Romney. I've been placed in a small primary school, St John's – perhaps you know it – it's about five miles from here. Anyway today was the start of my third week. I'm not sure what happened exactly; one minute I was standing happily reading a Bible story in assembly, felt a bit faint, and next thing I knew I was lying on the floor.'

'Had you been feeling unwell before that?' Dr Greene asked, taking hold of her wrist and feeling her pulse.

'I wasn't feeling very well this morning; felt a bit sick when I got up. I've been feeling pretty exhausted for the last few days in fact.' Kate replied, reflecting that, after the weekend, this morning seemed to have arrived long before the night could have run its course. She had really struggled to get up. If this teaching practice hadn't meant so much to her she would probably have stayed in bed.

'Did you have breakfast?' continued Dr Greene in an attempt to establish the cause.

'I managed a little porridge but, to be honest, my appetite seems to have gone. A lot of the children have come down with a tummy bug so maybe I've caught something from one of them and I've been working really hard. This teaching practice is really important to me you see; it means absolutely everything and I'm anxious to do really well. Maybe I've been overdoing it a bit.'

Kate reflected that her first two weeks had been exhausting but rewarding. She knew that she was doing well and already felt like a long established member of the small, close-knit team. She was under the care of Angela Taylor, herself only a couple of years older than Kate. Kate knew that Angela had taken to her, probably because she recognised a fellow spirit; an ambitious, intelligent and capable young woman, making her way is a male-dominated word. It was Angela who had hinted that there may be an opportunity for Kate. Joyce Armstrong, the neat, grey-haired matriarch was due to retire in the summer. It was already obvious that her focus was on a time when she could channel her controlling efforts into her garden, rather than the constant curtailment of half-grown farmers' sons, whose legal school leaving age and desire to learn anything more were sadly unsynchronised. Angela reckoned Kate should have an eye on her job. Kate knew that she had to do well and really impress the headmaster.

'Have you been sleeping okay?' continued Dr Greene, working through a systematic process of elimination.

'Not really, I suppose,' admitted Kate. 'But then I haven't been sleeping well for a few years. I find it difficult to get off and then seem to wake around four o'clock and can't get back off again. I've got used to doing without much sleep.'

Ever since her return to England, Kate had found that, despite her body craving sleep, she tossed and turned most of the night in fitful half-conscious slumber. In the darkness, and in a state of semi-awake alertness, her thoughts always turned to Art. She still longed for him, his touch, the smell of him, his very presence. The more she willed herself to sleep, the more her restless mind whirled. It was filled with endless thoughts about the nature of her love for him. Why did all other emotions, such as envy or hate, remain unchanged whether reciprocated by another or not? They could exist in complete isolation from their object. She could feel hatred without feeling hated, feel envious without feeling envied. There was no interdependence, no reliance on the feelings of another to bring the emotion to life in her. Love, however, she concluded, was a coin with two sides. To love and be loved by Art had brought her indescribable joy. Now, knowing she still loved him but without feeling his love in return, had changed the very essence of that emotion from one of unending joy to one of unrelenting pain; love it seemed could not exist in isolation. Was love like a tree falling in a forest –

it only made a sound if there was someone there to hear it; or a rainbow, only existing if someone was watching? Her mind would race in a never ending loop, forever wondering, before she would eventually find herself drifting off to sleep; the pain within deadening as her senses became nullified.

'I see,' responded Dr Greene. 'That's not so good, Mrs Willis. The body needs sleep to regenerate; it's most important. Well, hopefully it's nothing too serious, nothing some rest and a tonic won't cure. Have you any headache or dizziness now?

'I don't think so.'

'Have you ever fainted before?'

'Yes, a few times, when I was a child, but then I seemed to grow out of it,' Kate explained as Dr Greene took her blood pressure. 'Since then I've never actually fainted but I have felt faint a few times, I suppose, but that was only a couple of times when I got very hot and I was living in America. I was pregnant with my daughter at the time. I'm sure this is just because I haven't been sleeping well and I've picked up something. I really didn't want Mrs Steele to trouble you but she insisted. I seem to be putting everyone to so much trouble today.'

'No trouble. Mrs Willis, could you be pregnant again?' he queried nonchalantly as he continued to examine her.

He doesn't realise I'm no longer married, thought Kate.

'Doctor Greene, my husband and I are divorced.'

'Right, well perhaps it's not that then; it's always worth eliminating though. I often find that in women your age it's the underlying cause but somehow it's the last thing many expectant mothers think about.' He was about to continue his questioning when, with horror, the awful realisation began to dawn on Kate.

Oh God, I'd forgotten about that, it makes sense, it's just like it was before with Clare and before I had the miscarriage… the early signs… the increased sleeplessness… the tender breasts… the loss of appetite… the awful tiredness… the nausea and now the fainting. It never occurred to me; it just never occurred to me... it has to be. The awful truth started to dawn on her. She felt her mouth drying as she tried to swallow, but there was nothing there except the remaining taint of sick.

'Dr Greene, I'd forgotten, but now I think about it... it is possible...' she proffered tentatively.

He raised an eyebrow, waiting for her to continue.

'A remote chance but possible...' Kate knew that she was fighting the inevitable, but she needed to convince herself that it couldn't possibly be true. It was too awful to contemplate.

'What's possible? Do you mean that there's a chance you could be pregnant? Mrs Willis, I don't think you need me to tell you that if there is even the remotest chance then it's possible. Have you been menstruating?'

'I've never had a regular cycle, Dr Greene, it can be several months in between; I never know. It's always been like that, for me that's normal.'

'Have you any other symptoms. Come on, you've had a child already, Mrs Willis, how did you feel when you were pregnant before?' he asked rather more brusquely as his brow furrowed.

Kate thought she detected a note of disapproval in his sudden change of tone. No eulogy of congratulations was forthcoming from him, she suspected.

'Yes, I feel so stupid now, it all makes sense... now I think about it, the same symptoms are there... it just never occurred to me, it really didn't. How could I be so stupid?'

'I'll need to do a proper examination in due course,' he continued, 'but judging by the symptoms you've described, I think we can safely say, Mrs Willis, that there's every possibility that you're with child. If so, would you know how many weeks?'

'I know exactly, Dr Greene, it really was only once. The date is etched in my mind, it was the day of my father's funeral; the sixth of October.'

'The day of your father's funeral?' The crescendo in his voice accurately betrayed his judgmental assessment of the situation. He didn't need to spell it out, it was written across his face.

Out of context, the trail of events that had led to this revelation sounded so tawdry, so utterly removed from the reality in which Kate had found herself, on that awful, emotionally charged day. How could she even begin to explain to this stranger that she wasn't just another naïve girl who had casually 'got herself in trouble'; that it wasn't at all how he believed it to be? She had lived her life responsibly; it was one dreadful mistake that was all. She couldn't make excuses, it would all sound so weak and unnecessarily apologetic.

'Early days then, about seven or eight weeks I reckon,' he continued unemotionally.

'You'll be due around July, Mrs Willis – a summer baby. You need to come in to see me as soon as you feel up to it and get a proper check-up, though. I think you should take a couple of days off before you go back to the school. Plenty of fluids and rest in the meantime. I'll let myself out, but ask Mrs Steele to ring if you need to see me again urgently. Good day.'

She listened to his careful tread on the stairs and then the muffled sound of voices in the kitchen below.

Will he tell Mrs Steele? How on earth will she react to this? She'll be so disappointed in me. Kate lay staring at the ceiling trying to take it in, as her mind raced with the myriad of implications.

'What a nightmare,' she whispered aloud. She recalled how ecstatically she had received the news that she was pregnant with Clare, how excited Art had felt about this gift from God. This child, if it did exist, did not come as a gift, it felt like a disease, an unwelcome canker growing in her belly.

What am I going to do? How on earth will I be able to cope? A thousand desperate thoughts flooded her bewildered mind.

Perhaps it will be alright…it will turn out alright…nature will take its course… I've miscarried before, perhaps again. I could get rid of it, have an abortion. But where, how does one go about getting an abortion…where would I go, who would I ask? What am I thinking…I couldn't… I just couldn't… how could I begin to contemplate the death of a child, my child? I've got to get through this…oh no, my mother, what will this do to her? The shame of it, first the divorce and now this. I can't tell her, not so soon after Father, no, not now that she's alone…and Clare, how will Clare react? No, she'll be delighted… a brother or sister that's all she'll see… and I'm going to have to tell Bob…Bob…of course, he'll want to do the honourable thing. He may even be pleased… it's not what I would have chosen …not that… perhaps I have no option, beggars can't be choosers. A life with Bob sure doesn't hold much appeal… but then again he's kind, boring but kind, he'd make a good father… but a husband, my husband? Mr Madden …the school… they've all been so kind, what will I tell them? They'll want to know how I am, when I'm coming back. A few days rest that's all I need, there's no reason why I can't go back and finish my time there; it's only four more weeks. I won't even be showing by then. I was so small with Clare, even at the end, people could hardly tell. No, there is no reason why they need to know. I'll go back and continue as before. I'll have to tell the College though; I can't hide it for that long. What will they do? Will they understand? Will they even let me continue? Why not, the baby's due in the summer, there's no reason why I can't finish this year. At least the timing is good…it can't be the first pregnancy they've dealt with and it won't be the last. I'm doing well at college, I know I am, I get good reports; it'll be fine they'll understand. How ironic is that? All those other girls so free and easy with their favours getting away scot-free while I, living like a mother superior, get caught like this…the Devil's had the last laugh…

Her mind grass-hoppered around as she snatched at ever more desperate solutions. She turned her head to the sound of a gentle knock and Rita Steele's concerned face peeping round the door.

'How are you feeling? I've brought you another wee hot water jar, would you like something to eat? You probably haven't had anything since this morning. I've made some broth, would you like some? My mother swore by shin soup to get you up and running again. Dr Greene said to keep you warm and make sure you get some rest. Did he say what he thought it might be? Flu, I suppose.'

So he hadn't told her.

'He wasn't sure,' Kate answered truthfully. 'Thank you, I think I could eat something now, shall I come down?'

'You stay where you are, I'll be back up in no time. I'll not heat it up too much.'

Kate cuddled the jar for comfort. She's going to be so disappointed, she thought. She's been so kind to Mary and me; I hate the thought of letting her down. She so wanted her own child, prayed long and hard for many years, but it wasn't to be. She would have made such a great mother. Instead, she's left a childless widow while I'm carrying an unwanted child. Life's twists and turns can be so very cruel.

Kate could hear Mary's cheery voice from down below as she bounced through the front door.

'Hello, anybody home? Is that soup I smell? Hello, Mrs Steele, is Kate back yet? I've just got to tell her about today – what a disaster.'

'Sshh, Mrs Willis is in bed, Miss Coates, she fainted today and is resting.'

'What, actually fainted? Where, on teaching practice? Crikey, how is she?'

'Yes, at the school, the headmaster brought her back. Dr Greene has been and she's going to be fine. Probably picked up something from one of the children, that's all. You can take this soup to her if you're going up; she'll want to see you.'

'Blimey, what have you been up to?' Mary winked as she set the tray on the bed. She meant to make light of the situation but Kate couldn't help feeling the stab of accusation.

'Mary, I can't eat soup lying on my back, lift the tray please, it's going to spill,' Kate replied, irritated by the inadvertent but targeted remark.

'Sorry, didn't think. Good job I didn't follow my father's advice and go into nursing,' she said cheerfully. 'What's up with you then? Did you actually faint, like flat on your back faint?'

'Yes, Mary, I did, it wasn't very pleasant I can tell you. One minute I was standing reading about John the Baptist, next I was lying prone on the floor in front of the whole school.'

'Wow! That's the way to do it, kid. But you're going to be fine aren't you, what is it, flu?'

Kate stalled as she pondered over her reply. Do I confide in her? What if it turns out to be a false alarm, after all my chastising of her over her antics, she'll think I'm such a hypocrite. But then if anyone is going to be supportive it's Mary. There but for the grace of God, thought Kate.

She decided to make light of it. 'I'm sure it's nothing serious, a couple of days rest and I'll be up and about again. How was your day? I overheard your telling Mrs Steele that you'd had a disaster. I need cheering up, what happened?'

Mary burst out laughing. 'Oh Kate, you'll never believe it; it could only happen to me.'

Chapter 14

Exeter November 1955

'I will get it,' called Evelien cheerily, responding to the shrill ring of the phone as it echoed round the hall.

Jim followed her from the kitchen carrying a steaming cup of hot chocolate. He set it down on the little hall table as she mouthed with a puzzled look, 'It is Hans.'

Strange, thought Jim, hope nothing's wrong.

Evelien and Hans had long since resolved their differences over Eliezabeth and now his calls were as regular as clockwork. He rang his sister, without fail, on the first and third Sundays in the month. Evelien would await these calls with eager anticipation; each conversation with her brother would happily carry her through to the next one. She never complained, but Jim knew she still missed her family terribly and Eliezabeth in particular. In truth, she grieved for the Eliezabeth that had once been, and in Jim's opinion she still harboured the futile hope that one day the old Eliezabeth would return to her.

Jim hovered in the doorway, eavesdropping on the call. He couldn't understand the words, but he wanted to see if he could determine why Hans was calling his sister during the week; he was sure it must be something urgent. One look at Evelien's horror-filled, grief-stricken face told him what no words needed to; Hans was delivering some terrible news. He watched helplessly as Evelien's colour faded from pale to ashen and her tear-laden eyes turned to him in despair. It was blatantly obvious that something awful had happened.

'What is it, darling? Your parents?' he asked anxiously as she set down the phone and he rushed towards her. She couldn't speak. He rocked her as she desperately fought to regain her composure.

'It is Eliezabeth,' she croaked eventually, through hiccupping sobs. 'Oh Jim, I cannot believe it... she is dead.'

'What?' replied Jim incredulously. 'Oh no, not Eliezabeth. Darling, I'm so sorry,' he whispered as she clung to him and the sobbing intensified.

'Come on, you need to sit down,' he said decisively as he felt her full weight sink into his arms. He helped her into the sitting room and directed her towards the sofa. She slumped down in a daze, numbed by shock. She shivered involuntarily as Jim sat down beside her and wrapped her in his arms. The house suddenly felt filled with the full chill of autumn.

'What happened, Evelien? How on earth did she die? The morphine?'

'No. Hans found her this morning... she was lying in the bath, dead.' Evelien was struggling to speak.

'She drowned in the bath?' exclaimed Jim, desperately trying to deal with the enormity of what Evelien was saying and to make sense of it all.

'No, she did not drown... she killed herself...there was blood everywhere...' she wailed in agony, doubling over onto his lap.

Jim couldn't believe what he was hearing. He hugged her tightly, as much for his own comfort as for hers. What did she mean Eliezabeth had killed herself? They all thought she was getting better. The doctors were trying to wean her off the morphine at last. Why would she have killed herself now? His mind was spinning as he felt Evelien's heaving body shudder against him.

'Tell me how it happened.' he said quietly, as Evelien's sobbing eventually began to subside and he straightened her up. 'Can you talk about it?'

She pulled away from him and shook her head imperceptibly. He sat holding her hand as she slowly regained her composure.

'I'll get us a drink,' said Jim emphatically when he could bear the silence no longer. He stood up and poured them both a large Scotch. As he handed a glass to Evelien he noticed his hands were trembling. He flopped beside her and downed half of his.

'Well, at least she has peace now,' Evelien uttered coldly in a surprisingly strong voice, breaking the silence between them. 'The evils of the world can no longer touch her. Good for her!'

She raised then drained her glass. Jim looked at her anxiously. It was most unlike Evelien. She hardly ever drank and what was she saying? The rapid change in tone and the sentiments she was espousing were worrying him intensely. Her whole demeanour had suddenly stiffened and it was unnerving him.

She continued to speak in a purposeful but expressionless voice.

'I am glad she has done it... all her pain is gone. It is only those of us who are left who must suffer; forever wonder if we should have done more to help her...Do you know what she did?' She paused before continuing, pronouncing each word with exaggerated emphasis. 'She lay down in the bath and cut her wrists.'

As she spoke, she graphically enacted the scene. Jim felt the cold hand of death ripple down his spine. He emptied the remainder of his glass. He was rendered speechless.

'I will never forgive them, never,' Evelien spat out, her anger building with every word. 'Those bastards; they were not men, they were not human. They took my beautiful sister and condemned her to the cruellest of slow deaths. Well, she did not let them do that, did she?' she added with a hollow laugh. Jim looked at her in alarm. The voice that spoke was not Evelien's, rather that of a remote, objective observer. He felt like he needed another drink but didn't dare to move.

'I am glad. Now she is free; free from her memories, from her pain, from the morphine...' Evelien continued soullessly as she stared into space.

Jim was unsure how to react. He was shocked by the news but even more shocked by Evelien's response. He shifted uncomfortably. He would never have believed that such vitriol could emerge from the lips of his beloved, patient, gentle Evelien. He could barely believe that she was capable of such sentiments but he wanted to console, not condemn. He feared that his words of comfort would only succeed in making it worse for her and felt he could best communicate through touch. He squeezed her cold clenched fist in a gesture of love.

He wanted to know more, but didn't dare to ask. It occurred to him, with increasing disbelief that Evelien actually approved of Eliezabeth's actions; seemed to welcome them. For his part, he was deeply shocked that anyone he should know would actually commit suicide. He knew how difficult things had been for Eliezabeth, but when it came to it, it felt so wrong. He had to admit, however, that he felt a grudging admiration for Evelien's independence of thought. It was at times like this that he became most acutely aware that Evelien was not English by birth and that she saw life, and now as it happened death, very differently to him. She was not bound by the sub-conscious religious conventions that seemed to shackle even his relatively liberal thinking. Jim had to admit that he was astonished by her reaction; there was no hint of shame or words of condemnation; there was no suggestion that Eliezabeth had done anything wrong at all. It was obvious that Evelien felt profound grief for the loss of her sister, but she had pronounced no judgement in respect of the manner in which it had happened. If anything she seemed to approve; Eliezabeth had a right to live and a right to die as she saw fit. As he sat watching her Jim was ashamed to admit it, but he knew if it had been his sister he would have reacted very differently.

They were lucky to get a sailing at short notice. Two days after Hans' call they travelled to Harwich by train then caught a boat to Hoek van Holland. Hans picked them up and took them to his house in Rotterdam. The journey had been long, tiring and emotionally draining for both of them. Thankfully

Evelien's parents had decided that the funeral should be a quiet private affair, attended only by the immediate family. Neither of them could have faced the fuss of a large collective grieving. They cremated her body and each, in turn, lovingly scattered her ashes over the chill surface of the mighty Rhine. The river would carry her mortal remains from the living to the dead. As she watched them float away, Evelien couldn't help but hope that they would be carried to the sea and wash across, on a benevolent tide, to the shores of England. Perhaps the waters that for so long had separated them would finally bring them closer together again.

Evelien had remained remarkably composed and resolute throughout the tedious journey to Holland. Only when she met her parents, and observed how lost and life-weary they looked, had she finally cracked. She had fallen into their welcoming arms and wept torrid tears of shared sorrow. How she would have loved to have been able to bring them the happiest news, salve their pain, tell them that although they had lost Eliezabeth she was carrying the next generation for them, that there was a new life in her, that she was bearing their first grandchild. But she couldn't as there was no child, there was no sign of a child and she now doubted if there ever would be. With Hans a confirmed bachelor, Evelien now carried the family's sole hope of extending into another generation but, increasingly, that hope was ebbing away. It merely served to confirm Evelien's firmly held belief that each life lay in the lap of the gods. Mankind deluded itself with its claims to freedom. There were few paths of choice. So much less was ours to take and so much more was ours to accept; except, on that score, Eliezabeth had had the last laugh.

Chapter 15

Exeter, December 1955

'Well, Mrs Willis, a very successful teaching practice by all standards. I've seen the headmaster's report and I must say it's outstanding. He has awarded you a grade 'A' in every single area. Most unusual, as I know Joe Madden of old; he sets high standards and is not prone to awarding inflated grades. You have obviously impressed him very much indeed. Well done. I wish I could say the same for many of your colleagues, you're an example to all of them.'

Kate watched Dr Murphy's normally stern face break into a forced half-smile, as he continued to observe her over the half-moon glasses, perched precariously on the end of his nose as always. Since their first encounter, she had successfully managed to avoid him for most of her time at the College, only to discover, to her dismay, that he had been appointed as overseer of her final teaching practice. She had assumed it was because he had originally interviewed her.

He had visited the school on several occasions observing her lessons and both had managed to mellow their mutual distrust during that time. She even ventured to believe he might have developed a grudging respect. She thought back to the time when she had first met him, during that awful interview, how she had defiantly held her own against him when she had nothing to lose. Now she had everything to lose.

'I must say I had my doubts when we first met, Mrs Willis, not, you understand, about your professional potential, over which I had little doubt, but, how shall I put it, by...by the irregularities in your personal situation. I was persuaded by my younger colleagues, however, to overlook your unusual personal circumstances. I realise now that I may have been too hasty in forming my first impressions, you have the makings of an exceptional teacher and the profession can do nothing but benefit from your talent in the classroom. Unusually for me, I am pleased to admit that you have proved me wrong, especially regarding your...shall I call it your general demeanour while here at the College.

'I've been talking to Mr Madden and I think there is every likelihood of your gaining a position in the school, if that is somewhere you would like to go. I'd be happy to provide you with a glowing reference for there or anywhere else for that matter. Have you thought about where you would like to work when you've finished?'

Kate stared at him hardly believing what she was hearing. The irony of the timing hit her hard. Her stomach was churning. Six weeks ago, such praise and offers of support, from him, of all people, would have filled her with unimaginable pride and satisfaction; she had proved him wrong. Now his words of adulation only served to elevate her standing to a place from which the inevitable fall would be all the more painful and pronounced.

That she had achieved so much on teaching practice was solely down to her steely determination and the conviction that nothing, but nothing, would get in her way or stop her on the path to success. She was on the home straight. She had put her heart and soul into it, often fighting the awful sickening, omnipresent nausea through gritted teeth. No one at the school had suspected anything and if they did occasionally comment on how pale and tired she looked, they had reasonably concluded that it was probably due to the supreme efforts exerted by an immensely hard-working student. She had put any other life on hold, even foregoing visits back to Plymouth to see Clare and her mother. They realised how important this final teaching practice was to her, that she was tired at the weekends and needed to rest. She was looking forward to going home for Christmas and a well-earned rest a week after it finished. She was on the verge of exhaustion.

The week following her fainting incident she had gone to see Dr Greene, had received the confirmation she had dreaded and was, by now, about ten weeks pregnant. The news had come like an unexploded bomb; how often in the past had she listened fearfully to the whistling of a five hundred pounder dropping from above, hoping against hope that it wouldn't explode, but steeling herself for the inevitable bang. And what a bang it had been. She had reeled then rallied.

She had agonised over whether or not she should tell Bob. After hours of silent contemplation, she had eventually confided in Mary, who had shown a maturity of response that had moved Kate to tears. There had been no misplaced melodrama, no girlish giggling but only thoughtful empathetic support and Kate had felt it keenly; this unusual reversal of roles. They had concluded that Bob had a right to know, it was, after all, his child too.

She had arranged to meet up with him as soon as possible, before her courage totally deserted her. She had lifted the receiver, dialled boldly and tried to sound light and carefree when he answered, hoping the lilt in her voice was disguising the tremor. If he were surprised to hear from her, and noted her uncommon giddiness, he hadn't commented. He had seemed genuinely pleased and agreed that he would love to meet for lunch at the weekend. He expressed his surprise that she wasn't making the usual journey home; on all previous occasions, whenever he had tried to persuade her to stay around for the weekend, she had insisted that she missed Clare too much, needed to give her mother a break, and enjoyed getting home. He had readily accepted, as everyone else had, that at this time she was so focused on her teaching practice she didn't want to travel home as well.

'Nothing wrong is there?' he had queried when she got through to him, 'thought something else might have happened in the family, glad everything is fine. It will be lovely to see you Kate, you know it always is. No pressure, just like old times,' he had added as an afterthought.

It can never be like old times, Kate had thought.

'Yes, just like old times, look forward to seeing you,' she had replied cheerfully, knowing in fact that she was dreading it.

They had arranged to meet in the little café where he had first taken her when she came for her college interview. It had remained largely unchanged; Kate had not. Bowls of hardened sugar, tinged with tea, nudged against frosted salt and pepper pots. The aroma of freshly baked cakes jostled with the hint of smoking lard. Elderly ladies whispered in corners, students held hands across the greasy oil cloths sharing covert cigarettes. Kate had felt that all around her the jigsaw of life was picture-perfect, carefree and ordered as it should be, while her life was disintegrating into a thousand pieces.

'Bob, do you mind if we go for a walk when we've finished our lunch, there's something I'd like to discuss with you?' she had suggested tentatively.

He had looked up quizzically.

'If you like,' he had replied. 'Is everything alright, Kate, you're unusually quiet and morose? I was beginning to think that you regretted arranging to meet and would take the first opportunity to bolt the moment lunch was over.'

'Sorry, Bob, I don't mean to be rude, I've got a lot on my mind at the moment. I just want to talk to you about something that's come up, something that's troubling me.'

'Of course, Kate, you know me, always a listening ear,' he had leaned forward and squeezed her hand. She had left it resting on the table as he continued to stroke it.

He had paid the bill, without leaving a tip she had noticed, before putting his arm around her shoulder and ushering her out in front of him.

'Hello, Mr Poots, lovely crisp day isn't it,' he had remarked as they stepped aside to let another customer in. The man had raised his hat in recognition. 'Problem with this city, Kate, everyone knows everyone else.' He had seemed pleased with himself, however, hoping no doubt, that Kate would notice what a well-known and important figure he had become.

They had turned in the direction of the College and strolled through the gates of the municipal park. The grass was still glistening from the hoar frost that had survived all morning in the weak sunshine. The trees unclothed, were gently swaying in the slight breeze. Warps and wefts of the finest spider gauze blanketed the frosted bushes. The sound of laughing, squealing children cut across the calm and peaceful afternoon scene.

'Come on, Kate, what is it, what's bothering you?' Bob had broken their silence.

'I'm not quite sure how to tell you this, Bob; it's very difficult for me.'

He had stopped and looked straight towards her grinning. 'Come on, can't be that bad. You haven't met someone have you? You sly thing,' he had teased, elbowing her gently.

If only, she had thought.

'No, no, nothing like that Bob. It involves you in fact,' she had said cautiously.

'Me?'

'Yes. Do you remember the night of my father's funeral?'

'Remember it?' he had emitted a puerile snigger. 'Of course I remember it, how could I forget? Oh Kate, you're not still dwelling on that. I thought we'd agreed to let sleeping dogs lie, if that isn't too much of a pun.' He had laughed heartily at his own lame wit.

'Bob, please be serious, this is difficult enough as it is. It's just... well I've found out that I'm... that I'm pregnant with your baby.' She had said it straight.

The sides of his mouth had suddenly drooped as the smile disappeared and panic set in.

'What do you mean pregnant? You can't be…well not with mine anyway, we only did it that once. Are you sure it isn't a false alarm?'

'I'm quite sure, Bob; believe me, once is all it takes.'

'Well how can you even be sure it was that night and that I had anything to do with it?' he had added accusingly.

His words had slapped hard against her face and she had felt herself reeling from them.

'I can assure you it's yours. Believe it or not, I'm not in the habit of leaping in and out of men's beds. There's been no one else.' Kate had replied resentfully.

'But this is awful, I can't believe it. How can you be so definite?'

'I've been to the doctor; I've had the symptoms before remember. I'm about ten weeks pregnant, there's no doubt about it nor, as I've already said, is there any possibility that you're not the father.'

He had stood wide-eyed, pale and silent, trying to take it in; his mouth wide open, gaping like a gargoyle. His mind was swimming with the enormity of it. Eventually he had broken the silence.

'This will ruin me if it gets out.'

'Ruin you? How on earth could it ruin you?' Kate had struggled to maintain her composure. Whatever scenarios she had run through her head a thousand times, this was not one of them. She had finally convinced herself that he would be pleased and that her struggle would be with herself, whether or not to agree to marry him.

'Don't you see it will ruin my chance of promotion; any scandal would destroy my hopes of eventually becoming a manager, of getting my own branch, ruin everything I've worked so hard for. I can't let it slip away now. The bank would take a very dim view of this...of me. They expect their managers to live by a strict moral code.'

'A code, it would seem, it's perfectly okay to break as long as you don't get caught,' Kate had retorted pointedly.

'You'll have to get rid of it, Kate,' he had continued ignoring her jibe. 'That's the answer. I'm sure there are people who know where to go to get such things done, quietly and without anyone knowing. Can't you see it's for the best, for goodness sake, you've already got a child; you're divorced.' His voice was rising in barely disguised panic.

Kate had listened in horror, her anger rising.

'I'm well aware of that, Bob,' she had responded emphatically, 'I hardly need you to remind me.' She could barely form the words. She had tried to swallow but her mouth was arid dry.

'Well then, think about it, how on earth would you look after another one? You've almost finished your course, you'll be getting a job... you've just told me how well you're doing. Can't you see it's the obvious option... to keep it would ruin both of us. You must see it makes sense. No one need ever know – you can't tell at all by looking at you.' He had rambled in panic, without stopping to draw breath. Kate had flinched as he held his hands against her stomach and stretched her coat across her middle looking for signs of a tell-tale bump.

'See nothing at all. If you're quick, no one need ever know,' he had repeated triumphantly.

'Take…your…filthy…hands…off….me,' she had spat out slowly.

She could feel the red rage of her childhood descending.

'It's not an 'obvious option' as you so thoughtfully put it – for a start it's illegal,' she had snarled defiantly, barely able to control her temper. 'I could not, and would not get rid of it. It's a child we're talking about, flesh and blood; it's your child, my child for God's sake, not some ill-advised bank loan you want to off-load. Somehow I'd stupidly convinced myself you would react so differently, honourably, I suppose,' she had accused, her voice rising audibly with each stark statement. 'I should have realised. For as long as I've known you, your biggest concern has been how others might view you. It's not about doing the right thing with you, it's about being *seen* to do the right thing. It's all you care about… presenting a perfect image to the world. You're a fake! I foolishly believed you might even be pleased.'

'Pleased? Are you mad – how could I be pleased? I don't even like children. They're an expensive, yappy nuisance.'

'Well, you might have to get used to this one,' she'd yelled.

'No, it's your choice,' he had replied in a notably cold and measured tone. 'I'll help you to get rid of it, make enquiries, take you to where you need to go. I'll even pay for it if necessary, make sure it's done properly, that you're well cared for, but if you decide to continue with this selfish folly and have the brat, you're on your own; I don't want to know. I don't even want to be seen with you in this condition. This is a very small city and people will be only too quick to jump to, what in this case would be the right conclusion. I can't afford to take the chance.'

Kate had looked at him in disbelief as she fought the urge to slap his cowardly, pasty face.

'Don't worry, there's little chance of our being seen together. I doubt if I shall ever wish to see you again,' she had replied, regaining her composure.

She had stared at him in utter contempt, before turning and walking briskly towards the park gate. She had hoped it really would be the last time she set eyes on him, the despicable, selfish, weak bastard. Her cold cheeks had burned with the sting of hot tears.

Back in the warmth of Dr Murphy's cramped little room Kate sat and contemplated her response.

'Mrs Willis, I was asking if you've thought about where you would like to teach, will you go back home to Plymouth?' his words refocused her attention on the moment.

It's now or never, she thought. I've got to tell him, they're bound to start to notice after Christmas anyway. He obviously recognises my professional potential; I think he has even begun to like me. If anyone is going to raise a fuss it's going to be him. I suppose thinking about it, it's quite fortunate that I've had this chance to prove myself to him. How much will my personal circumstances matter? I've finished my teaching practice, it has gone really well, when I come back after Christmas it's the start of preparations for my exams, one more term and then I'll be leaving. What harm can it do? What difference could it possibly make to the College? I'll have gone, long before the baby is even born.

'Dr Murphy,' she began with an air of confidence she did not feel, 'thank you for your comments, I'm very flattered and it is very kind of you to say such things. I'm also very pleased that you've been able to set aside my unusual personal circumstances, as you so aptly put it, and have been able to judge me solely on my professional ability. I'm afraid I must ask you to do so again.'

He sat forward in his chair peering even lower from over his glasses.

'Dr Murphy,' she cleared her throat, 'I feel that it would be a common courtesy to let you, and therefore the College, know that I'm pregnant. The baby is not due until July, when I will, of course, have finished my studies and should hopefully therefore have little bearing on my success, or on my future career. I may, of course, need to delay applying for teaching posts for a while, but would be most grateful if you were prepared to provide me with the references you've so kindly offered now, at a future stage.'

She looked him straight in the eye hardly believing that, once more, she found herself confronting this most conventional of men with the most unconventional of news.

She felt her heart pounding in her chest as she swallowed hard waiting for his reply. He looked at her, his mouth slightly ajar, as he shook his head deliberately from side to side in apparent disbelief. It seemed an age before he replied, during which time Kate desperately sought to gauge his reaction. She couldn't tell; his face was otherwise motionless. Eventually he spoke.

'Mrs Willis, I can't believe what I am hearing or that you can convey this news to me, which has such grave personal consequences for you, with such apparent nonchalance. I see that, once again, I've been too hasty in my assessment of you and that indeed you are not the young woman of high principles that I had come to believe. I must retract my previous comments unreservedly and my offer of a reference. To allow you to come into this profession as a divorced woman caused me, amongst others, considerable concern, but as a collegiate we accepted that you were probably a victim of circumstance and therefore merited a second chance. But now, to present us with the proposition of allowing an unmarried mother, a fornicator, to take responsibility for the moral welfare of our children, well it's beyond comprehension. We put our trust in you and you have thrown it back in our faces. There is absolutely no possibility of your being allowed to finish your studies. In fact, the most honourable course you can take is to leave us immediately before you have the opportunity to contaminate the innocence of your fellow students. I am shocked and disappointed beyond words and must ask you to leave the College and its grounds immediately. We will expect written confirmation of your intention to terminate your studies.'

Kate was dumbstruck, speechless; each word had landed like a well-aimed punch. She couldn't even begin to take in what he was saying. To be required to leave and immediately; to throw away the last two and a half years, her future, Clare's future, it was beyond words. She had had to cope with Bob's unbelievable reaction to the news and now this.

As her mind rallied, her clarity of thought began to return and with it a sense of profound indignation. She had the sinking feeling that this was only the start of the obstacles she would face; uninformed reactions to a situation where, she firmly believed, she was taking the principled stance, maintaining the moral high ground. Well they could stick their pseudo-morality, their thin veil of propriety; she would abide by her own code and be proud of it. How dare he brand her a fornicator? What did he know about her personal life, the pompous ass? Was he judge and jury to pass such summary judgement on her? Did he even have the authority to require her to leave the College? She hadn't broken any rules, at least not any that she was aware of. She would leave his room immediately, not even attempt to justify her position, avoid inflaming him further. She would approach the College authorities and explain the circumstances; it would turn out fine. There could be no possible justification for his decision. That's what she would do.

She stood up slowly, pushed her hair neatly behind her ears, straightened her skirt, turned her back on him and tried to walk with dignity towards the door. Neither spoke. She was overwhelmed by the sense of déjà vu, but there was a flicker of hope; after all, previously it had turned out in her favour.

She was still shaking when she arrived back at Rita Steele's. She hoped Mary was at home. Mary, the girl, who on hearing Kate's news, had suddenly become a woman. She was displaying her true strength and maturity in the face of Kate's adversity. Mary, who reassured her that all would be well, convinced her that she had made the right choice in keeping the baby and that Bob Thompson wasn't worthy to have a child call him, Father. It was Mary who had given her the courage to face the College and to trust that it would all turn out fine. Mary, whom she now knew, would stick with her throughout it all.

Mary was in the little front sitting room, curled up in the cramped two-seater settee, bare footed, her legs folded under her, reading a magazine. The fire was dead and the room felt cold. Thankfully she was alone and could talk freely. Kate hadn't summoned sufficient courage to break the news to Rita Steele; she couldn't bear to allow that she would think less of her, or worse still, that she would ask her to leave the lodgings she had come to love as a second home. It would be a blow too far.

Mary looked up from her reading and didn't need to ask how it had gone.

'I'm sure you can appeal, Kate.' She tried to sound reassuring. 'Contaminate the other students, what rot. Does he honestly believe that he stands every day and lectures the Vestal Virgins? What century does he think he lives in? Come on, I'll help you to draft a letter. Presume you should write to the College Principal, Dr White; we can safely assume that by now old 'rigor mortis' Murphy has gone shuffling off to inform him.'

Kate managed a smile. She could always rely on Mary to lighten the mood. It was the moniker Mary had adopted for Dr Murphy the moment Kate had first pointed out her initial inquisitor.

'Mind you,' Mary continued, 'if the rumours I've heard are true, Dr White is a complete misnomer, to say the least.'

Kate was intrigued by the comment. 'What do you mean?'

'Well I don't like to gossip, but you must have heard the rumours.'

Kate had to admit that, no she hadn't; she didn't tend to focus much on college rumours, which were usually apocryphal tales, much embellished over a drink or two in the College Common Room. Mary was the conduit for anything she had heard.

'Well, I don't know for definite, of course, but I've heard the same story several times. Apparently his wife, who's a good twenty years younger than him, was a senior pupil at the boarding school where he taught before becoming a college lecturer. It was commonly understood that they were having some kind of intimate personal relationship while she was in the Sixth Form and he was Head of Boarding. They both maintained that the relationship only began after she left the school, and no one could prove differently, but it cast a shadow over his teaching career, which is why he left to come to the College. I was first told it by Joan Myers. Apparently, she went to the same school and her older sister was in his wife's form. Well you know how prim and po-faced she is, so

I think we can safely assume that there's some grain of truth in it. I believe it was common knowledge among the pupils at the school and in the local community. Created quite a scandal at the time I understand. You must have noticed what an old letch he is – talks to your chest not your face.'

Kate, of course, hadn't had quite as many face-to-face, or indeed face-to-chest, dealings with the College Principal as Mary had, to notice where he looked.

'Well, if it is true he can hardly stand in judgement of you,' protested Mary. 'Wait and see it will all be fine. Old 'rigor mortis' Murphy has got a bit above his station, in making such grand declarations, that's all.'

Kate wished she could be as confident.

On the final day of term, Kate was required to attend a hearing at the College. As she nervously entered the Principal's office she noticed that the auspicious panel confronting her, consisted of Dr Murphy, Dr White and Dr Campbell one of the few female senior lecturers. Dr Campbell smiled as she came in, while the other two remained impassive.

She sat down and began to present her case with dignity and composure.

'Thank you for affording me this opportunity to explain my situation,' she opened. 'May I begin by acknowledging that while there may be understandable concerns regarding my current condition, in no way will I allow it to overshadow my professionalism or my dedication to teaching. Contrary to the evidence in front of you, since my marriage ended in the most painful of circumstances for me, I've lived in a quiet way, devoting my time to my college studies and the care of my child. I take full responsibility for my own actions, I am after all a mature woman, but I find myself in this unfortunate position not as a result of reckless wantonness but as the result of a most regrettable one-off incident when I was emotionally very vulnerable, following the death of my father. I only ask that I may be allowed to finish my course and to qualify in a profession I have come to love and to which I believe I can bring so much. I would ask you to give me the chance to prove myself worthy of your trust and understanding.'

They questioned her at length, listening to her carefully constructed responses. Dr Campbell nodded throughout and smiled encouragingly in her direction, proving a much needed ally.

Kate was eventually asked to leave the room while they made their decision. She felt it was too close to call, but she believed that she would get Dr Campbell's support and Dr Murphy's dissent, so the decision would lie with Dr White. Surely a man who had suffered at the hands of accusers, himself, could not condemn her she reasoned.

Shaking with nerves she returned to hear the verdict. Dr White spoke for the panel.

'Mrs Willis, we have given your case due consideration. We acknowledge that your college work has been of an exceptional standard and that, apart from this most unfortunate event, your behaviour has been exemplary. Dr Campbell has spoken most favourably in your defence, Dr Murphy's views you know already. I find, therefore, that the decision regarding your future attendance at this College lies with me. As Principal I cannot be seen to condone any form of impropriety. I must set standards for all the students and send out a clear message that will discourage those of a, shall I call it, promiscuous nature from entering our profession. As you acknowledge, you are more mature and therefore experienced in the ways of the world than many of the other students. You should have recognised, therefore, that you had a responsibility to act as a role model. I believe that I must use this unfortunate incident to set an example to others, and as a result I require you to leave this College immediately on the grounds that your behaviour has brought it into disrepute.'

Kate gasped. She immediately saw that it was hopeless. Dr White continued to look her straight in the eye, Dr Murphy busily polished an imaginary smudge from his glasses, averting his gaze, Dr Campbell looked past her shocked and defeated. Kate couldn't speak; she could neither acknowledge their decision nor find the strength to stand her ground. The fight had gone out of her, she felt drained and alone. She rose slowly to leave.

Kate walked towards the door desperately trying to retain her dignity and maintain her composure. Dr Campbell followed and shook her hand, her tear-filled eyes brimming with unspoken sympathy; a lone voice, but the system had won.

To Kate, the verdict was nothing more than the outward and visible sign of inward invisible hypocrisy.

Chapter 16

Exeter, December 1955

Kate inserted her key into the lock and pressed her shoulder firmly against the door. As always, it resisted and creaked against the door post.

How many more times will I do this she thought with a horrible sinking feeling. I've got to tell Mrs Steele. Not yet though, I'll wait until I come back after the holidays, I can't bear to tell her before Christmas. I suppose I'll have to organise moving out then. She's bound to notice sooner or later and she'll wonder why I'm not attending college. I can't just leave every day and pretend to be heading off there. But first I've got to go home and face my mother.

She climbed the stairs and started the ritual of packing her small case for the journey home. She looked around the familiar little room with its cramped furniture neatly stacked against every available wall. It had become more than a home; it was a sanctuary where she felt safe and secure and now it would all have to come to an end. She was intending to get the 3.30 train back to Plymouth but had promised Mary that she would wait for her and let her know how she had got on. She glanced at the clock, time was getting tight.

'Come on, Mary, where on earth are you? I thought you'd be waiting for me to get back.' She spoke out loud. She felt irritable and tired. She heard the door open and Mary's familiar noisy entrance. As always, she dumped her bags at the front door before bounding up the stairs. Kate heard her slowing into a more dignified walk before she knocked on her door.

'Well?' she enquired as her anxious face peered round the bedroom door, followed by her hand holding an enormous bouquet of the freshest flowers.

Kate looked at her, looked at the bouquet and shook her head.

'Oh no, what on earth did they say?' Mary sat down on the edge of the bed, discreetly placing the bouquet on the floor as she did.

'They said I'd brought the College into disrepute and must leave immediately,' Kate spat out. She collapsed on the bed beside Mary and threw her arms around her. They held each other as in bereavement.

'Oh Mary, it's over for me, my hopes, my career, all my hard work. I can't believe it, I just can't believe it. I'm going to have to tell Mrs Steele and worst of all, my mother. What will either of them think? I can't believe this has happened to me – why me? A few minutes of mindless madness and I'm left to deal with the consequences for the rest of my life. Well I'll just have to get on with it. Take it on the chin, face up to it. But just now, I feel completely at a loss.'

Mary held her tight, stroking her back gently.

'I can't thank you enough for being so understanding, so strong for me. I'm not sure I could get through this without you.'

'It's nothing; I wish I could do more. I don't know how I can help, but I'm here if and when you need me. You know you only need to ask. The flowers were for you. I'm not quite sure why I felt the need to buy them. I suppose I just wanted you to know, well, you know…'

Kate hugged her hard. It didn't need to be said. 'I've got to go, Mary, or I'll miss my train. I don't want to see Mrs Steele just now. I'll face her after the holidays. I'll see you both then. Enjoy the break and wish her a happy Christmas from me.'

It occurred to Kate, only after she had said it, that she was no longer on a college break; she was unemployed and probably unemployable.

Kate contemplated her opening gambit on the journey home. Instead of feeling excited at the prospect of seeing Clare and her mother, enjoying the Christmas festivities, relaxing after a few long hard weeks, she was filled with dread at the thought of breaking the awful news to her mother. She couldn't begin to imagine how she would react. Disappointment, anger, understanding? It was hard to call. She had been surprised by her parents' supportive reaction to her marriage breakdown, particularly her mother's affectionate response, but then on that occasion she had been the blameless party. It was so different this time. Now she was the architect of her own foolish demise.

Kate felt the train shudder to a halt; she reached up to collect her case from the rack, pushed down the window, leant out, turned the handle and opened the door. She knew they would be waiting for her on the platform. She poked her head out of the door and saw both of them standing there hand in hand, waiting patiently. Clare seemed to have grown even taller; she was catching up on her grandmother, who in turn appeared to be shrinking.

Clare ran to meet her, arms outstretched, grinning excitedly. Sarah eventually caught up with them.

'You look worn out, dear. A good rest for you this Christmas, I think,' her mother commented, as she lifted one of her cases.

Kate hadn't seen either of them for several weeks. Clare's exuberant delight at seeing her mother only served to emphasise Sarah's unsentimental practicality.

'I think I'll have a lie down if you don't mind,' Kate declared, as soon as they arrived back at the house. 'You don't mind, do you, Mother? I'm pretty tired what with the journey and everything. I think teaching practice has finally caught up on me. I'll just have an hour then I'll help you with supper. Want to come up with me, darling? We can have a cuddle.'

Kate pulled Clare towards her and smelt her hair.

'Are you feeling alright?' her mother asked, searching Kate's face as she touched her arm.

'I'm fine thank you, just tired that's all.' Kate wondered if she were sending out subliminal signals that would betray her condition to an acutely perceptive mother.

'Sleep as long as you want, dear,' replied Sarah, 'supper can wait. We can chat when you come back down and you can tell me all about teaching practice. Did it really go well?'

'Very well, thank you. I promise, just an hour or so and then I'll tell you all about it.'

Kate climbed the familiar stairs with Clare in tow. They still creaked underfoot, she knew she was home. Her news could wait. She wanted to enjoy some time with both of them first before she had to face the inevitable. James was arriving home tomorrow; it seemed an age since she had last seen him. Someone else to tell. But first a happy family gathering before she shattered their peace; it surely wasn't too much to ask.

Kate woke to the sounds of her mother setting the table. She nudged a snoring Clare who was sleeping soundly beside her. She glanced at her watch; she had been asleep for nearly two hours. The first time she had managed to drift off immediately in weeks. She felt much better for it.

They chatted happily over supper as Kate was momentarily able to forget. Only the vacant chair, where her father had sat for so many years, detracted from the convivial scene. It was their first Christmas without him.

When she had put Clare to bed she came back down and flopped in the nearest armchair, casually drooping her arms over the side. Surprisingly for Kate, her mother offered her a brandy. It had been left over from the funeral. Equally surprisingly for her mother, Kate declined.

She glanced at her mother and smiled. She returned it fondly.

'Kate, I want to talk to you about something that's been on my mind for a few weeks now. I would have preferred to wait until after Christmas, but I want to discuss it before James comes home. It may affect him as well.'

Kate sat upright. 'Is something wrong, Mother, you're not ill or anything?' she asked anxiously.

'No, no it's nothing like that. In one way I'm quite excited about it, but I don't know that you will be. I hope so.'

Kate was intrigued. It was unlike her mother to be so obscure.

'After your father died I had a letter from your Aunt Elizabeth in Australia. She sent her condolences, of course, but she also suggested that I go out to visit her. Well, you know I've always wanted to see Australia, but your father wasn't too keen. I think he reckoned he'd travelled enough for one lifetime while in the Navy. I haven't seen her for over twenty years. I don't suppose you even remember her.'

'Vaguely,' replied Kate, 'she looked like you if I'm not mistaken. Is she the eldest of the family?'

'Yes, she was born when your grandmother was only nineteen; she married very young, of course,' Sarah added unnecessarily.

Kate was surprised, not only because of the relative spontaneity of her mother's decision, but that she wanted to travel so far at this stage in her life. She also couldn't see what contingencies her mother had made for Clare but knew that it was highly unlikely that she had not thought it through in precise detail. Perhaps she meant to leave travelling for a year or so.

'I can read your mind, Kate Aldworth, sorry, Willis, I mean. You're wondering about Clare and what's going to happen to her.'

Kate denied it.

'I haven't forgotten about Clare, of course. I wonder how you would feel if I took her with me? Think about it, Kate; it would be a marvellous experience for her, a whole different culture, the animals she will see, the landscapes, the way of life. I've always believed that education doesn't only occur in the classroom. At such a young age, she'll have experienced America, England and Australia – how wonderful for her. I would love to have had that chance at her age. She's such a bright, adaptable child; you know she'll soak it all up like a sponge. Elizabeth has already made enquiries and it would appear that she could attend a local school. It would be the same one Elizabeth's grandchildren go to. They're Clare's second cousins after all, so I'm sure she'll soon make friends with them and others of course. I do so want to go. Your father's presence still dwells here you know,' she commented looking around the room. 'A few months away from this house, which has so many constant reminders of your father, might do me good. What do you think?'

'A few months? How long are you intending to go for?'

Kate couldn't conceal her surprise. Her mother had spoken without stopping for breath in delivering such an uncharacteristic impassioned plea.

'Well it's such a long way and I may never see Elizabeth again, we're both rapidly getting older, your father's death has brought that fact home to me sharply. I thought we should make it worthwhile. I thought about going in February, catch the end of the Australian summer and then we would probably stay until July, which is their winter, of course. Clare would be back here before the summer holidays ended, which would allow her time to readjust before the start of a new term. Elizabeth wrote in her letter that her son Robert is getting married at the end of March and I would love to be there in time for his wedding; I've never even met him. What do you think? I know you'll miss Clare terribly, but I thought you would probably be working so hard when you go back, studying for your final exams, that it might actually be easier for you. I'm sure the time would fly by.'

Kate's mind was spinning. Of course she would miss Clare and her mother, but if they were away in a month's time, right through until the summer, it would buy her some time; time to consider what she should do about the baby. She could probably hide her condition until they left, and if they could be persuaded to stay until July, well by then she would have had the baby. God had not deserted her. It was a most unexpected chance.

She tried not to sound too enthusiastic. 'I think it's a great idea,' she replied. 'Of course I'll miss you, but what a great opportunity for Clare, for you both. The timing is great... I mean because of my exams and because Clare is at the right stage at school,' she added quickly.

She couldn't bear to spoil it all by admitting the truth, that there were no exams; that, in fact, she was mightily relieved they would not be around for the next few months.

'But that's wonderful, thank you, dear. I was so concerned about telling you. Of course, I'll pay for Clare's fare so you needn't worry about that. I do want to go, very much indeed, but I wasn't sure how you would feel about it. I thought you might consider that I was being rather self-indulgent. I didn't want to mention anything to James until I'd spoken to you. I'm hoping that he might come back and live in the house while I'm away. I'd feel happier if someone was staying in it, so much better than leaving it empty and you would have company at the weekends if you were travelling back. I haven't felt this excited since I was a little girl.'

Kate could hardly believe it was her mother who was talking, such was the sense of elation visibly etched on her face.

'I need to be quick,' Sarah continued, 'we haven't much time to plan it if we're to leave in February. I'm hoping James can help me as he's so much more experienced in these things. I'm actually thinking of going by aeroplane. Can you believe it? I know it's expensive, but the boat takes so long, we would spend half the time travelling.

'Your father's sudden death has made me realise a few things about life. We both worked so hard for so many years, saving our money for a rainy day, being careful especially in the difficult years just after the war, and now he's no longer even here to enjoy the benefit of it. If I don't do it now, I never will. Of course anything I've left, when I go, will go to both James and you, and Clare of course, you know that, but you're both so independent now. You about to embark on your new career, and I know James is doing well. I don't need to worry so much anymore. I don't often say it, but I'm so proud of both of you.'

Kate was finding the conversation intolerably difficult. She felt a total fraud. Uncontrollable, contradictory emotions were raging through her veins. Her every instinct was to be honest, forthright, reveal it all, confide in her mother, tell her that she had let her down, that she felt more frightened and alone than she had ever felt in her life, even more so than when she had first returned from America. She hated the deception. She was a child again; the child who had always longed to be a woman but now longed to be that child once more.

Ironically now, when more than ever before, she needed her mother's loving presence and needed to gain succour from Clare's unconditional love, she was willing them to be absent. She had no idea how she was going to get through this, where she would live, what she would do after the baby was born, to whom she could turn for advice, for guidance or for support. Her reality was so far removed from the vision of an exciting, independent future as presented to her by her mother. She was not secure, she had no career, she would have an extra mouth to feed; once again, in her short life she would have to face the judgements and prejudices of those whose lives were seemingly unblemished, wholesome and upright. Her mother, so undeservedly the vicarious victim, would once again have to face it all; the final confirmation for many, that Kate was a bad lot. The lemon-lipped whispers of her accusers; surely there was indecent haste about the marriage wasn't there? She disappeared to America then returned without him and a child in tow to boot. Divorced him didn't she? Now to crown it all she is birthing a bastard. Poor Sarah has her troubles to bear and her husband hardly cold in his grave.

It came to Kate, as clearly as if spoken by another, that she could not keep this child. She could not put her mother or Clare through the pain of it, for they would surely suffer as much as she herself would. She would give birth, but in the child's, her mother's, Clare's and probably in her own best interest, she would have to release it into the care of another. The painful realisation came as a relief. There could be no other way. Her mother and Clare need never know; no one that mattered need ever know.

Chapter 17

Exeter, January 1956

Kate turned her face to guard against the piercing snow flurry sweeping horizontally across the station platform. She tied her scarf around her neck, bent to pick up her case and proceeded to walk slowly towards the exit. It occurred to her that this might be the final time she would make this familiar journey. In a short while she would be back in Rita Steele's homely sanctuary, but for how long? She hoped Mary would have arrived by the time she got there. She had spent the whole of the Christmas festivities in false good humour, screaming inside. She had no one to talk to, no one to confide in and no one to reassure her that it would all turn out fine. She knew that she would have to confront Rita Steele almost immediately. Term was due to start in a couple of days' time. The rent was paid a month in advance, so she reckoned she had until the end of January to find somewhere to live for a couple of weeks. With her mother and Clare due to be out of the house by mid-February she could go back there and lie low. Art's parents were still sending her sufficient money to cope in the short term, so she could survive. Of course, that would mean she would have to tell James that she was moving home, but she hoped he would keep her confidence. But how could she hide it from the neighbours who were bound to notice her presence in the house as well as her expanding waistline? She tried to put it out of her mind as she struggled to breathe in the icy air.

Mary heard the door opening and rushed from the kitchen to meet her, throwing her arms around her neck.

'Happy New Year, Kate, it's great to see you. How's everything?' she asked, pointing towards Kate's belly, lowering her voice and mouthing that Mrs Steele was in the kitchen.

'Mmm, so, so,' replied Kate, 'it's great to see you too. Happy New Year, Mary; how was Christmas?'

'It was fine, thank you. Of course, my mother took every opportunity to remind me that the summer, and therefore the finals, would soon be upon us all. Sorry, I didn't think.' She stopped abruptly, realising what she had said.

'It's alright, Mary, I've come to terms with all of that. Can we talk? Come up to my room while I unpack.'

'Is that you, Mrs Willis?' called Rita Steele as she emerged from the kitchen, wiping her hands on her apron. 'I thought I heard the door. How are you? Family all well?'

'Yes, thank you, all well. It was difficult, of course, for my mother, what with it being the first Christmas without my father, but it was lovely to see everyone. How about you?'

'Very quiet. I spent Christmas Day with some of Stan's family but, apart from that, very quiet. Glad to be back?'

'Yes, thank you, I'm going to go up and unpack now if that's alright with you. I won't be long.'

'Think I'll do the same,' echoed Mary, looking at the mass of bags and cases dumped at the door. They both turned to go up the stairs.

'Well, tell me all about it, are you really alright? You look tired. What did they say, what are you going to do?'

'Oh Mary, it's been awful, pretending that everything is fine, that I'm coming back to recommence my studies, that I'll be back at the weekend, the same old routine.'

'You haven't told them?' Mary asked incredulously. 'They'll have to know sometime, you can't hide it from them forever?'

Kate recounted the fortuitous circumstances that meant she might be able to keep it all from her mother after all.

'Crikey, what a stroke of luck, you'll have to tell Rita Steele though. She'll wonder why you aren't going to the College every day.'

'Don't, Mary, I know. I dread that almost more than I dreaded telling my mother. She's been so good to us. How do you think she'll react? Do you think she might let me stay on until the end of the month?'

'I don't know. It's hard to say. She has a heart of gold, but she's pretty conventional, what with all that church going et cetera. I just don't know. When are you going to tell her?'

'I thought tonight. Could you make yourself scarce for a couple of hours? It's only fair that I let her know who is lodging in her house. I don't know what I'll do if she asks me to leave immediately. Any ideas?'

'Afraid not. Surely she would give you time to sort something else? I'm sure she would.'

'Well, we'll see, wish me luck.'

Kate entered the small kitchen and smiled as Rita Steele turned towards her and smiled in return.

'Cup of tea? Is it just yourself? I thought I heard the door opening, was that Miss Coates going out?'

'Yes, Mrs Steele, Mary has gone out to meet up with some of the others. It's just me, and yes, I'd love a cup of tea. When you've made it, could we have a chat about something that's come up?'

Rita Steele looked at her suspiciously. 'Of course. I lit a fire as it was your first night back. We can have it in the front room. It will be like it was the very first time you came to live with me. It only seems like yesterday.'

Kate went in and perched herself on the hard little sofa. The fire was burning brightly and filling the room with a cheer she could not relate to. Rita Steele came in and set down the neat tray and a plate of her home-made buns. Kate took the tea but declined anything to eat.

'Tea's too wet without something to eat,' Mrs Steele chuckled as she reached forward and helped herself. 'Now what was it you wanted to talk about? Nothing wrong I hope?' she queried, dusting the crumbs from her chest.

'Well, in fact there is, Mrs Steele. This is very difficult for me. Truth is I don't know where to start.'

Rita Steele paused from devouring her bun and looked up. 'The beginning is usually a good place,' she said kindly.

'Yes, the beginning, whenever that is,' sighed Kate. 'Well, I suppose it begins on the day of my father's funeral. You will remember, perhaps, that I didn't come back here until the following day. In fact, I'd come back to Exeter the previous evening. Bob Thompson gave me a lift in his car. The weather was awful, which delayed us, so it was very late by the time we got to Exeter. I didn't want to disturb you both by coming in so late so I accepted Bob's offer to stay at his house, in his spare room. I feel so ashamed telling you this, I don't want you to think badly of me, but the truth is, I was so emotional, I felt so alone and empty and Bob was there, a much needed source of comfort. I really don't know how it happened, it just did, and I regret it bitterly, but one thing led to another and the result is…. well, the sad fact is that I now find that I'm expecting his child.'

Kate felt herself blushing to her hair roots as she struggled to explain. She kept her gaze down as she twiddled nervously with the handle of her cup still full of, now tepid, tea. She dreaded the response; she couldn't bear to hear Rita Steele's words of disapproval. Kate was sure she would react badly. She wanted her to understand.

'I'm so ashamed, but I felt it was only right that I should explain. The thing is, I've been thrown out of the College and really don't know what I am going to do. I'll leave the house of course, as soon as I can. I'm not sure how much rent I'll still owe you, but I'll pay whatever you think. I don't want to leave you in the lurch.'

She looked up in response to a gentle hand squeezing her shoulder.

'It all makes sense to me now. I'm so glad you've told me, I was that worried about you. I knew something wasn't right. You weren't like yourself at all before Christmas; you'd lost your spark and looked that tired and drawn. What with you feeling unwell that day Dr Greene came, I didn't think it was flu, but I didn't want to pry. You poor, poor dear. I can't believe the College have thrown you out, after all your hard work and you so near finished. It must be awful for you. So what now? I suppose you and Mr Thompson will have to marry, and you want to go back to live with your mother and daughter until then. I'll miss you, you know. It won't be quite the same in the house; of course I'll still have Miss Coates, but it won't be the same. I hope you don't mind if I say this, but I've almost come to regard you as the daughter I never had. I'll miss you terribly.'

'Oh Mrs Steele, I can't tell you how relieved I am. I'm so touched by that, you've been so kind to us, to me in particular. I've been dreading telling you all over Christmas. I thought you would be angry, or disgusted, or disappointed in me, well to be honest I'm not sure what I thought. I was so worried; your opinion mattered a great deal to me. I'm just relieved you've taken it like this. You mustn't think, for a minute, that while I was living here I was leading a wanton life. I really wasn't, it just happened; it was stupid, so stupid, just one terrible mistake.'

'Sshh, you don't need to tell me anymore. I know that. It's the innocent ones get caught, that's what my mother always said. So when did you say you want to move out? I suppose you and Mr Thompson will be getting married soon, and you'll move into Mr Thompson's house once the wedding is over.'

'No, I'm afraid we're not going to get married; I'm on my own in this.'

'Oh dear, that's very brave, Mrs... look do you mind if I call you Kate? In the circumstances it seems far more suitable. Please, call me Rita, I see us as friends now,' she said with affection.

'Thank you, Rita, I see us as friends too. The truth is I'd much prefer you to call me Kate.'

Rita smiled. 'Well, of course, it has to be your choice not to get married,' she continued, 'and I suppose Mr Thompson will be there to give you a hand if you need it.'

'No I'm afraid to say it, but Bob and I have fallen out. We didn't see eye to eye on something. I'm not sure what I'm going to do yet, but Bob Thompson won't be involved.'

'That does make it very difficult for you. Is there no way you could get him to help out? It would be much better for you and I'm sure he would want to see the baby when it's born.'

'Rita, I wasn't going to tell anyone this, but especially you, as I know you think so highly of Bob, what with his arranging to get you lodgers and everything. I'm sure he has his reasons, but Bob has made it clear that, if I go ahead and have the baby, he doesn't want to know. There will be no wedding.'

'What do you mean, if you go ahead and have the baby? How can you not have it?' She looked confused. 'Oh, you mean he wants you to have an abortion?' Rita Steele's face filled with horror as realisation dawned. 'But how could he? His own flesh and blood. You're not thinking about it are you?' she added quickly.

'No, it's not for me. I couldn't do it, not in these circumstances. I can understand that for some women it is the only option, but it's not for me. I'm thinking of giving the baby up for adoption. The thought of it breaks my heart, but I have to be pragmatic. I can't afford to bring up another child on my own, especially now I have no career and no income. I can't ask my mother, it would be unfair on her. I haven't even told her about it; I can't, she's suffered enough on my behalf, the whispering neighbours, what with the divorce and everything and now so soon after my father's death. I can't land all this on her as well.'

'Oh Kate, I'm sure she would understand, support you, from what you've told me she seems such a sensible woman. You might be surprised by how she reacts.' A strange look passed over Rita Steele's face as she spoke.

'I can't tell her, Rita. I just can't face it. She'll be disappointed enough as it is that I won't be qualifying as a teacher. She'll think I've thrown away my future recklessly. You've been so unbelievably understanding, so kind, I can't thank you enough. I think there are many who would be only too quick to condemn me.'

'*Judge not lest ye be judged*,' replied Rita quietly, her voice barely audible. She hesitated before speaking. 'Kate, I'm going to tell you something that I've never spoken about to anyone in my life before. Not even Stan knew. It's extremely painful for me, but it might help you to decide what to do; to think about what is best for you. I suspect many a one's life is far more complicated than they let on; if you could look beneath that still, calm surface you'd find muddy waters flowing.' She looked uncomfortably across at Kate before speaking.

'The thing is, I discovered, quite by chance, when I'd just turned sixteen that I'm also an illegitimate child. There I've said it, illegitimate, born out of wedlock, a bastard. I could cope with that – there are worse things – but that's not all.' She struggled to continue, fighting back her tears. Kate instinctively reached over and took her hand. Rita smiled in gratitude.

'I feel that ashamed telling you this, as I said, I've never breathed a word to anyone else,' she continued hesitantly. 'The thing is…,' she paused as she looked towards Kate, 'well, I found out that Amy, who I'd always thought was my eldest sister, was in fact my mother. She was…' Rita hesitated as her eyes misted over, 'she was raped by her eldest brother, Ivan, when she was only fifteen.'

'Oh my God, Rita! How awful for her,' exclaimed Kate, covering her mouth with her hand, hardly believing what she was hearing.

'Raped by her own brother,' Rita repeated with conviction. 'In the same afternoon I discovered that my mother was my grandmother, my sister was my mother and my brother was not only my uncle, but my father. It sounds like some bad comedy when I say it like this, but it's far from funny. It's something I find very difficult to accept. I was horrified at the time and still am when I think about it. I'm sure that's why I was never able to have my own children.'

Kate sat in shock, unable to find the appropriate words of comfort. She took Rita's hand and squeezed it tightly. Rita took a deep breath before continuing. 'Anyway, as soon as it was discovered, the family did everything they could to hide the truth. They didn't want him to be exposed and the family's reputation to be dragged through the mud, so nothing was done about him. He got away with it. I've absolutely no doubt it wasn't the only time he done it. Amy was kept hid away, the 'guilty' party, closed up in the house until the baby was born. Another baby, born into a house of twelve children, hardly registered with the neighbours, but of course there was talk. Life carried on, just as it had, for everyone except Amy who was expected to live the lie, keep her mouth shut and get on with it.'

'What, they expected your sister, your mother I mean, to pretend that you weren't her child? She couldn't be your mother? But that's a terrible thing to do to anyone. How could they?' Kate was reeling from the full horror of the story.

'Quite easily it would seem. Amy watched me, as you say, her child, grow up as her sister. Her brother, Ivan, my father, God forbid, still lived with us; his presence round the house must have been the most awful constant reminder for her. He drank too much I remember, and he had a vicious temper; I often felt the back of his hand. I'd never liked him even before I learnt the truth.'

'But how on earth could his parents, your grandparents, have even thought about allowing him to continue living with you all? It's outrageous,' Kate could hardly contain her anger. 'Surely someone must have been able to confront him, to stop him.'

'I suppose they didn't want to do anything that might bring it all into the open. They were scared stiff that it would bring the family's name into disrepute. You see my family were very well known, well respected; they'd lived in the same wee townland for generations. But that's not all.'

She paused and glanced at Kate before speaking. 'When I was about six, Amy was found drowned in a remote quarry, miles from home…'

'Oh Rita, how dreadful,' Kate interjected, wide-eyed with disbelief.

'I was devastated… she'd always been that kind to me… I never got over it.' Rita continued quietly, her voice barely able to contain her sorrow. 'I was told, and had no reason to assume anything other than it was a tragic accident; although what she was doing up there was never explained to me. I missed her sorely; no one ever bothered about me the way she did. I was merely the youngest in a long line. My mother would never admit it to her dying day, but I'm convinced she took her own life. You see, Kate, Amy's life was sacrificed for the greater cause of upholding the family's reputation. I don't want you to make your decisions on the same basis. You must do what is best for you and for your child, not what's best for others.'

'God, Rita, that is the most terrible story I've ever heard; terrible for you, terrible for your mother… I mean for Amy. The injustice of it all – it makes me mad to even think about it. It's so unfair.'

'Yes, I agree, but that's how it was. He got away with it, didn't he? He continued on with his life as if nothing had happened, while Amy suffered. To the outside world, he was still the respectable farmer everyone had always assumed he was and it suited the family to let everyone think that. Personally, I couldn't bear to be anywhere near him so I left home almost as soon as I found out.'

'Good for you,' said Kate emphatically.

'He never married, you see, so he lived with us the whole time, carrying on just the same. Truth is, I was afraid that one day he would turn his attentions on me. I managed to get a boat to Liverpool and then went to stay with my mother's sister, Julia, who ran a wee guest house in Blackpool. That's where I met Stan. My Aunt Julia knew nothing about it and I never told her. I couldn't, it was so shameful. It has hung over me, like a constant black shadow all these years; there's hardly a day passes when I don't think about it. But I've managed to live with it this long and I'll take it to my grave. You must promise me, promise you'll never breathe a word of this to anyone. Promise me, Kate.'

'Of course; I would never betray your trust; I promise, no one will ever hear it from me,' reassured Kate. 'I'm so sorry, Rita, I can't begin to imagine what it's been like for you, the innocent party. I really can't. I suppose it's largely for the sake of my child, this innocent, that I think adoption is the best option. I know how difficult it is for Clare, the child without a father. This child will have the chance to grow up in a normal home, with two parents, without the label of illegitimacy hanging over them – no one need ever know. Perhaps I'm a hypocrite, and behaving like your family did, but I want to hide it from my mother, hide it from Clare, from prying neighbours. Voluntarily hide it away from everyone.'

'But, Kate, how can you possibly keep it hid from your mother? She's bound to notice sooner or later.'

Kate explained all. 'So you see,' she continued, 'if I can keep a low profile, just until they return, it might just be possible. I'll go back and live in my mother's house, I don't see an alternative. There's no doubt it's going to be difficult, so many eyes watching my every move, wondering why I'm not at college. I'm not really sure what to do, if I'm honest; I'm so tired I can hardly think.'

'Well, why don't you stay on here with me – that's if you would like to, of course? There's no reason why you should have to go back at all. Stay here until the baby's born, I can look after you and Dr Greene can continue attending to you. No one need ever know, except Miss Coates, of course, but I presume she knows already, what with college and everything.'

'Yes, I told her; Mary has been wonderful. Oh Rita, it might work. I'm not sure what I would do all day though; hanging around here under your feet, but it might work. Are you sure you want to be seen harbouring a loose woman?'

'I don't consider you a loose woman, Kate, you mustn't talk like that. You're as much a victim of circumstance as my own mother was. Bob Thompson is the disgrace here. I didn't say anything before, as I thought you were close, but the truth is I've never liked him that much, always thought he couldn't be trusted.'

Kate looked at her in surprise. In Rita she had found an unexpected and very welcome ally.

Chapter 18

Plymouth, February 1956

Clare could hardly contain her excitement as she held Kate tightly in a farewell embrace. Kate glanced over Clare's shoulder and smiled at her mother who returned a weak, apologetic smile.

'Come on, Clare, time to go,' Sarah stated purposefully.

It seemed so matter of fact and uncaring but Kate knew that, in her own inimitable manner, her mother was seeking to put a lid on the boiling emotions that were in danger of overheating in anticipation of the impending departure.

'We don't want to miss the aeroplane,' Sarah continued practically. 'I want to be at the airport in plenty of time. Say goodbye to your mother, Clare, and before you know it you'll be back together with such exciting stories to tell,' she added, as a softening afterthought.

Kate looked at her watch, it was hours before they were due to fly but, after all, they were on Sarah's schedule. James was taking them to station to catch the London train. The itinerary had been precisely worked out and the appointed time to leave had already come and gone; Kate could see that her mother was getting agitated.

'I'm going to miss you both so much. I can hardly believe the time has come for you to leave,' Kate interjected. 'The summer seems such a long time away, but I really hope you enjoy yourselves. Don't worry about James and me – we'll be fine here, and the house,' she added. 'You'd better get going. Write often and tell me all about what is happening. I don't want to miss a thing.'

Kate was struggling to maintain her composure as she observed Clare's expression vacillate between excitement and grief. They gave Kate a last quick hug before clambering into James' little car. The little Morris Minor set off in a plume of exhaust fumes as it struggled to move, burdened down by the weight of three passengers and six months' worth of luggage. As it climbed the hill and turned the corner at the end of the road, Kate watched Clare continuing to wave frantically through the small back window, smiling through her tears, until they were completely out of sight. Kate turned and walked back into the house, sad but strangely relieved. She stood in the silence, conscious that this was probably one of the few times she had ever been completely alone in the house of her birth. If not her parents, then James, and more latterly Clare, had been a constant presence.

She was drawn to her father's homely study and sat down gently in his large, leather Queen Anne armchair. While he was alive no one else sat in it; it was his most personal space. Kate recalled the many times she had curled up on his lap, a log fire burning brightly in the grate, as he read aloud his beloved classics. Over the years, the seat had moulded to his shape and still bore his imprint. The arms were blackened by the mindless caressing of his gentle hands. It felt warm to her touch. In this chair she could still feel his presence. She pressed her ear against the wing, seeking to draw from it his words of wisdom. She contemplated her next move. As yet she had not broached the subject with James who, she knew, fully expected that she would be sharing the house at weekends and in the holidays. She would have to explain the reason for her absence. She owed him that. He wouldn't be back for at least half an hour so she had time to sit in the stillness, enjoy the calm and consider how she would broach the subject.

The previous few weeks had flown past in a flurry of activity. There had been so much to organise, but Sarah had approached it with her customary cool efficiency. Kate was torn between dread that their departure would herald the long separation from Clare, with an even greater dread that her mother would notice that she was rapidly putting on weight. With Clare she had the smallest bump possible, even at the end of her pregnancy, but this child was already starting to protrude like a bass drum. She had relished the particularly cold winter that had enabled her to bulk up her naturally slim figure with layers of thick obscuring cardigans. She had played out the masquerade continuing to follow her usual routine which meant leaving for Exeter on Sunday evening and coming back on Friday. If she did notice, her mother hadn't commented that Kate was catching a much earlier train home on Fridays. Kate had decided that, if necessary, she would explain the unusual routine as a final term change of timetable. She hated the deception, fabricating stories about her week at college, second guessing what questions she might get asked and the pointless wasted time that she could have spent with Clare, but she was convinced that she had made the right decision. The sickness had settled and she was starting to feel much more able to cope.

Rita Steele had been a pillar of strength; she had even managed to find Kate a discreet job. It gave Kate a purpose, a reason to get up in the mornings and a feeling of independence and focus. For several years Rita had been a daily help for a local solicitor, John Reid, and his wife Susan. Rita had overheard John complaining to Susan that he needed some extra help in the office until the summer. He was finding it difficult to get the right person, someone bright enough to cope but who would be happy to work only when he needed additional support and for such a relatively short time. Rita had immediately thought of Kate, whom she considered would fit the bill admirably; she was reliable, bright and happy to work whatever hours John needed. It wouldn't pay very much, but it would give her meaningful employment until the baby was born, and more importantly keep her mind away from her worries.

Kate had started working with John Reid almost as soon as the new College term began. His busy, modern practice was only a short walk from Rita's house. She soon got into an easy routine and proved a quick and willing learner. She enjoyed interacting with his clients who were surprisingly friendly. They bordered on kindly interference in their keenness to find out more about the popular solicitor's new secretary. While in the office, she decided to wear her wedding ring again, conscious that her ever expanding waistline was proving a popular topic of conversation and that while she wore her ring it would remain one of congratulatory approval. She was also conscious of John Reid's professional standing. From the beginning, she had ensured that he was fully apprised of her situation and, although he had never demonstrated anything other than unequivocal support, she did not wish to be the cause of any unnecessary criticism or gossip directed towards him.

She had started to look forward to her times in the office and was disappointed on the days when John explained that he didn't need her. The work was interesting and relatively challenging. It wasn't teaching, but it had its merits. John Reid came to depend on her as he gained more and more confidence in her abilities. He started to pass work to her that would normally only go to an experienced secretary. She started to feel more optimistic about her future; she started to believe that she could cope no matter what happened, to believe that perhaps it would all work out fine. Rita and Mary were also proving wonderful; their uncompromising kindness gave her the strength to remain cheerful and to confront her fears.

Despite her outwardly happy demeanour, inwardly Kate could not escape the omnipresent thought that she needed to start arranging the adoption. She was now nearly five months pregnant, but she couldn't bring herself to make the first enquiries. Sub-consciously, procrastination was the only means of distancing herself from the permanency of her decision. While it remained in the future, it remained unconfirmed. Kate knew that once she started down this road there would be no turning back and she would be voluntarily relinquishing any right to her own child. The enormity of it overwhelmed her as she began to question if she really were doing the right thing.

She spent hours imagining the young married couple who would raise her child; the happy family unit blessed with the fruit of her womb. It seemed neither real nor imminent. She could hardly bring herself to accept the fact that a child, her flesh and blood could exist simultaneously in the world, completely independent and ignorant of her, its mother. Like her, this child would breathe the air, gaze at the moon, feel the warmth of the sun upon its face, but remain completely oblivious to her coexistence. She would never see that first precious smile, hear its first spoken words, wipe away childish tears, kiss better scabby knees; she would never experience the myriad of humdrum events that bind mother and child together but, in the normal course of things, pass by relatively unnoticed. She wasn't even sure where to start with the adoption, to whom she could talk or how she should go about arranging it. Rita and Mary, in this respect, were of little help and she was hardly in a position to ask around. She decided that she would speak to Dr Greene when she returned to Exeter; she concluded that he must have dealt with this situation and young women like her before.

Kate was sitting mulling it all over in her mind when she heard James' car pull up outside. She realised that she hadn't fully formulated her thoughts or considered how she would break the news to him. She decided to speak from the heart and hope that he could be trusted to maintain her confidence, not just for now but for the rest of their lives. She knew how unfair it was expecting him to become a duplicitous partner in a deception of her own making but she had little choice. She wasn't at all sure how he would react; James was an odd mixture of the conventional and the maverick.

He opened the door and called brightly from the hallway. 'Hello, are you still here, sis?'

'In the study,' Kate replied, with false cheer.

'What are you doing in here, sitting all forlorn?' he asked grinning at her. There was a warm, easy affection between them. 'Hard on you all this, I suppose,' he continued, 'what with Clare going to be away for so long. I'll miss them too. Who would have thought it? Imagine Mother heading off to Australia; there's life in the old girl yet, eh? So when are you heading back to Romney? Tonight I suppose,' he suggested, casually folding his arms as he leant against his father's desk.

Kate had been sitting with her legs dangling over the arm of the chair. She swivelled round and sat up straight. 'I wanted to talk to you about that, James, and something else, as it happens, but I'm not sure how you're going to react.'

His brow furrowed as he looked at her questioningly. He was sufficiently sensitive to notice the significant change in her demeanour. 'What is it?' he enquired, sitting down on the arm of the chair and placing his arm around her shoulder. 'Something's wrong.'

'Oh James, it's all such a mess, my mess,' Kate spilled out, trying to be strong.

'What is it?' He removed his arm and looked towards her.

'There's no other way. I'm going to have to tell you straight, but I'm trusting that you will never breathe a word of this to Mother, to anyone. Will you do that for me, James? Promise me, I know I shouldn't ask such a thing of you, but I can think of no other way.'

By now he had stood up and was gazing down at her, his face filled with concern as he turned to face her directly.

'What on earth is it? Are you in some sort of trouble?'

'I suppose I am, if you want to put it like that. Truth is, I'm not going back to Romney. I can't – they've thrown me out.'

'What? Thrown you out, why on earth have they done that? What have you done?' asked James aghast.

'Please don't judge me, I couldn't bear it if I lost your support as well. The truth is, well the truth is… I'm pregnant.'

His eyes widened in disbelief. 'Oh Kate, how come? Did you plan it?' he asked weakly, desperately searching for the right response.

'No, there was no plan. It was a stupid, stupid mistake that's all. A mistake that unfortunately has cost me everything. I need your help now more than anything in the world. You see I've decided I can't keep it.'

She noted his reaction.

'I don't mean I'm getting rid of it, I mean I'm going to put it up for adoption. I'm going to have the baby and no one, especially Mother and Clare, must ever know.'

'Blimey, are you sure? Why would you want to give away your child? I've seen you with Clare, how much she means to you, you're devoted to her. I know you, Kate; you couldn't give up your own child. Do you realise what you're saying? Have you really thought this through, what it means?'

'Believe me, James, I have thought of little else for the past four months,' she stated emphatically.

'But what about the father? What does he say about it? Surely he doesn't want to give away his own child?'

James was struggling to find the right words, to say the right thing.

She explained it all, not least Bob Thompson's dereliction of duty, as James looked on incredulously.

'I might have expected it of him. How on earth could he end up fathering anything? Sorry, shouldn't have said that... God if ever I get my hands on him... makes me mad. All I can say is he'd better stay well out of my way... always thought he was a lily-livered, louse,' James added vehemently.

'Forget him, he's not worth it, but you see, not only will there be no help forthcoming from that quarter, I really can't put Mother and Clare through it all. They've suffered enough on my behalf. I know she doesn't say much but Mother finds it really hard, what with the divorce and everything, and you've no idea how much Clare has suffered because of the situation. She asked me one day what being 'born the wrong side of the blanket' meant. I explained but had to press her to find out why she'd asked. She finally confessed to me what she'd been suffering at the hands of the other children. They taunt her with the most despicable, unfounded allegations, both behind her back and to her face. She just wanted reassurance that they weren't true. Some of them have told her that her father sent us back to England because he already had a wife in America, others that she doesn't really know who her father is at all and has invented one in America because she's illegitimate. The least offensive are the hurtful comments about our divorce. They're jealous of her, of course, because she's bright and talented, so they try to get at her in whatever way they can. It's hard to believe that children can be so unnecessarily cruel, but it's parental influence I fear. You know Clare, she's kind and sensitive; she doesn't know how to respond, how to stick up for herself. I'm afraid she feels it terribly, but she puts on a brave face for fear of upsetting me. I am determined that another child will not suffer such derision and, to make it worse, in this case the taunts to a large extent would be justified.

'I've thought long and hard about this, God knows I can hardly think about anything else any more. I've made up my mind, it's for the best, for Clare, for Mother, for me, but most of all it's best for the child, but I need your help. It's not fair to ask you, but I really do need you to promise me that you'll never breathe a word of this to Mother, or anyone else, ever. Do you promise?'

'You poor thing, you know I'll do it for you, anything, anything at all, just ask.'

'Thank you. You don't know how relieved I am to hear that. I know you were expecting me to be come back at the weekends, but I daren't be seen around here, not like this. Someone is bound to notice. Rita has agreed that I can say in Exeter, at least until after the baby is born; it's due in July. By the time Mother and Clare return, hopefully it will all be over. All I'll have to do then is somehow explain why I've given up teaching, but I'll worry about that once this is all out of the way. Now all I've got to do is visit Dr Greene to see if he can advise me about the adoption process. I don't even know where to start.'

He bent over and cradled his sister in his arms.

'It'll be fine, Kate. You'll see, it will all work out. If anyone deserves some good luck it's you. Why do these things always happen to the righteous, someone like you? God if I ever meet up with Bob Thompson again I won't be accountable for my actions.'

'Not if I get there first,' Kate half-laughed, half-cried. Her sense of relief was palpable.

Chapter 19

Exeter, March 1956

Dr Greene's surgery was alive with the remnants of winter colds and flu. The weather had warmed up slightly at the beginning of March, but a cold snap had returned unexpectedly, and brought with it the bitterest of northerly winds accompanied by a blanket of damp, grey clouds. The winds had carried with them a cocktail of sniffles and general malaise. Evelien sat in the surgery holding a crisp, white handkerchief to her nose, observing above it the steady trickle of patients entering and leaving the surgery. Her head throbbed and her limbs ached. Around her old men coughed and hacked to clear phlegm-filled chests, middle-aged women powdered red-tinged noses, but mostly she noticed the young mothers anxiously carrying their babes in arms.

She was feeling tired and morose. Every time she visited this surgery it brought back the painful memories of the countless hopeful visits; visits that inevitably transformed into unfulfilled quests to discover what could possibly prevent two, outwardly healthy, young people from conceiving the child they so desperately desired. In the ten years since they had married, each and every month Evelien had watched and waited for the cyclical flow to miraculously stop; a small sign that fate had finally granted her wish. With every month the onset of her bleeding triggered the subsequent onset of profound disappointment. Every intimate act with Jim was now surreptitiously motivated by her hope that perhaps, finally, this would be her time. Although she still loved Jim as much, if not more than when they first met, the act of making love to him no longer held any intrinsic enjoyment for her and had become a mechanical means to an end. Jim seemed to have come to terms with the situation and was enjoying their life together with or without a child; Evelien, however, had tried and failed miserably. They no longer talked about it. The overwhelming compulsion to conceive overshadowed her very existence; it filled her waking thoughts and her sleeping dreams.

Dr Greene had been wonderful, arranging every possible test available. There was no plausible explanation, 'just one of those things' they were told; their plight so casually dismissed by the experts, so bitterly felt by Evelien. She had tried to rise above it, accept her lot, focus on the positives in her life, but it constantly pulled her down like an invisible, malevolent force of gravity. She felt she was losing her zest for life.

Evelien had turned up at the surgery on the off chance that she could see Dr Greene. She had been feeling off colour for a few days, tired and nauseous. Her first thoughts were that perhaps, finally, her dreams had been answered. Her hopes had disappeared as quickly as the defiant red spots had appeared that very morning. She had immediately felt much worse, her throat had started to ache and she began to shiver then perspire in rotation. She had called into the surgery hoping to get something to relieve the symptoms, but it was so busy she had to wait her turn. She sat there miserably observing the mass of people around her, feeling utterly despondent and sorry for herself.

Finally she was called. Dr Greene quickly diagnosed tonsillitis and prescribed a combination of antibiotics, rest and fluids. As she got up to leave, he seemed to hesitate, then asked if she had a few minutes to spare. She sat down again and gazed across at him through bleary eyes; she was dying to get home and go to bed.

'Mrs Palmer,' he started, falteringly, 'I hope you don't mind my asking, but something has cropped up which may be of interest to you. I know how much you have longed, and indeed waited, for a child and I think I know you well enough now to speak candidly. May I ask if you and your husband have ever considered adoption?'

'Adoption?' Evelien croaked, her voice rising then disappearing as she spoke.

Dr Greene wasn't sure if her response was one of incredulity or simply due to her failure to understand the word.

'I mean, have you ever thought of bringing up someone else's child as your own? A full legal adoption would mean that the child would be yours in every way, except of course the obvious fact that you didn't actually give birth. The mother would relinquish, I mean sign away, any rights to the child. The baby would be yours to raise as your own. If you chose, the child need never know that you were not the natural parents.'

'I understand what adoption is Dr Greene, I am just surprised that you have asked the question. I have never really considered it. But how could it be possible, surely we would need to have registered, or requested it through some sort of authority? I don't know how these things work in England. I suppose I have not given up hope of having my own child. It never occurred to me to think about adoption.'

'What you say is true, but often doctors are the first point of contact. We have got to be realistic about the prospect of your having your own child now, considering your age, Mrs Palmer; you are nearly thirty-eight, I see. I think perhaps we need to accept that it is becoming less and less likely that you will ever become pregnant.'

The objective nature of his professional assessment hit Evelien intensely, but she was intrigued by his suggestion. She swallowed hard.

'Why do you ask me this, Dr Greene? What are you thinking of? Do you think that adoption is our best option and that we should register or whatever it is that we need to do?'

'No, I have something more specific in mind. I have a young woman in my care who is seeking to give up her child for adoption. The baby is due at the beginning of July. You will understand that, for reasons of patient confidentiality, I cannot tell you much about her circumstances. Suffice to say that she is a most agreeable and principled young woman from a very good family.'

'If that is true, Dr Greene, how can she even think about giving up her child?' Evelien retorted sharply. 'What possible circumstances could lead her to take such a terrible decision? It is not bearable for me to think about it, me who has suffered so much in my wish to have a child, and this woman quite happy to hand over hers so easily. How can she be a principled young woman; what sort of family would let her do it?'

'I understand that you might think that, Mrs Palmer, but believe me this has not been an easy decision for her – far from it. Her decision has been based on a selfless desire to do what is best for her child, to give it the best opportunity in life, an opportunity to be raised in the security of a loving family unit. She does not believe she can offer this herself. She's highly intelligent; in fact she was a student, training to be a teacher, before she found herself in this most unfortunate position. She was married before and already has a child to whom she is very attached. Giving up a child for adoption is a most difficult and soul-destroying decision for her, but she is most anxious that the baby should go to a caring and deserving couple. She is most particular about the choice of couple; a stable relationship and a nurturing environment are most important to her. I haven't mentioned anything to her yet, of course, but I immediately thought about you and your husband; I was waiting for an appropriate time to approach you. It is most fortunate that you have come to see me today – perhaps it is providence,' he smiled.

Evelien wasn't quite sure what providence meant, but she guessed it was a good thing.

'I do not know what to say, Dr Greene, it is most unexpected. I am quite taken by surprise. I do not think I will ever understand how any woman could give away her child; no matter what the circumstances, it seems impossible to me. You will understand this has come as quite a shock. I need time to think, time to talk to my husband. July you say; it is not that long to get used to the idee. I do not know what to think. I find myself pulled between finally accepting that it probably will not happen for me myself, and the exciting thought of having a baby to look after, to call my own. Imagine, my own child. July, it is so soon. I really do not know what to say,' she added wide-eyed, hardly able to take in what he was suggesting.

'Go home and talk it over with your husband, you need time to make sure it's the right decision for both of you. You never know, it might still happen and you will go on to have your own child – that can often happen once you stop fretting about it – but that doesn't preclude, I mean prevent you from adopting this one. It's a big step, a lifetime's commitment and not something to be undertaken lightly. I will, however, need to know quite soon as, if you decide not to proceed, I'll need to make other arrangements and of course, even if you do decide to go ahead, there is much to do. As you say, July is not that far away and, as I explained, the mother is very anxious to make sure that her baby goes to the right couple. She has entrusted me with that duty. I think she would more than approve of my choice. I'm sure that you would like her very much if you met her, but unfortunately that can't happen.'

Evelien left the surgery in a daze; she felt completely disconnected with the outside world. She wasn't sure whether it was due to the fishbowl effects of feeling unwell or the enormity and excitement of the prospect now laid before her. She couldn't wait to talk to Jim; she was sure that he would be as excited as her. Her headache had eased and she noticed that the sun had finally melted a hole in the clouds. She arrived home urging the hours to pass until Jim came home. As soon as she heard his key in the door she rushed out to meet him.

'Hello, what's up with you? I came back as early as I could, expecting to find you tucked up in bed.' Jim swept her into his arms and kissed her fondly. 'How are you feeling, darling?'

'Oh Jim, I feel much better, I could hardly wait for you to come home. I have been to see Dr Greene and have the most exciting news.'

'You're pregnant,' he exclaimed, grabbing her back into his arms and swinging her round in delight.

'No, Jim, I am not,' her voice dropped as she spoke.

Jim desperately tried to find the words to compensate for his tactless mistake. 'I'm sorry, Evelien, when I saw your excitement, I immediately thought... I'm sorry I didn't mean...' he stuttered.

'But what I have to tell you is nearly as good,' she interrupted brightly.

He set her down surprised by the positivity of her reaction to his mistaken assumption. He knew how desperately important it was to her to have a child, so he generally tried to avoid the topic all together, conscious that talking about it seemed to bring her even more pain.

'What do you mean, Evelien? You're not making sense? What did he say? Are you feeling better now?' Jim followed her into the kitchen confused but intrigued.

'Do you fancy a drink, Jim? Let's have a glass of something and I'll tell you all about it.'

He was even more intrigued. Jim poured a couple of glasses of whisky and sat down at the table. He noticed her hands were trembling.

'You're worrying me, Evelien, what on earth did he say? What's wrong with you?' Jim looked across towards her anxiously. Her face wore an enigmatic smile.

'It has been such a mixed-up day, happy and sad all at once. I am so excited by the thought; wait until you hear what I have to tell you. I can hardly believe it. I went to see Dr Greene. It seems that I have tonsillitis which is why I have been feeling poorly; it is a pretty mild dose I think, and I am feeling much better already. But that is not the important bit.

He knows how much we want a child, and he has still not ruled out the possibility that we might have our own baby one day, but you will never guess what he has suggested to me. I can hardly take it in.'

Jim was desperately trying to be patient, but he wished Evelien would get to the point. He held her hand tightly across the table anxiously waiting for her to speak.

'He knows of a young woman who is pregnant, expecting her baby in July; she is one of Dr Greene's patients. I do not really understand it all properly, but apparently she has decided to give up the baby for adoption as soon as it is born. Dr Greene has suggested that we adopt her baby. He thinks that we would be perfect. Oh Jim, what do you think? I know it would not be ours, as such, but I am sure we would come to love him or her as much as any child of our own. July, think about it, it is only a few months away. We would be a family at last. What do you think?'

By now she was gripping his hand hard; it felt hot and clammy. Her beautiful blue eyes were pleading with him to agree. Jim lifted his glass and drained it. He needed time to think, to provide a measured response, but was fearful that any delay would be read as negativity by Evelien. He knew how much this meant to her. At first he had wanted a child as much as she and had felt every disappointment as acutely as she. Lately, he had resigned himself to a life without children and was actually enjoying having Evelien exclusively to himself. One look at her beautiful face, however, the expectation in her eyes and he knew there was only one choice; he could never deny her this chance, it would be too cruel. He loved her with every fibre of his being and her happiness was the most important thing in the world to him; when she was happy, he was happy. He set down the empty glass and smiled across at her.

'I can think of nothing in the world I want more, darling. A family at last, it's everything we dreamed of.'

Evelien yelped, jumped up from her chair and wildly threw her arms around him, burying her face. He held her tight and felt the river of tears flowing down the nape of his neck washing away a decade's disappointment.

Despite, if anything, feeling even more under the weather, Evelien insisted that they should go to see Dr Greene the very next day. She was anxious that he would know how keen they were and she was concerned that he might begin to line up someone else. She couldn't wait to tell him of their decision. Jim was happy for her but felt rather swept away by events. He would like to have had the chance to really think things through, discuss the implications. It was such a big step; what if the adoption didn't work out? How would Evelien cope if the child didn't bond with her? How would it affect their rather comfortable life? There was so much to think about, but he could see that for Evelien there was no going back.

Dr Greene was delighted by their decision and started to put everything in motion. He explained that the formal application for adoption couldn't be made until the child was at least six weeks old and that it could then take several months after that to get the final adoption order that would make the baby legally theirs. The intention was, however, that assuming the mother agreed with his choice of potential parents, Evelien and Jim would have care of the baby almost as soon as it was born in July.

'But does that mean the mother could change her mind at any time during those first few months, that we might have to give the baby back?' Jim asked.

Evelien looked on in terror. 'I couldn't bear it; it would be as if the baby had died,' she exclaimed. 'Surely she would not change her mind not when she had gone that far. She could not be so cruel to allow us to have it and then take it back.'

'There is that possibility, Mr Palmer, it's a chance you have to take. Any rights to the child, during that time, must remain with the birth mother until she is quite sure that she has made the right decision,' Dr Greene replied gently.

The response fuelled Jim's concerns, but he could see that Evelien's mind was made up and nothing would deter her from this course of action. He did not want to put a damper on her enthusiasm and kept his thoughts to himself.

*

Dr Greene called at Mrs Steele's that same evening. Kate was sitting quietly, chatting in the kitchen with Mary and Rita when he arrived. He asked to speak to her in private. Kate glanced at Mary, pursing her lips as she followed Rita into the small front room. Rita put a match to the carefully laid fire, which caught immediately; the strong March winds creating the perfect draw.

'I'll leave you to it then.' Rita smiled at Kate, before closing the door quietly behind her.

Kate was sure she knew the reason for Dr Greene's unscheduled visit and faced him with a mixture of trepidation and interest. Every step on this painful journey was a step closer to its final, awful conclusion. Since their first inauspicious meeting, when she had found him cold and judgmental, the relationship had transformed into one of mutual respect. She had warmed to this experienced practitioner now nearing retirement. He was an old-school GP but he had an avuncular manner that reminded her of her father. He had shown her exceptional professional kindness and subsequently she had entrusted him with the most important decision of her life; the choice of her child's prospective parents.

He took both her hands in his and leant directly towards her.

'I think I have found the perfect couple for your baby,' he opened. 'They have both been patients of mine for many years and have longed for their own child as long as I have known them. Unfortunately, that has not happened for them, and it would seem unlikely that it will now as they are both in their late thirties. All I can tell you is that they got married at the end of the war and now live here in Exeter. They are very respectable.'

And by inference, I'm not, thought Kate. His words had delivered an unintentional sting.

'The husband is in a professional job; his wife used to be a nanny working abroad. They met during the war, while both were overseas I understand; they are well educated and travelled. If you could meet them, I know you would approve. They would provide a loving and secure home for your little one and I know he or she would be taken very good care of. At least you could be happy in the knowledge that your child is in the best possible hands,' continued Dr Greene enthusiastically, oblivious to his listener's inner turmoil and self-flagellation.

Kate was desperately trying to focus on his words, take it all in, but she felt a slight movement inside. The baby was making its presence felt, every kick hammering home the cruel reality that she would be handing over the rights to her precious child; this living, breathing part of her. This innocent would soon belong to someone else and she could never go back. If she were going to change her mind she needed to do it now.

'Dr Greene, I'm so grateful for everything you've done and are still doing for me. They sound perfect. Thank you. It's just that it all seems so final; I'm starting to doubt if I'm even doing the right thing at all. I'm questioning if I could actually go through with it if and when the time comes. I really don't know. My head tells me it's the right decision, my heart screams at me every minute, of every day, causing me to doubt my own judgement. It's the hardest decision I've ever had to make in my life, or I hope I ever will. I feel so confused.'

'It's quite natural that you should feel like this,' he replied sympathetically. 'You mustn't feel pressurised into making a decision that you may regret for the rest of your life. Adoption is permanent, forever. Their joy will undoubtedly be your pain, but we need to let them know if you've changed your mind.'

'I'm sorry, Dr Greene, I hadn't really given much thought to them and how they must be feeling about all of this. I suppose adoption will answer their prayers, bring the greatest happiness to them; they seem to have waited a very long time to have a child. It's all so unfair, isn't it? I know it's the right thing to do, deep down I know; it's just so very, very painful for me.' Kate sat back on the sofa and automatically placed her hand on her abdomen. Dr Greene watched and waited patiently for her to continue.

'No,' she said eventually, speaking with a conviction she didn't feel. 'I've started down this road and must continue; I have to be strong. This child will be much better off with someone else. I'm not in a position to provide for another child as I would want to. Even if I could, that's not really the main reason for my decision... no, decision made,' she stated emphatically. 'Please let them know that I still intend to go through with the adoption. I trust your judgement, Dr Greene, and if you think they're perfect, then I'm sure they are. Thank you for everything. I really can't thank you enough.' As he stood up he gently squeezed her hand; she acknowledged the gesture with a resigned smile.

*

Jim and Evelien received the news with trepidation and delight respectively. There now appeared to be no turning back for any of the protagonists. Ecstasy, anxiety and agony; the confluence of emotions flowing in this complex interplay.

Chapter 20

Monday, 25th June 1956

Kate woke with a start as she felt a sharp rip tear through her body. The warm, watery gush between her legs confirmed that she wasn't dreaming. She placed her hand on the mattress beneath her; it was wet to her touch and she knew immediately that her waters had broken. It shocked her. The baby had decided to arrive two weeks early.

'Rita, Rita, can you hear me? I need your help,' she called, trying to remain calm.

She wasn't sure if she should get up and try to make it down the single flight of stairs to Rita's room or try knocking on the ceiling. The mattress was getting ruined. Kate waited but there was no sign of movement from the room below. Rita was a heavy sleeper. Kate groaned as she stood up and made her way gingerly down the stairs. She could hear Rita snoring as she walked towards her room. She knocked on the door tentatively before entering and approaching the side of the bed. She shook her gently.

'Rita, Rita, wake up please, the baby's coming.'

Rita woke immediately, startled by the presence in her room.

'What is it, what's wrong?' she exclaimed in alarm, sitting up quickly.

'It's the baby, Rita. Can you call Dr Greene for me please? My waters have broken. I'm sorry, the mattress is ruined, I'm afraid.'

'What? Oh, never mind about that. I'll call him immediately. I hope he gets here before the baby arrives. Why is it coming so soon? It isn't due for a fortnight. I think you should go back to bed in case it arrives while you're standing there. I'll come straight up to you when I've called him. What do I need to do?' Rita garbled in a panic, leaping out of bed and reaching for her dressing gown. She dashed down the second flight of stairs. As Kate made her way back to the bedroom she heard Rita frantically phoning Dr Greene. Kate had the slightest cramps but otherwise felt fine.

Having finished her final exams, Mary had reluctantly left the house already, and gone back to live with her parents. She no longer had a valid excuse for staying on at Rita's now that she had finished college. At both hers and Rita's insistence, Kate had moved into Mary's room, which was larger and brighter. Mary was intending to come back to stay with them for a couple of days once the baby was born. She had successfully kept Kate's pregnancy hidden from the prying eyes of her domineering mother, whose views on the subject they could all happily do without.

Dr Greene had insisted that he should attend the birth. Kate had grown enormous with this pregnancy and he was concerned that she was carrying an exceptionally large baby. He had recommended that the baby should be born in hospital, but Kate wanted it to remain low key and as quiet as possible so, after much debate, they had agreed that it would be born at Rita's.

Rita arrived back in the bedroom puffed and flushed. 'I've put on the kettle, though to be honest I'm not quite sure why,' she gabbled.

'Calm down, Rita,' Kate laughed, 'it'll be ages yet, babies unfortunately don't come that quickly. Remember, I've already had one. What you can do, please, is get the rubber sheet for the bed; I feel bad enough as it is.'

Dr Greene arrived within the hour and settled an over-excited Rita. Kate was surprisingly calm although the pain was becoming increasingly frequent and unbearable. She had already decided that she was going to commit to memory every precious minute of the experience; this would form part of the copperplate of memories upon which she would rely for the rest of her life. She wanted to feel it all.

Dr Greene carried out an initial assessment and was surprised how widely she was dilated already. He had expected to make an initial visit and then return when he had sorted out his morning surgery patients.

'I don't think this is going to take very long so I need to stay with you,' he smiled as he wiped a cool cloth over her brow. Rita was standing, needlessly wringing and re-wringing an old towel in her hands, keen to help but feeling utterly useless.

The baby's arrival was precipitous and excruciatingly painful. As Kate sobbed, Dr Greene placed the small wailing bundle on her still large abdomen.

'It's a boy,' Dr Greene stated simply, 'a perfect, but surprisingly small boy.'

As Kate cradled the bloodstained baby she noticed his concerned expression. She was still in considerable pain; the contractions hadn't eased.

'What is it, Dr Greene? Is there something wrong with the baby?' she asked alarmed.

'No, no, not at all, he's absolutely fine, but I need to examine you again.'

She felt him press on her abdomen as his eyes widened.

'Mrs Willis, there's one still in there. You've been expecting twins.'

Kate and Rita gasped in unison.

Ten minutes later Kate was also cradling her daughter. She raised her head off the pillow and gazed in wonderment at the little lives uniquely created by her. She held out her fingers as two tiny hands, edged with miniature fingernails instinctively curled around them. The babies lay across her chest, their legs intertwined in nature's perfect tessellation. Her heart wept.

'Two of them... two of them,' she uttered hoarsely. 'God has been doubly cruel.'

Kate could barely speak such was her sense of desolation.

'How can I possibly give away two of them?' she continued as Rita looked on awkwardly, not sure whether to offer the customary congratulations or words of condolence.

Rita looked disconsolately at Dr Greene; surely some means could be found to enable Kate to keep her children.

'I'm not sure I can go through with it, Dr Greene, I'm really not sure. I want to keep them for a little while, a few days; just a few days, please allow me that.' Kate looked at him pleadingly.

This seminal moment had been the subject of much debate throughout the term of the pregnancy. Dr Greene had been very open to many of Kate's wishes, but had strongly advised her that she should hand the babies over as soon as they were born. To bond with them would make an already difficult situation agonisingly painful, he believed. It was the perceived wisdom, but Kate had struggled to make a decision on the matter. The babies' early arrival had caught them all unawares; Kate hadn't even begun to reach her final conclusion. Their physical presence, however, had finally made up her mind; she couldn't hand them over, at least not yet; she needed time to think.

Dr Greene was in a quandary. He needed to know Kate's intentions. Now that there were two babies he didn't know if the Palmers would take both of them, or if indeed he would need to find another couple, and quickly. In many ways, Kate's delay gave him the time he would need, but professionally he felt it was a bad decision for her. It would make the final separation, if indeed it came to that, almost intolerable. If she did decide to keep them then he would have to break the agonising news to Evelien and Jim Palmer. He would have raised their hopes unnecessarily and would be the bearer of the most cruel of let downs.

'I must say, it's against my better judgement but, yes, perhaps for a few days,' he conceded. 'I advise you not to become too close to them though. I don't want to rush your decision, you obviously need more time to think, but you'll understand that I also need to consider the other couple involved and to let them know as soon as possible. We might even need to arrange a second couple if they don't want to adopt both babies, I need…'

'No, Dr Greene,' Kate interrupted emphatically, 'that's not something I will allow under any circumstances. They stay together. Look at them. They're as one. If I do go through with the adoption, it's on the clear understanding that it's both babies together or neither.'

'I understand,' replied Dr Greene slightly agitated.

In the past few months he had got to know and understand this remarkably strong, principled young woman, who had already been through so much. He had developed enormous sympathy for her, but he needed a decision. An already complicated situation was turning out to be incredibly difficult.

'I think it would be best to inform the other couple that you've had twins. I will let them know that you're keeping the babies for a few days and are still undecided, but I need to find out if they are prepared to have both of them if the circumstances do arise. They won't have been expecting this news so soon and will need to make their own preparations, especially now that there are two babies involved. Are you happy for me to do that at least?'

Kate agreed with the proviso that she could change her mind. She was acutely aware of the distress she was causing to a vulnerable and well-meaning couple but, for once in her life, she needed to be completely selfish. She was drained from the physical and emotional effort of the births and was finding it hard to think straight. She needed to talk it through with those whose advice she could trust most: Rita, Mary and James.

Kate was amazed by Rita's ingenuity. She had created a perfect sized cot from the bottom drawer of the large chest in Kate's old room. She had lined it with blankets borrowed from the Reids. It made a perfect but temporary nest for her children, sardined in head to toe.

Kate handed the babies over to Dr Greene and Rita. They were washed then dressed in borrowed baby clothes. Kate closed her eyes as exhaustion took hold but sleep refused to come. She only half-slept, ever alert to the cries of need from her newborns.

*

Dr Greene planned how he was going to break the news to Jim and Evelien. He wished that he could have brought the happy news as a fait accompli. Mrs Palmer answered the door, but fortunately Mr Palmer was also at home. She was surprised to see him and immediately assumed that something was wrong.

'No, nothing wrong, although I do have some surprising news,' Dr Greene assured her as he was invited in and sat down. His words had been carefully thought through.

'I have some good news and some potentially not so good. We've had a bit of surprise earlier today. The mother went into labour two weeks early. Everything though has gone very well, there were no complications. I have to tell you, however, she's had twins, a boy and a girl.'

Evelien whooped in delight; Jim paled slightly.

'Two. But that's twice as good as one,' cooed Evelien, before noticing Dr Greene's stern look. It stopped her in her tracks. 'But surely she would want them both to be adopted together, we could have both babies couldn't we, Jim?' Evelien continued falteringly.

Jim remained silent, slightly dazed by the unexpected turn of events.

'Well, yes, in fact, she's adamant that if she goes through with the adoption, then both babies must remain together,' continued Dr Greene.

'You said *if* she goes through with the adoption, so is there still some doubt?' Jim asked cautiously, anxiously observing Evelien's crestfallen face.

'You can imagine how difficult this is for her', Dr Greene tried to explain tactfully. 'It's the most heart-rending decision for anyone at the best of times, but to give birth to twins has made it is unbelievably hard for her. She just wants a little time, a few days with them before she finally decides. I'm so sorry I can't tell you this with a greater degree of certainty. Can I take it, however, that you would be prepared to have both babies if she does decide to go through with it? That would be a pre-requisite I'm afraid. I'm sure she'll decide quite quickly, she's very conscious of how difficult this is for you and doesn't wish to prolong your ordeal.'

Evelien looked across at Jim. She was devastated by the prospect that it could all fall through. He felt deeply for her.

'She sounds like an extremely good and honourable young woman, Dr Greene,' said Jim, realising how awkward the situation must be for him. 'Please assure her that we'd be delighted to have both babies; we wouldn't think about separating them. I can't begin to imagine what she's going through, and of course, she must be allowed enough time to make the right decision. It would far worse for her, for us, and probably for the children, if she changed her mind once we'd had them for even a short time. I don't pretend that we'll not be hugely disappointed if she decides to keep them but, after all, she is their mother and she must do what's best for her and her children. Could I ask you though, especially for Evelien's sake, to let us know as soon as you can?'

Dr Greene left the house acutely conscious that, in this awful situation, one party could not win without the other party losing. He wasn't at all sure how it would turn out but one thing was certain, he would be professionally involved in picking up the pieces of one or other of the young women involved.

*

The next day James and Mary descended simultaneously. Like Rita before them, they were torn between sentiments of congratulations and sympathy. Kate was relieved to see both of them; there was so much to talk about. James sat beside the bed holding his niece and nephew like an old hand. Mary clutched them like a pair of precious china dolls. Kate watched on in distress. Her decision making oscillated like a creaking pendulum, as she rationally tried to assess both sets of none too appealing options. She spoke candidly to her companions, gathered around her like the three wise men visiting the infant Jesus. Both options were as highly problematic as they were highly desirable.

'Kate, the decision has to be yours but, of course, we'll all support you in whatever you decide to do,' James reassured her. 'Perhaps it would help you to think about what advice you would give someone else who was in the same situation?'

'To do what's best for the babies,' Kate replied without hesitation, looking at her children.

'And what do you think that is?' he continued.

'To grow up in a secure home where they'll be loved and cared for by two devoted parents and won't have to suffer any of the petty prejudices or social stigma they would if they stayed with me.'

She looked at each of her companions in turn, realising that she had made her decision, one that came from the heart as well as the head. 'I have to do it for them, don't I?'

No one spoke. They sat in awkward silence. It was a question no one felt able to answer. They could not and would not assert undue influence. There was no right answer. It had to be Kate's decision and hers alone.

'There's really no other option, is there?' Kate said, breaking the silence, her voice cracking. 'I need to do it, I'll have to tell Dr Greene so that he can let their new parents know…'

The words caused her to stop suddenly, 'their new parents'.

Legally, perhaps, she thought, but I'll always be their mother.

*

Evelien was enraptured by the news brought by Dr Greene; Jim was pleased, especially for his wife, but the niggling concerns remained. Dr Greene explained that the mother would be bringing the babies into his surgery in two days' time, by which time they would be four days old. He would contact Jim and Evelien when it was time to come to collect them. It didn't give them much time to prepare, but they were sure that they could manage it.

Two days seemed like a lifetime to Evelien, a blink of an eye to Kate.

Chapter 21

29th June 1956

Evelien gently pushed back the blankets and gingerly stepped onto the bedroom floor. She could hear Jim's rhythmical breathing as she turned the handle and slowly opened the bedroom door. Its slight squeak did not waken him, thankfully. She slowly descended the stairs, carefully negotiating each tread. She put the kettle on to boil. The supreme silence was broken by the tuning up of the dawn chorus as it began to strike its first chords. Evelien glanced at the clock, it was 4.45; dawn was breaking. Arms resting on the table, she sipped a cup of steaming hot chocolate; she had never mastered the British love of tea.

Her eyes were fixed on the large Silver Cross pram parked in the corner; its presence overwhelming the small room. Unoccupied it appeared so lifeless, a large, inanimate intrusion into the ordered life she had built with Jim. She longed for it to stir, a small sign that they had arrived, that it was not a dream and that it had all come true. Well she would know today, the waiting finally over. Jim had been so incredibly supportive; he knew how desperately she needed it to happen and how devastated she would be if it all fell through. He had enthusiastically joined her in making the final preparations, willingly buying everything she felt they needed and more, rushing around at the last moment in response to the bombshell that they could now expect two babies and much sooner than planned. And yet, throughout it all, he had remained oddly detached.

She heard Jim's step on the stairs.

'What on earth are you doing up at this time, darling?' he asked as he pushed open the door. 'Come back to bed, you're going to need all the sleep you can get when you have two hungry mouths to feed in the middle of the night,' he yawned, as he sat down at the table beside her.

'*If*,' she replied rather more testily than she intended. She looked at him apologetically.

'Evelien, darling, don't say that,' he replied stung by her tone. He lifted his pipe and started to fill it. 'What time did Dr Greene say he would call us?' he continued puffing as he spoke.

'After twelve,' she answered contritely. 'I am sorry, Jim, I did not mean to sound so sharp, it is just that I cannot bear the uncertainty, the thought that we might have prepared it all for nothing. I should not take it out on you. I am tired, that is all. Do you really think she will go through with it?'

Privately Jim was not at all convinced that the mother would be able to go through with it, either now or at a later stage. He had an awful premonition that she would change her mind, keep them while she still could. He wanted to protect Evelien; he knew that to have them and lose them would be much worse than never to have had them at all.

'I hope so, darling, but we must be prepared to discover that she's decided to keep them. Can you imagine what she's going through this morning, how she must be feeling? I wouldn't think she has slept that much either.'

Evelien was too ashamed to admit that she hadn't given much thought to the mother's feelings; she was too caught up in the cauldron of her own emotions. Jim's constant cautioning that she should steel herself for possible disappointment, not raise her hopes too high, had taken the edge off her excitement. She wished he would not have such doubts. She had to conclude that by the time the sun set again she would have gone through either the best or worst possible day of her life. The waiting was intolerable, she couldn't think about going back to sleep.

*

Mary called quietly at Kate's bedroom door unwilling to waken the sleeping babies.

'Kate, are you awake, may I come in?'

'Come in, Mary,' she replied listlessly.

Mary crept in to find Kate sitting on a pillow on the floor, leaning back against the wall nursing both babies. They slept silently in her arms. She looked dreadful; red-tinged eyes encircled by black pools of sleeplessness. At her feet lay two photographs neither of which Mary had ever seen before. She picked them up and studied them. There was one of Kate and Art on their wedding day and another of her parents with James and Clare.

'I needed them all with me last night, my entire family, everyone I've ever really loved. Half of them still alive, yet destined to be taken from me.'

Mary set the photographs on the bed, conscious that she was intruding, inadvertently, on Kate's most private thoughts.

'Have you been to bed at all?' she asked gently.

Kate looked up and shook her head. 'I couldn't bear to sleep and miss my last moments with them. What time is it?'

'Eight o'clock, I didn't want to wake you too early. You know we're due at Dr Greene's surgery at twelve o'clock? I'll ask Rita to make you some breakfast, you look washed out.'

'Thanks, Mary, but I'm not hungry, perhaps something to drink, that's all. I'll get up and bath the babies. Can you take them for me please, and put them back in their cot, such as it is?'

Kate struggled to her feet. Pins and needles pricked the aching arms that had remained motionless most of the night, encircling the warm little bodies, refusing to set them down.

She ran a lukewarm bath and, taking them in turn, dipped each child in the soothing water. She dried them carefully then slowly dressed them for the final time. Mary and Rita had bought a set of clothes for each baby; Kate felt like she was placing them in their shrouds. She cut a neat lock of freshly washed hair from each child, carefully securing each with a length of cotton thread; a blond lock in blue, a black lock in pink. She placed each scroll of hair in an empty matchbox.

'At least I'll always have this little part of you,' she whispered to them, as she set it down.

Kate had hardly slept or eaten for the past two days, reluctant to let the babies out of her sight. She was utterly exhausted, but had declined the offers of help freely offered by James, Mary and Rita, determined to keep going by herself until the final moment.

James had arranged to take Mary and Kate to Dr Greene's. At 11.45, Kate and Mary each carried a child to the waiting car and climbed into the back. Rita remained inside; she couldn't face the final goodbye. As they pulled up outside the surgery Mary rested her hand on Kate's shoulder.

'Let James go in with you, Kate, I'm not sure that I can. I'll say goodbye to them here and wait for when you return. You need to be with family now.'

James shot her a grateful glance.

Dr Greene watched from the window as James carefully carried his niece and Kate her son. There was no one else around apart from two kindly looking nurses waiting awkwardly in the reception area. The small party followed Dr Greene into his surgery. Kate took both babies in her arms and tenderly cradled them together for the last time. She bent over inhaling their unique sweet scent, subconsciously arousing that primordial bond between mother and child. The aroma filled her nostrils as she felt her pulse quicken. Her tears fell, christening each child with the sign of a mother's love.

'Kate, it's time, give them to the nurses, they're waiting patiently.' James spoke softly, wrapping both arms around the family trio. Kate hesitated before turning round and nodding; she couldn't find any words.

The nurses gently lifted them from her arms, as Dr Greene opened the door for them. Kate's gaze burned into their backs as they carried her precious bundles towards the open doorway. She felt that her entrails had been ripped from the depths of her abdomen, like a bee stinging its victim; she was dying inside. As they turned to go through the door, Kate noticed a small pink arm protruding from the side, bobbing in unison with the nurse's gait. She was transfixed, convinced that her child was waving goodbye.

'Au revoir, my darlings; be happy,' she mouthed. 'I vow to you, one day I'll find you and we shall be together again.'

The room was filled with a silence that transcended human sympathy. As the door closed behind them, blocking her final view, Kate heard a faint cry. Medals of milk oozed from her breasts and seeped through her blouse; two silent circles testimony to the force of maternal instinct. The room began to swim as the familiar blackness descended causing her legs to buckle.

'I think I'm going to faint,' she cried, as she felt herself falling.

Dr Greene swung round as James reached over and caught her. He guided her towards a chair.

'Keep you head down, Mrs Willis, I'll fetch you some water.'

Dr Greene rushed towards the door.

'Do as he says, Kate, rest your head on the desk.'

Kate half consciously obeyed.

James sat in Dr Greene's chair, leaned across the desk towards her and stroked her hand. Her face was ashen, her lips a faint blue. James glanced down at the buff coloured file sitting on the desk in front of him and stared at the title:

'ADOPTION NOTES WILLIS/PALMER.'

He glanced across at Kate, who was still groaning, her eyes half-closed, and then towards the open door. There was no one about. He hesitated before furtively opening the file; his heart was racing as his eyes rapidly scanned the typed notes. There was little time. He stopped dead as his gaze was drawn to the most critical piece of information he would ever read:

James and Evelien Palmer, 19 Chestnut Grove, Exeter.

He committed it to memory, noting the unusual spelling of the woman's name, before he quickly closed the file and repositioned it exactly as he'd found it. He crept back guiltily towards Kate, and crouched down beside her as Dr Greene returned with the water. Dr Greene handed him the glass and James gave Kate a sip of water; his hand was shaking.

'She's hardly eaten or slept for four days, Dr Greene; no wonder she nearly fainted,' explained James in concern.

'Mrs Willis, I'm going to give you something that will knock you out for twenty-four hours. Make sure she takes it, Mr Aldworth. You must rest and eat properly, it's most important to help you on the road to recovery. I'll call to see you tomorrow; presumably you'll be staying with Mrs Steele for a while.'

Kate stared at him dumbstruck.

'Yes, we plan to be there until Sunday, Dr Greene, and then Kate is coming back home to Plymouth with me. Her daughter Clare and our mother are returning from Australia in just over three weeks' time,' explained James on their behalf.

'Good, you must try to focus on that, Mrs Willis, and look forward to spending time with your other daughter. You will never forget them, but over time you will remember less. It will get easier, I promise you, but it's important that you start to get on with the rest of your life. I don't need to tell you that I'm here whenever you need me.'

James thanked him as he lifted Kate from the chair. She leant heavily on him as she walked disconsolately to the car where Mary was waiting for them. She fell into Mary's caring arms and wept dry tears; there were none left to shed.

By the time they returned, Rita had succeeded in tidying Kate's room, returning the homemade cot to its rightful place in the chest of drawers. She had lifted out the soft baby blankets and gently washed them to remove the telltale posset patches. With selfless compassion Rita had removed every possible, painful reminder; the damp towels, the miniature garments, the discarded boxes and packaging littering the floor and dressing table. The detritus from four days continuous occupation had been thoughtfully cleared away, burnt or binned.

Kate returned to find her room unfamiliarly neat and tidy. She thanked Rita, but privately wished she had left it as it was, filled with their presence, imbued with their scent. There was nothing left of them. She looked for the matchbox; she needed to touch and smell the precious locks of hair, her only tangible connection. It was gone, burnt on the pyre of Rita's best intentions. By the cruellest act of kindness, Rita had unwittingly erased Kate's most manifest memory. Kate was distraught, the final blow struck by the woman she had come to love as a second mother, but she could never tell her. Sobbing hysterically, she grabbed the pills; she needed to sleep, to eliminate consciousness. She felt that she never wanted to wake again.

*

Jim looked across to Evelien as the phone's shrill ring cut across their conversation. The clock had chimed 12.30. 'Shall I answer it?' Jim asked nervously, setting down his pipe. Evelien nodded.

'But that's marvellous news, Dr Greene, thank you for letting us know, so we're to come to the surgery at half past one. We'll be there. Evelien will be delighted. I can't thank you enough.'

Evelien leapt from her chair as Jim arrived back in the kitchen. His grinning face confirmed what she had overheard. Tears of unbridled joy began to flow.

An hour later they walked into the surgery, strangely apprehensive. Dr Greene met them and shook their hands.

'Congratulations', he smiled, 'you are about to become parents. It's the most important role you will ever undertake and I'm so pleased for you.'

'Thank you, Dr Greene. Are they here? May we see them?' asked Evelien impatiently.

'They are indeed, Mrs Palmer, the nurses have just finished feeding them. Follow me.'

Jim and Evelien entered the warm, sun-filled room to find each nurse sitting holding a sleeping baby. Hand in hand they walked towards their son and daughter, hearts pounding.

'But they're beautiful,' Evelien gasped, 'may we hold them?'

Jim was mesmerised, he had not expected such miniature perfection. Small carefully carved toes peeped from under a crisp white blanket, delicate eyelashes brushed against flawless peachy skin, a tiny thumb protruded from a perfect bow mouth as it comforted the sleeping child. He was captivated. As they held their children for the first time Jim's reservations melted away. He realised that his words of caution had fallen on his own deaf ears. Like Evelien, he was enraptured and he couldn't imagine ever giving them back. He couldn't wait to take them home, to get to know them, to become their father and to form the family Evelien had craved.

*

Kate finally woke late the following day. They had left her alone, conscious of her need to sleep, to recover, to be allowed to forget. She groaned as her waking thoughts returned to her missing children; her head was pounding, her heart was breaking. Would the crushing pain ever go away?

Mary had waited until Kate awoke; she was returning home but left promising to visit her as soon as she could.

They were all leaving her. The following day she faced the final trauma of leaving Rita's house for the last time. As they embraced, Rita handed over her parting gift. Kate opened the carefully wrapped parcel to reveal a miniature calf-skinned bible. There was a handwritten bookmark inserted between the fragile gold-edged pages:

Isaiah 66: verse 13
As a mother comforts her child so will I comfort you;
and you will be comforted over Jerusalem.

Kate looked at Rita, choked. 'Thank you, it's beautiful, I will cherish it for ever,' she croaked.

'It was mine, a gift from Amy, my mother, for my baptism; it deserves a special owner so I wanted you to have it,' Rita explained simply.

'You're a good woman, Rita Steele; a guiding light for me and, in your own quiet way, an example to all of us. I can never thank you enough for your friendship, your forgiveness and your wisdom. I'll miss you terribly.'

Kate bent over and wrapped her arms around the forlorn figure standing before her.

'Enough of that, now off you go, before I make a complete eejit of myself,' Rita retorted trying to sound cheerful through her sniffles. 'You take care of yourself my wee girl and don't be long before you come back to see me.'

Rita held her tightly as James opened the boot, carefully placing Kate's large American case inside. Kate slowly climbed in beside him, wound down the window and hugged Rita again though the opening. Rita watched in silence as they drove off, before walking back towards her lonely little terrace.

Chapter 22

Plymouth, 22nd July 1956

Kate stood before the full length mirror and miserably observed her reflection. She studied the gaunt face frowning back and sighed. Her once enviable figure had metamorphosed from corpulent to skeletal in the course of a few turbulent weeks. The dress she had chosen, in a vain attempt to look her best, hung on her frame like a coat on a hook. No amount of rouge or powder could disguise the tragedy being played out within. And now today, when they returned from Australia, she would have to put on the mask, re-enact the role of loving mother, of dutiful daughter, of the respectable young woman they believed her to be. She felt a fraud, a bit part player in a most deliberate deception.

For the past three weeks she had woken every day with the expectation that, by its close, the weight of guilt would have lifted a little; that life would start to hold some appeal, that she could, once again, enjoy the most basic pleasures – food, laughter, even her own thoughts. It was not to be. Every day ended as the previous one had begun. She felt that she was intruding on the world, an unwelcome guest, an outsider, a trespasser and she despised herself for it.

Kate contemplated their return. Of course she was pleased to see them, to hold her child again, to share in their excitement, but she also knew that their return would herald the beginning of the rest of her life; a fabricated life, constantly weaving a web of deceit, hoping that it would never unravel. She feared that seeing Clare again, that living breathing embodiment of herself, would reopen the barely healed wounds, remind her of what she had lost, confirm that she had made the most awful mistake. From the moment she had handed them over, her mind had been flooded with waves of doubt. Every minute, of every day, she agonised over her decision, doubted her motives and questioned her judgement. She had used James again and again as her gauge, her sounding board.

'What have I done, James? I don't even know where they're living. How on earth did I get into this mess? How could I ever have let this happen to me and with Bob bloody Thompson of all people? I must have been mad. How will I ever know if I've done the right thing or not? I keep wondering where they are now; who has my children. Do you think it really was best for them or simply easier for me?'

Inwardly and outwardly the questioning had been relentless. James was suffering from his own crushing guilt. He knew he had some of the answers she so desperately sought; he had seen what he ought not to have seen and he was holding it back. He had shared his guilty discovery with Mary and Rita, seeking advice and reassurance that he was doing the right thing in keeping it from her. They had unanimously agreed that Kate needed time to accept her decision, make a clean break. Ignorance was her protection – she should not be told. He was convinced it was the right course of action, but it was proving incredibly hard in the face of her anguish, an anguish he had the power to salve.

Kate watched the clock tick by as she sat at the kitchen table drumming her fingers, nervously awaiting their arrival. She looked around the carefully scrubbed kitchen; would it pass muster? They were due at three o'clock; in less than half an hour. It was ridiculous – she was waiting for her family, the people she knew and loved best in the world, yet she felt that she was facing her execution. As she heard James' car pull up outside she rushed out to meet them, her face fixed in fake enthusiasm.

They greeted each other with endless chatter, hugs and commotion. Clare clung to her mother like a limpet to a stone. Kate matched their unbridled need to talk, and tell all, with her own need for silence and concealment. She told them everything she needed to, without saying anything much at all. She realised that over the past six months their lives could not have travelled more divergent paths. She listened, shared their exuberance, forced herself to participate, all the while waiting for the inevitable question.

'Sorry, Kate, here we are rabbiting on about our adventures and we haven't even asked what's been happening with you,' her mother stated, suddenly shifting from the sole topic of conversation. 'You must have so much to tell us. You've lost weight, far too thin I should say, I hope you haven't been working too hard for your exams. How did they go? Very well I'm sure. Any sign of a job yet?'

Kate felt her stomach churn; the moment of truth had arrived. Over and over in her mind she had carefully crafted her response to the one question she dreaded, but which she knew would inevitably crop up. Her reply would start to spin the first strand of the complex web she would be forever forced to weave; unless she told the truth, of course.

'Oh, plenty of time to talk about that later,' she replied hoping to deflect the question, delay the inevitable, 'I'm enjoying hearing all about your adventures too much. Come on, there must be far more to tell. Did the new cine camera work?'

She tried to make light of it, maintain the momentum, but something in her voice gave her away. Her mother looked at her askance, she knew her child; she also knew to leave it for the moment.

The afternoon passed into evening and into early night, until Clare finally conceded that she needed to go to bed. Sarah was also exhausted, her body clock craved sleep but she knew Kate had something to tell; there was something amiss.

Four years after her return from America, Kate found herself reliving the most unwelcome déjà vu as she descended the stairs steeling herself to confront her mother with the most difficult revelation. James had made his excuses and left them alone; he couldn't trust himself to live the lie in the face of his mother's direct questioning. Kate wasn't sure she could either. She sat down desperately trying to steady her nerves as she prepared for the greatest performance of her life.

'All quiet on the Western Front, thankfully, she's fallen asleep. You must be exhausted too, Mother, why don't you go to bed?' Kate started lightly, trying to buy herself some time. Her mother wasn't fooled.

'Come on, what's troubling you, Kate? I'm worried about you. I didn't want to say anything in front of Clare, but you look ill. What's wrong?'

'I'm fine, really I am; perhaps I've lost a little weight,' she started brightly. 'There's nothing wrong exactly. I've changed my mind about something that's all. I don't expect you'll understand this, Mother, but I've decided that teaching isn't for me after all. I didn't finish my exams. I left Romney not long after you left for Australia. I'm doing something else now.' She tried to sound upbeat and matter of fact but was filled with apprehension.

Sarah looked at her, shocked.

'But why? I thought you were doing so well, that your heart was set on teaching. What on earth has made you change your mind? Something has happened, I know it has.'

The disappointment and disbelief in her mother's voice were tangible; she wasn't buying it and Kate knew it. She was going to have to brazen it out and pretty damn convincingly.

'I don't quite know when I decided, it just crept up on me. I suppose it was sometime during my last teaching practice when I finally realised that it wasn't for me,' she explained as nonchalantly as she could muster. 'I could no longer imagine myself teaching in twenty years' time, that's all; it just seemed so pointless to continue.' At least, she felt, there was a grain of truth in this.

'But to leave your course so close to the end, why on earth didn't you at least finish your exams? You'd almost finished;

you never know you might have come to realise that you were mistaken. At least then you could have reconsidered at a later date. It doesn't make sense, after all you've worked for the past three years, the sacrifices you've made, we've all made. It seems so irrational, so irresponsible, so unlike you.'

The comment made Kate smart. The carefully crafted response rehearsed over and over to be presented with conviction, now seemed weak and unconvincing. She decided that she needed to put forward her point once and for all, and make it eminently clear to her mother that the subject was closed for further discussion. If she didn't achieve that, then there was every chance that she would crack, confess all and disclose what she must keep hidden forever. It was the lesser of two evils.

'I don't suppose it makes much sense to you, Mother, but I've made my decision and have to stand by it now for better or worse, there's no going back. I'm sorry if you're disappointed, I wouldn't have wished that, but I must live my own life. As it happens I have found another job that I think suits me better.'

Sarah was finding it hard to maintain self-control; she had to remind herself that Kate was no longer the petulant, independent child she had so often confronted, but a mature woman, with her own child and her own mind. She was sure there was more to it than she was being told, but perhaps it was better that she didn't know. It was obvious that Kate was not for budging.

'And what possible wonderful career awaits you with no qualifications to speak of?' she asked rather more sarcastically than she intended.

Kate refused to rise to the challenge. 'I'm training to be a legal secretary. I've been working with a solicitor in Exeter since Christmas, a Mr John Reid, who has now found a position for me here in Plymouth, in the offices of an old friend of his, Guy Prosser. They read law together at Oxford before joining the RAF at the beginning of the war. They both flew Spitfires in the Battle of Britain; apparently Guy Prosser was awarded the DFC. I don't know the details, but you'd like him, I know you would. I start there next Monday, in a week's time. It is a good job and I think I've done really well to get it.'

'I don't care whether I would like him or not, I can hardly believe what I'm hearing. Just when I think I'm finally beginning to understand you, you whip the rug from under me again with yet another rash decision. I just hope you know what you are doing, because I can't see it. Why on earth would you throw away three years of study on a whim? It's beyond comprehension. I'm sure there's more to it than you're telling me. You must know that your father would have thoroughly disapproved. I'm sure he would have plenty to say on the matter if he were still alive.'

This was a blow too far, the last thing Kate needed was to be clothed in even more guilt, especially where it concerned her father. She refused to be drawn into a war of words that she could never win.

'He's not here, Mother, so don't you dare drag my father into this. Who knows what he would have thought? He would have wanted me to be happy, I know that, which is more than you seem to do.' Kate could feel the unfettered temper of her youth rising. She swallowed, breathing deeply as she tried to maintain control before continuing. 'Please,' she reasoned, 'can we leave it at that, before either of us says something we'll come to regret?' She hoped she spoke sufficiently emphatically to signify an end to the subject. 'It's done and I hope you can be happy for me. If not, then please accept what can't be changed.'

They both understood that much had been left unsaid and would have to remain so. Kate knew that she had upset her mother, but she needed the subject to remain taboo, a potential source of conflict, a topic forever to be avoided if she were to prevent the need for future explanation; if indeed she were ever to carry off this charade.

Kate started with Prosser and Jones the following Monday. Her mother grudgingly admired the dress she had carefully chosen to wear. It added inches to her diminishing waistline, curved what nature had straightened out. She was keen to look her best – smart and professional. When she woke early in the morning, the sun was already shining brightly. It was a perfect English summer's day, so she decided to walk the mile or so to the office. She was standing patiently outside the building nervously reapplying her lipstick, when Guy Prosser pulled up noisily in a little cream sports car. He waved cheerily through the open roof as he skilfully parked the car perfectly level with the pavement.

'Hello, you're early,' he called, 'must get you a key of your own if you're going to arrive with the dawn chorus.'

He smiled as he opened the door, smoothing down a mass of wavy brown hair that had developed bouffant proportions as a result of its morning blast. Kate giggled. It was the first time she had heard herself laugh in weeks. It felt good.

'Good morning, Mr Prosser,' she replied, 'I didn't want to be late on my first morning. Lovely car and the perfect day for it. What is it?'

'It's an MGA. Bit flash I know, but hard not to enjoy on a day like today. I'll take you for a drive in it later if you like, that's if the sun continues to shine.'

Kate felt herself blush. There was something about him that unnerved her, that reminded her of Art. Perhaps it was his easy-going charm and confident manner, she wasn't sure. At her interview she knew he had warmed to her, she had been self-consciously aware of it. She wouldn't admit it to herself, but she was excited by the prospect of meeting him again. She chastised herself for her foolishness; he was merely displaying his perfect manners, openly polite and welcoming to his newest member of staff. A quick glance in the mirror confirmed it; she was a bony replica of herself, a haggard shadow of womanhood, a fraud, no one could look at her and think otherwise. Yet she had found herself taking extraordinary care over her appearance this morning; it was the first time she had cared about being a woman since arriving back in England.

'I'd love to, Mr Prosser, thank you; I've never been in a sports car before.' The words appeared from nowhere, her lips had formed them, not her mind; it was an instinctive response devoid of conscious thought. She immediately regretted it, she had revealed her cards; it was too soon, she had come across as eager and impulsive and she should have been more guarded.

'Good, that's settled. Now let's see what excitement today brings shall we, divorced, diddled or died, take your pick,' he laughed, as he opened the office door, standing aside to let her enter first. She was confused; she knew that she shouldn't read anything into his invitation. John Reid had described him perfectly; polite, funny, annoyingly handsome but, at thirty-six, a confirmed bachelor. He was being charming, that was all, and she needed to refocus her attention, remain detached and get to grips with the job.

Chapter 23

August 1956

The practice consisted of two partners, Guy Prosser and Meredith Jones, supported by Annabel Wright, the senior secretary, and Kate, for now the office junior. Annabel was, in fact, a couple of years younger than Kate but she knew the ropes having worked in the office since before the end of the war. Annabel had been surprised to be offered the position of senior secretary following the retirement of Kate's predecessor Gladys Goodwin, and initially faced her new role with apprehension and self-doubt. Kate made a welcome change from Gladys, however, as she was someone with whom she could relax and be herself. With Gladys, she had always felt like she an errant school girl who'd forgotten her homework. Kate's first impressions of Annabel were of a rather sweet but intense mouse, who was clearly uncomfortable with her new found status and she felt for her. In Kate, Annabel found a willing and quick tutee, one who not only put her at ease but was only too happy to defer to her superior years of experience. They hit it off immediately, developing a mutual regard as they rebuilt each other's confidence. Gradually, the office began to ring with peals of laughter largely focused on the good humoured banter bowled by Guy Prosser and batted by Kate. The days, then weeks, started to fly by. Kate felt her mood lifting with each day that passed, as her mind began to fill with thoughts beyond her grief. She felt her spirit return; the butterfly had begun to emerge from the chrysalis. She was starting to remember less.

The initial pleasure drive in the little sports car had gradually evolved into a regular lift. At first she had accepted his offer when it was raining, when she had needed to work late, when he was going her way anyway. Gradually she realised it had become a regular event with no need for contrived excuses. Kate had fought against her feelings with every weapon in her protective armoury; she had erected every shield of common sense, but she knew she was falling in love. It was stupid, reckless and leaving her vulnerable to inevitable disappointment. She needed to check her feelings and control her passions, but she was finding it impossible. She was sure he felt something in return, but he had remained so guarded, so completely in control, she began to doubt her instincts. She had started to regain her figure as the bloom on her cheeks and her inner radiance returned. At last she could look in the mirror and approve the reflection, smile at herself, begin to like and admire herself once more.

His first move came completely out of the blue one otherwise unremarkable afternoon in late August. 'Mrs Willis,' he announced with a dramatic flourish to an astonished Kate and a bewildered Annabel, 'do you like the theatre, the Bard to be precise? Two tickets to *A Midsummer Night's Dream* and no Hermia to accompany Lysander. I wonder would you like to undertake the role?'

Kate's heart began to race as she struggled to maintain her composure; she wished she could remember the plot. It was typical of him, making light of the invitation, announcing it in front of Annabel when he could have asked her in private, but she was sure there was a hidden meaning. If only she could remember the plot.

'I'm not sure, Mr Prosser,' she replied with false indifference, 'as it happens I love the theatre, Shakespeare in particular, but it depends, I'm not sure that I'm available for auditions. When did you say the performance was?'

She noted with some amusement his swift deflation, his pricked confidence.

'A week on Saturday,' he replied suitably subdued. 'I know it's short notice, but I was hoping you might be free, unless of course Miss Wright would like to come.'

Annabel looked at him in horror. Kate smothered a giggle. She wasn't sure whether Annabel's reaction was due to the thought of an entire evening alone with Guy Prosser or an entire evening in the company of Shakespeare. Kate knew that he was toying with her; it was a game of cat and mouse, but was he hunter or prey? She tried to play it cool, but she was flipping cartwheels inside.

'It's a very kind offer. Do you mind if I let you know tomorrow, Mr Prosser?' she replied calmly.

He looked at her suspiciously, trying to gauge her reaction; he wanted her to be as excited as he was, but he should have known better. She would never be so obvious. She intrigued him, infuriated him, aroused emotions he had never felt before. He had tried to remain detached; so far he had successfully avoided the trap that had caught so many others of his acquaintance. He valued his independence. Kate Willis had managed to lay the noose without even knowing it and he was becoming ensnared. What was more, he found that he was happy to let her, but she was hard to read this infuriatingly intelligent, independent, enigmatic, glorious woman. He was besotted – she filled his mind. He had felt it from the first moment she had walked into his office; how dare she turn his world upside down?

Of course she agreed. She only needed to check that her mother was prepared to look after Clare. She thought she may object, but then a night at the theatre was hardly daring.

As soon as she got home she scoured her father's office, hunting the shelves for the collected works of Shakespeare. Hermia and Lysander; what was their connection? Was he sending her a cryptic message? She spent the evening immersed in the play. Lysander loves Hermia, Hermia loves Lysander, Lysander desires Helena and renounces a stunned Hermia… what did it mean? What was he telling her if indeed anything at all? Was she trying to read too much into it? Perhaps he'd got the ticket for someone else and been let down; he simply had no one else to share it with, she reasoned.

Kate dressed and redressed a dozen times. Her room was strewn with rejected garments as the contents of her drawers spilled over the floor. She was seventeen again, carefully choosing her outfit for her first evening with Art and that seminal date at The Officers' Club, thirteen long years ago. She felt the first pricks of guilt as she observed herself in the mirror, recognising that her thoughts were no longer of Art. She knew she still loved him, and always would, but now, perhaps, she could finally close that chapter. His parents still wrote to her but less frequently; perhaps they also wanted her to forget and to get on with the rest of her life. They all knew that Art was never going to recover. He was living a half-life locked in his own horror, institutionalised and unaware of the world around him. He no longer recognised his parents or anyone else. Kate and Clare were completely unknown to him.

And now, once more, she was nervously looking forward to spending an evening with an intelligent, handsome man. Looking back, it was her youth and innocence that had caused her most concern; now it was her experience. She'd been honest with Guy Prosser, up to a point, declared that she'd been married and that she had a child, but what about the rest of it? If it did develop into something more, would she forever have to weave her web? Would he ever understand, ever accept?

She sighed with frustration. In America she could have settled on any one of a dozen suitable outfits, now her wardrobe seemed dated and shabby. She realised that she hadn't had cause to dress formally for at least four or five years. There was nothing else for it. She was going to have to spend the weekend looking for something to wear.

'You look lovely, Mummy,' Clare announced as Kate strolled into the kitchen on the appointed evening. Sarah lifted her head from her book and smiled.

'You do dear, very lovely indeed. I hope you enjoy yourself. What time are you expecting to leave?'

'At seven o'clock. Guy, I mean Mr Prosser is collecting me at seven. Do you mind if he doesn't come in to meet you?

It feels rather awkward; you see I don't want to suggest that I think it's a date.'

Sarah and Kate had reached détente. Kate knew her mother would never fully accept her decision about Romney, or her explanation, but Sarah had to admit that in the past few weeks Kate had seemed happier and healthier than ever before. She had regained her lovely figure and her lustre; the spirited girl who'd left for America had finally come back. At first, Sarah had expressed her reservations about what she regarded as a highly improper crossing over of their professional and social relationship. Guy Prosser was Kate's boss; it seemed inappropriate, but looking at her daughter standing before her now she couldn't begrudge her a second chance of happiness.

Guy arrived just before seven. Kate waited until he had rung the door bell, she didn't want to appear too keen. She noticed the look of admiration as he ran his eye over her slim figure. Clare had helped her to choose well and she knew that she looked her best.

'You look beautiful, Mrs Willis,' he stated simply as he held out his arm to lead her to the car. 'Do you think, for the purposes of this evening, Mr Prosser could dispense with Mrs Willis and instead Kate could accompany Guy on this trip to fairyland?'

'Kate would be very happy to dispense with Mr Prosser,' she replied. He looked at her alarmed before they both dissolved in laughter. He curled her hand around his forearm and placed his own on top of it. She squeezed his arm affectionately as he patted her hand in return, only releasing it to open the passenger door for her.

For Kate, a mediocre performance on stage passed in a haze of excitement in the stalls. She was beguiled by his handsome face, his perfect manners and his learned interpretation of the play. Kate had always found it confusing and contrived but, oh, what would she give now for a visit from her very own Puck? It ended much too soon. He drove her home and pulled up outside her mother's house. Was that it then? Had she imagined his admiration, did Mrs Willis and Mr Prosser return to their rightful roles on Monday?

'I can't tell you how much I've enjoyed tonight,' he started cautiously, fingering the steering wheel when he had turned off the engine. 'I know it wasn't the very best of performances, but for me it was the very best of evenings. Did you enjoy it?'

He looked across at her uncertain how she would respond. He was in virgin territory; Kate, ironically, was the old hand. 'I really enjoyed it too, thank you,' she replied. 'But I enjoyed the company more.'

His face lit up buoyed by her encouragement. 'You don't know how relieved I am to hear you say that. Would I be expecting too much to hope that we could do something together again soon? How about dinner some evening this week, perhaps; I could take you after work and make an evening of it. I know just the place.'

Kate's head was in a spin. She wanted to scream, 'Yes, yes I'd love to,' but she needed time to think about what she was doing in giving him encouragement, in re-embarking on a relationship. It was what her heart wanted more than anything, but her conscience was cautioning her to hold back, to delay. She had convinced herself that he was enjoying the company of the woman he assumed her to be, the Kate she presented to the world – the professional, carefree, fun loving, dutiful mother. The Kate who didn't actually exist. She needed time to think about what she was doing. For the first time in years she had momentarily allowed herself to become the feisty young woman, full of hope and expectation, who had departed the shores of England for the excitement of Boston. But she knew she was no longer that carefree girl; she was cloaked in a sackcloth of guilt and remorse and it would weigh on her forever. As she studied his expectant face she almost lost her resolve but, although it pained her greatly, she knew she had to remain strong.

'Guy, I'm sorry, I'm not sure that I can make it to dinner during the week, it's difficult what with my daughter, you see…' She was trying to let him down without discouraging him; it sounded like such a weak excuse.

His face fell before lifting again with a strained smile. 'Of course, I didn't think,' he interrupted. 'I'm sorry, I'm rushing you, another time then perhaps?'

'Yes, thank you, I'd like that,' she replied simply. He looked bemused, unsure whether she really meant it or was merely being polite. Perhaps he had misread her and she didn't feel the same way he did. He walked her to the door.

'Good night, Kate, thank you for a lovely evening. I'll see you at the office.'

'Thank you, I really did enjoy myself,' she replied. She noticed that he hadn't offered to give her a lift on Monday. He gave her an awkward embrace then politely waited until she had searched in her handbag and found her key. Kate opened the door glancing up towards Clare's window. She saw the curtain twitch; she was being observed. She sighed as she went in.

She crept up the stairs, carefully avoiding the giveaway creaks. She lay down on her bed and stared at the ceiling. It was late but she felt wide awake and knew there was little chance of sleep. Would this cup of sorrow ever pass she pondered? It was clear that he liked her, and that he wanted more than her professional friendship; it was all she had hoped for, what she had imagined. But he was focusing on a façade, Kate the actress, the great performer. How would he feel when she removed the mask, when he was confronted with the hidden face, the fallen woman, the mother who had abandoned her babies? How could he possibly like her then? She could hide it from him, he need never know the truth, but she knew that she was falling in love with him and she could never live the lie. She needed him to love her, despite her flaws, and she needed to know that he understood; there could be no secrets between them. She couldn't give him anymore encouragement without telling him the truth, it was only fair and then he could decide for himself; he could decide from a position of knowledge. She would have to face up to the possibility that she would lose him completely, lose his respect; that she might even lose the job she loved, but it was risk she had to take.

The next morning Kate fielded Clare's insatiable curiosity with the barest of details.

'I saw them kissing, Grandma,' she announced in front of a mortified Kate.

'You see too much, young lady,' came Sarah's curt reply. 'What were you doing out of bed spying through the window?' Sarah raised her eyebrows knowingly towards Kate in an unexpected show of solidarity.

'We weren't kissing as it happens, nosy-parker. Mr Prosser gave me a hug, like you do to your friends, that's all.'

'So you're *friends*, is that what you call it, Mummy?' she replied mockingly.

Kate didn't want to get into a detailed discussion regarding the nature of the relationship, though she was pleased that Clare was showing signs of approval rather than resentment. Sarah didn't press her. Kate anticipated meeting him again the next day with a mixture of excitement and anxiety. They had agreed that it would be best if, in the office, they returned to their more formal nomenclature. She would be Mrs Willis once more and he Mr Prosser. Was that how it was going to be from now on, formal friends? Kate felt she had blown her chances, embarrassed him and thrown him off her scent forever.

Kate, as usual, was the first to arrive at the office. She sat down at her desk and started to type the pile of notes left over from Friday. Meredith Jones' handwriting was difficult to decipher and focused all her attention. She didn't hear the door opening as Guy came in. He saw her crouching over the notes, concentrating hard on the task in hand; it was obvious that she was unaware of his presence.

243

He hesitated before closing the door with a bang. She jumped with a start, dropping the notes as she swung round towards him.

'Blimey you gave me a fright,' she uttered, laughing, placing the back of her hand on her forehead in a mock faint. It was the crack in the ice they both needed.

'Sorry Kate, I mean, Mrs Willis, I think the wind must have caught it. Bit jumpy aren't we?' he grinned back. 'I was hoping I'd catch you alone. I just want to say something before the others arrive in. The thing is, I really, really enjoyed Saturday evening with you, but I don't want you to feel obliged to repeat the experience just to keep the boss happy. I'm delighted you've come to work with us here. I hope that we've become good friends, and if that's all you want then that's fine with me.'

His tanned face was wrinkled as he concentrated on his carefully rehearsed words. He looked so handsome, so concerned, like an awkward schoolboy building up the courage to ask her out on a first date. Her resolve disappeared.

'Actually I don't want us to be just good friends,' she replied smiling. 'I really enjoyed being with you on Saturday as well and I'd love to repeat the experience.'

He beamed. 'Fantastic, you don't know how relieved I am to hear you say that. I was thinking about it all day yesterday; I was sure that I'd frightened you off. How about lunch next Saturday, that's if you're not planning to spend it with your daughter, of course?'

'Lunch on Saturday would be great, I'm sure my mother will help me out,' she replied enthusiastically. 'Something to look forward to.'

He rubbed his hands in exaggerated glee before bending to give her a peck on the cheek.

'Mr Prosser,' she remonstrated in mock disapproval, 'not in the office, please!'

He winked at her and laughed, before disappearing into his own office.

The following Saturday morning, Kate shielded her eyes from the glaring sun as she skipped towards the car. She reached in her bag and donned her large American sun glasses, as he revved away. She covered her hair with a silk headscarf as the wind whistled over the small windscreen. She felt like Grace Kelly. The road was remarkably busy as they drove out of the city leaving the weekend hustle and bustle in their wake. They bounced along bumpy country roads until he suddenly turned off into a small wooded lane, pulling up sharply as he switched off the engine. It was in the middle of nowhere. Kate gazed at him over the top of her glasses, looking puzzled.

'*I know a bank where the wild thyme blows, where oxlips and the nodding violet grows*,' he grinned. 'Lunch is served, madam.'

He jumped out, opened the boot and pulled out the contents; a large chequered rug, a battered wicker picnic basket, two glasses and a bottle of wine. She smiled before lifting the rug and throwing it over her arm.

'Oh is it, milord?' she answered curtsying. They strolled hand in hand over a field of freshly mown hay, breathing in the delicate unfamiliar scents before descending a small mossy bank that led down to a clear flowing river. A cathedral of willow arched across it, casting its shadow along the length of the bank. It was magical, like Titania's bower. He placed the rug on a patch of dry grass and opened the basket. Kate watched entranced.

'My little secret haven,' he explained, 'I've been coming here since I was a boy. I used to sit here and fish with my father. My father and the owner, Sam Gourley, fought in the first war together and they've remained close friends. It's my most private place. I've never brought anyone else here.'

Kate was moved by the gesture, but it confirmed that she had no right to be there; that he would regret sharing it with her once he knew the truth. He expertly popped the cork and handed her the glass. As she lit a cigarette, he noticed her hand was shaking.

'Hey, can't believe I have that much of an effect,' he teased. 'Have some more.' He jokingly began to top up the glass. He opened his jacket and pulled out an engraved silver cigar case. He lit a cigar and leaned back on the rug, smiling, deep in thought.

'I hope I'm not spoiling it all,' he started hesitantly, as he blew a puff of smoke in the air, 'truth is, Mrs Willis, I think I'm in danger of falling in love with you. Like Helena, you have bewitched me with your very own potion of pansy juice, but I doubt if you ever meant to.' Kate's heart thumped. She paused.

'No, I think Puck got it right this time,' she replied smiling, 'there was no mistake.'

He leaned over and pulled her gently towards him. He kissed her tenderly, a gentleman's kiss, his desire constrained only by good manners.

'Guy, I need to tell you something, something terrible about me, something you don't know,' Kate stuttered pulling away from him.

He sat upright and turned towards her, his face filled with concern; she looked so flustered and uncomfortable. He took a swig from the glass and watched as Kate followed his lead.

'While our relationship was merely professional I didn't feel I needed to tell you this,' she continued nervously. 'I would never have let it affect my work. But now it's different, you've a right to know everything about me.'

She drained her glass and held it out. He refilled it and set the bottle down slowly.

'Kate, you don't need to do this. I don't have a right to know everything about you. If it helps, I've always known there was something in your past; that something painful had happened to you. When John first told me about you, he explained that you had left Romney College suddenly, without finishing your studies, that you had personal reasons for doing so and would need time to adjust. He wouldn't betray your trust and I didn't push him. He spoke really highly of you. I've known him a very long time, and we've been through a great deal together, so I reckoned if he could recommend you, then that was good enough for me. From the moment I first met you I knew he was right, and I reached my own conclusions. I didn't ask you then, and I don't need to know now, but I saw the pain in your pale, thin face when you walked into the office. As far as I'm concerned I'm happy with the woman I've got to know over the past few weeks. It will make no difference to how I feel about you. You don't have to tell me anything.'

'But I do. I don't want there to be any secrets, nothing that could ever come between us. I don't want to start something with you, feeling that I have to hide the truth. I don't want you to think you are with another Kate, someone you think you know, someone who isn't me.'

She told him everything, the hard, cold truth. It pained her unimaginably to relive it, but she forced herself to do it. She spared no details of what she herself described as her callous, cold-hearted choice. He would know her as she knew herself.

'They're my children and I will never know them,' she lamented. 'That's the worst bit, not even knowing their names or where they are, having to accept that they will never know of me; they'll grow up named by another, thinking they were born to another. I've deceived my mother, my daughter, so many people I know and love and I hate myself for it. I can't deceive you too. I can't allow you to fall in love with someone who doesn't exist.'

She'd spoken freely, while maintaining her dignity. She'd told it to him straight, now he knew everything. She couldn't bear to look at him, to see his reaction; he had remained so quiet throughout she was sure he was appalled by her.

'I told you, it makes no difference at all to me,' he replied softly, 'except I'm glad you've told me. Now you can share your burden. It seems to me that you're an amazingly strong, beautiful, selfless woman who has made a terrible sacrifice for the sake of her children. I cannot begin to understand your pain, but I know it will be unbearable for I do not recognise the cold, cowardly, calculating, woman you've portrayed to me. Believe me, it's not the woman sitting in front of me, the woman with whom I'm falling in love.'

He held out his hands, pulled her towards him and wrapping his arms around her shoulders, he drew her in before gently kissing her hair. They sat in silence watching as the water trickled over the glistening stones. The sound of birdsong echoed round the glade; she felt the wind's cooling breath brush across her cheeks. She felt the warmth of the sun shining on her back. Neither spoke, lost in their thoughts. Kate realised that from this moment on she could forever face her future.

Chapter 24

16th October 1956

Evelien bent over the cot and carefully tucked the blankets round each of her sleeping children. She ran her finger along each velvet cheek and glanced up at Jim who was leaning over the edge, peering affectionately at his son and daughter.

'They look so peaceful like that. Have you noticed how their little legs are always intertwined?' he asked. 'Do you know I think this is my favourite time of the day – well, that's apart from waking up beside you every morning,' he added smiling.

He put his arm around her waist and kissed her gently, 'I love you, Evelien Palmer, and I love my family. I'm happier than I've ever been in my life, just seeing them lying there, watching you with them. Well, I never thought I would enjoy being a father so much.' He hesitated before continuing. 'I wish tomorrow was over and we knew once and for all if it's all going to last, if they will finally become ours forever. But, Evelien, remember no matter what happens, what decision she makes, I shall always love you; I'll always have you and you'll always have me.'

Evelien's face remained impassive but she nodded gently in response. He embraced her again tenderly before they tiptoed across the landing towards their own bedroom. They undressed in silence and got into bed, shivering in the cool October air. Both lay staring at the ceiling, acutely aware of the others' tension. Evelien was the first to break the silence.

'What if she changes her mind and we lose them? I could not bear it if she changed her mind, now when we are this close to having them as our own. Do you not think these have been the longest four months of our lives?'

Jim reached over and squeezed her hand. There was nothing he could say to reassure her; they both had to face the reality that the decision might go against them and had to keep a check on their hopes.

They had applied for the adoption at the first possible opportunity, which was six weeks after the babies had been born. They couldn't have imagined how unbearably difficult the wait would be. They accepted the congratulations heaped upon them by family and friends with guarded appreciation, for both were permanently weighed down by the realisation that the twins might never be theirs. They felt pangs of guilt as they listened to the admiring comments of total strangers who debated whether the beautiful twins, wrapped up snugly in their pram, resembled their mother or father more. They were conscious that they were claiming ownership of another woman's children, but it already felt like they were theirs. And now, hopefully, after four interminable months the agonising wait would be over; the decision would be made, the formalities finalised and the final stamp of approval given. They could breathe a sigh of relief and start to enjoy the rest of their lives as a fully fledged family. They dreaded and anticipated the decision in equal measure. It was unbearable.

*

Kate played with her food, pushing peas around her plate. Guy watched her as he polished off the last mouthful. He wiped his mouth with his napkin and set it down.

'Not hungry, darling?' he asked with concern.

'I'm sorry but I seem to have lost my appetite. I must appear very ungrateful, but I just don't seem to be able to face anything to eat. I'm afraid I'm not very good company tonight.'

Guy had taken her out to dinner at one of his favourite restaurants. He was hoping to distract her from her blackest thoughts. He realised that she was on the brink of a precipice, approaching the point of no return. This was the final opportunity for her to turn back, to stop the process, to take her children back and it was distressing her greatly. He wished he could do something to help.

'It's fine, I understand. Is there anything I can do?' he asked sympathetically.

'Help me to know that I'm doing the right thing,' she replied plaintively. 'Sitting here with you in this lovely place, it all seems so different. I feel that I've acted too rashly, that I've made the wrong decision, that I should admit my mistake and take back my beautiful babies. And then I'll go home and see Clare and I'll remember what it's like for her to grow up without a father around, the labels that define her. And how can I now, suddenly out of the blue, present the world with her fatherless brother and sister and throw even more fuel on the fires of shallow ignorant prejudice? She would wonder why I'd deceived her, deceived them all; confirm that I was an unfit mother. But that's my own cowardice talking.'

She paused, setting down her knife and fork before continuing. 'I've also got to think about them, haven't I? I mean the couple, whoever they are, who must think of my children as their own. They've cared for them for four months when I've not and surely they will have grown to love them by now, I know I would. Dr Greene explained it all to me, how they've waited ten years for a child of their own, it just didn't happen for them. They were absolutely overjoyed when they discovered that I'd had twins. 'Twice as good,' they said, apparently. How then could I be so cruel as to take this chance away from them, when they think they're theirs? It would be so wrong wouldn't it? I should never have considered going down this road, raised their hopes if I were going to change my mind. Oh Guy, I don't know what to do – I'm just so confused. I no longer know whose interests I'm seeking to serve because they all seem so at odds.'

He reached across and took her hand. 'Darling, I can't advise you what to do. What I can tell you though, is the fact that you're sitting here agonising over your decision proves to me that you are the principled woman I love. You've not mentioned your own feelings once; your concern is for your babies, for Clare, for your mother, for this other couple whom you've never even met; for everyone but yourself. Where do your needs come into this?'

'My needs, Guy,' she replied lethargically. 'My needs are to be convinced that I'm doing the right thing for my children and I mean all my children, all three of them.'

'So what is the right thing, for Clare and for your twins?' Guy coaxed gently.

She sighed as she lit a cigarette, slowly exhaling a plume of white smoke.

'I wish I knew. I suppose for Clare it's to leave things as they are, not complicate her life even more than it is already. For my twins, not to create those complications in the first place, which I suppose means leaving them where they are; leave them in the care of a couple who will love them and give them a life of relative normality.' She paused, drawing on her cigarette again. 'I should go through with it, shouldn't I? I just don't know what to do for the best. I thought I had decided, but I really don't know.'

Her eyes glistened as she spoke. Guy squeezed her hand across the table in sympathy. He ached for her and wanted to take away the pain, make it all alright for her, but he knew that she needed to do this alone and to reach her own conclusions.

She didn't say it, but Kate knew that meeting Guy had made the final decision even more difficult. When she'd handed them over, she had felt completely alone, there was no one who could share the burden and it had seemed the only viable option. It was too early to say, but perhaps now all that had changed. It added a further complication to an already impossible decision.

*

Evelien wept as they were told the news. Jim cradled her in his arms fighting back his own tears. They looked at each other shaking their heads in disbelief. Now they knew; the final decision had been made, but they couldn't take it in. The twins' mother had done the honourable thing. She had handed her children into their care; the final documentation had been signed by her on Wednesday 17th October 1956, and the adoption certificate had been issued. Richard and Helen Palmer had been delivered to them and their family life could begin in earnest.

*

Kate clung to Clare like she never wanted to let her go. She was now her only child incarnate. She held her, smelt her, gazed at her, listened to her rhythmical breathing, brushed her lips against her salty skin; she needed to excite every sense and to know that her child was with her. Clare wriggled uncomfortably in her mother's arms with the self-conscious objections of a ten-year-old. Kate reluctantly let her go but she had had her fill; finally perhaps she could put her demons to bed.

Chapter 25

July 1957

Kate stood on the foredeck, threw her head back and allowed the force of the air to lift her arms. She felt like a swallow in flight. The wind tousled her hair as the taste of the sea dissolved on her lips. In front of her the sea bubbled its foam, splitting open as the boat cut its path. She looked round sharply as Guy shouted the warning that he was going about. She braced herself as the boat curved round, listening to the heavy clunk of the mainsail as the mast swung across into position. She staggered back towards the stern, gripping the guard rail tightly, swaying in time with the boat. She laughed as she stumbled down beside Guy, who was fighting with the tiller in an effort to maintain their course. The wind was picking up and had changed direction. It was causing the yacht to pitch and roll.

'I think we should head in, what do you think, John? We're getting up quite a swell and we don't want Kate to be completely put off on her first trip.'

John Reid nodded, looking towards the sky he noticed the stream of grey clouds that were starting to roll in from the west.

'Yes, think you're right there, Guy; what do you reckon, Susan, had enough? We can head towards Lulworth Cove and anchor for the night; should be there in about an hour.'

Susan nodded gratefully as she handed Kate a gin and tonic. 'You don't know how thankful I am that you're on this trip. Usually I'm left to the mercy of the elements and my husband's steely determination to reach his destination come what may. Sailing glamorous? Don't you believe it, a wind-blown, queasy, galley slave that's my usual role,' she protested, pulling a face, before handing John a drink as well.

'Admit it, you love it, almost as much as I love you,' he retorted before giving her a peck on the cheek.

Kate and Guy had been invited to spend the weekend on the Reid's brand new yacht and jumped at the chance. John and Susan were intending to spend a couple of weeks exploring the south coast and were keen to share the excitement with their friends. Guy had done some sailing with John at Oxford, but had to admit that he felt much more at home in the cockpit of a Spitfire. Still, it was a great opportunity to see them both again and spend some idyllic time with Kate; an entire weekend's sailing off the south coast was the perfect opportunity. They finished work early on Friday, packed the car and drove down to meet the Reids at Poole Harbour.

John and Susan were delighted, if not a little surprised when, the previous autumn, Guy had sheepishly admitted to them that Kate had become much more to him than an excellent secretary. In hindsight, Guy suspected that he may have been the willing victim of a deliberate conspiracy, hatched by Susan and executed by John.

With the help of his partner Meredith Jones, he had succeeded in establishing a lucrative and highly respected solicitors' practice. He was determined to enjoy the fruits of his labour to the full, working and playing hard and revelling in the freedom afforded to him by bachelorhood. He had lost none of his youthful vigour and relished tackling the most physical and mental of challenges. He spent his winters skiing in Norway and his summers climbing in the Alps. The previous year, an almost fatal attempt on the north face of the Eiger had merely served to spur him on to try again. He was irresistibly drawn towards the next perilous challenge, fuelled by a voracious hunger to prove, to no one but himself, that he could do it. It was this insatiable inner drive that had seen him gain a First from Oxford, seen him safely through the War, moulded his business, dictated his hobbies and influenced his general outlook on life. He had watched in bewilderment as, one by one, his former comrades in arms had shackled themselves to the responsibilities of marriage and fatherhood. It was not for him. Not for him, that was, until the moment a tall, sad-looking beauty had entered his world. She had changed it, and him, forever. He now knew what true fulfilment meant; he could finally stop searching, stop pushing himself to the limit. With her, he had found himself at last.

The party sailed into the shelter of the beautiful little horseshoe cove and dropped anchor offshore. As they had approached the entrance, they noticed that the dark clouds that had threatened to dampen their enthusiasm had blown out to sea, and the wind had dropped to a warm, brisk summer breeze.

They ate on the boat, happily chatting as they drank bottles of white wine cooled by the sea. As they sat contentedly gazing towards the narrow entrance and the horizon beyond, Guy leant over the edge and pulled on a small rope until a bottle of Bollinger emerged with a plop from its briny refrigerator.

'Fancy a trip to the shore, my darling?' he asked holding up the bottle in anticipation. Susan and John exchanged knowing glances.

'I'd love to but is there enough room for everyone? I'm not sure there's even room in there for two of us.' queried Kate, glancing at the little rowing boat they had trailed behind them all day.

'We're quite happy sitting here watching the sun go down, aren't we, darling?' asked John rhetorically, putting his arm round his wife. 'No we're fine, you two young love birds go off by yourselves. Though on second thoughts, as you say, it is a lovely balmy evening and the cove does look very inviting…' he added mischievously. Susan dug him in the ribs.

Kate stepped cautiously into the little rowing boat. Dramatically she had feared that it was tied there in case the yacht sank; it hadn't occurred to her that it could serve a much more romantic purpose in carrying them to the shore.

She sat down and leant back against the stern as Guy attached the oars to the rowlocks and pulled away towards the shore. He had packed a rug, the champagne and two glasses. They landed and dragged the boat up the narrow, deserted pebbly beach. A wall of chalky cliffs loomed up ahead encircling them in its arms.

'Durdle Door's in that direction,' explained Guy pointing to the west, 'and over there is Fossil Forest. The cove is a masterpiece of natural sculpture, carved by the sea.' Kate looked at him in admiration.

'It's beautiful, so peaceful. I feel like you've brought me into another world,' she observed, gazing round the sweep of the cove in awe.

The sun was setting, like a Turner seascape, in a blaze of ochre and cadmium red; the moon was smiling through the scattered clouds. The air felt warm as it breathed across the shore.

Guy flicked a rug unto the beach with one hand, straightened it out and sat down, still deftly holding the bottle of champagne. Kate flopped beside him raising the two glasses above her head as she fell back unto the rug. They sat gazing out to sea watching the moored yachts bobbing gently, listening to the gentle clink of halyard on mast vaguely audible in the now still air. Kate lit a cigarette and leant back against him, inhaling the smell of the sea mingled with fresh tobacco.

The champagne cork flew off into the fading light as Guy filled her glass with the frothy juice. She took a sip and sighed in contentment. They sat watching in silence as the sun finally set and the moon took over, lighting up the cove like an outdoor theatre.

'Heavenly, isn't it.' Kate whispered. 'The perfect end to a perfect day; the sound of the sea, a beautiful sunset, cold champagne... you. Do you know, I think I'm a little bit tipsy,' she giggled as she leant over and kissed him, tasting the sweet liquid on his lips. 'I love you so much.'

He balanced his empty glass on the rug and sat up kneeling before her. She looked at him sleepily, smiling languorously as he bent to kiss her. He smiled at her before he reached in his pocket and surreptitiously pulled out a small, red leather box.

'Darling Kate, it is the most beautiful evening, but there's something else that would make it even more perfect for me,' he started nervously. 'I love you more than I can ever tell you, my beautiful girl. Would you do me the incredible honour of becoming my wife?'

She sat up noticing the box for the first time. Her pulse raced as he opened it and the contents glinted in the bright moonlight. He took out a stunning diamond solitaire and paused as he held it over her finger. His hand was trembling. Kate's tipsiness vanished in an instant as the reality of what he'd asked her began to sink in. She gazed at him with her dark brown eyes as tears welled up and trickled over her cheeks.

'I'd love to be your wife, Guy,' she replied ecstatically. 'I can think of nothing in the world I would love more.'

He slipped the ring on her finger and kissed her passionately.

'Thank you, my darling, darling, Kate. I can't believe you've said yes. I'm so happy I can't tell you. I love you so much. Come on, let's go back and share our news with John and Susan, I can't wait to tell them.'

She looked at him suspiciously. 'And of course they would know nothing about this already, would they Guy Prosser?'

'Absolutely nothing at all,' he replied in fake innocence, grinning widely as he kissed her again. She laughed and leant on him as she attempted to stand; the champagne and emotion of the evening had taken their toll.

They giggled like school children as Guy struggled to row the small boat towards the yacht, fighting against the dizzying effects of the swell and the grape. They clambered aboard, falling onto the deck where John and Susan were waiting for them expectantly.

'Well?' asked Susan giving the game away immediately.

'Well what,' asked Kate, smiling naïvely, hiding her hand behind her back. Susan looked at Guy and raised her eyebrows. He nodded grinning.

'Is this what you mean?' Kate laughed, pulling her hand from behind her back and extending her finger, 'but, of course, Susan knew nothing about this, did she, Guy?'

Susan hugged her warmly in delight. John shook Guy's hand before cracking open another bottle of Champagne.

'To the one we thought had got away and his beautiful captor,' he cheered, raising his glass and emptying it in one as Susan followed his lead.

They decided to get married in September; they couldn't wait any longer to be husband and wife. They both wanted a small affair attended by their immediate families and a few close friends only. They booked the register office in Plymouth for the 14th September at eleven o'clock.

From their very first meeting Guy had shown remarkable sensitivity to Clare's needs, ever conscious that she might feel he was seeking to usurp her father. He was also anxious that she should not think her mother's attentions, until now lovingly lavished solely on her, were being diluted by her feelings for him. He insisted that when they were together, Clare should be given her place, included in their activities and involved in their conversations. As a result of his slow and thoughtful integration, Clare had started to demand that Guy should be included in everything; that it wasn't any fun without him. It amused Kate, who teased her daughter that she was highly insulted. Clare greeted the news of their betrothal with elation, especially when asked to be the only bridesmaid. Guy had filled the enormous gap left by her absent father. Kate's mother was relieved that, finally, it seemed Kate's life was heading in a direction that met with her full approval. Kate had been absolutely correct in her prediction; her mother had taken to Guy from their very first meeting.

For Kate it meant another chance of happiness, but it was more than that. She had loved Art with every fibre of her being, and still grieved bitterly for the husband she'd lost to the ravages of mental illness. It had seemed impossible that she should ever find love again and certainly not with a man who would even come close to Art. But in Guy she had met her soul mate; the two halves had been melded together and rejoined as one. They had an easy consciousness together, barely needing to explain what the other was thinking or feeling. Their time together was filled with laughter and love but always with an edge of challenge and lively debate that served to stimulate their fertile minds.

Their marriage was witnessed by the intimate party of Guy's parents, his brother Giles, Kate's mother, James, Clare, Rita, Mary, Annabel, Meredith Jones and John and Susan Reid. Sarah had expressed her surprise that Kate wasn't intending to invite one of her oldest friends, Bob Thompson.

'But Kate,' she'd protested, 'you've known him such a long time, since you were children. He was so good to you when you were living in Exeter; it was a relief to me to know that if you needed a friend he was there. He introduced you to Mrs Steele and look how he helped us all at your father's funeral. He's alone now that his parents have died. I don't understand why you haven't thought to include him; he's been a faithful friend to all of us for so long. You used to be so close.'

Her mother had unknowingly twisted a knife. Kate wanted to scream, to expose him for what he really was – a self-serving coward. A man whose first thoughts were for himself alone; a sham who had deserted her when she most needed help. Instead she made her excuse, simply explaining that they had invited enough people and it might be awkward for both Guy and Bob. Sarah had shrugged her shoulders and complied.

Kate looked radiant on the day, dressed in an elegant, cream crepe suit. Her happiness was almost complete. As she sat at the wedding breakfast and happily surveyed the faces of all the people she loved most in the world, her closest friends and her dear family, she reflected sadly on two empty spaces. Her world could never be completely whole.

The inner circle of confidants, Mary, James, Rita, John and Susan, those who had seen her through the worst of her pain, supported her at her lowest ebb, privately proposed a toast to a welcome ally, Old Father Time. He'd healed many of Kate's running sores, brought her renewed happiness and allowed her to get on with the rest of her life. They cheered enthusiastically as the happy couple set off in the little cream car to an accompanying cacophony of rattling tins. 'To ward off evil spirits,' James had explained to Clare as she carefully helped him to tie them to the bumper. He hoped that Kate's demons could now be laid to rest forever. He had his own demons, however, and was still wracked with guilt knowing that he had kept the twins whereabouts hidden from her. He cornered Mary and Rita as soon as the car disappeared out of sight and they could talk alone. They concluded that it would be best to share his secret with Guy and leave it to him to decide. James was delighted to pass the burden.

They honeymooned in Paris, spending two glorious weeks strolling along the leafy boulevards, soaking up the rich Parisian culture, loving each other. They climbed to the top of the Eiffel Tower and gazed along the Seine.

'It's a beautiful river scene, isn't it, but yet to me not quite the most beautiful,' Guy explained wistfully. 'Do you realise, darling, that I haven't given you your wedding present yet.'

'I don't need a wedding present, I have you, that's present enough, n'est-ce pas?' she said softly.

'Peut-être,' he replied, 'but I don't think that is quite enough. I have something else in mind for you. Unfortunately, I couldn't wrap it up and bring it with me otherwise I would have. I was going to wait until we were back in England, but standing up here, looking down at the Seine, well I think you should have it now.'

Kate looked at him intrigued.

'Remember where we were when I first told you that I was falling in love with you?'

'Yes, of course, I remember exactly where we were, at 'Titania's bower', on a glorious sunny summer's day; you brought a picnic. But what on earth has made you think about that? You're being very mysterious, my darling husband.'

'Well it's no longer Titania's bower, it's yours. It's your wedding present.'

'It's what? But how, what do you mean?' she queried, her excitement mounting.

'I mean I've bought it for you. I told Sam Gourley that I wanted it for my wife as her wedding present, so he agreed to sell it to me. You're the proud owner of a stretch of river bank and ten lush acres. I hope it will bring you good fortune.'

Kate's squeals of delight could be heard drifting across the Parisian sky. To her it was the most romantic of romantic gestures, from the man she now knew she loved as she had loved no other.

Chapter 26

Exeter, September 1960

Richard rubbed his little hand around the inside of his collar and wriggled his neck uncomfortably to relieve the stiffness of the crisp new shirt. As usual, his socks had managed to collapse and settle around his ankles, like a pair of rolled up sleeves. Evelien sighed, bent over and pulled them up again, neatly turning over the tops before pulling down the edges of his grey shorts.

'Got your bag for school?' she enquired, knowing the answer before she received it.

'Here it is, Mummy,' replied Helen triumphantly, as she handed it to her brother.

Evelien and Jim surveyed their children as they stood before them dressed, for the first time, in their smart new school uniforms.

'I can't believe it, their first day at school; where on earth have the last four years gone?' remarked Jim as he held up his camera. 'Come on a photograph for posterity – stand bedside your sister, Richard, and hold her hand. Say cheese.'

Richard grimaced as he reluctantly did as he was asked. Helen smiled enthusiastically.

They couldn't be more different, thought Evelien as she looked on with pride. It was hard to believe that they had been borne by the same woman. It amused her greatly every time she was asked if her twins were identical. It was not only a biological impossibility she thought, but one look at them would have corrected any possible doubt. Richard was boisterous, stubborn and only happy when he was charging about outside kicking his ball and scraping his knees. Helen was quiet and studious, neat and tidy, happy to sit for hours inside drawing or making puzzles. Helen had the blackest hair, yet her eyes were the most striking turquoise blue, while Richard was almost blond with large dark brown eyes. Like all children they had their squabbles, but Richard was immensely protective of his much more timid and shyer sister. He had been instructed by his parents to look after her on this their first day, and he was proud to have been invested with the responsibility.

They had brought Jim and Evelien immeasurable joy, enriching their lives more than they could ever have expected. They had disagreed about telling their children the truth regarding their origins. Jim believed that they should be told that they were adopted, from the very beginning; then they would always know that they had been specially chosen because their parents had wanted them so much. Evelien didn't agree. She didn't want anything to come between her and her children's love. She had finally conceded, but very reluctantly. She wasn't at all convinced. Up until now, any difference hadn't seemed to register much with the children, especially as Evelien avoided the topic whenever possible and few people actually knew. Evelien was anxious that now when they were going to school, and mingling with new friends, they would begin to understand more and accept less. She feared that they would realise they were different and resent her for it. It added to the normal maternal anxieties about leaving her babies to school for the first time.

Jim bent down and hugged them both. 'Remember, I want to hear all about it when I get home, every single detail.'

He kissed Evelien and headed out the door, humming. Evelien walked the short distance to school, proudly holding each of her children by the hand. She felt strangely nervous for them; this day was proving to be a trial for her as much as for them. She led them into the small, well-lit classroom where they were met by their teacher, Mrs Bates, a kindly looking woman in her late forties. Evelien helped them to find their seats, looking down in amazement at the minute chairs neatly positioned side by side, each one neatly tucked under a miniature desk. A label with their names, Richard and Helen Palmer, had been Sellotaped to the top of one of them. On every desk there was a tin containing the fattest pencils Evelien had ever seen, as well as an assortment of brightly coloured crayons.

'I thought I'd let them sit beside each other, just for a week or so until they have settled in,' Mrs Bates explained. 'Now don't you worry, Mrs Palmer, they'll be fine. I find it's much, much worse for the mothers than it is for the children. It will be time to pick them up before you know it. Quite the little man, isn't he?' she said with amusement, looking across towards Richard who, hands in pockets, was showing Helen and a number of the other children where they should hang their coats and leave their bags. Evelien smiled.

'Very different to each other, aren't they? One has got your blond hair and the other your blue eyes; perhaps they look like your husband. Excuse me please, Mrs Palmer, I think I might have a bit of a job on my hands,' she suddenly announced as she glanced around the room, which by now was filled with the sounds of wailing children and weeping mothers.

Evelien didn't want to correct her mistaken assumption; they were her children and that was all she needed to know. It did matter to her, though, it mattered a great deal. Each small, seemingly innocent, incident added to a constant niggling fear. It was a fear borne from the belief that they were hers only by default and that one day she would eventually lose them to their birth mother; the law of nature would draw them back to the woman who'd borne them and supersede any law of man. It made her overly protective of them and paranoid. Again and again, Jim had tried to reassure her that their identity had been protected, that their birth mother had no idea who they were, or where they were, and that Dr Greene had been ever so careful. In any case, she was the mother they loved, the woman that they would stay with forever. She should relax and enjoy her children. Her head told her he was right, her heart couldn't concede. It was a constant worry.

Evelien thanked Mrs Bates and left the room quietly without disturbing her children further. Richard was in his element bossing the other children around, while Helen was standing happily looking at the shelves of library books. She knew they were going to be absolutely fine. Their birth mother, she reflected, wherever she was, should be immensely proud of what she'd done with them. She wondered which of their features they did take after her.

*

Kate breathed deeply in an effort to stave off the next wave of excruciating pain. Guy paced up and down the hospital corridor anxiously waiting for news. Kate had been in labour for over five hours and the wait was interminable. He was convinced that something was wrong. Kate had ballooned to unrecognisable proportions, almost from the moment she had overwhelmed him with the news, in March that she thought she was pregnant once more. He couldn't believe that her perfectly smooth skin could stretch so much without splitting open. To him though, she had never looked lovelier as her normally slim body developed curves and a voluptuousness he wouldn't have thought possible. There was little doubt in the doctor's mind that she was expecting twins once again, and it added a complication to the birth that worried him sick. Why was it taking so long?

He turned round sharply as he heard the sound of a nurse's brisk step approach from behind. One look at her face told him everything he needed to know. The waiting was over.

'Mr Prosser?' she started smiling. 'You are the proud father of two healthy twin boys. Your wife is very tired, it was a difficult birth, but she did remarkably well, all things considered. Would you like to see your sons?'

'My sons?' replied Guy in astonishment, the words sounded wonderful. 'My sons,' he repeated as if the classification shouldn't quite be ascribed to him. 'Of course, I'd love to, thank you.'

He walked into the delivery room in a daze, hardly knowing what to expect. Kate lay on the bed looking pale and exhausted but amazingly beautiful. He leant over the bed and kissed her tenderly. 'I love you,' he whispered in her ear. Resting on each arm was a wrinkled bundle of pink baby. He smiled and kissed each one on the forehead. 'My sons,' he said quietly as he gently touched each head. 'My beautiful boys in the arms of my beautiful wife. I am a very lucky man.' He was moved beyond words.

Kate stayed in hospital for a full week. The babies were small and slightly jaundiced but otherwise they were thriving and Kate was enjoying every exhausting minute with them, as she drank in their smell and caressed their soft, warm bodies. She was relishing the unadulterated joy of motherhood. Periodically, however, the unique scents and sounds of her newborns, unleashed a flood of painful memories as she was transported back to the time when she had last experienced them. She was overcome by an overwhelming sense of loss. She clung to her sons comforting herself that this time it was fine to bond; this time it was for good. She could enjoy these children today, tomorrow, the next day and for the rest of her life. She grieved for her lost children, she grieved for the loss of the careless girl she had once been; she despaired of a society that would so readily condemn her.

Eventually Kate was allowed home. Guy and Clare had prepared everything for the homecoming, each revelling in the excitement. Guy had secretly arranged for the babies' room to be redecorated as a surprise for Kate. He ensured Clare was not left out. She was allowed complete control of not only the choice of paper and curtains, but also a complete overhaul of her own room as well. Clare was ecstatic that, at last, she had become a big sister.

She fussed over her baby brothers with the enthusiasm of a fourteen-year-old girl, herself on the brink of young adulthood. In the afternoon, Kate's mother, her cousin Rose and James arrived laden with presents. The house was a whirl of visitors, congratulations and joy. Kate, the outcast, had become Kate the icon.

'Any names yet?' asked James holding one of his nephews. 'We can't keep calling them 'the twins' forever.' He blushed as he noticed Kate's expression and realised his mistake. This was not the first time the term had been used. He looked at her apologetically.

'I was wondering the same,' added Sarah rocking the other baby.

'Well, after much debate, we've finally agreed,' replied Guy. 'Do you want to tell your mother, Kate?'

'I think it's a case of keep it in the families, isn't it, Guy? They're to be named after their maternal and paternal grandfathers. James you're holding Matthew Thomas and Mum you're holding Michael James. I hope you're pleased.'

'I couldn't be more pleased, your father would be delighted. I wish he could be here to see them. Not one, but two grandsons at last,' she responded.

Kate carefully avoided Guy's and James' gaze. If only you knew, she thought uncomfortably.

She was relieved when everyone left and she was finally able to flop on the sofa. Clare had already helped her to bath the babies and now all her children were tucked up in bed, sleeping soundly. At last she was able to spend some time alone with Guy, but she was very tired and feeling morose. The day had reignited another trail of difficult memories. She had brought these babies home, she had introduced them to her family; she had wholly incorporated them into her life. She was finding the whole experience a bewildering contradiction of extreme joy and extreme pain.

Guy brought her a cup of tea, which she sipped slowly as she smoked her final cigarette of the day.

'Are you alright, darling?' he asked with concern as he sat beside her. 'You don't seem yourself.'

'Thank you, I'm fine. I'd forgotten how tiring it all is, the sleepless nights, the early wake up calls. Of course I only had it for four days with them...' she tailed off.

'With whom?' he asked puzzled.

'With my other 'twins', as James so thoughtfully reminded me,' she added irritably, gazing wistfully into the distance. 'It's brought it all back to me; just now bathing our boys with Clare, feeding them, tucking them in, kissing them goodnight. It's brought it all back. It feels like there's a gaping hole that can never be filled. When my mother talked about how happy she was to have her first grandson, I felt like a bit of me had died inside. I didn't dare to look at James or you. I wanted to tell her that she already has a grandson and another granddaughter for that matter, but of course I couldn't. Once again, it's hammered home to me that I live this enormous lie. And then when we told her their names, it was as if the boys had finally developed their unique identities, come into their own, they were real little people and part of this family. And then I realised, I have two more children and I don't even know their names. Do you know, Guy, I think it would help so much if I at least knew their names. They would not forever be known to me, to James, to you, as the anonymous 'twins'; as if they didn't actually exist. I'm sorry, I shouldn't bother you with all of this – it's my problem and I need to get over it. It should be such a happy time for you and I'm spoiling it. Perhaps it's the baby blues talking... I just wish I knew their names. I don't know why but it just feels like it would help.'

Guy put his arm around her shoulders and held her close. He sat deep in thought, a rush of options running through his mind. He could see her intense pain.

'There may be a way, Kate,' he eventually said softly.

'A way for what?' she asked wearily.

'A way to find out their names, if it's that important to you, and you think it would help, there may be a way.'

Kate sat bolt upright. 'But how? How on earth could we find out their names? Dr Greene was so careful not to tell me anything. What are you talking about, Guy, how could I find out their names?' she demanded in a state of agitation.

'Darling, I wasn't sure if I should tell you this and I hope to God that I'm doing the right thing, but I think you have a right to know.'

'Know what, Guy? What have you not told me?' She was starting to get distressed.

'James told me that just after you handed over your babies, at Dr Greene's surgery that day, you felt faint; is that right?' She nodded vigorously.

'Well, apparently when Dr Greene left the surgery briefly, to get you some water I believe, James noticed the adoption file sitting on his desk. He read it, Kate.' She gasped, clutching her hand to her mouth, wide-eyed.

'He saw the names of the couple who adopted your babies.'

Kate sat, shocked to the core.

'He saw their file. But why did he hide it from me? Why have you all hidden this from me, who else knows for God's sake? How could you be so cruel? You of all people, Guy, I thought you loved me,' she shouted.

Her accusation hurt him deeply but he understood it was spoken in anger.

'Of course I love you, it's because I love you so much that I didn't tell you. We thought it would bring it all back to you, open up old wounds and that you needed to be able to look forward, not to be reminded of the past. We did it for the best of motives. James told me just after we got married; he felt I should decide whether you should be told or not. I thought then that it was right to keep it from you, I couldn't see how it would help, but now I think you should know.'

'I can't believe what you're telling me, you know their names and you've kept them from me. What are they, what are they called?' she shouted, becoming frantic.

'I only know their surname,' he replied softly, 'their Christian names weren't on the form. It was too soon for that.

Their name is Palmer, darling. The couple who adopted them are called Evelien and James Palmer.'

Kate sat in a daze. She was trembling but was desperately trying to calm down and to take it all in.

'I can't believe it, Palmer, their name is Palmer,' she repeated slowly shaking her head. 'All this time you knew and you didn't tell me. I can't believe that you knew and you didn't tell me. Well, it's something I suppose, but it's not enough. I need to know their Christian names as well.'

'But why, Kate, what good will it serve to know?' Guy asked with growing concern.

'I need to know, I can't really explain why; I just need to know. I suppose it's important for me to know them as the rest of the world knows them. I feel excluded, cheated somehow. Other people knowing what I don't. I realise that I'm not making much sense, it's really hard to explain, but I feel that I can never truly rest until I know their names.'

'There is a way we could find out,' he continued cautiously, against his better judgement. 'We know the names and the address of the adoptive parents, and the date, of course. We could go to London to a building called Somerset House and ask to see a copy of the adoption records. It could be done quite easily.'

'You know the address as well, where they're living? Tell me then, where are they?' She was starting to get agitated again and was hardly listening to what he was saying to her.

'Well, all we know is where they were four years ago; they were living in Exeter. The address then was Chestnut Grove, I can't remember the number but James knows.'

'But I know where that is, I've seen it. It's not far from the park – there's a school near there where one of the girls from the College did her final teaching practice. I've walked past that road many times. It's really nice there, Guy. They built new houses after the war. They're living in Chestnut Grove, I can't believe it. Well at least I know they're living somewhere nice, somewhere respectable. Four years ago you say, so, of course they could have moved by now, but if they moved into a new house… Guy, it's just occurred to me, it's September and they're four now, they'll have started school; that school I mentioned, probably. It would make sense, it's only about a couple of hundred yards away. Just think, I may know which school they go to. Someone I know could be teaching there now, perhaps actually teaching them. I might know their teacher. Just think about it, Guy, I know where they're living. I could go to see them,' she exclaimed excitedly.

'Please, darling, don't get carried away, think about what you're saying. They belong to another couple now and you have your own family to care for, Clare, Matthew and Michael. Don't open the old wounds that time has taken so long to heal.'

'I'm sorry, it's just that they seem so much closer now, more real to me. I know I gave away my rights to them, but they're still my children, my flesh and blood; I gave birth to them. Please could we at least find out their names? Just that and then I'll be happy.'

Guy wasn't convinced that he had done the right thing. Would it end, if he helped her to find out their names? He couldn't be at all sure, but it had been his suggestion; it was he who had raised her expectations so he would have to go through with it.

'Just their names and no more, promise me, Kate. I'll go to London with you to find out their names, but that is all,' he conceded. She nodded in agreement. It was a start.

Kate was impatient to get the records as soon as possible, so she insisted that they travel to London the following week. Guy had urged her to slow down, to think about what she was doing, to wait until the boys were older, but her mind was made up and he realised how utterly stubborn she could be. In truth, he had an ominous feeling about the whole matter.

They needed an excuse to be away, to be in London, so he concocted a story for Kate's mother that he wanted to buy Kate a piece of jewellery as a surprise, and would prefer to get it in London. Her mother, although disapproving that they were leaving the twins alone so soon and all for the sake of buying a trinket, kept her opinions to herself. She was happy to look after her three grandchildren for the day.

They caught an early train, arriving in at Paddington by ten o'clock before taking the underground to Charing Cross. Kate had never been to London before, but Guy's attempts to engage her in any conversation about the cultural landmarks they passed on their journey were dismissed by her singularity of purpose, which was to get to Somerset House as quickly and directly as possible. She walked into the spectacular neo-classical building, oblivious to its architectural magnificence or historical significance. They made their way to the North Wing as instructed. Guy had made all the necessary preliminary enquires so within half an hour she was presented with the documentation she so desperately sought, the culmination of her quest. He sat by her side, holding her hand, as with trepidation she was handed each certificate. The names were noted in neat handwriting.

'It's Helen and Richard,' she said simply, swallowing hard. 'Helen and Richard Palmer. I like those names. I think they've chosen well, don't you? Thank you, Guy, you don't know how much this means to me.'

She was overcome by emotion. She sat staring at the certificates. As she read each name it felt like she was being formally introduced to her children for the very first time; they finally had an identity. It brought the enormity of what she had done home to her. It had opened the old wounds as Guy had dreaded.

'I think we should leave now, darling, we've got what we came for. I hope it's given you the comfort you needed. Let's go and have some lunch.' Guy suggested kindly. Kate didn't feel in the least bit hungry, but she knew that she needed to leave. She had a final look at the file.

'Why do you think her name is spelt like that?'
'Whose, darling?'

'The mother. E-V-E-L-I-E-N,' she spelt out. 'Strange don't you think?'

'Is that strange? I hadn't noticed. Perhaps it's foreign.'

'Perhaps,' replied Kate softly, as she handed back the file. She walked from the building deep in thought, the day was taking its toll and she was feeling tired, but she didn't want to spoil it for Guy who was keen to make the most of an unexpected trip to London. He knew that he needed to lighten her mood, to distract her thoughts and focus her attention in another direction.

They had lunch at Simpson's. Kate's malaise started to lift with each glass of chilled white wine. She began to feel quite decadent, drinking at lunchtime, relaxing in London while her mother struggled to look after her two demanding babies. She missed them but was enjoying having some time completely alone with Guy. As they emerged into the street she began to notice the vibrant colours and sounds of the bustling city. It seemed so liberated. Kate saw in the faces of the young men and woman the girl she used to be, the girl she would have wanted to be, free and utterly at ease with herself. She began to feel old at thirty-four.

'Come on, I want to take you somewhere,' urged Guy as he took her hand and started to stride off with uncharacteristic purpose. He slowed when they turned into Regent Street, gazing around looking for his chosen location. He finally stopped outside his destination and gestured her inside. She glanced up at the sign, 'Mappin and Webb'.

'Oh Guy, what is this?' she asked, her excitement building.

'I wanted to get something for you, for the woman I love and now the mother of my beautiful sons. I want you to choose something really nice. I thought perhaps you might like an eternity ring,' he explained grinning.

Kate entered the jewellers in a state of awe – she was a child again. She left the shop an hour and a half later wearing a ring set with round, brilliant cut, white diamonds. She was speechless; it had been a day of roller coaster emotions. She felt that her life was one of the most extreme contradictions; ill fate and good fortune her lot in equal measure.

They arrived back late. Kate's mother was exhausted and was delighted to hear them returning at last. She admired the ring with the cool enthusiasm she generally applied to gifts. She was very fond of her son-in-law but thought that he overindulged Kate. Kate couldn't wait to look in on her sons and Clare.

'They've only just gone off to sleep; I think they realised that you weren't there. Don't wake them,' her mother chastised mildly. Kate felt the hint of reproach, presumably in respect of her unwarranted absence. She didn't care if she woke them because she wanted to hold them; she needed to feel them alive in her arms. She went into their room and lifted each sleeping child in turn. She took comfort from their wails; they'd missed her. With them, she was able to fulfil her full role as loving mother, providing help and succour to her children whenever they needed her.

'Has today helped?' asked Guy tentatively, when she finally got the boys back to sleep and they were downstairs alone.

'I think so. I suppose I feel that at last I can put names to faces, although of course much older faces than when I last saw them. I often imagine what they might look like now. They were so different when they were born; ebony and ivory. Richard was very blond and Helen was really dark.' She stopped speaking, acutely aware that it was the first time she had actually used their names. No, if she were honest with herself, today hadn't helped at all; in fact it had only served to bring them to life again. If anything it had strengthened her resolve to see them in the flesh.

'Yes, darling, thank you it has helped a lot; finally put my mind at rest,' she replied guardedly. 'I can't thank you enough for sorting everything for me and for my beautiful ring. I'm a very lucky woman. I love you,' she added smiling.

'I love you too. I'm so relieved, I thought it might open old wounds and, I've got to admit, I was worried that it wouldn't be enough. I'm so glad it has settled things for you; hopefully now you can put it all to bed, get on with life and enjoy the boys.' Guy put his feet up on a footstool and smiled with contentment.

Kate sat quietly. There were some things best left unsaid.

Chapter 27

Plymouth, October 1960

'Is that the doorbell?' asked Guy glancing at the clock as he set his mug of morning coffee on the table. 'Eight o'clock on a Saturday, who on earth is calling at this time in the morning?'

He got up from the table and returned carrying a large soft parcel. 'Only the postman; it's for you, darling. Secret admirer?' he teased as he set it down.

'If only,' laughed Kate, setting down a bottle of warm baby milk before she ripped off the string and brown paper.

'Bet they're from Rita,' she said, as she lifted out a couple of delicate, hand crocheted shawls. 'They're lovely aren't they? She's obviously been busy, bless her. There's a card and a letter addressed to both of us.'

Kate handed over the card as she started to read the letter. 'She's sprained her ankle otherwise she would have brought the present in person. She'd love to see the babies, but she's finding it difficult to get around, although from what she says some of her friends from the church have been helping her.'

'She's a good woman, Kate – bit holy and conventional if I may say so – but a good woman,' Guy mused as he read the card with its addendum. '*Suffer the little children to come unto me, and forbid them not: for of such is the kingdom of God.*'

'Perhaps there's more to her than meets the eye,' challenged Kate, defending Rita fiercely. 'Think you might find she's not as conventional as she likes us and the rest of the world to believe. Don't call her 'holy', Guy, it sounds like a criticism; Rita lives by her strong beliefs in a quiet unassuming way, that's all.'

'I'll take your word for it,' Guy answered doubtfully, setting the card on the table.

'Do you know,' Kate started tentatively as she continued to feed the babies, 'I think I'll drive over to Exeter and take the boys with me to thank her in person and see how she is. She said she'd love to see them.'

'Good idea, why don't we all go tomorrow, take Clare and make a day of it,' suggested Guy enthusiastically.

Kate stalled before continuing. 'Could do I suppose. Mind you, Sunday probably isn't the best day to go. She's always so tied up with church things and visiting Stan's family and it's a bit short notice for her. Think I'd rather go during the week sometime.'

'She won't be going out if she's sprained her ankle, surely? Just thought it would be easier for you, rather than having to go all that way with the boys on your own. You're not used to driving such a long way. Why don't you take your mother with you then, if you prefer to go during the week, and she can help you?' suggested Guy thoughtfully.

'Well we'll see. It's a good idea, but Mother doesn't really know Rita and she's so house-proud, she'd feel she had to fuss about, spring cleaning before we came and what with her sprained ankle and everything that wouldn't be fair on her. She won't mind so much if it's just me. Anyway we can talk more freely if it's just the two of us... I'll probably need my mother to keep Clare after school for me; I doubt if I'll be back in time and I'd feel I have to rush away if we were both there. I'll be fine driving, the Rover is easy. Could you take Clare to school on your way to work for me?'

Kate was feeling guilty, she was conscious that she was spouting a stream of pretty lame excuses. The truth was she wanted to go to Exeter alone.

'Well, if you insist, but I think you're making it all unnecessarily difficult for yourself, darling,' replied Guy, acquiescing.

Kate was up early the following Wednesday morning and had bathed and fed the twins before anyone else emerged. She hadn't slept well and was feeling tired and agitated.

She wanted to get on the road, as soon as possible, and was uncharacteristically irritable with Clare and Guy who seemed to be dawdling unnecessarily over their breakfast.

'Come on you two, hurry up, or you're going to be late for school and I don't want to be late setting off,' she snapped.

Guy looked at his watch in surprise. 'What's eating you this morning, darling, it's only a quarter to eight and we've plenty of time?' he remarked reasonably.

'Sorry,' she replied sheepishly, 'I didn't sleep very well. I'm feeling a bit over tired, that's all. Take your time, it's not that late.'

'Why don't you go on then, get on the road early and then you won't be back so late. Clare and I can sort everything out here, can't we?' he nodded towards his stepdaughter looking for agreement. 'We'll help you to load up the car. Come on, Clare, you carry the wheels and I'll bring the carry cot.'

He packed the boot, before placing the twins on the back seat. 'Drive carefully, won't you, and we'll see you this evening. What time do you think you'll be back?' he asked, as he kissed her tenderly on the cheek.

'I will. I'll be back around tea time probably, but I'm not sure exactly when. Mother is going to come over to the house, once she's picked Clare up from school, so she can sort something for you to eat if I'm a bit late.'

She waved goodbye to them, aware as she set off that she felt on edge and nervy. She hadn't been back to Exeter, let alone Rita's house, for over four years; not since she had handed over the twins and she was feeling the pain of the memories as they began to flood back and threatened to overwhelm her. Every mile she drove towards her destination brought the agony back that bit more acutely. She drove overcautiously, conscious of the precious load she now carried on the back seat. She was aware how little she had driven outside of Plymouth and she was finding the country roads narrow and claustrophobic. She felt she needed to negotiate every twist and turn with the utmost care. She had learned to drive in

America, in a much larger car than the family Rover, but there, the wide open roads seemed to part naturally allowing the traffic to pass through freely. Now she felt hemmed in as the road, overhung by a thick canopy of trees, seemed to narrow and lower as it led into the distance. The journey was long and tedious; the twins were getting restless in the back. They were hungry and in need of a change. She was thoroughly regretting her decision to venture out alone by the time she finally hit the outskirts of the city, an hour and a half later. She arrived at Rita's house tired and emotional. She breathed a sigh of relief as she parked the car outside on the road. She left the twins in the back and walked to the door to check Rita was in. She knocked it with a sense of trepidation; her hand was shaking. It seemed like an age before she heard Rita turning the lock. She stood trembling on the other side, fighting back her emotions as the door was dragged back and she was greeted by the smiling face of her close friend and confidante.

'Kate, what on earth is it?' asked Rita, alarmed by the unexpected reception. 'Has something happened to the twins? Where are they?' She walked into the street in a panic, hobbling on a stick and obviously in considerable pain.

'They're fine, they're fine. I left them in the car; I'll fetch them in. I'm sorry, Rita, it's lovely to see you,' gabbled Kate, as she leant over and gave Rita an affectionate hug. 'I'm sorry, as soon as I was standing outside your door something seemed to snap inside. It's silly I know. I didn't mean to alarm you, I couldn't help myself. I'm fine, we all are. Really I am and I'm very pleased to be here.'

Kate wiped her eyes with the back of her hand as she walked to the car to fetch the boys. She struggled to lift the heavy cot off the back seat then staggered up the short drive, presenting them to Rita with pride. By now both babies were howling.

'My boys,' she stated simply.

'Well, there's nothing wrong with their lungs. Two beautiful wee babbies, and snugly wrapped in my shawls.

Och, aren't they like you?' remarked Rita, peering into the cot and smiling with pride.

'Do you mean they can howl?' laughed Kate regaining her composure.

'You know very well what I mean, come on in with you, it's good to see you smile,' retorted Rita in mock indignation, as she limped back into the house shaking her head.

Kate was finding it hard to be back in the house that held so many difficult memories, but nevertheless she felt relaxed and at ease with Rita. She knew that, for once, she could completely let down her guard and chat to her friend without the fear of inadvertent betrayal. It was a rare opportunity to speak freely and openly about everything. They fell into easy conversation and within an hour had caught up on every possible area of common interest.

They chatted about the family, events in Plymouth and the massive clear up following the floods that had hit Exeter earlier in the month. Neither as yet, had mentioned the unmentionable; they had both skilfully tiptoed around the subject of her first born twins. Kate did not want to admit to Rita what she now knew about them and Rita did not want to cause Kate unnecessary pain by bringing up the past. Kate was profoundly and uncomfortably aware that she was keeping some of her most exciting news – the fact that she knew their names and where they lived – from one of the few people with whom she could share it. She couldn't justify her omission with a clear conscience.

Rita fussed over the babies and fussed over Kate. She had made Kate a pot of her signature shin-bone soup and they sat contentedly eating and chatting. The tastes and smell invoked the most painful memories for Kate as she recollected the many times Rita had provided similar comfort in a bowl of steaming broth. She tried to put them out of her mind and concentrate on enjoying her time with the woman she viewed as a surrogate mother. After lunch, Kate fed the boys and placed them in their cot for their afternoon nap. She noticed that Rita was nodding off in her chair.

'Sorry, I'm not sleeping very well at the moment, my ankle gives me that much pain in bed,' apologised Rita as she woke with a start.

'Tell you what,' suggested Kate brightly, 'why don't you go and have a lie down for a while and I'll take the boys out for a walk. It's a lovely day and the park will be full of autumn colour. It's not that far and the fresh air will do us all good after being cooped up in the car for so long.'

Rita was relieved, her ankle was throbbing and she was exhausted. It was lovely to see Kate, as always, but she was struggling to maintain her enthusiasm.

Kate got the wheel base from the car and set the carrycot on top. She wrapped each baby in one of Rita's shawls and covered them with a couple of blankets. The sun was shining as its watery warmth heated a perfect autumn day. As she set off, she glanced at her watch; it was twenty to two. She reckoned it would take about fifteen minutes to walk to the park, so she set off at a brisk pace enjoying the fresh air. As she walked along to the sound of the pram crunching the golden leaves, she absorbed the familiar sights and sounds of the city in which she had spent nearly three years of her life. It all seemed like a distant memory; a time she had learned to put to the back of her mind, as the happiness of her current life had moved to the forefront. She turned the corner at the end of the street and walked along the road that led to the side entrance of the park. For the first time, in a very long time, Bob Thompson's pasty face flashed before her. Rita had carefully avoided any reference to him and she realised that she had no idea where he was or what he was doing. She was happy to keep it that way.

The last time she had seen him, they had been in this park. She was beginning to think that this visit back to Exeter had not been such a great idea after all; there were too many ghosts that needed to remain exorcised. As she walked towards the end of the road, deep in thought, she noticed, straight ahead of her, a small assembly of women happily chatting. They were standing outside the primary school. She glanced at her watch; it was approaching two o'clock. Her heart began to thump.

'Home time for the infants,' she said to herself out loud.

She walked towards the group trying to convince herself that she was merely on her way to the park, taking her children for some fresh air, that she just happened upon the group waiting for their children. She wasn't doing anything wrong, she wasn't doing anything out of the ordinary – she was blameless. She slowed her step as she approached the gathering. She stopped outside and observed the mass of tiny bodies emerging enthusiastically from behind the school doors, their faces lighting up like sunbeams as they were reunited with their mothers. She stood watching them, mesmerised. She scoured the faces, desperately seeking out a brother and sister; one blond one dark. She watched and waited viewing them all with the guilt of a voyeur. Nothing of note. She was beginning to attract the attention of the other mothers for whom she was an unfamiliar face. They assumed she was waiting for someone. She didn't want to talk to anyone as she didn't want to have to explain why she was standing there. She had no legitimate reason to be there. The longer she stood the more self-conscious she became; she needed to leave. As she turned and started to walk towards the park, half relieved, half bitterly disappointed, she felt the thump of a ball as it crashed against the wheels of the pram. It made her jump.

'Sorry, Miss.' The small, high-pitched voice was childish and contrite. She turned round towards its owner. The face that met her was framed with short, soft blond hair; a pair of large brown eyes stared out as the guilty child prepared himself for the expected remonstration.

'Richard,' called a woman's voice from behind them, crossly.

Kate fixed her gaze on him hardly able to speak.

'Richard, your name is Richard?' she whispered as she reached forward and placed her hand on his head. It felt warm and familiar. He recoiled as if she were about to strike him.

She stood in a trance, fixated on him, as time started to slow. He stood staring back at her unsure what to do or say next. They both stood completely still, looking straight at each other, neither speaking.

'Oh dear, I am terribly sorry, you must say apologies to the lady, Richard. He is always kicking his ball around. I hope he did not wake your baby. Say you are sorry to the lady,' repeated his mother, as she caught up with them.

The sound of her voice brought Kate back, as she regained full awareness and withdrew her hand. She looked at the woman, a small, slim blond with striking blue eyes and a faint accent. She was holding hands with a shy, dark haired girl. By now, both of them were bending over and looking into the carrycot.

'Goodness, it is twins. Look, Helen, twins just like Richard and you are. Good, they are still asleep. What are their names?' she asked pleasantly, looking round and smiling at Kate.

Kate felt a shot of adrenaline surge through her body. Her hands began to shake; her legs felt like they were melting beneath her. She stood pale and motionless, as she gripped the handle of the pram for support. She couldn't speak. She couldn't move.

'Are you alright, madam, you have become very white?' asked the woman anxiously, taking Kate by the elbow and looking into her staring eyes. Kate reached forward automatically and laid her other hand gently on the small girl's head. Her mother stood beside her transfixed, wary and unsure what to do or say next. An uncomfortable silence existed amongst them all.

'I'm fine,' Kate eventually answered in a monotone voice, as she slowly removed her hand. 'I'm fine. I think I have walked too far.' She turned the pram and started to walk back towards Rita's without saying anything else.

'What was wrong with that lady, Mummy? She scared me. Why did she put her hand on me like that?' asked Helen, looking up towards her mother's puzzled face. Evelien hadn't moved. She was staring at the woman's back, still not quite sure what she had witnessed. Richard stood awkwardly, holding his ball, biting his lip aware that something had happened to upset the woman and assuming that he was at fault.

'I do not know, but she was very strange. Do not worry, she has gone now. Did she say anything to you, Richard?'

He shrugged his shoulders, unsure if she had spoken to him or not. Evelien couldn't put her finger on it, but her instincts were warning her that there had been something unusual, almost sinister about the incident and she felt a growing sense of unease. The woman had placed her hand on Helen almost as if she knew her. She had kept it there and not spoken. Why had that peculiar look crossed her face? Why had she gone so pale and quiet all of a sudden? It was most disconcerting. The woman's odd behaviour unnerved her and it was obvious that the children had picked up something strange as well. They were still watching her, wide-eyed and wary as she walked away from them.

Evelien suddenly felt the need to get them back to the security of home and as quickly as possible. She took both children by the hand and started to drag them along the pavement.

They half-walked, half-ran in her wake as their little legs tried to keep up with her unusually rapid pace. By now her mind was racing with possibilities, her alarm and paranoia increasing with every step she took. She looked over her shoulder to check that the woman and her pram weren't following them. She could see them crossing the road in the distance. She waited until they were completely out of sight before turning into the street that led to the house. She opened the door, rapidly closing it behind them all as if she were shutting out an intruder. She leant against it and turned to both children.

'Richard, why can you not be more careful, and both of you, I have told you before you must not talk to strangers.'

They stood shocked by the force of their mother's scolding. They weren't at all sure what they had done to upset her so much. She sent them upstairs to their room to get changed. She needed time alone to think, to calm down; she knew she was upsetting them.

She sat at the table anxiously gripping the edge of the cloth. She tried to recall the sequence of events, to reason with herself that she was must be over-reacting to the most innocuous of situations. She looked perfectly normal, quite nice really, so why had she behaved so oddly and made them all feel so uncomfortable? It had been the most bizarre incident and it didn't make sense. Evelien couldn't get the strange look that had crossed the woman's face out of her mind. There had been something visceral in the way she had touched Helen. Why would she do that and then not say anything to her? Who was she and where had she come from? What did she want? Evelien tried to think if she had seen her somewhere before, but she was pretty sure she hadn't. Who on earth could she be? She desperately tried to keep her fears at bay, as an array of explanations flashed through her mind. Perhaps she hadn't been feeling well, that was why she was so pale and quiet, After all the babies were very young, she had probably walked too far with them and was tired. She ran through a host of reasonable explanations. She refused to allow the worst possibility of all to come into her mind, but it kept coming back. It didn't bear thinking about, and anyway, it couldn't have been *her* she reasoned, how could it be? Dr Greene had been so careful and she was sure he had said their mother had been a student at college… in that case she would only be in her early twenties and this was a mature woman, who had her own children… but then again she had twins, she was obviously prone to having twins. The more she thought about it, the more insidiously the possibility crept up on her. She couldn't eliminate it completely. Perhaps Dr Greene had got it wrong… that wasn't likely though. But then why else would she have behaved as she had? It was a plausible explanation. It was feasible. But then somehow she would have had to know who Helen and Richard were. She tried to think back, was she imagining it or had she also touched Richard's head. She couldn't remember; she had been looking at the pram, worried that he had disturbed the babies and she wasn't really looking at him. She tried to hear Jim's voice of reason, but she couldn't help it; she was becoming more and more convinced that they had encountered the children's natural mother. It must have been her – it would explain everything. And if that were the case, it was doubtful that it was merely serendipity but far more likely a carefully executed plan, and she was stalking them. That must be it. She had been waiting outside the school for them perhaps hoping to snatch them away. It was what she had warned Jim would happen; now he might believe her. It was her worst nightmare, they weren't safe and from now on she would have to watch her children day and night. She sat at the table working herself into a state of extreme agitation. She wanted to call Jim and tell him to come home immediately, to warn him that she needed to hide them all away.

*

Kate walked back towards Rita's deep in thought. She was sure she had seen her children; she was elated. She sought to convince herself that that was all that mattered. Except she knew it wasn't, because she knew she had transgressed. Their mother had realised who she was, she was sure of it. She felt confused, ashamed and excited. She had touched them, reconnected with them momentarily, but she knew that she had overstepped the mark; she had committed a moral indiscretion. She had given up all rights to them long ago and they were no longer her children, but for that brief moment she had reclaimed them. She felt that she could never confess to Guy; she could never confess to anyone. She berated herself, knowing that she should never do it again, but like a reformed alcoholic she had imbibed and, having done it once, she wondered could she resist temptation again.

She left Rita's almost as soon as she returned from the walk, suddenly anxious to get back to Plymouth and conscious that Rita was tired and in pain. She didn't want to discuss the walk with her; she didn't want to discuss anything. They embraced fondly promising to meet again soon. As she drove home, she felt like an adulteress preparing to confront her husband for the very first time, desperate to conceal her guilty secret. She had never hidden anything from Guy before. Right from the beginning it had been important to her that he should know everything. She was in uncomfortable, unfamiliar territory, as if an invisible wedge had been hammered between them. She didn't want her relationship with Guy, as with so many others, to be clouded by the constant need to maintain her guard. She struggled with her conscience. Should she tell him and pretend that it had all happened by chance? She knew he would quickly see through that, would know she had planned it and wonder why she had wanted to deceive him. She had been too eager to travel alone. If she confessed, and told him the truth, she knew he would be bitterly disappointed in her and probably angry; after all she had promised him that she would be content just to discover their names. She had let him down, she had let herself down and she felt it intensely. Moreover she realised, only too well, that the mother would probably deduce who she was. She had blindly gone through with it instinctively, impetuously, following a hunch, but she hadn't thought through the consequences, the aftermath, the implications for Guy, herself or most importantly, the mother.

*

Evelien had worked herself into a frenzy by the time Jim arrived home. The children had remained in their rooms, quietly hiding away. He was completely taken unawares, met at the door by a verbal tornado.

'She was there, she was there,' Evelien screamed. 'I know it was her, she touched them, she had come to take them away, but I was there so she could not, but she will come back, I know she will. They are not safe. How could she know where they were? Who told her? Dr Greene promised. We will have to move, move from this house, from Exeter, take them out of the school.'

'Evelien, what is it? Who was there? What has happened? Calm down you'll frighten the children. What has happened, tell me, you're worrying me.' He tried to restrain her in his arms as she pummelled his chest. 'For God's sake, calm down, tell me what's happened. Where are the children?' he shouted sharply as he led her into the kitchen and forced her into a chair. She started to calm, tears streaming down her swollen and reddened face.

She was sobered by the sound of his raised voice; it was sharp and unfamiliar.

'At the school, there was a woman with a pram, she put her hand on their heads, she was looking at them, I know it was her, the mother,' she blurted out in between semi-hysterical sobs.

'Evelien, where are the children now?' he asked again firmly.

'They are in their bedrooms. I sent them to their bedrooms. Jim, I know it was her, she was there, I am not mistaken, I know I am not.'

'Be reasonable, think about it, you don't know it was their mother. You saw a woman with a pram, she put her hands on their heads, she's a mother for God's sake, she was admiring them and that's all. Darling, you're imagining things. She can't know where they are, you know she can't. Tell me what exactly did she do?'

Evelien rattled out everything that had happened. She managed to calm down as the events unfolded. It all sounded so lame when she recounted it, actually sounded quite normal, there was nothing particularly out of the ordinary, but in her heart she was convinced that she had been confronted by their mother. There was no proof – the woman hadn't done anything particularly untoward. She had admired her children, briefly laid her hand on their heads, and on the surface it would appear that was all, but she knew differently. There had been something odd about her behaviour. She knew Jim thought she was being melodramatic and would never be convinced that she had legitimate fears, but she also knew that, if necessary, she would protect her children with the ferocity of an animal.

*

Kate arrived back in Plymouth, tired and mightily relieved to be home. Clare bounded out to meet her, happy to have her back, followed more slowly by her grandmother. They helped her to empty the car and carry everything into the house, politely enquiring about her day. She had hoped Guy would be home early, so she could hide under the cover of her mother's presence and have the perfect excuse for not revealing everything about the day's events straightaway. Her mother declined an invitation to stay for supper, so she was soon left alone with her children and her conscience. She heard his car arrive in the drive as she fed the babies. He came in grinning, happy to see her and the boys back safely.

'Great, you're back, darling. I was worried that you were going to be much later.' He kissed her fondly before bending over and kissing his sons and Clare. 'Good day? How's Rita?' She answered both questions truthfully but succinctly.

Kate spent the evening in a state of fake normality, idly chatting about nothing in particular. Underneath she was desperately wrestling with her conscience. She knew if she didn't tell Guy now, then it would be doubly difficult at another stage. She couldn't decide for the best, she hated her current life full of deceptions and the last thing she wanted was to deceive him. Thankfully Clare was still awake so there was time to decide.

'Goodnight, Mummy and Daddy,' Clare announced, coming down dressed in her pyjamas. 'See you in the morning.' Kate loved to hear Clare call Guy, 'Daddy'.

They were left alone. She listened to the clock tick quietly on the mantelpiece. She sat surreptitiously glancing at Guy who was smoking his pipe and reading a book. She lit a cigarette and sat in the chair picking at her cuticles, gazing at the brightly burning fire.

Guy looked across at her and smiled. 'You're fidgety tonight, what's up?' he asked, as he set down his book.

She looked him straight in the face, at his handsome, gentle, concerned face. 'Am I?' she answered. 'I've something on my mind that's all.'

'Sounds mysterious,' he replied continuing to smile.

'I know you're going to be angry with me, but I can't keep it from you. I don't want there to be any secrets between us,' she started her voice shaking.

He sat forward, frowning.

'Please don't be cross with me. I took the twins for a walk to the park today. We passed the primary school I told you about, when the children were getting out. I won't lie to you. I knew it was likely to coincide with our walk. I did it deliberately, that's why I wanted to go to Exeter alone. I knew you would be against it.' She couldn't meet his gaze.

'No, Kate, I can't believe you've done this, you promised me.' He sounded shocked, disappointed, disbelieving all in one.

'I'm sorry. I know I did, but that's not all,' she continued with a defiance she didn't feel. 'I saw them, Guy, I saw them with their mother. I'm sure I'm not mistaken. A blond boy and a dark haired girl, she called them by their names; she said they were twins, she had a strange accent. I touched them on their heads – I actually touched them with my hand. I'm sorry, I know I promised and I feel so ashamed; I don't think I really knew what I was doing. I just had to go. I didn't think I'd actually see them – I wasn't even sure they went to that school. It was a chance in a million. Please don't be cross with me, please understand, I had to go, I had to see that they were alright.'

'I should have realised,' he said his voice rising. 'I couldn't understand why you were making it all so difficult for yourself. You weren't going to tell me, were you? What changed your mind, did you think I would find out?' he demanded accusingly, as the reality of it sank in. 'I can't believe this. I'm so disappointed in you, Kate; you promised me, just their names, you said. I wouldn't have gone through with it, taken you to London if I'd suspected you would do anything so stupid. You had no right. They're someone else's children now. Did she see you touching them? Did you tell her who you were? Please God, tell me you didn't tell her who you were?' he asked frantically.

'No, of course not,' she answered defiantly. 'But I think she knew,' she added shamefacedly.

'What? Oh my God, Kate, I can't believe what you're telling me. What on earth have you done? Do you actually realise what you've done? The effect this will have on that poor woman, forever wondering if you're watching her, watching the children. I've acted professionally for lots of women who've adopted children and, believe me, their abiding fear is that they'll lose them; that they will eventually be drawn back to their birth mother. They are no longer your children – you have no legal right to them. She is as surely their mother now as if she had given birth to them. You must promise me that you will never repeat this folly, never. Swear it to me. I mean it, Kate, on your honour.' By now he was almost shouting at her, desperately trying to control his temper.

'I'm so sorry,' she replied with contrition. 'I know everything you've said is right. I knew it myself that's why I told you. I didn't think it through fully, really I didn't. I got swept away by the idea as soon as Rita's present arrived. Please don't be cross with me, I can't bear it. You've never raised your voice like that before, I don't like it. I promise I won't do it again. I'll leave her alone to bring up my... I mean her children. I promise, Guy, I swear it. Please don't be cross with me. Please try to understand I meant her no harm.' She felt the full force of his censure hitting her like a hurricane; it made her gasp for air.

Kate knew she had a lot of ground to make up. She was shocked by the extent of his anger but was mightily relieved she had told him. She loved him too much to deceive him. They sat without speaking, both staring at the flames as they danced and leapt up the chimney. For Kate it was hell; for Guy it was a welcome distraction. He had never felt so angry in his life. Will I never learn, she asked herself, will I ever be able to control my impulses?

They sat in silence, one seething; one suffering. Kate didn't know what to do or say to make amends. She desperately wanted him to sit beside her, take her in his arms and tell her he understood that she had made a silly mistake, one that should never be repeated, but that, despite it all, he still loved her. It wasn't going to happen, however; she knew that she had abused his trust and that in all probability she would never fully regain it.

Eventually he rose from his chair and abruptly wished her goodnight. He left the room without kissing her. It was the first time in their married life he had gone to bed without her. Kate had never seen him look so angry before. She felt that a chasm had opened up in the understanding between them and she wasn't sure that it could ever be fully bridged. She sat feeling utterly dejected, utterly alone and ashamed, knowing that, once again, she was the mistress of her own misery.

Chapter 28

Plymouth, July 1980

'Couldn't eat another bite, Mum, that was delicious, thank you,' remarked Matthew loudly, as he ostentatiously wiped his mouth with his napkin.

'Would you like anything more to eat, Rita?' asked Kate looking at her friend affectionately. 'There's plenty if you would like some.'

Rita declined, setting her knife and fork neatly on her plate. Guy got up from the table and brought out another bottle of wine. He poured a little into Rita's glass ignoring her half-hearted remonstrations as she cupped her hand over the glass.

'You'll have me tipsy,' she chortled. Kate noticed how wrinkled her hands and face had become. Rita sat in her chair, looking small and pinched, an old lady still slightly uncomfortable in the formality and fuss of the large family gathering. She was wearing her Sunday best dress. Kate noticed she had powdered her face and she was sure that there was a slight trace of lipstick on her lips. Her snow white hair had been recently permed, no doubt for the occasion of her trip to Plymouth. She never knew Rita's actual age, but Kate reckoned she was now in her late seventies at least. The years were starting to show on the outside, but she was still defiantly sprightly and obviously hadn't conceded to the trappings and slowing down of old age.

Kate looked round the table with satisfaction, noticing the collection of empty plates. She smiled, happy to have her brood about her for once. Rita had travelled down by train the night before and was staying with them for a couple of days. Clare, with her husband Mark and their two young children, Susan four and Jess two, had driven across from Liskeard, arriving just before lunch. The twins Matthew and Michael were at home for the summer holidays. The table was alive with convivial chatter as they simultaneously sought to catch up on months of each other's news. The twins, as always, were vying to outdo each other as they argued about the merits of their respective courses and dynamic student lives. Both were following in their father's footsteps and reading law. Matthew was at Exeter and Michael at Birmingham. As they sparred and riled in jest, Kate couldn't help noticing how very different they were to each other. Matthew confident, athletic and outgoing had recently been promoted to Junior Under Officer for this, his second year in the University's Officer Training Corps. He was full of exaggerated stories about his antics during their recent summer camp at Westdown, with boasts of sleepless nights and wild parties, intravenous drips and heat exhaustion as they sweltered and collapsed on the plains of Salisbury.

Michael, so much quieter and thoughtful, listened with a healthy degree of scepticism. He was artistic and musical, sensitive to others and what was going on around him. He could think of nothing worse than dressing up and running around playing soldiers with a bunch of jumped up capitalists. He had strong socialist beliefs and had chosen to take digs in one of the most deprived areas of the city to 'live the life'. He smiled mischievously as he described the CND march he had recently joined; an event that was met with howls of derision by Matthew and set the two brothers off into yet another heated debate.

'Give it a rest you two, Rita doesn't want to have to listen to your Boy's Own, Che Guevara stories or whatever they are,' challenged Clare, glowering at them.

'Your sister's right boys, come on, what's for pud, Kate? Need a hand? The boys are only too happy to help aren't you?' interjected Guy, as he started to clear the plates, proud of the lively minds his sons had developed.

Clare and her family left almost immediately after lunch in their typical whirl of fuss and goodbyes. It was a beautiful afternoon so everyone else, enjoying the peace, decamped to the garden and dozed in the bright sunshine. The garden was full of the vibrant colours and perfumes of summer. Kate had worked wonders with it, turning an overgrown morass into a perfect English garden. A canvas of bright-faced sunflowers peeped out from behind rows of pink hollyhocks, which cradled beds of white and purple asters. In the foreground, a carpet of yellow marigolds merged with the lush green baize of the lawn. The scent of lavender and roses wafted across in the gentle breeze.

'Bliss isn't it? Nothing quite like a lazy Sunday afternoon to wash away your woes,' sighed Guy, as he stretched out and placed his straw hat on the bridge of his nose. He watched the boys, who were playing cricket as competitively as ever, bowling and batting the ball with gusto, as he drew on a freshly lit cigar. He hadn't the energy to join them.

Kate nodded. 'I agree. I love having the family around me and I include you in that, Rita. You know I've always thought of you as my other mother and now, since my own has died, you're the only one I've left.' She reached over and squeezed her hand. 'We've been through a lot together over the years, haven't we?' she added, glancing at her knowingly.

'Yes we have, but you came through it all admirably,' Rita whispered, returning the squeeze and checking to see that the boys were out of earshot.

'Oh, don't worry,' remarked Kate, noticing Rita's reluctance to speak openly. 'I've told the boys and Clare about my first twins. I thought they had a right to know, they're all adults now. I told them a few months ago, soon after Mother died. While she was alive, I didn't want to tell them; I didn't want them to have to hide it from her. I didn't think that would be fair on them. They took it remarkably well; in fact, I think I actually went up in Matthew's estimation, not quite the prude he took me to be. Clare was the most shocked, but that was only because she was alive, of course, when it all happened. She couldn't believe that I'd managed to keep it hidden so well. Also I think having her own children now somehow made it all the more real for her. She couldn't imagine how I could have done it. They asked me if I'd ever tried to find them; I think Michael, in particular, would be quite keen. It's not every day, after all, you discover that you have an extra brother and sister.'

'You haven't been trying to find them, have you?' asked Rita, alarmed that she might have to admit to knowing what James had told her in confidence years previously regarding their whereabouts. Kate glanced at Guy, who raised his eyebrows urging her to continue. Kate had noticed Rita shifting in her chair and guessed what was troubling her.

'Rita, I know James told you about discovering the file with their new parents' name and address…' started Kate.

Rita promptly interrupted her. 'He asked me not to tell you, I hope I did the right thing. We weren't sure whether or not to tell you but I thought it best if you could let go of the past. I'm sorry, if you think I should have told you, but I did it with the best intentions,' she rattled out self-consciously, assuming that Kate was about to chastise her for keeping it hidden.

'Rita, it's fine, I know you did, you all did. I have a confession to make, I'm afraid. I'm sorry, I've never told you this before. Oh dear, I suppose thinking about it now, I realise that for all these years you have been keeping it secret afraid to tell me when I knew all along. I think I owe you the apology. Guy told me about the file just after the boys were born. I've known for over twenty years, but that's not all.'

Kate recounted the events as they had happened in Exeter twenty years previously. She told Rita all about the search for their names, the trip to Exeter, the contrived walk to the park, the meeting with them and their mother, Guy's angry response.

'The thing is, Rita,' she continued, 'I promised Guy I wouldn't do it again and I've kept my word, I've never attempted to get in touch, I've left them in peace, though of course I think about them all the time. They were twenty-four in June; it's always hard around their birthday. They're adults themselves now. Do you remember, one was so blond and the other so dark. I wonder what they look like now, if they've taken after me or, God forbid, their father.'

'Who takes after you?' chirped in Matthew, as he caught the tail end of the conversation and clunked her gently on the back with the side of the cricket bat. 'Who's the unlucky one, Michael or me?'

'Neither actually, big ears, I was talking about your half-brother and sister,' replied Kate emphatically, pretending to smack him. 'I was telling Rita that I'd told you about your half-brother and sister and was wondering if they looked like me or their father.'

Both boys sat down at the table and joined in. The topic still held a great degree of fascination for them; the incredible tale had cast their mother in a completely new light. It was so hard to imagine that the woman sitting beside them, the epitome of respectability, had once been forced to take such a drastic and covert decision. It seemed like she had lived in another world, on another planet, but they couldn't understand why anyone had cared so much. All she had done was get pregnant, what was the big deal? In their opinion it was an inconvenience perhaps, but a hanging offence most definitely not.

'What did he look like?' piped up Matthew.

'Who do you mean?' asked Kate.

'The father, what did he look like?' he asked again carelessly. Guy pulled a face at him to shut up; he didn't think it was an appropriate question.

There was an embarrassed silence before Rita spoke hesitantly. 'I wasn't sure whether I should tell you this or not, but he was in the local paper recently. There was a photograph. I cut it out. I thought perhaps I would show it to you. It's in my bag upstairs. Should I get it?'

Kate grimaced, Guy shifted in his chair, Michael looked uncomfortable but Matthew nodded with enthusiasm.

'Why not, give us a laugh,' remarked Kate, breaking the uncomfortable silence, as she lifted her wine glass and gulped down the remains. Rita was beginning to regret that she had said anything in the first place, but she got up to fetch the cutting. She returned with it and handed it over apprehensively.

Kate took it with a bold flourish, preparing to confront the face of the man she hadn't laid eyes on for nearly twenty-five years. She unfolded it feeling surprisingly nervous, acutely aware that there were four pairs of curious eyes fixed on her. She pulled a face in disgust as she read the bold heading. His pasty face stared out at her, greyer and older, but there was no mistaking the smug look.

Local Bank Manager Presents War Memorial Window to mark 35th Anniversary

Local Barclays Bank Manager, Mr Bob Thompson and his wife Edith have made a most generous presentation of a new stained glass War Memorial Window to St Mark's Church. The original window was destroyed during an air raid in 1942. Mr Thompson is a native of Plymouth, but has lived and worked in Exeter since 1952. During the service of dedication Mr Thompson explained, 'I was most disappointed that, for health reasons, I was unable to serve my country during the 1939-45 war. I suppose in presenting this window I feel that I have finally been able to do my bit, in remembering those from this parish who lost their life in that terrible war.' In reply, the rector, the Reverend Cyril Rodgers said, 'Mr Thompson is a most generous patron and an example to us all. He is a dedicated member of the congregation, freely giving of his time and has served as both rector's and people's churchwarden.'

Kate couldn't read anymore. She handed it to Matthew.

'There you go, have a look at him. Example to us all,' she fumed. 'Yes a perfect example of hypocrisy, self-promotion and self-satisfaction. Oh, he'll love this; the unreserved adulation. It was always about show for him. It didn't matter what the truth was, just as long as he could save face and turn it to his advantage. He's a fake. Do his bit indeed. He was delighted when he didn't have to join up, the coward; thought it would give him an opportunity to get ahead in the bank. Well that's all worked out perfectly for him. God help the poor woman who got saddled with him,' she ranted. 'Get me another drink please, Guy, will you, I think I need it,' she urged holding out her glass.

No one spoke but Kate started to laugh. 'What a complete and utter pillock. Can you believe him? Those poor kids; I hope they never discover the true identity of their father. What on earth was I thinking of at the time; if you want to know the truth, absolutely nothing.'

'That's the spirit, Mum. Here, Michael, have a shufty at that. Don't think you have too much competition to worry about Dad,' goaded Matthew handing the cutting to his brother grinning. 'Lucky escape, I think Mum.'

Rita breathed a sigh of relief. She was feeling guilty for having brought up the subject of Bob Thompson in the first place. Now the photo was breaking the tension as everyone gently ribbed Kate.

'Do you think they still live in Exeter? If so it would be possible to find them, wouldn't it?' suggested Michael kindly, looking at the photo of their father. 'They're grown up now, surely they can make their own decision about whether they would like to meet us or not. Where did you say they lived?'

'19 Chestnut Grove,' replied Rita without thinking. The address was etched in her mind. She didn't think this was the time to confess that, on many occasions, she had walked along that way and stood watching the house from a distance on the off chance of spotting them.

Kate felt like a ghost had trodden on her grave. She had put any thoughts of finding them out of her mind for so long, but Michael's well intended suggestion had opened a sluice of unwelcome emotions.

'I think it best to leave well alone, Michael. I know you think it would be doing your mother a kindness, but it really is best to leave things as they are. Don't you think so, Kate?' asked Guy anxiously, worried that the conversation was taking a turn for the worse. He wanted to change the subject; they had dwelt on it long enough and he could see it was starting to upset Kate.

Kate didn't reply. She didn't want to leave well alone, but she couldn't betray her deepest cravings. She had never overcome her addiction to finding them and she knew she never would. She merely controlled it, day by day, month by month, year by year but that was all. It was a constant companion. Michael sat in quiet contemplation.

'Come on boys, challenge you to a game of clock golf,' Guy suggested, rising from his chair and wishing to change the topic of conversation. Kate shot him a grateful look.

Rita left the following Tuesday. The house returned to normality as the boys headed off to their summer jobs and Guy disappeared to the office. Kate enjoyed the quiet solitude of the day, as she pottered in her garden. She usually met friends for lunch on a Tuesday, but there was little doubt that Sunday's events had been very unsettling and she didn't feel like going this week. The photo of Bob Thompson had reminded her of her own mortality and the fact that she was also growing older. She had hardly recognised the aged, grey-haired man who had once been a baby-faced boy. She needed to put it out of her mind again. She had promised Guy that she would not make contact and, no matter what validity there was in what Michael had said, she wouldn't break her word. Guy had noticed that she was talking about them more and she knew he was concerned that she would fail to control her impulses once again. He had forgiven her long ago, but she knew he had never forgotten, and that she had never really fully regained his trust when it came to this matter. She would reassure him tonight that she would keep her word. The trouble was she had also made a vow to her twins as they were carried from her on that awful day. She had vowed to find them and it had long troubled her.

Matthew and Michael had arranged to meet for a pint after work, and met in a busy city pub. Matthew had his eye on a girl they had seen in there several times before and he fancied his chances. He had little problem attracting women and he made the most of it. He had inherited the best features of both his parents. Michael had had the same girlfriend, Jayne, since Freshers' Week, but she was working in a Kibbutz for the summer and he was feeling at a loose end. He wasn't interested in ogling at other women. He didn't really want to meet Matthew knowing that he would turn it into a macho drinking competition and one that he was bound to lose, but he wanted the opportunity to talk to him alone about something that had been playing on his mind.

Michael was already standing at the bar, quietly sipping a pint when he heard Matthew's voice boom cross the room. Never one to make a quiet entrance when a loud one would do, he swaggered up and slapped his brother smartly between the shoulder blades.

'Your shout, bro, pint of whatever you're having,' he announced loudly, as he clattered a stool across the floor and sat down. He looked around the bar seeking out the main object of his visit. There was no sign of her, but there were plenty more opportunities.

'Ever notice that the length of the hem is directly proportional to the strength of the sun; here's to the summer,' he joked as he raised his glass and downed half of it in one. His head turned as he clocked a rather attractive pair of long tanned legs sauntering past in a skirt that could pass for a belt. Michael followed his look discreetly, wishing his brother could control his more lascivious behaviour. The girl was obviously with someone else. Matthew finished his pint and ordered another two.

'So what was so secretive that you had to drag me along here?' he asked, half-interested, as he continued to scour the room.

'It's about Mum. I wanted to get your view on something I've been thinking about for a while. For God's sake,

Matthew, will you stop leering at every bit of skirt that passes and listen, this is serious,' he challenged. He hated it when Matthew was in one of his stupid supercilious moods. He didn't seem to take anything seriously and this was important to him. Matthew turned back and stared at him wide-eyed with exaggerated interest.

'The thing is,' Michael continued, ignoring his brother's idiotic expression, 'I think I would like to get in touch with our half-brother and sister, see if they're interested in meeting us. What do you think?'

'I think you're bonkers, brother. What if we don't like them and they turn out to be a couple of complete geeks? We can hardly make contact and then decide sorry 'not quite our type, darling' and decide to ignore them. Why on earth do you want to go down that road?' he asked, lifting his glass.

'I'm not sure really. It just seems like the right thing to do, that's all. I think it would mean a great deal to Mum.'

'Oh yeah, and when they decide they want nothing to do with her, how will she feel then, you plonker?'

'I wasn't going to say anything to her until we saw how it turned out. If they don't want to meet, she need never know anything about it. It's worth a try though don't you think?'

'I think you're mad, but if it means that much to you go ahead, just don't involve me. Hey, that's more like it, look who's arrived, sorry, brother, bit of business to attend to.' He hopped off the stool, pint in hand and sidled up to his unsuspecting victim. Michael watched him briefly, finished his own drink and left.

*

Evelien sat in a state of shock hardly hearing what Helen and Richard were telling her. Both had come to visit her unexpectedly. Richard was clutching the letter she had forwarded to him a few weeks earlier. For the past twenty-four years she had dreaded this moment, ever fearful that it would arrive but hoping against hope that it wouldn't. She had never forgotten the strange encounter outside the school and that odd woman with her faraway look. For months afterwards she had watched her children day and night, refused to allow them to go into the street to play, had warned them over and over not to talk to strangers, refused to allow them to walk the short distance home alone when they so desperately wanted to assert their independence.

She was convinced that over the years someone was watching the house, observing them, waiting for the chance to snatch them away. Several times she had seen a stranger standing alone at the end of the road. She knew it wasn't the same woman she had met before, she would surely know her if she saw her again, but it was just as disconcerting. This one was older and smaller, almost bird like. She didn't meet anyone, didn't talk to anyone, didn't seem to have any reason to be there, other than to watch and wait.

Evelien had protected them so fiercely that she was unknowingly imprisoning them behind the bars of their own fears. They would cry out in the night if they heard the slightest creak, run to her if a stranger smiled at them; they had become timorous and insular. She was causing them more harm than any stranger ever could. Jim had reluctantly intervened and made her see sense for, although he sympathised greatly with his wife, he could see what she was doing to their children. Gradually over the years, as the children grew, she relaxed knowing that they could fend for themselves, but the fear had never really gone away. She was convinced that, even if she never came to reclaim them, they would eventually leave her under their own volition. They had been lent to her that was all; they were only hers until it was time to give them back. That time it seemed had come. They had been contacted by someone who claimed to be their half-brother.

'How can we even be sure that he is your brother and how on the earth did he know where we lived, or who we are?' she asked, as her heart pounded.

'He doesn't say,' replied Richard, rereading the letter. 'All he says is that he believes he may be our half-brother, that his mother was a student here in Exeter in 1956 when she became pregnant and that she had twins who she put up for adoption. He believes that we're those twins; he knows our names. The address to reply to is in Birmingham of all places. Blimey, I think I know that area. I've been near there and it's pretty rough if I may say so. Not somewhere you would want to walk about alone on a dark night. He mentions a Dr Greene. Does that name mean anything to you?'

'He mentions Dr Greene? Yes, he was the doctor who arranged everything, but I cannot believe he would ever have betrayed us,' she stated decisively. She paused before adding forlornly. 'What do you want to do? I won't stand in your way if you want to make contact with him; it is your right. How I wish your father was still alive. He would have known what to do.'

Her heart sank and her eyes misted over as she remembered the man whom, for so many years, had been her strength and her voice of reason. She missed him terribly; she had loved him from the moment she first laid eyes on him. He had appeared so gallant, so proper in Bill's presence, but she knew there had been an instant attraction between them, and that he had felt it as surely as she did. She had fought against her feelings, ever conscious that she was betraying the man she had promised to marry, but in her heart she knew that Bill could never compare to Jim. Her doubts had been confirmed on a balmy beach; that perfect oasis in a war torn world. Jim had felt as guilty about the relationship as she had – after all, Bill was an old friend and had put his trust in him.

They had both agreed that they should tell Bill as soon as possible. Jim had chivalrously offered to write to him and take the blame, but Evelien had insisted that it should come from her. She had steeled herself to write to her fiancé with the most devastating of news – to tell him that she no longer wished to marry him. She had deliberated for days over whether or not to tell him the whole truth. Jim felt that he should know, she had thought it would hurt him even more. In what possible way could she frame it to cause him the least pain? In the end she had told him everything, having been convinced by Jim that he would find out anyway. He never replied. Six weeks later she had received official notification that he had been killed when his ship, HMS Britomart, was hit by friendly fire off the coast of Normandy. With his parents having died in the London blitz, he had named the woman who was to be his wife as his next of kin. She never discovered whether he died having received her letter or not. She had wept bitterly for the decent man who had lost both the woman he loved and his life at the hands of an ally.

And then Jim had been cruelly snatched from her, long before his allotted time, lost to the ravages of lung cancer. Now she was in danger of losing her children and would be left completely alone. She wanted to yell at them, remind them that it was she who had loved them, cared and suffered for them, not some other woman who had abandoned them and forgotten all about them until it suited her to take them back. But deep down she knew that it had to be their decision; she could not command their love through coercion. It was up to them to decide. She feared their answer; she could hardly bear to listen.

'We've talked about it, Mum. We weren't even sure that we should tell you about this at all, in fact. I thought we shouldn't but Helen thought you would want to know,' Richard started.

'I only thought that you had a right to know,' Helen interjected, jumping in quickly in her own defence. 'As far as we're concerned, Mum, and we both agree, you're our mother, the one we both love and always will. This other woman is simply some woman who bore us. She means nothing to us.' She walked over to Evelien and hugged her. Richard joined her. They stood together, a silent tripod bound by the ties of a mother's love. She had never felt their embrace more keenly.

'Thank you, thank you,' she repeated slowly, hardly believing what they had said. Her sense of relief was tangible. 'I would never have stood in your way, stopped you from meeting her if you had wanted to, but you will never know how much this means to me my darlings. You will never know.'

'There's something else we want to suggest,' continued Helen. 'Why don't you sell the house and move down to Cornwall to live beside Adam, Alice and me? There's no reason for you to stay here now, all on your own. You'd be able to see your granddaughter every day, live beside the sea as you've always wanted to. We've seen the perfect cottage.'

'Helen's right, added Richard. 'Once I've finished Sandhurst I could be posted anywhere so there's no point in you staying here, so far from Helen and her family. It makes perfect sense. It would also mean no one could ever contact us again, they wouldn't know where we lived. You could put it out of your mind for ever – we all could.'

Evelien looked at her children as her heart swelled with love for them. She had been very lucky; they were her life, the centre of her world. The offer was daunting but tempting. It was true, she did feel lonely living on her own, but it was the home she had set up with Jim, where she had raised her children and it held so many precious memories she was loath to leave it. She was so proud of what they had achieved together. Helen was now a fully qualified nurse, married to Adam, and living with her baby near Penzance. Richard had graduated from university the previous year and had almost finished his officer training, so now perhaps it was time to move on and take on the mantle of a grandmother. She didn't need to think about it for long.

'I will do it. I will move to the sea, sell the house,' she pronounced with conviction, to the surprise of her children. 'It will be a new dawn for me as I head towards my sunset years. Come on, I want to hear all about this cottage.'

*

Michael waited in expectation for a reply, his hopes raised then dashed with every letter that arrived. Months and nothing had come. He had decided to give the address of his student digs as he didn't want his mother to discover anything about it. He had warned his flatmates to keep an eye out for anything addressed to him, to be careful not to ditch it with all the other junk, but no one had seen anything. As time trailed on his hopes died and he realised that it was more and more unlikely he was going to hear anything. He was bitterly disappointed. He had hoped it would be a wonderful surprise for his mother, maybe in time for Christmas. Perhaps Matthew was right and he had been mad to try; perhaps they didn't live there anymore and hadn't received it; perhaps they had and didn't want to know; perhaps he should let the ghosts of the past remain at rest. He wasn't at all sure, however, that he should or indeed could; it had become an obsession for him.

What could he do to discover why they hadn't replied? It was obvious – he would convert Matthew to the cause. After all he lived in Exeter, so he could easily check if they still lived at that address. All he had to do was look them up in the phone directory. Even better, if he got the number he could ring and see who answered. It took a bit of persuading; Matthew was reluctant to get involved in what he thought was a harebrained scheme, but Michael persisted and eventually he was in possession of the number. Good – it was still registered to Palmer. They were in luck. He lifted the phone, not entirely sure what he would say when it was answered.

'Exeter 42687,' said a woman's voice. Michael checked the number; it was correct.

'Oh hello, I'm not sure if I've got the right number, who am I speaking to, please?' he asked tentatively.

'Who are you looking for?' came the cautious reply.

'I'm looking for the Palmer residence,' he replied semi-confidently.

'I'm sorry, they don't live here anymore, moved out a couple of weeks ago. We live here now.'

Michael's heart sank. He decided to take a flyer on it, after all there was nothing to lose.

'I'm sorry to trouble you. I was at school with Richard Palmer but unfortunately we've lost contact. I'm trying to get in touch with him as we're having a reunion. I don't suppose you would have a forwarding address, would you?'

'Afraid not. Odd, but they didn't seem to want to leave one. Somewhere in Cornwall I think, well the mother that is. The son, your friend I presume, is in the Army now I believe; just finished officer training, but that's all I know. Sorry I can't be of more help. Do you want to leave your name in case they contact me?'

'No… no it's fine thank you. I'll try to see if anyone else might know where he is. I'm sorry to disturb you, goodbye,' replied Michael crestfallen. He set the phone down slowly. They had been there until two weeks ago, well, the mother had; he had missed them by two weeks. Why hadn't he thought to get the number earlier? If only Matthew hadn't delayed; he'd arsed about for at least three weeks, the idiot. But if they were there up until two weeks ago they must have got the letter – they simply didn't want to reply. They hadn't even left a forwarding address, didn't seem to want to by all accounts. Was that because they knew he was trying to get in touch? If so, they had covered their tracks well and the trail had gone cold. It was over; he couldn't see how he could ever make contact now. Where would he start? He was glad he hadn't said anything to his mother, raising her hopes only to dash them again, but for himself he was devastated.

Chapter 29

14th September 2001

Richard Palmer glanced towards his sister Helen, and forced a resigned smile. Only the sound of their mother's erratic breathing, and the steady tick of the clock, cut across the silence that pervaded the bedroom. Evelien's lungs, like a pair of worn out bellows, wheezed and rattled as they fought to suck in sufficient air to keep her alive; each shallow breath managing to snatch less and less of the life giving compound. For over twenty torturous hours her children had listened agonisingly to every desperate gasp, willing each one to be her last, hoping it wasn't. They had watched the hands on the bedside clock open and close, with monotonous predictability, as they semaphored the ending of her life. Richard and Helen had refused to leave the side of the mother they loved as surely as if she had borne them herself. In their selfless, exhausting, vigil they had fulfilled their vow; they had not abandoned her.

'Did you know,' remarked Helen, as she absentmindedly fingered her mother's wedding ring and broke the silence between them, 'she's never taken this off, not once since the day and hour Dad placed in on her finger.' The ring rotated freely on its wearer's skeletal finger.

'I didn't know that,' replied Richard with a modicum of tired interest.

'She considered it would bring them bad luck, might cause a rift between them,' Helen continued.

'Jeez, I've never known two people more in love than those two. Totally devoted to each other,' reflected Richard. 'If you think about it, Dad was still a relatively young man when he died. Do you remember how he used to talk about his kitbag of three score years and ten; joked every birthday that it was getting that bit lighter. Never got to empty his, did he?

'No, suppose he didn't… They deserved so much longer together, didn't they?'

'Yeah, they did…she was never quite the same after he died, was she?' remarked Richard sighing.

'No, not really… lost a lot of her spark. The last twenty-one years must have seemed incredibly long and lonely for her, although I think it helped that she was living down here close to us. She really loved being near the sea, being an Oma, surrounded by her grandchildren, but I honestly think she was simply biding her time, waiting for the day she could be with Dad again…not that she ever really believed in an afterlife, certainly not a heaven, but I think she's always hoped there just might be some special place where she could be with him again.'

'I know, forever hedging her bets... He was the love of her life wasn't he, and she his for that matter. Love at first sight for both of them, despite the fact she was already engaged to someone else…he swept her off her feet and stole her away from another man. Hard to believe of him, he always seemed so proper about such things. I suppose that's why he never really wanted to discuss it… think he always felt incredibly guilty about it, don't you?' suggested Richard.

Helen shrugged carelessly in reply.

'Strange they should both succumb to lung cancer,' continued Richard aimlessly. 'The consequence of two misspent youths I suppose; fondness for a pipe and fondness for the sun. Although I'm not sure how that works – how can you start with skin cancer and end up with it in your lungs?'

'It's called metastatic melanoma if you really want the medical terminology. But know what, I honestly think, if they could, they would do it all again, exactly the same; quality over quantity every time,' Helen added, hoping her brother wouldn't push her for further explanation on complicated medical conditions; she was beyond tired.

They gazed at the gaunt figure lying before them. Evelien's beautiful face had collapsed onto the cheekbones beneath; her eyes had plunged into the depths of the sockets that had once held them proudly aloft; the overall diminishing effect made her nose appear much too long for the space it occupied. The smooth unblemished skin, that had once moulded her perfect body, had eventually been her undoing. Malignant melanoma had done its work and, by the time it was discovered, there was nothing anyone could do.

'Perhaps she had one regret…' Richard proffered tentatively as the conversation began to wane.

'What's that?' enquired his sister half engaging in the conversation, drunk with fatigue.

'Well… I'm sure, she would love to have had his children, given birth to her own…'

'We're her children,' interrupted Helen abruptly, brightening suddenly. She was immensely irritated by the comment. 'She's never treated us any differently. I've never felt any different…Why, have you?' she enquired accusingly.

'No, not really I suppose,' he replied defensively, slightly taken aback by the ferocity of her reaction, 'but I'm sure it was never quite the same for them, or for us. We don't look like either of them for a start.'

'So what. Flesh and blood that's all,' challenged Helen. 'As far as I'm concerned no one, but no one, could ever have been more of a mother and father to us. They devoted their lives to us. You know they did… anyway, I don't think this is an appropriate conversation; she's still with us, for God's sake!' Helen's eyes flared in exasperation at her brother's complete insensitivity. Exhaustion and desolation were taking their toll.

'But she can't hear us,' he protested.

'That's not the point,' retorted Helen tartly.

'Sorry, you're right… shouldn't have said that. Too tired to think properly, I expect,' Richard responded, suitably chastened and glancing guiltily at his mother.

Richard and Helen rarely talked about their adoption, but it hovered over them like an invisible spectre. Very occasionally something unexpected would bring it into focus once more; like the letter that had arrived, years earlier, from an alleged half-brother. Helen had resented the intrusion, Richard had been mildly curious – Evelien's distress, however, had been tangible. She had lost her husband only a few months before, and now, she believed she was in danger of losing her children.

Ever since that fateful day, when she had been confronted by the strange woman with the pram, Evelien had remained convinced that eventually, nature would supersede nurture and they would return to their natural mother. Hardly a day passed when the thought hadn't occurred to her. It had taken some of the sheen off her enjoyment of the children. When they had made the unanimous decision that she should make a completely fresh start and move to Cornwall, she had been delighted, convinced that it would ward off the possibility of any further contact. They had left a forwarding address with a trusted neighbour who could get in touch with Evelien if there was something urgent, but that was it. Quite possibly the new occupants of 19 Chestnut Grove, Exeter thought the arrangements irregular, but they had respected the wishes of the elderly vendor who obviously wished to keep her future whereabouts to herself. Evelien's move to Cornwall had brought her physically closer to her daughter and grandchildren and mentally removed her from the dread of discovery. It had brought a degree of security and comfort to her autumn years. She had finally allowed herself to believe that her children were truly hers and hers alone.

Brother and sister sat quietly, lost in their thoughts once more, watching and waiting as Evelien's breathing became more and more laboured; the gap between each breath more and more protracted. They both knew it couldn't be long, but neither could bring themselves to say it. The wait was interminable but the end agonisingly close. Her cancer-riddled body was fighting its last fight. It could do no more.

They turned their heads, in unison, as they heard the sound of the door being pushed open gently, and watched as Ellen Harkness peered round.

'Any change?' she asked with professional empathy as she approached the bed and took Evelien's icy, weightless hand in hers. She glanced at her fob watch and felt for a pulse.

'It can't be too long now,' she answered quietly in response to their silent enquiry. 'Her pulse is steadily weakening and there's quite a change in her breathing.'

'Yes, I've noticed a considerable change too, just in the last half hour or so,' commented Helen, speaking as one professional to another.

'Would you like me to stay with you?' asked Ellen sensitively.

'I think we would like to be alone with her, if you don't mind,' Helen ventured, looking at Richard for confirmation. He nodded compliantly, as he weakly smiled at Ellen in a gesture of gratitude.

'Of course,' said Ellen, touching the end of the bed and feeling the outline of Evelien's stick thin legs through the covers. It was an unspoken gesture of goodbye.

Ellen left the room discreetly. Richard and Helen sat, lost in their memories. Flanking their mother, each had unconsciously taken hold of a hand as automatically as they had in childhood. For years they had walked beside her, received her selfless, unconditional love, as she had protected and guided them along the way; now, it was their turn to support her on her final journey. Evelien groaned a deep throaty whimper. Her children stared. For a brief moment each was convinced that she was about to open her eyes but instead, she snatched her final gulp of air and fell silent. The clock ticked on.

Richard looked at Helen hardly believing that it was finally over. He saw silent tears of sorrow trickling down his sister's face. It was all the confirmation he needed. He stood up, bent over, and gently kissed his mother on the cheek. She didn't move. For as long as he could remember she had responded to his every touch with gestures of exuberant affection. This kiss was met with cold indifference. It shocked him deeply. He suddenly felt completely alone.

His sister reached over and, with the tips of her fingers, gently drew her mother's hair across her forehead; nature's alchemist had long since turned Evelien's golden locks to silver. Helen took her mother's still, cold hand and held it to her lips. 'Goodbye, Mum,' she whispered. 'Go to him. He's been waiting for you for a very long time.' She set the hand gently on the cover, stood up and embraced Richard. Brother and sister stood side by side, silently gazing at the lifeless body that had once filled their lives with such joy. They were rocked by grief.

Nine days later two lone figures picked their way cautiously over the slippery rocks that led to Gurnard's Head and the north coast of Cornwall. The sun was beginning to sink in the evening sky, casting its coloured beams across the horizon as it had for millennia. A light southerly breeze was blowing, causing the waves to gently lap against the rocks below. It was a perfect September evening, warm and clear. On this rocky promontory Evelien had long since discovered her spiritual home. She had felt its primeval call from the very first time she had ventured along the treacherous path, teetered at the edge and gazed into the watery depths below. Supernatural forces had held her spellbound and drawn her closer to Jim; she had felt his presence here in this sacred place, heard his whisper in the waves below. She knew she had found their final resting place.

Richard and Helen walked warily towards the edge of the steep cliff, stopped, looked at each other then nodded in an unspoken act of solidarity. Each slowly opened the urn they had so precariously carried along the headland and, in an act of silent dedication, gently shook the precious contents into the evening air. Their parents' earthly remains danced in the breeze, floated over the edge, and sank into the waters below.

The waves drew them together and pirouetted them towards their watery grave. In death, as in life, Jim and Evelien Palmer had become as one.

Chapter 30

14th September 2002

'Happy Anniversary, darling,' Guy breathed in Kate's ear as he cuddled her to him. She slowly awoke to the sound of his voice and the comforting feel of his arms around her waist. It took her a moment to realise where she was; the bed felt strange. A choir of birdsong was drifting through the open window, as the sweet treble of the blackbird sang in counterpoint to the corncrake's hoarse bass. It confirmed that it was still early morning. The light curtains were barely able to hold back the early autumn sunshine as it fought to flood the room. She glanced at her bedside clock and groaned; it was only 6.30.

'Thank you,' she replied sleepily. 'Happy Anniversary. What on earth are you doing awake at this time?'

'Watching you, wondering how on earth I could be so lucky to have been married to someone so beautiful for forty-five years. Know what, it's a lovely day, shame to waste it. I think I might get up and make some coffee. Fancy some?'

She nodded reluctantly. Another three hours in bed seemed much more attractive, but she didn't want to hurt his feelings. She watched as he got out of bed, still relatively fresh and agile at eighty-one. She shook her head, partly in frustration, partly in admiration.

They had travelled down from Plymouth the previous day. On each anniversary he had brought her to her bower. It was their private haven and they rarely invited anyone else, even the children. Forty years previously he had built a small summer house for her, positioning it as close as possible to the riverbank. Often, if she lay quietly, she could hear the gentle melody of the water as it babbled over the stones, but this morning the birds were drowning out its song. She contemplated getting up to join him.

'Ridiculous time in the morning', she said aloud, smiling to herself. She stayed in bed and let him bring the coffee in to her. They lay in bed chatting contentedly, finishing their coffee before both fell back into a deep sleep.

Four hours later, Kate was standing in her dressing gown, making scrambled egg and bacon, when she heard his car return. She sighed; it was always a relief to know he had got back safely. He walked into the kitchen carrying the papers and a bottle of champagne.

'Never too old,' he said mischievously as he popped it open and pinched her buttock. The contents spilled onto the tiled floor in a pool of bubbles. Kate glanced down, grabbed a glass and shoved it under the lip of the bottle.

'Sorry about that, bit of a butterfingers, eh? Well here's to us and another forty-five years,' he quipped as he lifted the glass, his hand shaking slightly. She kissed him fondly on the cheek and took a sip.

'Happy Anniversary, darling,' she replied. 'Shall we have breakfast outside? It really is the most beautiful morning. If you bring the papers and drinks, I'll bring the plates.'

They sat in the warm sunshine, eating, drinking and chatting as they glanced at the papers. Guy jumped as Kate's fork suddenly dropped on her plate, chipping the edge.

'Oh my God!' she yelped. 'I don't believe it, listen to this.'

He looked at her in alarm as she started to read, her voice visibly shaking.

IN MEMORIAM
Palmer – Evelien died 14th September 2001. Formerly of Rotterdam and Exeter. Widow of Jim and much loved mother of Helen and Richard...

Kate crumpled the paper and handed it over, wildly tapping her forefinger on the notice. Guy looked at her intently from over the top of his glasses, as he took the paper and spread it on the table in front of him. He straightened it and started to read.

'It must be her, it's too big a coincidence to be anyone else, it all fits, the strange spelling of her name, the children,' Kate continued breathlessly. 'Formerly of Rotterdam – so she was Dutch. That explains it. Why formerly of Exeter? Does that mean because she is now dead or because she'd moved? Widow of Jim, don't you see, it means they're both dead, Guy. She's been dead for a year now, they're both dead. Don't you see what this means?'

'No, Kate, I don't see what it means,' he replied levelly, knowing exactly what she was implying.

'It means that I can find them; at last I'm free to find them. I promised you I wouldn't, but that was only while she was alive; it doesn't count now. I promised because I didn't want to upset her, that's the only reason. I've always wanted to find them and I've never given up hope. It's everything I dreamt of and now I can do it with a clear conscience. I can find them, Guy, I can find them, we know the address in Exeter – I can write and see if they want to meet. Oh, I'm so excited. This is the best news possible, the best anniversary ever.'

Guy set down the paper. He looked at her apprehensively. Her face was aglow. She was beaming with delight, as excited as a child on Christmas morning. He couldn't share her sentiments; his every instinct warned him that this was a road she should not travel. He could only see a trail of despair and disappointment looming ahead; disappointment that she wouldn't find them, disappointment that if she did they wouldn't want to know her, disappointment that they would meet and realise it was a terrible mistake, that they weren't what she hoped. It was fraught with dangerous possibilities, alleys to which Kate was blind; she couldn't or wouldn't see them.

'Slow down, darling, think about what you're saying. Please, you need to think carefully about this, you're in danger of opening Pandora's Box. Your unbridled curiosity could spread a great deal of pain, for you can't close it once it's open. I know how much this means to you, honestly I do, and I know you've kept a lid on your hopes for all these years, but you must remember there are many others involved in this too.'

'But you can't really understand what it's been like for me all these years,' she protested. 'I read once that we define ourselves by the memories we choose to enter in the scrapbook of life. Mine is full of memories I would wish to forget. I have so many regrets; I don't like the person I see when I look back on my life. I'm seventy-six now and as I get older I have less and less time to make amends. I cannot begin to describe the pain I have felt all these years, forever wondering. I know I cannot die in peace unless I find them, unless I have the chance to explain to them why I gave them away; to seek their forgiveness. I just want to know that they're okay and happy, that's all. Is that too much to ask?'

'But, darling, you've got to think about Richard and Helen and how they might feel about a whole new family suddenly popping up out of the blue. For all we know they've never been told. And what about Matthew, Michael and Clare and their children? It affects them too. They're their half-brother and sister after all. We need to think about this carefully Kate. It might turn out well, give you the peace you seek, but it could also turn out to be the most enormous mistake.'

She heard, but she wasn't listening. Her mind was filled with optimistic images of their meeting; she had the clearest picture of how it would be. She wanted to leave immediately and start the process without delay. She looked across at Guy. His brow was furrowed with concern; he was looking at her pleading with her to slow down, to think it all through carefully, but he could see that it was a lost cause.

They had been planning to spend a few days at the summer house, relax and get away from it all, while the weather remained so good. Now, Guy was fully aware that she would stay only to humour him and that her mind was elsewhere;

her focus was on the sequence of future events. He tried to reason with her, make her understand the enormity of what she was doing, the implications for so many people but, as he had discovered so often before, when her mind was made up there was very little he could do to change it. She was adamant and impatient to get back. He finally agreed that she could go as far as to talk it through with the children, sound them out, but he made her promise that if they had a problem with it at any stage, she would bow to their wishes. She had reluctantly conceded, but only because she was pretty sure they could be persuaded.

No sooner was Kate home than she had convened a family meeting. A week later everyone was gathered together at the house. She had planned her strategy carefully and she knew how to put forward a powerful argument. She considered what her children's reactions might be. Michael was sensitive like his father, but wholly unconventional. To their great amusement, as a sixth former, he had persuaded his ultra-conservative public school that, in the interests of balance, the library should take *The Morning Star* alongside *The Times* and *The Telegraph*. He had won his argument, caused a sensation and become something of a cause célèbre amongst his fellow pupils. He still had that rebellious streak. He would be supportive, she knew he would.

Matthew was much more conservative, but he was a man of the world and, so long as events didn't impinge on his more hedonistic pleasures, he would be happy. He was likely to be ambivalent. Of the three of them, Clare was by far the most serious. Kate often thought she had been born a century too late and was far too prudish. Of course, she had been the most affected by the revelations, perhaps because she felt she had been deliberately deceived. As far as the boys were concerned their mother had simply never got around to telling them, but Clare had been there from the beginning. She had been witness to her mother's presentation of the case for leaving college; a case Clare now viewed as perjury. The facts of the matter could not be ignored; her mother had given birth to five children by three different fathers. It seemed indecent. It had brought back the pain and humiliation she had felt as a child; the outsider who had vehemently defended her mother against the ignorant accusations of those who believed they had a right to condemn. Somehow that defence now appeared hollow, fraudulent and she wondered in what else she had been deceived; it was as if she had colluded with a lie and been a willing conspirator. She felt let down. She didn't like to talk about the whole incident and Kate knew it. Clare was likely to resist.

Kate greeted them all warmly as they arrived in the usual flurry of noise and banter. Three generations spilled over into every room. There was Clare her husband Mark and two girls, Jess and Susan, Michael and his wife Jayne and last to arrive, Matthew with his partner Becky and young son Tom. She had given no explanation for the family get together, but they had taken it as an opportunity for a delayed celebration of their wedding anniversary and arrived laden with bottles and gifts. Kate wasn't at all sure how to bring up the subject as they chatted amiably about nothing in particular. She wasn't keen to bring it up in the presence of her grandchildren. Luckily the older girls had soon had enough and decided to take their young cousin to the park. It was the opportunity Kate needed.

'Isn't it lovely for all of us to be together again? I don't suppose it's happened since Christmas,' she started, as the adults sat together drinking coffee, digesting their large meal.

'Thank you for the presents everyone. I can't believe we've been married for forty-five years.'

'I bet Dad can,' joked Matthew. Guy nodded sagely.

Kate ignored the jibe and lit a cigarette before speaking. 'I want to talk to you all about something, before the children get back. I have a proposition to make which I hope you will all agree is a good idea. I would like to see if we can make contact with your half-brother and sister.' She drew on her cigarette and surveyed their faces for reactions. Clare pursed her lips, Matthew nudged Becky with typical irreverence, but it was Michael's reaction that disappointed her most. She had been sure that he would have greeted the suggestion with enthusiasm, but he had cast a glance at Jayne and sat looking glum.

'Well that has obviously gone down pretty well,' Kate interjected sardonically, as she read the mood. 'I thought that at least you, Michael, would be pleased; you seemed so keen when I first told you about them.' He remained impassive, unsure how to explain that he had tried already.

'But why now, Mum?' asked Matthew. 'I thought you had decided against it.'

Kate explained the change in circumstances. 'So you see,' she concluded, 'now that we know the mother and father are dead, all the obstacles have been removed.'

'It wasn't just the mother and father that were an obstacle,' added Clare solemnly, 'this affects all of us. What if we don't like them, if they don't like us, what then? Can't we just be happy the way we are, just the three of us; at least we know what we're dealing with.'

'They're our flesh and blood, Clare, we can't get away from that and we know how much it would mean to Mum, that's the most important thing in this. Personally, I've always wanted to make contact, I just don't think it's going to be that easy, Mum, even if we can agree that it's a good idea,' added Michael cautiously, looking at Matthew.

'But we know where they lived, we know their names, it can't be that difficult,' contested Kate. 'All we have to do is to write to the address we know in Exeter. Someone must be able to get a letter to them; one or other of them might still live there or whoever does will probably know where they are. Are we at least in agreement that we should try?' She looked round the room in expectation, seeking to judge the mood of the supporters or dissenters. Clare remained unusually quiet;

Matthew looked again at Michael, willing him to explain. Becky, Jayne and Mark looked like they had accidentally overheard a conversation to which they shouldn't be privy, and sat in awkward silence. Kate had never discussed her past in their presence before, but she obviously assumed that they knew. Kate was disheartened by the lack of enthusiasm. Michael spoke eventually.

'Mum there's something you should know,' he started, looking sheepish. 'Help me here, Matthew, you know all about this; we didn't tell you at the time but…and we did it for the best of reasons of course,' he stuttered. 'Well, the thing is, I did try to get in touch with them, soon after you told us in 1980.' There was an uncomfortable silence of conspiracy amongst those who knew; Clare, Matthew and Michael.

'What?' replied Kate, in disbelief, 'You did what? What happened? Did you manage to make contact? Did you meet them? For God's sake, Michael, why didn't you tell me? What did you do, what happened? Tell me.' She looked pale and shocked.

'I wrote a letter and sent it to the house. I addressed it to Richard Palmer, but I didn't get a reply.'

'But they might not have got it, they may not have known anything about it,' interrupted Kate, frantically. 'Are you sure you had the right address, 19 Chestnut Grove, Exeter.'

'Yes I'm sure, Mum. When I didn't hear anything for ages, I asked Matthew to find out their telephone number. I rang it, but the mother had moved out just a couple of weeks earlier. She didn't leave a forwarding address and I got the distinct impression from the new owner that she didn't want to be found. I'm sure she got the letter, Mum, there's no reason why she wouldn't have and presumably she either read it or passed it to him. I just think they didn't want to make contact, that's all. So even if we do agree, I don't know how we could even begin to find out where they are now and it's very possible that they wouldn't want to know anyway. All I know is that Richard Palmer had joined the Army; the woman I spoke to on the phone told me he'd just completed officer training. I just don't want you to be disappointed.'

Kate was devastated. It had never occurred to her that they wouldn't want to meet; it was an anathema to her. Reuniting with them had meant so much, for so long; she had naïvely assumed it would be the same for them, no matter what Guy had cautioned. She was their mother so they must have felt the same bonds. She couldn't believe they would have willingly given up the chance of meeting her. They mustn't have got the letter; the mother had intervened and destroyed it without telling them, it was the only logical conclusion. She sat, desperately trying to maintain her composure, while the rest of the family looked on uncomfortably, unsure quite what to say next.

'Well, I think it's worth a try,' she said softly, breaking the tension. 'Unless anyone objects, I think it's definitely worth a try. There's not a day passes when I don't think about what I did. I've never been able to get them out of my head. I just want to know that they are okay and that they have had a happy life. What's the worst thing can happen? We don't find them; well, then I'm no worse off. We find them and they don't want to know; well, I can stop the years of wondering, I'll have had my answer. We meet and it doesn't work out; well, we've all lived this long without each other, we can do it again. But there is also the distinct possibility you'll find that you have a brother and sister whom you wish you had always known, and that I will regain the children I lost so long ago. I could have grandchildren I know nothing about and you could have nieces and nephews. Please, I've got to try if I am ever to get peace. Don't you think it's at least worth a try?'

She looked at them, pleading, hoping, determined.

'Well I think it is, though I haven't a clue where we should start,' replied Michael, enthusiastically.

'I'm happy whatever you decide,' added Matthew to please her.

They all looked towards Clare; the casting vote rested with her. She felt their eyes boring into her.

'I'm really not convinced. If I'm honest I have a bad feeling about it,' she protested, 'but if it means that much to you, Mum, and everyone else seems to have made up their mind, I won't stand in your way. I just hope it doesn't all end in tears.' Kate smiled at her in relieved gratitude.

Guy's heart sank a little; like Clare he was not convinced. He was anxious because he believed that Kate had built up an unrealistic picture of what any reunion would be like. There was every possibility, as Clare had pointed out, that it would all end in tears and he would be the one left to dry them. There also remained the unresolved problem of how they were going to reignite a trail that had gone completely cold. Where on earth could they start to locate them? There was nothing particularly unusual about their names. They could be anywhere. Guy tried to think of any legal processes that would help. They could try to write to the previous address but that had proved unsuccessful previously. It was Matthew, for once, who unexpectedly provided a possible solution

'He's in the Army, you say, an officer. It's obvious; get hold of the Army List.'

'The what?' asked Kate.

'The Army List – it provides details of promotions and postings. If we get a copy of that, we can find out if there is a Richard Palmer listed. It's a long shot, but we could then write to his unit and see if it's him. It's a start. May not throw up anything but, hey, we've nothing to lose.'

'But where would you get a copy of that; is it not confidential?' asked Michael, amazed that Matthew had shown such a degree of interest or originality. Perhaps Major Blimp and his weekend soldiering could prove worthwhile after all, though Michael would never understand its appeal.

'Leave it to me,' Matthew replied chirpily, 'I'll ask next time I'm in the unit; should be there next Wednesday. I'll let you know how I get on, but are we all agreed that we're going to go ahead with this?'

'Yes, you dolt and don't dither over it this time, or he'll have retired by the time you get round to it,' goaded Michael, ribbing his brother.

To Kate's amazement, ten days later Matthew rang. She had been sitting quietly playing backgammon with Guy on a Wednesday evening. Of course she rarely won, but she enjoyed seeing his enormous intellect in action and it kept her own brain agile.

'Hi Mum, it's me. Guess what? I've got it, I've got the List.' Kate's heart leapt, she held her hand over the phone and mouthed to Guy, who walked over immediately and sat beside her. He knew how much it meant to her. He watched her face anxiously trying to read what was being said.

'There's some good news and some not so good,' he continued, as Kate frowned. Guy took her hand.

'There's a Richard Palmer listed, the dates fit; he was commissioned in 1980 but unfortunately he left four years ago in the rank of Major. His last posting is listed as Northern Ireland, of all places. Rita would have been amused at that.'

'So what does that mean?' asked Kate, her hopes dashed. 'Presumably we can't trace him through the Army then. Damn we've missed him again. Why do I feel someone up there is conspiring against me, punishing me?' Guy watched her expression interpreting the conversation correctly, as he squeezed her hand more tightly.

'Well, there might be another way,' he continued. 'I spoke to some of the admin guys here when we realised he'd left, and they've suggested that we contact the Army Pensions Office in Glasgow. They won't divulge his address, of course, but they have suggested that if you write and enclose a letter for Major Richard Palmer then they could forward it on. Our Adjutant rang for me today and spoke to a Captain Brown in the Pensions Office. I've got the address for you to send it to her. I'll tell you what, I'll pop round on Saturday with Becky, before we head off on holiday; it's virtually on the way to the airport. I can help you draft the letter to her if you like.'

'And you think they would actually do that for me?' asked Kate, astonished.

'Well, they said they would, but there's no guarantee. Let's hope they have a current address for him. Anyway you think about what you want to write in your letter to Richard, and I'll come over and help you with the letter to the Pensions Office. We'll see you about two – does that suit?'

'Yes, of course. Thank you, Matthew. I can't thank you enough and I'd love to see both of you. Don't you want to come earlier and have some lunch with us?'

'No thanks. If I know Becky we'll be packing for hours. See you Saturday then, glad I could help. Take care.'

Kate replaced the receiver and sat down slowly, strangely unsettled by the conversation. Like a deaf interpreter, Guy had gleaned bits and pieces of the conversation from Kate's gestures and facial movements, but he was dying to know the details. As she started to tell him how the chain of events was about to be set in motion, the enormity of what she was doing hit her like a steam train. Now she could understand why Clare had been so cautious. For the first time ever she started to doubt the wisdom of her actions. Up until this point it had seemed like an exciting adventure. Now it seemed like a step into the most treacherous territory; one potentially fraught with danger and disappointment. She would have to write a letter to her lost children. What on earth would she say to them? How could she even begin to explain the inexplicable? How could they even begin to understand the moral pressures that had borne down on her? Would they conclude that she had given them away lightly, merely for her own convenience? Looking back she wondered why on earth it had seemed such an issue; why had it mattered so much? Like Bob Thompson before her, had she trodden the path of a hypocrite?

Chapter 31

Plymouth, 5th October 2002

To the casual observer, it was an event so wholly unremarkable it barely merited a cursory glance; but not to Kate, who understood the grim consequences of ill judgements and rash decisions only too well. Too often it seemed, despite her best intentions, she had merely succeeded in directing her life along a pitiful path rutted with pain, regret and profound guilt. And now she was on the brink of making the final crucial decision; a decision she prayed would, at last, chart a course to absolution and deliver the inner peace she so desperately craved. But it was a risk, for she knew that there was every possibility she was merely paving the way to further recrimination and bitter disappointment, and there was no means of knowing how it would transpire. She shuddered as she felt the cold breath of fate exhale on her once more.

She lingered beside the post box, needlessly checking the address she had so carefully copied onto the crisp white envelope, but it bought her some precious time; time to change her mind, walk away, and leave well alone. She had noticed neither the darkening sky nor the tears of soft autumn rain that had begun to fall, until they started to smudge the ink and threatened to deface her clear, neat hand writing. It prompted her to act. She reached forward, placed the letter deep inside the narrow slot and held it aloft. She heaved a deep reproachful sigh as she withdrew her trembling hand and with it the precious missive. She simply couldn't let it go. She stood, gripped by indecision, blankly staring at the box with her hand still hovering in the slot.

She turned her head, begrudgingly, in response to a muted, attention-seeking cough and was confronted by a tall willowy woman flanked by two young children, a girl and a boy. Each child was standing in eager anticipation, impatiently holding their mother in one hand and a picture postcard in the other. Kate briefly glanced at the woman before lowering her gaze towards the smiling, expectant children. Her heart skipped a beat as she felt her hand open automatically, and the letter dropped from her grasp. It was gone.

'I'm sorry, I didn't realise you were waiting,' she muttered tersely, her mind still focused on the letter now nestling at the bottom of the box. The young woman smiled in silent response. Kate nodded in polite acknowledgement, touched the box for luck, then slowly turned to cross the road.

Head down, deep in thought she picked her way along the soggy, leaf-strewn pavement. As she reached the corner she glanced back. The trio had gone. In the distance, the bright red pillar box stood alone in silent witness, Kate's darkest secret enclosed within its bowels. A postman was kneeling on the damp ground, mindlessly shuffling the contents into a thick grey sack. Kate suddenly felt an overwhelming urge to run back, to explain that she had made a terrible mistake and needed to retrieve the letter, but it was hopeless; she was too old and it was too far. All she could do was stand and stare. She watched, powerless, as the postman stood up, closed the little door and carelessly tossed the sack into the back of his van. Then he was gone.

Kate was gripped by sensations of relief and trepidation in equal measure as she remained gazing into the distance, oblivious to the rain now tumbling down on her from above. Her thoughts, firmly focused on the past, were jolted into the present by the muffled sound of her mobile phone. She fumbled in her pocket and pulled out the wretched thing.

'Hello,' she answered cautiously, hoping she had pressed the right button.

'Oh, hi Mum, it's only me. That's novel, you've got it switched on for once.'

Kate grimaced but ignored the impertinence.

'Are you on your way back yet? We were hoping to get off soon.'

'Hello, Matthew, yes on my way now. Sorry, I didn't realise you were in such a hurry.'

'Well we weren't, but Becky has decided she wants to stop and get some things for the flight which means we're a bit tight on time now, but we don't want to leave without saying goodbye. How long do you think you'll be? Oh, nearly forgot, did you actually post it?'

'Yes, of course I posted it,' she replied indignantly.

He continued on breezily, her reply barely registering with him. 'Listen, do you want us to drive over to meet you? You must be getting soaked. Did you even take an umbrella with you?'

'No, I forgot to bring one, but I'm fine thank you. I'm just round the corner, almost home; honestly there's no need to come to meet me,' insisted Kate.

'Okay then, if you're sure. Tell you what, Becky and I will start loading the car which will speed us up a bit.'

'That's fine; I'll see you at the house. I should be there in about five minutes,' Kate replied.

'Alright, see you in a moment. Bye.'

Such an inane conversation reflected Kate as she struggled to turn off the phone, realising that she was still trembling. How unemotional and matter of fact he'd sounded; so like his grandmother in moments of significance. He must have known how high the stakes were, what it all meant to her; why couldn't he be more like his twin?

His detached, dispassionate, enquiry seemed to rasp awkwardly against the emotional charges still pulsing through her body. She knew only too well that moments earlier she had been on the verge of turning back without posting it at all; she had thought to tear up the carefully constructed letter. Maybe it was the sight of those children that had helped to steel her resolve, but she was riddled with doubt. What if her revelations destroyed years of cherished memories, and he hadn't known the truth about her? What right did she have to wreak havoc in someone else's life simply to salve her own conscience?

'What have I done?' she whispered to herself in harsh admonishment.

A torrent of turbulent thoughts tossed round her head as she began to walk more briskly towards the house. She turned into the gravel driveway, raised her still shaking hand and waved in silent greeting to Matthew and Becky who were standing in the pouring rain rapidly shoving their bags into the large boot. Becky ran towards her, kissed her warmly on the cheek, Matthew hastily embraced her, both jumped into the car and then they were off.

Nothing in their world had changed.

Kate dashed into the house, chucked her dripping coat over a chair, sat down and lit a cigarette in a fruitless effort to calm her jangling nerves. She wished Guy would hurry up and come home; she badly needed both his company and his reassurance. She'd expected him to be back at least an hour ago, long before Matthew and Becky left. He'd be disappointed that he'd missed them. What on earth was keeping him? It occurred to her just how much she worried each and every time he went out in the car – she was sure his reactions were slowing. She hated the effects of getting old; the changing face reflected in the mirror, the momentary delay before names trundled into her mind, the struggle to read the newspaper; all the cumulative telltale signs that shouted old age. She tried to call his mobile but irritatingly, it was constantly going to voicemail.

She stood up and looked through the window checking, for the third time in as many minutes, to see if he had arrived. She knew it was irrational, but then these days so many of her thoughts were. She sat down and lit another cigarette. She lifted a magazine and flicked through the well-thumbed pages but they held little interest. She set it down and sat back in her chair, listening to the silence, scanning the room with fresh eyes. All around her were the familiar trappings of a life of privilege; the original oil paintings, the tasteful antiques, some acquired from their parents, others lovingly chosen by them both. She loved each and every one of them; they held so many precious memories of their life together in this happy family home. Yet she knew that, despite everything they meant to her, she would have forgone them all for a life that had included all her children. Baubles, that's what they were, meaningless baubles that had brought only superficial and transitory satisfaction. In that moment, more than ever before, she realised that deep, spiritual contentment would forever elude her until the moment she was happily reunited with her children. Her life had been, and would be forever, tainted by their loss. The unshakeable conviction that, one day, she would find them again had sustained her through the darkest times. Now, the moment of truth was almost upon her and she would finally know if her dreams were to be fulfilled. It suddenly dawned on her, with a sense of increasing dismay, just how much those dreams in themselves had been an enduring source of solace and now even those could be taken from her. She would be left with nothing. She wished Guy would hurry up; what on earth was keeping him? She lit another cigarette.

At last she heard the comforting roar of the engine as Guy over-revved into the driveway. She smiled in both relief and amusement. The young man, who had so skilfully drawn up outside his office in the flash little sports car, now struggled to gauge the width of the gates as he manoeuvred the large saloon towards the garage. She went to the door to greet him, smiling in welcome.

'Sorry, got held up on the motorway and discovered the battery on my phone had gone flat, so I couldn't ring you to let you know. Have I missed Matthew?' asked Guy, clambering stiffly from the car.

'Yes, they left about half an hour ago. Becky needed to get some last-minute things before they headed to the airport. They'll call us when they arrive in Rome. Good meeting?' she asked, glad to have him back. They kissed lightly before linking arms and walking back towards the house.

'Well, as usual, all talk and very little action, such is the way of Rotary committees. Anyway, far more important, what about you? Did Matthew help you with the letter and did you actually post it?' he asked, half expecting a no to both questions.

'Yes he did, and yes I posted it,' she replied determinedly. She had detected his note of scepticism. 'I must admit though,' she added sheepishly, 'when it actually came to it, I very nearly chickened out but, there you go, it's done and I suppose all I can do now is wait, though to be honest, I don't think I can bear the suspense. What if I never hear anything at all? I won't know if it's because it didn't arrive or because they ignored it, just like when Michael tried, although I've always suspected that the mother had a hand in that, and that can't happen now.'

'Kate, that's unkind,' Guy chastised gently, as he pushed open the front door and guided her inside.

She grimaced in acknowledgement as she brushed past him and walked into the hall.

'Perhaps,' she conceded, 'but I was thinking I should ring Matthew to get whoever it was he spoke to in his unit to contact the Army Pensions office in a day or so, just to see if it got that far at least, to see if they forwarded it. Oh Guy, after so many years of wishing for this, more than anything in the world, I really don't know if I've done the right thing. What do you think?' she asked wearily, walking into the kitchen and flopping down in the nearest chair. She suddenly felt drained.

'I think you should relax and wait to see what happens. Matthew's going to be in Rome on holiday, the last thing he wants to have to do is organise a call to a Pensions Office in Glasgow from there. Kate, you've waited forty-six years, a couple of weeks won't make much difference, will it?' he added, looking down at her sad, pale face with the most profound concern. He stood behind her, placed both hands on her shoulders and squeezed her gently, hesitating before continuing. 'Don't raise your expectations too high, darling. If you expect the worst, then anything else will be a bonus. I don't want to see you getting hurt. Come on, I'll make you some tea,' he finished brightly, rubbing his hands together in exaggerated glee.

'Why is it that at every traumatic juncture in my life someone has offered me a cup of tea, as if that's the answer to all the world's woes?' she asked half irritated, half in jest.

'Can't do any harm, can it, anyway, I'm parched,' he replied as he set off towards the kettle.

Kate rested her elbows on the table. A couple of weeks, she thought to herself. I can't wait a couple of weeks, I'll have gone mad by then. She could hear her mother's pearls of wisdom ringing in her ears, 'patience is a virtue, Kate'. Well she may have tried to live a virtuous life, but patience had never featured in it before and was unlikely to materialise now.

*

The rain was pounding noisily on the Velux window directly above the bed, as Richard Palmer reached over to switch off the alarm. He groaned, stretched his arms above his head and looked across at his still sleeping wife, Rachel. He nudged her gently in the ribs.

'What time is it,' she asked sleepily, as she turned her head towards him, one eye still closed to shut out the light.

'Seven o'clock. Do you want to have the first shower and I'll get Nicola her breakfast?'

The morning routine soon got into full swing as they busied themselves washing, feeding and dressing, always with an eye on the clock. Rachel sat at the dressing table, carefully applying her make-up while letting her hair dry naturally. She picked up the dryer to give it a final blast. From the corner of her eye, she saw Richard come into the room and sit down on the bed, but took no particular notice as she continued to look in the mirror. He called her name gently, but she didn't hear him. She switched off the dryer, looked at her watch then got up quickly to check if Nicola had finished dressing; there was no guarantee that any effort would have been made at all in that direction and time was moving on.

'Rachel,' he called again in a strained voice, as she headed for the door. She noticed the unusual tone in his voice. When she looked back, she saw that he was slumped on the bed reading a letter intently.

'What is it?' she asked, coming to sit beside him, alarmed that he had received bad news.

'Read this,' he said, handing over the letter. Rachel noticed a slight tremor in his hand. She took the letter and looked at him quizzically. His face appeared pinched and drawn. She started to read.

> 4 Clara Road,
> Plymouth,
> PL3 5BP
> Tel 0 1752288669
> 5th October 2002
>
> Dear Richard
>
> It has been extremely difficult for me to put pen to paper, but I hope that you will understand how much it means to me to finally make contact with you and that what I say in this letter comes from the heart. I also hope that what I disclose will not come as a shock to you, and that you are already aware of the true nature of your relationship to your parents, Jim and Evelien Palmer.
>
> I believe that I'm your natural mother. I gave birth to twins, a boy and a girl on 25th June 1956, in Exeter. Helped by a Dr Greene, I gave those children up for adoption on 29th June, a day that is forever etched in my memory. The adoption was finalised on 17th October 1956. If this seems to coincide with what you understand about your

past then I believe you may be one of those twins, and I have found you at last.

In making contact with you, please understand that I would never seek to replace the mother who has cared for and loved you all your life, but I too have never forgotten, or stopped loving, the beautiful babies that I regretfully felt compelled to give into her care. I was able to look after you myself for only a fleeting four days, but the memories of that precious time have lived with me as a constant companion ever since. Not a day passes when I don't think about you both and wonder how you are.

I never met your parents but I know Dr Greene will have chosen well and this knowledge has brought a great deal of comfort to me for the past forty-six years. I know I gave up all rights to be called your mother a long time ago but I never gave up loving you, my children, or hoping that, one day, we would meet again. From the most painful moment when I handed you over, I have been waiting for an appropriate time to make contact and I hope that this is it.

If you can find it in your heart to forgive me, and would be happy to get in touch, then you would bring me such happiness and peace. If you decide that it is not something you care to do, I will understand and accept your decision. All I would ask, please, is that you would let me know you got my letter so that I can stop my quest. My address and telephone number are at the top if you wish to make contact.

I do hope I hear from you and that I will have the chance to meet with you both again; it would mean so very much to me.

With love
 Kate Prosser

Rachel sat staring at the letter. 'Goodness, what a surprise; what are you going to do?' she asked sympathetically, handing over the letter.

'I don't know,' he replied scanning the contents once more. 'It's really shaken me. I can hardly believe it. Someone saying he was our half-brother tried to get in touch with us years ago; we just ignored it as it upset Mum so much. I've always thought of her simply as the woman who bore me, not my actual mother, but to see her handwriting, well somehow it makes her more real, more flesh and blood; my flesh and blood come to think of it. She says here she doesn't want to replace Mum; well, Mum will always be Mum as far as I'm concerned. She seems genuine enough though, doesn't she; but what if she turns out to be like Vera Duckworth?' he said flippantly, feigning disgust, in an effort to disguise the torrent of emotions threatening to overwhelm him. 'I don't know what to do, what do you think?'

'Crikey, I'm not sure what to say. Obviously your mother is no longer with us so she can't get upset now, but it's still a big thing. You can't very well meet and then just forget about it if you don't like her,' Rachel cautioned, taking the letter to read it again. She looked up, her brow creased in thought. 'How would you feel if you discovered she was ill and she died and you never met? Would that bother you?' she asked, trying to be helpful.

Richard hesitated before answering. 'I suppose, if I'm honest, it would. I think I would regret not having met her.'

'Maybe that's your answer then.'

'Perhaps it is,' he said simply. 'Of course Helen will have her own thoughts; she's affected by this as well, and Nicola,' he added as an afterthought.

'Yes, strange to think, isn't it, that she's actually Nicola's grandmother and yet she has never known her either? Look, you were formally adopted in October, on the 17th; I didn't know that. It's the anniversary in a couple of days,' Rachel added. 'Just going on what she says here, she seems really nice. It's well written and thoughtful, but I really don't want to influence you either way, it has to be your decision. It must have been very difficult for her to write it. Come to think of it, how on earth did she know you were here?'

'Right enough. Look at the post mark. Glasgow, 14th October,' noted Richard picking up and examining the envelope. 'But her address is Plymouth and the letter is dated the 5th. That's taken a while to get here. And why was her letter inside another envelope with just my name on it? Why would she have posted it in Glasgow? Unless it went to someone else first, of course, and they posted it on,' Richard mused.

'Perhaps. But then how would someone else have had our address? If she knew they had it, why didn't she just get it from them herself? Look though, the writing on the outside envelope is different from the letter. How on earth did she, or someone else, track you down after all these years? It's worth contacting her just to satisfy our curiosity on that score. Hey, look at the time, we'd better get a move on. May we talk about it tonight? Nicola, are you ready yet?' she called across the landing, unaware that he would have liked to discuss it a great deal more.

They agreed to think about it during the day and ring Helen in the evening to get her thoughts, but there was little doubt it had been an unsettling morning. Richard couldn't get it out of his mind all day. If he had thought about it at all before, he had assumed that she had given them up easily, merely for her own convenience; she had felt nothing for them and that was that. But the letter, the hint at her pain and loss, provided a totally different perspective. It had sparked in his imagination images of their last time together and what it must have been like for her. It stirred intense feelings in him; for the first time she started to take on the form of his natural mother, not some nondescript woman who had merely provided a womb for the first nine months of his life.

He found himself talking about it incessantly to his colleagues at work, discussing his personal life in a way he had never done so before. It was intriguing stuff and he realised what a major impact the letter had had on him. It had become all-consuming and he couldn't wait to talk to

Helen. For him it no longer was a question of 'if' they should meet but 'when', but he suspected Helen might not feel the same. She had always been so close to their mother and he reckoned that she would see it as a betrayal. He would be bitterly disappointed, but would have to bow to her wishes. To meet her would have a much bigger impact on them both than not meeting, so the weight of the decision had to lie with Helen. He willed the day away but, like a watched pot, it had never appeared to take so long.

He arrived home promptly. Nicola and Rachel were already there and had started to cook dinner, but he didn't feel in the slightest bit hungry. Throughout the day his emotions had felt like they were on fire. He was experiencing sensations that were completely alien to him, and he didn't know how to respond. He had successfully absorbed the knocks and pressures of Sandhurst like a punch bag, emerged unscathed, but what he was experiencing now felt like nothing he had ever faced before. He was wholly disconcerted and excited in one. He had never known how to talk about his feelings regarding his adoption, so he had disguised them with flippant schoolboy hypotheses about how his natural mother had come to be 'up the duff'. He hadn't really considered her much until this flood gate had opened and as the day progressed, an obsession to return to her overtook him. It was only seven o'clock but he wondered if Helen would be home yet. He couldn't wait any longer, so he lifted the phone to ring her.

Helen was surprised to get a call from her brother, especially on a Tuesday evening, and immediately assumed that either something was wrong, or that he wanted something from her. She had just finished an exhausting twelve-hour shift on the geriatric ward of her local hospital and felt completely bushed. She was planning to have a quiet evening watching TV, a hot bath and an early night. If she were honest, the last thing she needed was some problem with Richard, or his family, but she responded to his voice with a professional's fixed interest.

'Hello, Richard, how are things with you then?' she answered with false enthusiasm.

'Oh, fair to middling,' he answered with his customary reply. 'What have you been up to today?' He wanted to dive in, ask her view on the situation immediately, but he had been told in endless work appraisals that he was too abrupt and direct and lacked social niceties. It didn't come naturally, but he was trying to change.

'Same old, same old, you know. Working too hard, earning too little, nothing new there then. What about you?' she asked tiredly.

Enough of the chit chat, he thought, time for action. 'Helen, I've had the most extraordinary day. I need your view on something. I got a letter this morning. It was from this woman called Kate Prosser, who believes she's our natural mother; she wants to meet us. She knew our names, date of birth, where we were born, when we were adopted, even the name of that doctor Mum used to talk about. It seems genuine enough. She lives in Plymouth. I haven't been able to get it out of my head all day. What do you think? If I'm honest, I'd like to contact her.'

There was silence on the other end, as Helen absorbed what he was telling her.

'Hello, are you still there?' he asked after a second or two.

'Yes, still here. I'm just trying to get to grips with what you said. How on earth did she track you down?'

'I don't know, it doesn't matter does it?' he replied, frustrated that she should consider that to be the most important thing. 'Well, what do you think? Should we get in touch?'

'I thought we'd agreed we didn't want anything to do with her; we promised Mum.'

'I know. That was my first reaction too, but I've thought about it, in fact I've thought about little else all day. Would you at least consider it?'

'It doesn't sit well with me, Richard, it seems so disloyal. Why on earth do you want to get in contact with her anyway? Leave well alone, I think. To be honest, I've enough on my plate without having to worry about some woman I may discover I don't even like. I'm perfectly happy with my memories of the Mum we've always known and I don't want to do anything to spoil those.'

Richard's heart sank. He had made up his mind to contact Kate and didn't want to be thwarted in his mission, but at the same time he knew he needed to have Helen's backing; it affected her too, and her children. He struggled to find a logical argument to persuade her why they should go through with it and then he remembered that Helen was more likely to be swayed by an appeal to her emotions. He desperately tried to think how he could put it to her.

'Would you like to hear what she's written in her letter? Would you like me to read it to you?' he asked, reckoning that she might be persuaded by Kate's words, rather than his own. If only she could become as real to his sister as she had to him, when he'd first read her letter, then she might consider it. In Richard's mind he now saw Kate as a woman of strong convictions, a woman who had suffered greatly all her life. Her raw emotion was implied rather than stated, but unusually he had been sensitive enough to read between the lines and had felt her painful loss. He felt it for himself too. She had gripped his heart with both hands and wasn't letting go. He slowly read the letter to Helen. She listened without interrupting.

Again there was silence when he had finished reading. He had to clear his throat before he was able to check again that she was still on the line. Helen had the most irritating habit of delaying before she spoke; everything had to be thought through so carefully before she voiced her view.

'She sounds so sad doesn't she? I didn't expect her to feel like that about us. I wonder why she gave us away in the first place; it sounds like she did so reluctantly, doesn't it?'

'Yes, that's what I thought.'

'I've never looked at it like that before. It seems it would mean a lot to her if we got in touch. I suppose we should at least acknowledge that we got her letter. It would be cruel to leave her hanging, wondering if it had arrived, I wouldn't like to do that to her. But if she knows we got it and we decide not to meet she'll wonder why– that seems a bit unkind too don't you think? Although it would be awful to meet her and then decide we didn't want anything more to do with her, almost better not to meet at all, although I still can't help feeling guilty about Mum and how she would feel about this.'

'Is that the only reason you wouldn't want to meet her?' asked Richard, trying to be patient with his sister but thinking how illogical it was to consider the feelings of someone who could no longer feel anything. Memory was one thing, illogical obstacles another.

'I suppose so,' replied Helen, without conviction.

'Would you mind if I contacted her, possibly arranged to meet her on my own? I don't want to force you into something you don't want to do, but I would really like to meet her.'

There was a pause before Helen continued. 'No, I don't think it would be right to meet her on your own, if you're going to meet her then I think I ought to be there as well. She handed us over together so she should find us again together. I think it should be both of us or neither. Look, let me think about it for a day or two will you and I'll get back to you. I'm too tired to think straight at the moment, I've had a pretty crap day and to be honest I'm knackered. I'll call you in a day or so and let you know, I promise.'

Richard set the phone down, totally frustrated. He loved his sister; for most of his life she had been the only blood relative he had, but they had always been so different. She took an age to decide anything. Every angle was considered with the precision of a draftsman. There was nothing for it he would have to wait until she had dithered sufficiently over her decision. He just couldn't see what the big deal was. If it didn't work out, well they didn't need to have anything more to do with her but at least they would have tried and satisfied both sets of curiosity. If it did, and he hoped it would, well, great for all of them. It seemed so simple.

*

Kate felt like she was living in the throes of a never-ending nightmare; each hour seemed to pass in slow motion as time crawled torturously by. Every day she waited with a mixture of anxiety and expectation for the letter or phone call that would end her agony. It was twelve days since she had posted it and still she had heard nothing. She had posted first class on Saturday 5th, so she reckoned it must have arrived in Glasgow by the following Tuesday at the very latest. She knew Captain Brown had been expecting it, so it shouldn't have taken her more than a couple of days at most to forward it; all she had to do was look up the address and pop it in the post. It should have arrived with Richard by Friday 11th or Saturday 12th at the latest. Today was the 17th, five days later, so he must have got it by now. He wasn't going to respond. It was the only logical conclusion.

Of all the days since she had posted it, she was feeling particularly low today. It was one of the three torturous dates that, if she had the power, she would wave a wand and magically leap-frog over. They were the anniversaries of the day the twins were born, the day she handed them over to Dr Greene and today the 17th, almost worst of all, the day when she had signed away all rights to them and knew there was no turning back. For years she had passed each of these days in a state of self-enforced numbness, hardly conscious of what she was doing or saying as she tried to block out the pain and memories they induced.

Today it was as if a knife had been thrust in her guts and as each hour passed some malicious force was shoving it an inch further in. She wished they would finish the job properly and she would no longer feel anything. Sometimes on these days she went back to bed and slept most of it away, but today she needed to stay awake. Sometimes Guy tried his best to keep her mind on other matters, taking her out for lunch or dinner or to the theatre – anything to occupy her mind and lift her melancholy – but today was different. For over a week she had refused to leave the house at all, in case the phone rang and she missed him.

'Darling, I know you don't want to miss a call from him, but you can't go on like this indefinitely,' Guy reasoned. 'What if you never hear anything? He'll leave a message on the answer phone, surely, or ring again if you aren't in.' She couldn't be persuaded. She would watch and wait while there was still a chance and perhaps it hadn't been that long; he could still contact her. She couldn't contemplate the alternative.

*

Richard ploughed his way through two difficult days before the phone eventually rang at eight o'clock and Helen's voice came over the line. She started with the usual social chatter before he managed to pin her down on the most important issue, which was whether or not she agreed to contact Kate Prosser.

'Well I've given it a great deal of thought,' she continued, ' and, yes, I'd like to go through with it I think, though to be honest I'm still not convinced. What do you think? It's just I'm worried that either she'll be disappointed in us, or we'll be disappointed in her. And I still feel so guilty about Mum. Oh, I really don't know what to do. I tell you what, you decide and I'll go along with it,' she finished, indefinitely.

'I told you, I've already decided that I want to go through with it. I want to contact her. Are you saying you're happy with that?' he replied in exasperation.

'Yes, I think so…yes, go ahead and contact her, I think you should. I'm happy with that. Are you going to write to her or ring her?'

'Ring her – it's much quicker,' he answered, much relieved and keen to get on with it in case she changed her mind again or he lost his nerve.

'What on earth are you going to say to her? I can't imagine how she'll feel when you call her,' she said, adding to his angst.

'I don't know, play it by ear I suppose. I'll try now once we've finished. Thanks, Helen, I was worried you would say no. I'll ring you back if I manage to get through. Do you know the thought of it has made me quite nervous; maybe I have more genes in common with you than I think. I'll hopefully be calling you back in a while.'

'No, call me either way otherwise I'll be sitting here wondering what's happening. I'm dying to know what she says. Make sure you call me back, won't you? Good luck. Bye. Promise you'll call me back now,' she finished as he said goodbye.

Richard set the receiver down slowly and steeled himself to lift it again. It was one of the most difficult challenges he had ever faced. His throat dried as beads of sweat oozed from his forehead like a bunch of transpiring lilies. His heart started to pound and his hands shake as he lifted the receiver and started to dial.

Chapter 32

Plymouth, evening 17th October 2002

'I'm afraid I've had enough for one day, Guy, I've got a rotten headache so I'm going to take a couple of paracetemol and go to bed early. You don't mind, do you?' Kate asked, touching her forehead with the tips of her fingers and frowning.

'Not at all, darling, you go on up and I'll get them for you. You look drained. Hope you feel better in the morning. Sleep well.' They kissed fondly before she wearily climbed the stairs. Guy watched her go his heart filled with love and sorrow. He knew she had placed all her hopes on hearing from her son, but it looked like hope was fading. Guy had to agree that if Richard Palmer had been going to respond he would probably have done so by now. He bitterly regretted telling her that he knew how to find them. If he had kept his own counsel she might have held her hopes in check and lived happily with the love of the three children she knew.

For Kate, the strain of the past two weeks had finally taken its toll. She felt like a prisoner on Death Row, never knowing whether to be thankful for another day of hope or angry that they hadn't made up their mind to finally end her misery. Today had been the worst of all, as hope diminished and she began to accept the finality of her decision of forty-six years ago, which now seemed to be irrevocable. As she lay in bed, exhausted, staring at the ceiling, unable to sleep, she reached a decision. She had to lay the ghosts of the past to rest and accept that her search was over. She had tried to fulfil her vow to her children, but there was little more she could do. It was wrong to continue to seek them if they wished to remain unknown to her. She had to respect their decision, but her heart felt like it was breaking, her head like it was splitting open. She craved sleep, she was overwhelmed by the desire to sink into a deep unconsciousness that would numb all feeling and enable her to awaken whole.

She started to doze, falling into that state of semi-awareness where all sounds are dulled and the world feels like it is pulling away. She dreamt that she was at her beloved bower. She had spent the day playing happily with her twins, Richard and Helen, on the river bank. She had left them to sleep on the far side while she went in to rest; she felt so tired. The sun, which had been shining all day, had suddenly disappeared behind a sky of dark clouds which had started to gather in sheets of menacing grey. She could hear a strange but familiar voice. It was Art, young and handsome like when she first met him. He was calling her. He was with her twins on the far side. He was standing begging her to cross to fetch them all. His arms were held out in entreaty but she could find no way across.

His cries for help became more and more desperate as she ran up and down the bank searching for a bridge. She spotted one and ran to cross it, but it dissolved in front of her as soon as she stepped out. She almost reached another one, but it too vanished before her eyes. She could find no way to get to them as the mist began to descend and they disappeared in front of her eyes. The river was transforming before her, its gentle flow was being whipped into a torrent, threatening to swamp them. The water was churning up the stinking black sediment that for years had lain undisturbed and was tossing it carelessly on the riverbank. They were stranded as the river started to break its bank, threatening to pull them all in and swallow them in its hungry depths. She was trying to jump in, to swim across to save them, but someone was holding her back. Over the deafening sound of the wind and the water she could hear Guy's voice, begging her to stop. 'There's nothing you can do, leave them, forget about them. Kate, Kate.' His voice was imploring her to stay where she was. She was frantically trying to shake him off, but he had a firm grip of her arm.

She woke with a start to find Guy leaning over and gently shaking her. He was holding the phone, covering the mouthpiece with his hand.

'Kate, Kate, it's the phone for you. Are you awake? Can you take it? It's Richard Palmer.'

It took her a moment to fully regain consciousness. She wasn't sure what he'd said, what was real and what was still part of her nightmare. She sat up groggily.

'What did you say?'

'It's Richard Palmer. Can you speak or do you want to call him back?'

She looked at Guy, who was grinning wildly. Bewildered, she took the phone, pushed back her hair and answered hesitantly.

'Hello, Kate Prosser speaking.' She listened for the reply.

'Oh hello, my name is Richard Palmer.' His voice sounded calm but unsure. 'I got a letter from you. You asked me to contact you.' He paused as Kate waited anxiously, 'I believe you may be my natural mother. What you wrote all fits, the dates, my parents' names, the places everything. I believe that I'm your son.'

Kate was glad of the bed's firm support beneath her weakening body. In that instant her strength had been sucked out, like an earthquake drawing the sea from the shore to be followed by an adrenaline tsunami. She couldn't find her voice. She was rendered speechless.

'Hello, are you still there?' he asked with concern.

'Yes' she replied breathlessly. 'Yes I'm still here. It's just I can't believe you've called me, that you've answered my letter. Forgive me, yes I'm still here. I'm so pleased you called. You don't know what this means to me, how long I've dreamed of this moment and now I don't know what to say. Thank you, thank you,' she replied, gradually finding her voice.

'I don't really know what to say either, except that I'm very glad to talk to you too. I can hardly believe it either. Are you okay? The chap who answered said you'd gone to bed early, I told him not to disturb you, but he insisted that you would want to take the call.'

'Yes, oh yes, I'm absolutely fine thank you. I just can't quite take it in that I'm actually talking to you after all this time. I'm really not quite sure what to say.' She noticed that her headache had lifted, her energy was returning and her thinking becoming clearer. 'How are you and your sister? Helen, isn't it? Where are you both living?'

'Yes, it's Helen. We're both fine thank you. I live in Northern Ireland; my wife Rachel is from here. I was in the Army and we settled here after I left. We live near Belfast. We have a daughter Nicola who's nine. Helen, my sister, lives in Cornwall with her husband Alex. She has three daughters, Annie, Jessica and Alice.'

Kate could hardly comprehend it; she had four granddaughters whom she knew nothing about. Almost a complete family in itself.

'How lovely. Well, I live in Plymouth. You have an older sister Clare and two younger brothers, Matthew and Michael. Clare has two children, Susan and Jess, while Matthew has a son, Tom. I married the boys' father in 1957 a year after you were born, his name is Guy; it was he who answered the phone. Clare is their and your half-sister. It all sounds so complicated when I say it like this, doesn't it? One day, perhaps, I'll get the chance to explain it all to you in person, and to Helen,' she added.

It took five minutes of stilted social conversation to cover forty-six years' worth of family news and relationships. Neither felt comfortable addressing the most intimate circumstances that had led to the adoption; the conversation had remained artificially formal and uncomfortable for both. They instinctively knew that such revelations should wait until another day, perhaps until they could meet and discuss them in person, but they also both felt that the words spoken between them were merely the vehicle through which they had reconnected at the most subliminal level. They finished the conversation promising to ring each other again in a few days. Both felt drained but elated.

Kate set down the phone. She lay in the bed motionless, hardly daring to believe what had happened. She was in a state of emotional meltdown. She gripped the bedclothes in an effort to reconnect with reality to know that she was living in the present, that the world around her was real and that she wasn't still asleep.

Guy had remained at a discreet distance downstairs, dying to know what was being said but conscious of her need for privacy. It was an intimate moment for the woman he loved more than anyone on earth and he knew she needed her space. He came upstairs when he heard her finish. He wanted to check that she was okay.

*

Richard set down the phone and sat on the kitchen chair totally shell-shocked. It had been the single most defining moment of his entire life. There was nothing else that had ever come close, except perhaps the birth of his own child, but even then he couldn't be sure. He was completely discomfited, lost in the involuntary feelings currently pulsing through his body. He had lost all sense of proportion, his body no longer felt like his own. He heard Rachel coming into the kitchen, but he didn't know how to respond to her. Of course, she wanted to know what Kate had said, what she sounded like but didn't she understand that what she was asking him was mindless? It didn't matter what he had discovered about her, what she was like, how she sounded, what mattered was that he had rediscovered his mother. The woman in whose womb he had lain for nine months, the woman whose genes had formed him, the woman who was the source of his existence, the reason for his being. Why didn't she ask him how he felt, what it meant to him? Didn't she understand the significance of what had happened to him?

'She sounded really nice; she told me I have two half-brothers and a half-sister. She would like to meet us,' he rattled off automatically, keen to move the conversation away and satisfy her curiosity. He needed to call Helen, he had promised; she, at least, he hoped would understand.

He called her straightaway. He couldn't wait to talk to her, to tell her that they had rediscovered their mother. He couldn't think of anything that had ever excited him as much. Helen received the news cautiously. She still felt that she was betraying the memory of their parents, particularly their mother; as if she were a willing conspirator in some shameful deception. She was interested in the details, the news about her unexpected close relations, but the event did not rock her as it had Richard. She maintained a professional aloofness, perhaps drawing on the skills developed over many years of nursing that enabled her to remain detached from the most painful of emotional situations.

'She would like to meet us. What do you think?' Richard enthused, 'I'd really like to, Helen, as soon as possible; she sounds so interesting. I'm happy to fly over, meet you in Plymouth, take a few days off work, bring Rachel and Nicola with me and make a long weekend of it. It'll be great. Would you be happy to meet us there?'

His enthusiasm was somewhat dampened by her controlled reserve. She wanted to think about it, not rush into anything she would come to regret. He felt like he was pushing water uphill – why couldn't she be more spontaneous, take a chance and go with the flow? There was nothing for it, he would have to wait.

Three weeks later, Richard, Rachel and Nicola walked across the concourse at Belfast City Airport and boarded a flight for Exeter. Rachel and Nicola were looking forward to an unexpected weekend break. For them, it offered a couple of days to look round Drake's City; a chance to see first-hand the landmarks that until now had remained as two dimensional descriptions in a history book.

They landed at Exeter an hour late. They collected their luggage, which seemed to take forever to hit the carousel. They queued for their hire car, regretting the decision to go with the airline's preferred provider; everyone else, it seemed had made the same decision. They finally set off on the relatively short journey across to Plymouth. The journey was slow, intense and deeply frustrating. Richard had forgotten how dense the traffic was on the A38 on a Friday evening. As he crawled along he felt his irritation building and his patience diminishing. Ever since he had left the house nearly four hours earlier, he had felt on edge and irritable, he just wanted to get there and achieve his objective. They had agreed to meet Helen at the station. Despite their long delay, she still hadn't arrived. He checked the time and called her on her mobile.

'Hi, on my way don't worry. I missed the first train; I'll be there in about half an hour,' she answered, without any hint of apology.

Richard marched off towards a small station café, with the family in tow. They paid for an overpriced, under-heated coffee and some sandwiches. Nicola didn't like them. Richard sat at the table drumming his fingers, saying little as he waited for his sister in a state of barely controlled agitation. Eventually her train pulled in and they walked to meet her. Richard and Helen embraced stiffly; Rachel kissed her warmly while Nicola took her aunt's hand and held it tightly as they walked towards the hire car. Richard started the engine and waited for Rachel's precise instructions, revving away as she navigated towards the hotel.

They had arranged to meet the following morning at Kate's house. She had suggested that they should then go out for lunch together. Kate hardly slept a wink; Richard slept fitfully, Helen like a log. Rachel and Nicola had tactfully decided to allow them to meet alone and intended to spend the morning exploring the Barbican and the city's aquarium. Guy had also decided to take his leave and let them rediscover each other alone. All the protagonists, whether directly or indirectly involved, were feeling anxious and nervous for themselves or others.

Helen and Richard set off armed with the directions that had been meticulously written out and sent through by Kate. Richard was soon feeling thoroughly exasperated as Helen's navigational skills were tested to their limit; she hardly seemed to know her left from her right. They got completely lost, arriving back at the point from where they had set out twenty minutes earlier. Richard finally conceded that he would have to stop at a garage to ask directions. He hated it, seeing it as a sign of weakness, and only did so as a last desperate measure. They were going to be late and Helen had forgotten to bring Kate's phone number. He had checked when they set out and been reassured to the contrary.

He drove along gripping the steering wheel in frustration, annoyed with Helen, unable to alert Kate and anxious that they were going to be late. It was already 11.40 and they had been due at eleven o'clock. At long last he turned the car into a neat, tree-lined avenue as he spotted the road sign Clara Road nestling in the greenery along a stone wall. He drove along slowly craning his neck in an effort to spot number four. The black, cast iron number was screwed to the side of a large, heavy, wooden gate. It had been left wide open in a gesture of welcome. He drove in slowly and parked in the driveway. He turned off the engine and turned to Helen.

'Ready for this?' he asked her, his voice shaking. She nodded.

He opened the car and stepped out onto the neat gravel driveway, drying the palms of his hands discreetly down the front of his trousers. Helen pulled down the vanity mirror and touched up her lipstick. She ran her hands through her hair and opened the car door stepping out after him. He came round to her side and took her arm as if to reassure her, but in reality to steady his own nerves. The gravel crunched beneath their feet as they strode towards the front door together. Richard placed his finger on the button and heard the shrill ring of the doorbell.

Kate had been pacing up and down the hallway for the past forty minutes and had just sat down. Watching the minutes tick slowly by, she had become more and more convinced that they had changed their mind. They were already forty minutes late. They weren't coming. She had brushed and rebrushed her hair, checked and rechecked her appearance in the mirror, willing the grey hair and wrinkles to disappear. She had finally sat down in an effort to settle her nerves. She was dying for a cigarette, but she had washed her hair, brushed her teeth, put on fresh clothes and opened the windows. She didn't want their first impressions of her to be that of an ageing hag, tainted by the stench of stale tobacco. She was becoming more and more agitated and, if they didn't arrive soon, she knew her willpower would weaken and she would light up.

She jumped from her chair alerted by the shrill sound of the bell. She hadn't heard a car. She had been sure that she would hear their arrival, allowing her a few precious moments to calm down. She steadied herself and walked towards the door. Through the small side pane of opaque glass she could see the outline of two figures, one tall, one short, standing side by side holding hands in perfect silhouette. Her legs would hardly propel her forward. She reached up and turned the lock opening the door to them.

Three hearts pounded like battle drums in the chests of the three main players as they embarked on the final act, of this, the greatest of all melodramas. No one spoke, no one moved as they stood in rapt attention unsure how to proceed, how to break the crushing tension. Kate was spellbound. Eventually, Helen shifted. She dropped Richard's hand and without saying a word stepped forward and fell into the arms of her mother. Richard followed suit. They stood clinging to each other like the sole survivors of the apocalypse, alone in their own little world, each drawing strength and comfort from one another. Kate breathed in their scent, felt the warmth of their bodies as they encircled her slight frame with their strong adult arms. They drew apart slightly abashed and smiled at each other.

'Thank you, thank you,' she said, choked. 'Thank you for coming all this way and for agreeing to meet me. Come in, please come in.' They both nodded silently and followed her into the hallway unable to respond to her words.

Kate showed them into the drawing room. Richard and Helen sat on the sofa together, like two shy children in the presence of a formidable maiden aunt. Kate wanted to sit in between them but thought better of it. They all needed time to adjust, to get to know each other, to relax.

'Would you like some tea or coffee,' she offered, 'or perhaps something stronger?'

Coffee would be lovely, thank you,' replied Richard. 'Yes that would be great, thank you,' added Helen. 'Would you like a hand?'

Kate felt she needed a few moments alone to compose herself. 'No, thank you, I just need to boil the kettle; it's all ready.'

She returned with a tray to find Richard and Helen gazing at the small silver-framed photograph of Guy, Clare, Matthew and Michael, which had been sitting on the table beside them.

'I presume these are your other children, our half-siblings. Doesn't this one look like you, Richard,' observed Helen pointing to the photo.

'Yes, that's Matthew, the eldest of the twins, that's Michael and Clare. Guy is the handsome one at the back,' she added, smiling as she pointed to each one.

'You mean the one who looks like me, isn't?' retorted Richard with a grin.

It was the start of the unfreezing; they had found a subject to connect them. They started to unwind and allow their true personalities to come forward. Kate handed out the coffee and offered them some scones. They both declined. Their appetites had escaped them for the moment.

'Would you mind terribly if I had a cigarette? I'm happy to have it outside if you prefer,' asked Richard rather awkwardly.

'Oh, thank goodness for that,' replied Kate, with a sigh of relief. 'I'm dying for one too, but I wasn't sure if you would approve. Let me get you an ashtray and I'll join you. Helen?'

'No, thank you,' she replied, 'I'm trying to give them up, but I don't mind if you do.'

Kate came back and lit up drawing deeply on its comforting cocktail as she sat back in her chair. Silence descended again as they drank their coffee and smoked. They so much wanted to discover all about each other, but each was sensitive to the other's right to privacy.

'I'd like to hear about your families if you're happy to tell me. Have you any photographs?' Kate asked tentatively. They exchanged details, photographs and chatted comfortably about the safest of topics, their family, their jobs, their homes. The most uncomfortable revelations would have to come, but not yet.

'Let's go for lunch,' Kate suggested after a while when the conversation had started to flag. 'There's a great little pub about three miles from here, just into the countryside. I'm happy to drive us there.'

'Not at all, I'll drive us,' offered Richard, 'just show me the way. Hopefully your navigation is slightly better than Helen's. Sorry again that we were so late arriving.' Helen looked at him through narrowed eyes. He winked in reply and smiled.

Twenty minutes later they arrived at the pub with its thatched roof and intimate alcoves. They sat at a reserved table with a bottle of chilled Sauvignon Blanc, looking at the extensive menu. The change to neutral ground, the effects of the alcohol and the passage of time started to take effect, as they began to relax into each other's company.

They ordered their food. Kate sat between them. She felt like she was in the middle of a surreal dream. Her heart was swelling with pride and joy. She knew that she needed to tell them the events of 1956; the events that had led to their adoption. They had a right to know.

'This is going to be very difficult for me, perhaps for us all, but I want to tell you how it all came about, how I ended up giving you away. Are you happy to know?' They both nodded; they were desperate to know, but hadn't wanted to push her.

'It really was the most painful and agonising decision I have ever had to make, and I've lived with it ever since, until now that is. As I sit here, with you, I not only feel that an enormous burden has been lifted off my shoulders, but like some benevolent force is carrying me along. Having both of you here with me, my children...well, I can hardly explain.'

Richard automatically took her hand in his and squeezed it gently, as Helen took her other.

'I want you to know everything. I'm not sure how much you know already about how it all happened, how much your parents knew or told you.'

'We knew that you were a student and that a Dr Greene organised the adoption. He was both your and our parents' doctor I believe, but that's about it really,' explained Richard.

'Yes that's all true, but there is so much more. Sitting here explaining it to you in 2002 and looking back at that time now, well it almost seems like I have straddled two lifetimes. Things were very different then, attitudes, expectations, pressures; it's hard to understand it all now. I'm not sure it will make much sense to you, but I'll try to explain. Please believe me, I'm not trying to defend myself, I just feel I need to explain why I did what I did.

'I married an American soldier, Art Willis, at the end of the war. We were very much in love. My parents, your grandparents, I suppose, were very much against the idea. Although they liked Art, they hadn't wanted me to get married as they thought I was too young, too reckless in giving up the chance to go to college, disappearing off to America with someone I hardly knew. They warned me that I would regret it. I thought they were far too conventional, too set in their ways and just wanted some freedom to fly my wings. I felt so stifled at home.

'Anyway, I moved to America in 1946. We had Clare soon after and a great life together for several years, but then Art became seriously ill. He had been badly affected by the war, mentally I mean, and I felt I had to leave him and come back to England to protect Clare. He's dead now; he lived for a few years in a mental institution in Boston, but he died young.

'We got divorced soon after I came back to England. On the surface of it, my parents were very understanding, but I knew that behind the reassurances there was a case of 'we told you so'. My mother, in particular, found my divorce very difficult, it was shaming for her. Believe it or not, divorce was still relatively uncommon in those days and had never blighted our family. Clare also suffered from relentless teasing. She was a child with no father, but she wasn't an orphan, like so many others around her. What they couldn't understand about her, they made up. The other children accused her of being illegitimate, of not knowing who her father was; told her he had abandoned her because he didn't want her. I felt so guilty that I had brought all this on her and on my parents.

'A year or so later I decided to go back to college and was lucky to be accepted at Romney; it's not that far from where you grew up in Exeter, so you may know it. I really felt that my life had got back on track. I was doing really well, although I missed Art terribly. Then my father died. I was very close to my father. I was terribly upset and felt very alone and vulnerable. This is the embarrassing bit I'm afraid, but I'll spare you the details. After his funeral, I got a lift back to Exeter with an old childhood friend called Bob Thompson. It sounds terrible when I explain it to you like this.'

Kate took a sip from her glass and then re-held Helen's hand. She noticed that they were both listening intently to her every word.

'Anyway, as I said, I was still very upset, we had a few drinks and…well… one thing led to another. I'll spare you the details, but the fact is he's your father. When I told him about the pregnancy he didn't want to know. He said I should have an abortion, asked if I was sure it was his; of course, we didn't know at that stage there were two of you. It was awful. I'm sorry to have to tell you this about him as he is your father, after all. I haven't seen him since that day, although he still lives in Exeter, I believe. To make matters worse, the College threw me out as soon as I let them know, told me I was a bad influence on the other students and that I wasn't fit to be a teacher. I forgot to tell you, they hadn't been too impressed that I was divorced in the first place.'

'That's ridiculous. Did people really still have those attitudes then?' asked Richard incredulously. 'From what I've read, I thought the war years had encouraged free love, lowered inhibitions, if anything.'

'Yes, unfortunately, you're right. To a large extent society openly condemned in public what the individual enjoyed in private. It was a complete sham. Many a bride was what we at college used to call a 'retread virgin', a miracle transformation going up the aisle. Still that's how it was.'

Richard and Helen laughed. It helped to ease the tension.

'I already had Clare, I was divorced, I had no prospects and now I was pregnant. I didn't want you to go through what Clare had suffered as a child with no father. I also couldn't place the burden on my mother who had recently lost my father and Clare who already had suffered so much. I didn't know what to do. It was terrible. It may seem to you now that I gave up too easily, but I really tried to do what I thought was right. I decided that adoption would be best for you, for my mother, for Clare and I suppose, if I'm honest, for me.

'I spoke to Dr Greene and he knew about your parents, how they'd wanted a child for so long. It seemed like a good solution and to me they seemed ideal. You were born in the house I stayed in as a student in Exeter. I was allowed to keep you for four days only. I can't begin to tell you what it was like loving you with all my heart, yet knowing that I was going to have to hand you over. It was torture. On the day we'd agreed with your parents, I took you to Dr Greene's surgery with my brother, James. I had to hand you over to the nurses who took you away. It was absolutely awful. The last sight of you is etched in my memory like a photograph. As they carried you from me I vowed I would find you again and now I have.'

Kate stopped and reached for her handkerchief. She had remembered to get a freshly laundered one for once. She blew her nose. Helen reached for a tissue.

'I nearly fainted when I handed you over. I was distraught thinking I might never see you again. Even now I can hardly think about it. Dr Greene kindly went to get me some water, and while he was away, my brother, James, saw your file; it contained your parents' names and address. He should never have seen it. I, in fact, didn't know anything about it until several years later; no one had wanted to tell me. When I found out I was desperate to know more. Guy took me to London, to Somerset House where they held all the records. We found out your names. It was wonderful. I felt like I'd almost found you, it was like I knew you once again. I had to promise him though that I'd leave it at that, once I knew your names. I'm afraid I have a confession to make, and I feel very guilty about this; I went to Exeter when you were about four or so. When I saw your address I thought that you would probably attend the primary school near the park. I went there and stood outside…'

'The strange woman with the pram, who touched us; it was you. Don't you remember, Richard, we were very small?'

exclaimed Helen, interrupting Kate as the recollection of the event and realisation dawned on her. 'It was you, wasn't it?'

Kate nodded uncomfortably. 'I'm sorry. I know it was very wrong of me. You remember it then. I was pretty sure it was you at the time and now I know for certain. I didn't mean you, or your mother, any harm, I really didn't. I was desperate to see you both, that's all. I realised afterwards that I shouldn't have done it, that I had no right to, that it might have upset your mother. I never did it again I promise. Did she realise who I was?'

'She never actually said anything to us, but for a long time after that she was very strange. Do you remember, Richard, we wanted to walk to school alone and she wouldn't let us? She kept warning us about strangers. Thinking about it I suppose that's why. Yes, it makes sense she must have known,' finished Helen. Kate wasn't sure if there was a note of disapproval in her response.

'I'm even more sorry then. She didn't deserve to be upset. I would never have wanted that. I hoped afterwards that she wouldn't suspect who I was, I really did. What was she like?'

Up until that point neither of them had described their parents. They felt awkward talking about them to Kate, but guilty that they had avoided all mention of them.

'They were both very loving parents to us, kind and generous. We miss them both an awful lot,' said Helen a bit defensively.

'I'm glad, I'm sure I would have liked them,' replied Kate.

'They would have liked you too,' added Richard, aware that Helen might have appeared rather abrupt.

'I didn't seek you out after that. I kept my promise, although I found out recently that Michael sent a letter some years ago. I knew nothing about it. I don't even know if you got it.'

'Yes, we did, I'm afraid,' replied Richard. It was his turn to feel uncomfortable.

'Did your mother know about it?'

'Yes, I have to be honest with you, she did. She was very upset at the time. Her greatest dread was that she would lose us to you. Out of respect for her we didn't reply,' explained Helen.

'I'm sorry, if I'd known I wouldn't have let him send it. I only wrote when I saw the notice in the paper last month, the memorial notice of her death. I'm sorry that she died. I knew then that you had lost your father as well. Had they been ill?' asked Kate sympathetically.

'Yes, they both died of cancer, Dad some time ago and Mum just last year. It's hard to believe that they're both gone now.' Richard said wistfully. 'But we're intrigued, how did you track us down? Mum moved from our old address in Exeter a long, long, time ago. How did you know where to find me? The letter had a Glasgow post mark. Why Glasgow?'

'The Army Pensions office. I wrote to them and asked them to forward it to you. Michael rang your old house number in Exeter, the time he sent the first letter – he wanted to see if you still lived there. The new owner explained that your mother had moved but that you were in the Army. Matthew's in the TA, so it was he who thought to look up the Army List to see where you were. It said you had left, but he knew what to do.'

'Of course. That explains it. Very clever, very clever indeed,' said Richard impressed by the effort and detective work that had gone in to finding them. 'And here we are.'

'Yes, here you are. I can't put into words what it means to me. I hope what I've told you helps you to understand. I didn't give you up lightly. If I could have seen a way around it I would. I never even told my mother. I couldn't. She died not knowing anything about you. I only told Clare and the boys years later. I would never try to replace your mother. She'll always be your Mum. Why don't you call me Kate? It seems appropriate; the boys call me that all the time,' Kate suggested.

'Thank you, Kate. I think I can speak for Helen when I say that we're really glad to have met you, too. I can't quite believe I'm sitting here, talking to my natural mother; it's bizarre. You've been through so much, it all makes sense now. I think we have a lot of time to make up, the rest of our lives to get to know each other,' said Richard, smiling across at her.

'Thank you, I'm glad you understand. I hope that you can also find it in your hearts someday to forgive me.' She paused before continuing. 'Would you like to meet with your brothers and sister?' she asked, not sure if she were rushing things.

'I'd love to, but is that possible?' answered Richard eagerly. 'What do you say, Helen?'

'They're all coming to my house tonight. They were hoping you would want to meet them. I also think, though they didn't tell me this of course... well, I think they thought that if this hadn't gone quite to plan that I might need some company. They would love to meet you and Rachel and Nicola, of course. They're all coming about seven o'clock with their children. My brother, James, is also hoping to be there. Shall I tell them that you're coming? Do you think you could cope?' she asked in anticipation.

Richard looked across at Helen.

'We'd love to come,' she said to a beaming Kate.

Richard took Kate back to her house. They both walked her to the door and embraced her fondly before driving off promising to return later.

'Born fifty years before her time, I reckon. Didn't you think she was wonderful?' Richard commented to Helen as he drove away. She nodded but didn't reply.

They arrived back at the hotel to change and to collect Rachel and Nicola. Richard was in a state of extreme excitement. Helen was finding it more difficult to adjust. She had been extremely close to Evelien and still harboured deep-seated feelings of guilt, but she had to admit that the experience had been life changing and that Kate was a remarkable woman. Richard was enamoured. All thoughts of Vera Duckworth had vanished. He had discovered that his mother was an elegant, attractive and intelligent woman. He couldn't wait to meet the rest of the family.

One look at his face told Rachel everything she needed to know. She couldn't shut him up as he gabbled out the details of their encounter. He explained to a bemused Nicola that they were going out to meet her 'Granny Kate'.

'But I already have a granny,' she protested, 'and the other one died.'

You're lucky you still have two; this is a special, extra granny.' She wasn't convinced, but accepted his description without the need for too much explanation.

At 7.30 exactly, Helen, Rachel, Nicola and Richard arrived at Clara Road. The driveway was filled with cars; every window was ablaze with light. They walked with false confidence towards the door. The sound of laughter and music carried across the still night air.

Richard pressed the bell boldly. Kate came to the door smiling. Richard and Helen fondly embraced her, Rachel shook her hand, while Nicola stood shyly behind her mother. Kate smiled at her granddaughter for the first time, thinking how much she looked like Clare's eldest. Hovering behind Kate was a tall, and still handsome, older man.

'This is Guy,' Kate explained. 'Guy, I'd like you to meet my children, Helen and Richard. This is Richard's wife Rachel and their daughter Nicola.' Guy kissed the girls on the cheek and shook hands warmly with Richard.

Together they walked nervously into the drawing room where they were met by a sea of warm and welcoming faces. Kate proudly introduced each family member to their brother, sister, aunt, uncle, niece, nephew, cousin or in-law. Matthew thrust a glass of wine into each of his brother's and sister's hands. The room was filled with a convivial mixture of conversation, music and laughter.

As Kate looked around the room, her heart bursting with joy, surrounded by all the people she loved, she realised that with Art, then with Guy and her children, she had led the most enviable of lives. Until this point she would have described it as a beautiful jigsaw, carefully constructed from all the pieces of her individual personal experiences. It had been a lifetime's work, almost finished except for two lost pieces. Today she had found them and could finally slot them into their rightful places. Her picture was complete.